WITHOUT LIGHT

MEGAN A. ROCKWELL

For permissions, inquiries, or to learn more about the author and upcoming works, visit:
www.meganarockwell.com

First Edition
Self-published in the United States of America

ISBN: 979-8-9923328-1-0

Cover Illustration by Zayane Abdou Mhoussine
Cover Design by Megan A. Rockwell
Editing by Laura Pu-Syska www.lapsstudio.com

Printed in the United States of America

Dedication

For the girls who turned broken trust into unbreakable strength. When the world went dark, you didn't just survive—you became the light. Keep shining; the shadows don't stand a chance.

THE WORLD OF

DOBIA

BRAWN

◆ THE MOUTH
*ENTRANCE TO THE DEPTHS

SERTODA

SEA OF

SANCTIONED.

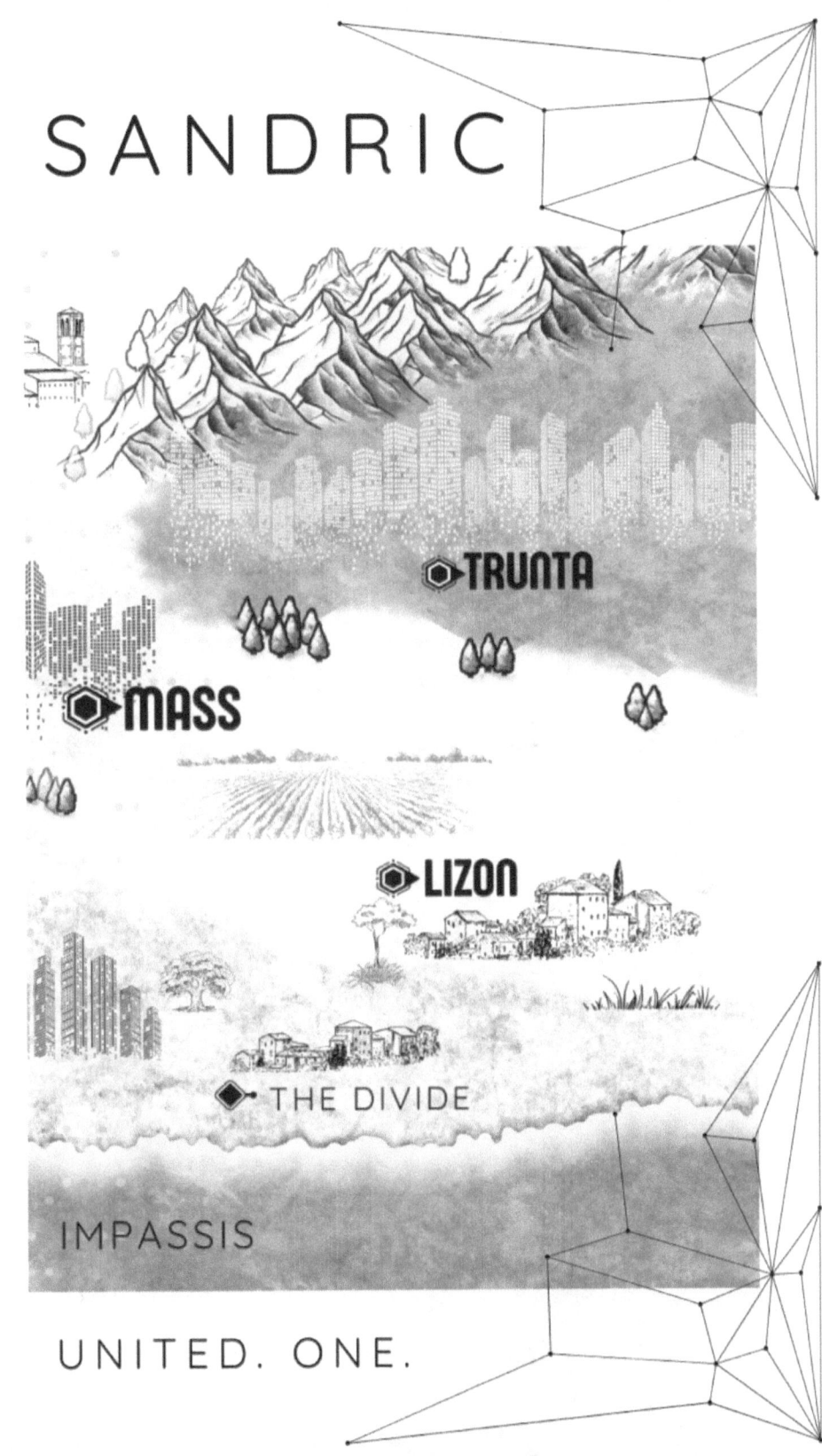

Prologue

HOPHSTED

The moon hung low. Its waning crescent carved through the mist like a tarnished blade. Wilhelmina and I always found solace in these waters. The creak of the hull and the lapping waves were our lullaby. Tonight, the gravitational pull would leave the tides lower, the approaching storm promising to swell the waters just enough. If the sea rose as we hoped, it would create a passage to the hidden depths, where ancient secrets waited to be uncovered. The sea roared with an unnatural fury, as if sensing the importance of the night about to unravel before us.

The storm arrived just as we predicted, summoned from the depths of the dark sky like an omen. The first crack of lightning split the night, tearing through the darkness like the rending of a great veil. The ship, a sturdy vessel we sailed many times, groaned under the weight of the tempest. I clasped the wheel as the cold sea splashed against my face, its salt mingling with the sweat of anticipation.

Wilhelmina stood by my side, her face illuminated by the storm's erratic flashing lights. Her eyes, always so full of life and conviction, were clouded with concern. "Hophsted, something's not right," she shouted over the wind's roar.

"What is it?" I asked, bracing myself as the ship lurched. We knew this search wouldn't be easy, but something in her tone unsettled me. The dark, monstrous waves surged, as if the sea itself had turned against us.

"I don't know," her voice barely audible above the din, "but—I feel like we're being watched."

I dismissed her fears as the product of the storm's chaos, but as I turned to check the ship's compass, my heart sank. The needle spun. A chill crawled up my spine. I tightened my grip on the wheel.

The storm intensified. At the height of its fury, a shadow emerged from the water. I thought it was an illusion conjured by the blinding rain and wind. Yet as it drew closer, the reality of it hit me. A sleek, dark vessel cut through the waves, larger and more imposing than our mid-size craft. Its hull moved silent with unsettling precision, closing in on us like a predator homing in on its prey.

A sharp sense of dread washed over me. "Wilhelmina!" I shouted, but the squall swallowed her name. Her face pale as the moonlight. Her beautiful, celestial blue eyes wide with fear.

The mysterious craft intercepted us before we knew it. Figures moved aboard their ship with a ghostly surge. Balaclava masks, revealing only their eyes, concealed their expressions. The larger vessel dwarfed ours, allowing them to throw down ropes and hooks, securing our boat with ease. They boarded with speed, their movements so fluid they seemed almost from another world.

I grabbed the flare gun beneath my seat, my hands trembling as I fumbled to aim through the pelting rain. The flare cracked into the sky, but the storm raged and I doubted anyone would see it from this far out. Wilhelmina, already in motion, grabbed a heavy fishing net from the deck, her eyes fierce with determination. She swung the net with all her strength, aiming to entangle the nearest intruder. But the invaders were relentless, their numbers overwhelming. They rushed forward like a dark tide. A masked figure sidestepped her attack and seized her wrist, yanking her off balance. Another invader knocked the net away, leaving her vulnerable as they descended upon us. I watched as the one still grasping her wrist shoved her arm behind her back, immobilizing any further efforts.

"Get away from her!" I yelled, my voice erupting with raw fury as I lunged forward grabbing an oar, ready to beat them senseless.

I caught glimpses of their cold, calculating eyes above the black of the masks. No hesitation marked their movements. They came for us, with a clear purpose: to destroy.

I swung the heavy oar at the closest invader, adrenaline coursing through me as I connected with a solid thud. More invaders surged forward, overpowering us. We were soon subdued, bound, and gagged, rendered helpless against their strength.

As I lay on the deck, dazed by the storm and crashing waves, a spotlight from the mast of their boat flooded my face. I squinted, glimpsing the figure directing the others, his features lost in the glare.

I called out to Wilhelmina, but the gag stifled my efforts. I watched as she struggled, her eyes locked with mine in frantic, wordless communication. We were doomed, but a part of me clung to hope that somehow, we would escape this nightmare and see our children again.

That hope vanished like a wisp of smoke as an intruder approached Wilhelmina. They grabbed her by the back of the neck with brutal force, and I thrashed against the ropes binding me, despair fueling my struggle. I strained and kicked, pleading with my eyes as I fought against the restraints, the fibers cutting into my skin.

In a final, piercing glance, I could see her lips moving. Whispering a silent plea. Then the intruder moved their other hand to her chin, twisting her neck with a vicious wrench. A sharp pain shot through me as a boot slammed into my back, forcing the air from my lungs and sending agony coursing through my body.

She crumpled to the deck.

Sound ceased to exist.

My heart pounded and blood rushed in my ears.

A primal scream tore from my throat. Rage and grief warred within me. I strained against my bonds, desperate to reach her, to hold her one last time. Tears blurred my vision.

The leader of the group knelt beside me, his voice a gravelly hiss in my ear. "This is what happens to those who defy us." His words were a final, cruel confirmation. As he rose, he gestured to one of his soldiers, who moved toward the compartment near the wheel. I barely registered the flash of the blade before a sharp, searing pain exploded in my side.

I gasped for air, my thoughts clouding as the soldier returned, clutching my leather-bound notebook—a testament of my life's work. A blackened haze crept into the edges of my vision, as I forced myself to look at her one last time.

Even in death her face was the epitome of my peace, the last sight before the world slipped away.

The Sea of Impassis and the Origins of the Land:

The Sea of Impassis holds a reverence in the hearts of Sandric's people, as it is not merely water but a cradle of existence. From its depths, the first of us are said to have risen—not in a blaze of conquest, but in the quiet shaping of the world itself. Life began there, in the merging of sea and land, where the contours of Sertoda were molded by hands long forgotten.

Yet the Sea of Impassis is more than the source of life—it is a keeper of secrets. Ancient lore speaks of its hidden passageways, where only those who understand the tides may find entry to The Depths.

I have often walked its shores, listening to the rhythmic pull of the water, feeling connected to those who shaped this land with such delicate force. The echoes of their laughter, their creation, seem to ride upon the waves, reminding me that our history is as fluid as the sea itself.

In pursuit of truth and understanding,

—H. Wilhoph

Chapter One

BETTA

I never wanted this role, but Sandric doesn't give a shit what any of us want.

I stood before the window lining the far side of the room, overlooking the sprawling skyline where steel and concrete blurred into the horizon. A distorted reflection stared back—golden eyes, once calculated and sharp had become more vacant by the day. Behind me, the small council sat in dead silence around the sleek obsidian conference table. The muted quiet a reminder of their powerlessness in the system.

The ceiling-mounted speakers hissed to life, static stretching through the stillness until the familiar mechanical voice hit our ears:

```
Your directives have been delivered. Check
your personal devices following this brief-
ing. The upcoming reading of the election
results is crucial. Ensure all details
of the ceremony are executed precisely.
The broadcast will be monitored by media
representatives. It is imperative that
the Surviving Aide maintains a flawless
image, as any deviation could compromise
```

the intended narrative.

I glanced out toward the world again. The heart of Mass formed a maze of gleaming towers, their glass exteriors reflecting the clouds that threatened rain. The city had become a sprawling testament to innovation. The once-primitive streets now buzzed with electric vehicles and pedestrians plugged into their personal devices ignored life happening around them. Neon lights and digital billboards blinked holographic advertisements, their messages vying for attention.

As I scanned the city a few stories above ground level, a large, brightly colored digital screen drew me in. A news clip flickered to life, the headline reading, BREAKING NEWS: DOBIAN INTELLECT GARON FIORE REVOLUTIONIZES TECH SPACE. My breath caught as the camera zoomed in on Garon. His long, silver hair flowed past his shoulders in braids, and his sharp jawline framed a face that could spark a thousand rebellions with just one of those devastatingly sexy grins. He exuded the kind of confidence and intelligence that promised he'd meet me toe-to-toe in wit and banter, effortlessly outclassing every man I'd ever let into my bed. And honestly, I'd savor every second of the challenge.

I knew his name well—everyone did. Garon Fiore. The tech prodigy from Dobia, a territory traditionally slow to adopt the cutting-edge advancements seen in neighboring Trunta. Dobia gained a reputation for its simplicity, resisting the rapid pace of change that consumed the rest of Sandric. For Garon to make headlines here, in Mass of all places, felt surreal. His presence on that screen served as a statement—Dobia no longer lingered in the shadows of their mountainous territory.

I tore my curiosity from the beautiful man on the screen and glanced down at the street below. A woman strolled along the pavement, twirling a bright yellow umbrella despite the somber gray sky. She moved with an ease I couldn't remember feeling, her small smile radiating a carefree spirit so foreign it seemed unreal. What would it be like to trade places with her?

For a fleeting moment, I indulged in the fantasy—a life where my world wasn't restrained. Where choices were simple, and burdens didn't crush. I'd jump from this window if it meant tasting that kind of freedom. Or, perhaps, if it meant falling into something warmer. Stronger. Like the arms of the silver haired stranger who had no idea how easily he consumed my thoughts.

The Surviving Aide of Sandric. *I survived*, but it was never that simple. Leadership here didn't reward governance—it demanded endurance. Only the Sanctioned were deemed strong enough to withstand what Sandric required. And withstand it, I did, but not by much. This land perfected the art of breaking its people, and soon, the newly elected representatives from our five territories would face the true cost of their victory. Survival didn't hinge on skill or strategy but on how much of yourself you were willing to sacrifice. There was no escape.

I turned from the glass, letting my gaze sweep over the dove-gray walls and polished surfaces, their design meant to convey order and stability, a detail I had learned over my time here. They made me sick. My attention finally settled on my small council. Three sat before me, their idle expressions betraying a lack of genuine engagement.

The briefing forged ahead, the voice droning on with the same emotionless cadence as the room of so-called officials:

```
The media's role is to project the image
we craft, and no interviews beyond the
predetermined protocol are permitted. The
integrity of the presentation must be
upheld without exception. Remember, the
appearance of fairness is paramount, and
```

```
any breach in protocol will be met with
severe repercussions.
```

I heard it too many times over the past five years: the threat of consequences. To an outsider, they would sound like empty noise from a supervisor having a bad day, but those inside knew all too well what happened when you crossed a line. I already teetered on that razor's edge. Rebellion simmered, not yet rooted in my heart. But feigning amenability? It grew tiresome.

The five-year term of an electee represented Sandric's five territories—Sertoda, Lizon, Brawn, Dobia, and Trunta. At the end of every term, three new representatives were elected from each territory. These representatives best embodied the qualities of the three pivotal roles of Sandric's top leaders. The fifteen electees in total, would be whisked away to Mass, the central city, to compete in *The Sanctioning*. And The Sanctioning? Oh, just a brutal, unforgiving process, shrouded in secrecy, that would determine who of the electees was truly worthy to lead.

I crossed my arms over my chest, pressing them against my ribs as I struggled to reconcile with the naivety of my past understanding of leadership. We were taught that the three highest positions of power, known as *The Sanctioned*, were not just titles but the ultimate measure of achievement in Sandric society. The seats were held by those who embodied intelligence, tenacity, and strength—individuals who rose above all others through the mysterious trial process. The Noble Warrior, The Perpetual Sense, and The Surviving Aide—each role crucial to the future of Sandric.

The message concluded with a final, bitter reminder:

```
Failure to adhere to these guidelines
```

```
will result in immediate and severe conse-
quences. Ensure complete compliance. Obe-
dience above all.


Sanctioned. United. One.
```

The small council's eyes shifted in unison, their attention zeroing in on me with a rigid intensity. The air crackled with tension, as if every piece of hardware watched us. The facility served to ensure control, efficiency, and observation—a place where power moved unseen, while the city's pulse thrummed below. I turned away from the window, leaving behind the warmth of the sun as it finally broke through the clouds and bathed my face. Turning away from the thought of escape, I finally took my seat at the head of the long table.

"Betta," a voice interrupted my reverie. Councilor Shen stared at me from his seat, his face a mask of flat, monotone detachment. I tried to remember where he originated from.

Lizon, perhaps?

Yes, Lizon.

He served as their Surviving Aide representative, of course—a role he once embraced with youthful zeal. Now, that zeal evaporated, leaving a dull shell of duty in its place. Like the others in this room, Shen and I once held the same title, Surviving Aide Elect.

These briefings, involving all the title bearers from our term, gathered us under the pretense that we were shaping the future together. Just like the Noble Warriors met with their own, engineering methods of combat, and the Perpetual Senses gathered to exchange their so-called '*brilliant insights*', we Surviving Aides merely simulated influence.

It was all smoke and mirrors. The notion of collaboration—of forging laws and policies—nothing more than a constructed illusion.

The truth?

The decisions that mattered were made elsewhere, far beyond our reach. We were pieces on a game board, moved by meticulously crafted rules we held no say in.

My mind drifted toward the absence of a familiar face, and before Shen could speak again I asked, "Where's Councilwoman Quintus?"

His mouth tightened into a thin line; the subtle budge almost imperceptible. "Held in the simulation chamber for her *compliance session*."

A chill ran through me. *Of course... consequences.*

She would return. A little more lifeless, but roughly still intact. My mind drifted to the Perpetual Sense council—permanently short one member. Their loss, unspoken yet impossible for me to ignore.

A Sertodan.

Someone close to me.

His absence left a gaping wound in my heart. A vacancy that could never be filled. Yet the anger, the disgust that burned in me whenever I thought of what happened to him, writhed under a placid mask.

And to think, a new group would come in, never knowing the possibility that they could succumb to the same fate.

"I need to discuss the upcoming election results ceremony with you and a potential issue," Shen finally said, his voice devoid of inflection. "The situation in Dobia is growing more volatile."

I raised an eyebrow. "Volatile? How?"

Shen's stare remained as impassive as his voice. "There's increasing unrest over the fact that Dobia's representatives have never moved on to a Sanctioned position. Rumors of insurrection are spreading. They're claiming that The Sanctioning is rigged, and there's fear that the lack of a Dobian leader could ignite serious unrest in their territory."

I exhaled slowly, twisting in my chair, my sight longing to be back on the city's sprawling panorama. "That's just great. It sounds like I'll

11

be sitting on a powder keg. Let Draven and his team pretend to sort it out—this isn't my problem."

My role as the Surviving Aide didn't just come with a pretty little title; it came with a *Cird-damned* performance. I served as the celestial face of Sandric, the one who strode onto the stage to deliver the sanitized narrative of our so-called order. The Surviving Aide represented not just a position but a constructed symbol of virtue and sacrifice. Elected for heroism, bestowed with an ethereal grace that concealed the relentless grind of reality. In this charade, my role became the beacon of hope and compliance, even as the world outside teetered on the brink of chaos.

Let the Noble Warrior handle the conspiracy.

Shen stiffened, waiting for a more reassuring response.

"I'll inform Draven about these potential threats," I said, my voice edged with irritation. "It seems I'm obliged to drag him into this mess. I'll seek his input and take it into account as we slog through this farce of a ceremony."

Each council member nodded, their faces briefly revealing unease at my mocking words before their practiced mask of indifference slid back into place. That flash of apprehension said enough. Deep down, beneath layers of conditioning, they knew the truth of it: we were the maintenance workers, ensuring Sandric's machine churned out its next batch of representatives without pause or conscience.

I wrapped up the meeting with a terse reminder of the stakes involved should compliance not be upheld.

As I turned to leave, my attention locked onto two public relations aides lingering by the door. The blonde, sharp-featured and in her mid-twenties, stood with an air of self-assurance. Beside her, an equally young brunette with a more aloof demeanor glanced my way, her dark eyes gleaming with quiet judgment. They exchanged a fleeting, knowing glance, their whispers just loud enough for me to hear.

The blonde aide muttered, "Betta's toeing the line. I wonder how long until they make an example of her?"

The brunette sneered, leaning in, "Oh, absolutely. When you dare ruffle Sandric's precious feathers, you can bet the consequences will be brutal and immediate. Betta's about to get a front-row seat to just how harsh Sandric enforcement can be if she doesn't fix that attitude."

In a different world, perhaps we might have been peers, but in this one, the divide between us remained all too apparent.

As I made my way to the door, their smug little jabs barely phased me. I flipped my hair over my shoulder as I turned back, lips curling into a smirk. "If Sandric's planning to make me their next big cautionary tale, they'd better come with more than a dull blade. I'm not easy to break, sweetheart." With that, I shoved the door open, leaving their pathetic grins in the dust.

As I headed toward the elevators, a grim thought threatened my conviction. In my final days, if an opportunity to speak out about my experience arose, would I have the courage to seize it? Or would I let fear silence me, just like so many others before? The seed of dissent, buried and ignored for so long, emerged time and again as a persistent, unsettling presence.

The uncertainty coiled around my core—would I ever escape this twisted web, or would I remain ensnared in Sandric's grip forever?

The elevator doors slid open with an all-too-cheerful chime, revealing two armed guards standing at attention, their faces blank as slate. I raised an eyebrow, suppressing a groan. *Ah, yes. My personal escort.*

"Well, isn't this delightful," I mumbled, stepping inside as they flanked me. "All I'm missing now is a crown and an entourage. Maybe you guys could carry me to my next obligation. No? Too much?"

The guards remained silent, their expressions set in stone. One of them pressed the button, and the elevator jolted to life. I threw a glance at the cuter one. "Do you think they'll roll out a red carpet for me? Or is it straight to the next round of '*mandatory fun*'?"

Nothing. Not even a blink.

"Tough crowd," I sighed, leaning back against the cold wall. "You guys are about as lively as a Cird-damn funeral."

The elevator hummed as it descended. Whatever grim duty awaited me, I wouldn't make it easy for them. If Sandric believed I would walk quietly into my next task, they faced a rude awakening.

The Creation of Borders:

The borders of Sandric's territories were never arbitrary. They were forged out of necessity—defined not by lines on a map, but by the land itself. Brawn's harsh deserts collided with Sertoda's verdant fields, while Dobia's soaring mountains naturally warded off encroachment. These divisions reflect a survival born out of scarcity, each region's people fighting to claim their space in a world where abundance remained perpetually out of reach.

Borders are more than geographical—they represent the uneasy peace between ways of life as different as fire and water. I wonder if these boundaries, carved in strife, will ever soften, or if they will forever remain scars of our past.

In pursuit of truth and understanding,

—H. Wilhoph

Chapter Two

LEVITY

"Levity, why are you always so serious?" Evie—Sprout, as I affectionately called my youngest sister—leaned out of the sidecar, her hand slicing through the air as if she were playing with the wind.

"I'm not serious," I said, breathless as the tires crunched over another patch of loose gravel. "Just thinking about all the things we need at the market."

I focused instead on the strain of pedaling over Lizon's uneven gravel roads. Every bump jarred the bike, and the extra weight from the sidecar turned each pedal stroke into a struggle against thick mud. My legs burned, but stopping remained out of the question—not with a steep hill left to climb.

Evie sighed, dipping her hand just above the ground passing beneath us. "You always say that. But I know you're thinking about something else."

I pressed my lips together and kept my eyes on the path. She was right, as usual. My thoughts were a constant storm of worries, from keeping our family afloat to the endless demands of our lives in Sertoda. But at that moment, I could only focus on the painful stretch of road in front of us and the relief that would wash over me once we crested the hill.

"Almost there," I muttered, more to myself than to her, as I pushed harder on the pedals. The electric portion of the bike would have made this easier, but every bit of energy stored in it needed to be conserved.

The top of the hill came into view, revealing Lizon's vast landscape. Terraced fields flowed in geometric rows, bordered by stands of slender bamboo and trees with delicate, fan-shaped leaves that cast shifting patterns on the ground below. The soft mossy paths wound through fields, lending an ancient, peaceful quality to the scene. As we reached the crest, I breathed a sigh of relief, feeling the pedals lighten as gravity took over and gravel turned to packed dirt, allowing me a brief, rare moment of calm as we coasted downhill.

"How did you get so strong, Sprout?" I asked, turning my head to watch her as she laughed, lifting both hands into the wind now that we were gliding with little effort.

"I learned from you," she said, as if it were the most obvious thing in the world.

I smiled, yet I knew her words carried a significance she might not grasp. I fell short of the strength she believed I possessed. No matter how hard I tried, I always felt we were one step away from the next struggle.

The "land people" as they were called, produced the majority of the fresh food for Sandric's different regions. I aimed to travel the rocky road to Lizon only once a month to procure food for our family, but the boys' appetites were growing heartier by the day, due to teenage growth spurts. This marked my second trip in two weeks.

As we rolled down the last stretch of the hill, Lizon's sprawling open-air market unfolded into a field of vibrant lines of stands and stalls. The smell of fresh produce and delicate, steaming pastries filled the air, mingling with the earthy scent of the turned soil. No trace of the saltiness that hung in the air back in Sertoda lingered here.

"Look, Levity! They've got peaches again!" Evie's excitement spilled out as she pointed to a stall piled high with ripe fruit.

I slowed the bike to a stop and parked near the entrance of the market. "We'll see if we have enough left over after we get what we need," I said, unclipping her from the sidecar. With endless energy she jumped out and tugged me toward the stands.

At almost eight years old, she exuded a precious innocence I envied. The boys would turn sixteen this year, and Blue turned ten last spring. Evie appeared untouched by the weight of responsibility soon to descend upon her like crushing stones.

"We need potatoes, beans, rice, and onions," I reminded her, fully aware her mind already drifted toward the peaches and fresh-baked rolls she adored. "We can't get distracted, okay?"

Evie wrinkled her nose but nodded, skipping ahead, her hand brushing the tops of wildflowers that lined the path.

The market bustled with activity: farmers chatted with customers, children dashed between stalls, and a hum of quiet laughter filled the air. Evie weaved between the shoppers, and I kept a steady eye on her as she darted toward the colorful displays.

"Lev! They've got purple carrots!" she said, her eyes wide as she dashed back and tugged at my arm.

"Not today, Sprout. Just the basics."

We made our way through the crowd, pausing only when I spotted a familiar stall near the back. The middle-age woman who ran it waved as we approached. Her straw hat perched precariously against her straight, dark hair with silver streaks.

"How much are potatoes going for in Sertoda these days?" she asked. The corners of her upturned eyes crinkled as she smiled warm as always.

"Eight kilowatts for just one five-pound sack," I replied with an exasperated sigh. "It lasts us less than a week. We can buy one at a time."

The government allocated each household's energy earnings based on their contribution to society. You worked more, you earned more.

18

Families in poverty, like ours, received less than one thousand kilowatts each month in assistance. The boys helped out by doing odd jobs around our small town, earning a few kilo coins and bartering trades, although our equally impoverished neighbors offered little in return. Now that Evie was old enough to be left in the half-hearted care of Blue, I could join the workforce for the first time to increase our income by the end of the year.

The woman carefully placed two sacks of potatoes into the worn canvas bag I brought with me. *I could work in a store, ringing up groceries and bagging them,* I thought, but even that seemed like a stretch. I never held a job in my life—unless raising my siblings counted—and I doubted anyone would be interested in hiring someone whose only skill involved ensuring kids ate on time and didn't run off to the ocean unsupervised. What else could I do? Stock shelves? Smile at customers? I could barely manage to get through the day without falling apart. How would I convince anyone I excelled at anything when I didn't even believe it myself?

"Are you stocked up on candles? I have eight sticks on sale for a kilo and a half."

"No, thank you. We're okay for now," I replied, taking my bag from her and dropping six kilo coins into her palm. Double the potatoes for two coins less. I offered a polite smile before stepping away from the stall.

We spent more time in Lizon than necessary, but Evie made it impossible to leave. Her curiosity led us from one stand to another, marveling at the displays of fresh produce. We sampled crisp, honey-sweet pears, warm steamed buns with a hint of spice, and soft cheeses wrapped in delicate leaves, the taste of Lizon lingering on our tongues. Evie's energy was contagious—at each new stall, she'd tug at my hand, her laughter mixing with the gentle clinking of ceramic bowls and soft chatter around us. Despite my practical mindset, I found myself giving in to the market's charm.

At one point, she'd even convinced me to try a sweet plum, despite my insistence that we stick to the essentials. The fruit melted in my mouth, its juice running down my chin as I tried to keep up with her endless ramblings about which stand sold the shiniest apples or where we could find the freshest butter.

A sweet nostalgic scent of fresh baked goods filled the air. I could almost feel Mama's finger dusting a sprinkle of white flour down the bridge of my nose, just as she did during my childhood. She'd taught me how to bake the bread of Piety every Sunday. We'd mix flour, salt, water, and wild yeast by hand—our family's tribute to the ocean that gave way to land for us to prosper. She always insisted it remained our duty, as good Sertoda people, to honor that history and give back. The bread symbolized the blessings we'd been gifted, sent out to sea in baskets for communion with the waves.

I smiled at the memory, but a squeal from Evie brought reality back into focus. We visited nearly every vendor, and although the people of Lizon were welcoming, the market seemed quieter than usual, as if anxiety lingered in the air. I noticed a few uneasy glances exchanged between the farmers, their conversations dropping to whispers. Something weighed on their minds, though I couldn't place what.

Evie, oblivious to it all, skipped ahead, her face lit with delight at every discovery. I didn't want to spoil her fun with my worries.

"Can we go to the beach?" Evie asked suddenly, her big brown eyes wide with hope.

"We've already been here too long," I sighed, adjusting the bags of produce over my shoulder. "We need to get home before it gets late."

"Please, Levity? Just for a little while!" She bounced on her toes, her enthusiasm impossible to ignore. "It's right on the way home! Just a quick dip, I promise! Besides, you always say we should make the most of our trips."

I shook my head, but her words softened me. "Fine," I muttered. "But just for a little while. No swimming too far out. And you owe me next time I need help around the house."

Evie's face lit up with a toothless grin, and before I could change my mind, she grabbed my hand and dragged me back to our bike.

The salty breeze hit us long before we saw the ocean, its comforting scent wrapping around us as we stepped off the road. The rhythmic crash of waves reached our ears next, with their sound came the familiar tension creeping into my shoulders. Evie raced to the shoreline, already kicking off her shoes.

We stopped at our usual spot; it was a quiet patch away from the crowds, where the cliffs blocked most of the wind. Evie waded into the water, her dress half-hazardly discarded. A shiver crawled down my spine as her delicate arms sliced through the sunbathed waves. She seemed so free, so unaffected by the burdens I carried. Evie's laughter mingled with the thunder of the surf, a fleeting moment of joy amid the anxiety building in me.

As I settled in on the shore to watch, I dug my toes deeper into the sand, the small grains yielding softly around my bare feet. She dove into a wave and my heart raced. Each second Evie spent underwater stretched out for an eternity.

She surfaced and paused to fiddle with a cluster of seaweed floating like a lost raft. Droplets of seawater cascaded from her thick brown curls, returning to the ocean below. She adjusted the seaweed nest before gently guiding it to the shore.

Shielding my eyes from the sun's glare on the ocean's surface, I called out to her, "Evie, ten more minutes, then we need to return home to your brothers. I'm sure they've turned the cottage upside down by now."

Evie waved back, the sound of delight carrying on the wind and disappearing against a seagull's calling, yet she remained distant, as if oblivious to the urgency in my voice. She once again dove into an approaching wave, letting it wash over her.

I held my breath until I saw her nose breach the air.

The year Evie rushed into our world, our parents left it, leaving her to navigate life without their warmth, their stories, or their gentle embrace. As her oldest sister, I often found myself questioning my own influence over her development. How could my guidance have shaped this kind of character? Doubt chipped away at me, whispering my inadequacies and insecurities. Unlike me, who had the privilege of sixteen precious years with our parents, Evie held not one memory of their love.

A twinge of guilt built in my stomach. Even as Evie grew into a girl of remarkable spirit, I wished she had known our parents as I did—heard their voices, felt their presence.

Two intertwined souls. Their love for each other, for our land and people, for our family, echoed through my memory even as I sat beneath the warm sun, melding into the beach.

Pop whispered in Mama's ear as he tucked his arms around her waist, swaying their bodies together to a silent tune:

"She is my ocean.

Wild and free.

Warm and cool.

Ragged and smooth.

All-encompassing.

She has wrapped around every inch of my being and we are one."

My birth began the legacy of Wilhelmina and Hophsted, the Wilhoph people of Sertoda.

Levity Wilhoph, the firstborn.

I pushed back onto my elbows, the sand cradling my weight as I watched Evie's small figure dip and dart through the waves like she belonged to the sea itself. The sun bathed the beach in a golden hue, and its warmth seeped into my skin. For a moment, I allowed myself to relax, the tension in my muscles easing.

Mama and Pop, I mused, always showered me with attention during my awkward adolescent years. They'd celebrate the tiniest milestones as if I'd conquered the world. I imagined them now, seeing Evie—gliding through the water with the grace of a dolphin. How proud they'd be.

I stretched my legs out in the sand, the gritty texture grounding me in the present. At Sprout's age, I could barely walk without tripping over myself, let alone command the ocean like Evie. She moved with little effort, while I had always been a series of stumbles and false starts, desperate for the approval they seemed so willing to give. My fingers absentmindedly combed through the sand, trailing lines like the ones Pop used to draw in the air when he spoke of the lore and fables of Sandric history.

Look right across the waves, my darling, he'd say, his heavy brow lifting with that fervor only he could muster. *Do you see it? The Holy Sea of Impassis.*

Pop, a professor of cultural studies at Sertoda University in the heart of the city, had a way of making our history feel alive and tangible. He could make you feel as though the legends were waiting, just beneath the surface, for you to uncover.

I smiled at the memory, squinting toward the horizon as if searching for that mystical place myself.

I don't see it, I always replied, shielding my eyes from the glare bouncing off the water.

It's there—you have to feel it. It's where our people arose and where they'll rise again. His voice would rumble like a distant storm, full of certainty. I never saw what he saw, but I believed in it because he did.

A sudden splash jerked me from my thoughts. Evie's petite frame bobbed in the distance, her body surrendering to the waves, letting the current pull her closer to shore. She'd grown so much, yet she still seemed weightless, like driftwood carried on the tide.

Pop would've been delighted. I remembered the days we'd spend together on our boat, the sun beating down as he taught me about fishing, the sea, and its creatures. It didn't matter if I failed; he always saw something in me I couldn't.

But now, lying on this beach, the same one we used to visit together, I felt that pressure again—the burden of his expectations. I'd never become the person he'd wanted me to be, and the more I tried, the more I fell short.

I glanced back at Evie. She tackled life headfirst in a way I never could, with no fear. I envied her for that. I wondered how much of that came from being so young, from never knowing the pressure of responsibility like I did.

Evie flopped onto the sand, arms and legs sprawled like a starfish. Her chest rose and fell as she lay there, staring up at the sky.

The wind picked up swirling the scent of saltwater and seaweed into the air.

Mama tried to teach me softness, balancing out Pop's intensity. She taught me to plant, to tend to the herbs that healed and the vegetables that sustained us. I pressed my palms against the sand. The grains reminded me of the way the dirt felt under my nails tending our little garden. I'd help Mama prune our native plants: the *viondra*—with its calming, silver-tipped leaves—and the *azureth*, its stunning blue petals vibrant against the soil, their sharp citrus scent cutting through fatigue. To

24

Mama, whether baking or tending her garden, life was about the gentle art of giving back. She saw patience and nurturing in every rising loaf and unfurling leaf—this deep connection between our people and the land. She believed in the power of growth, even if I struggled to grasp it.

Another gust of wind blew past, and I shivered despite the warm sun. I stared out at the waves again as Evie rolled onto her side, sand clinging to her wet skin. How much longer could I maintain the illusion of belonging here, acting as if I possessed the same capabilities, the same substance as Evie or the rest of my siblings? The truth always lingered beneath the surface.

I gathered our belongings and brushed the sand out of her linen dress. Our secret stop should have given the boys ample time to have dinner well underway by the time we reached home. It was the only task I gave with strict instructions.

"You never join me." She pouted, raising her core and flopping it down on the wet sand, mimicking a fish out of water.

"And you know I don't like to swim." I grabbed my boots, slipped them on, and dusted them off. I laced the ties, not missing a ring and pulled the bow tight above my ankle. I rolled the cuffs on my dark green pants back down to their intended length.

"A dress would be prettier on you. You might even catch the eye of Thomas if you would wear one to communion Sunday."

"What an imagination! Thomas hasn't been to communion since moving to the city. Enough. Get dressed."

I'd heard the comment more times than I cared to count—and not just from my sister. But dresses were as impractical as they were uncomfortable, especially with my unending chore pile. The bike ride to the fish market alone would make anything more than trousers unbearable. Besides, what did it matter if I caught the eye of someone like Thomas? That impulsive night years ago was one he'd probably forgotten by morning. Just a passing moment for him, a bit of excitement before he left for the city, but one that had lingered stubbornly in my own thoughts.

No, there was no point dwelling on it. He barely knew my name then, and now he was something like a legend. A well-loved, charming kind of man every family wanted. My baggage was far too heavy for any man in Sertoda, especially one with his perfect reputation.

I gathered my long, dark coils and twisted them up, securing them with a clam-shaped clip. The idea of Thomas even noticing me—really noticing, and not after one too many hard drinks—was… was laughable. A small chuckle slipped out as I tucked my chin down, the self-deprecating thought settling around me like an old coat. On my best days, I was passable, plain at worst. In the city of Sertoda, there were women with striking curves and undeniable beauty, women who didn't carry the weight of half-buried troubles like I did. Women suited to a man of Thomas's standing, with his easy charm and kind demeanor. No, he wouldn't give a second thought my way.

Evie tugged the linen dress over her head. From the bottom of the long skirt, a wet undergarment fell out. She wiggled her olive-complected arms through the capped sleeves, picked up the sea-soaked clothes, and offered them to me.

I stuffed it in my bag, certain the dry contents inside would soon be soggy, too.

After cleaning up our makeshift pallet in the sand, we walked back to the rocky ledge where I parked our bike. Evie tucked into my sidecar with her small frame. I adjusted the bags of beans, grain, and the colorful crops of veggies around her, so they wouldn't be bruised as they jostled around.

Our humble family cottage—one of many shabby homes scattered across The Divide—sat on a small, unassuming parcel of land. Mama's garden flourished in the small yard, a patchwork of greens and blooms that I tended to this day. This rare oasis of color brightened the rugged, weathered structures of our neighborhood. The ocean waves' constant murmuring could still be heard, a reminder of the beach that lay over the hill.

Pop would often pause at the garden gate, watching the flowers sway in the sea breeze as he spoke with reverence about our home's history, weaving tales of the first Sertoda settlers. He told us our cottage occupied sacred ground, a symbol of honor, even as its modest appearance remained overshadowed by the city's gleaming architecture.

Pop's stories often veered into the realm of grandeur, his pride in our heritage palpable. Yet, I suspected his tales were a way to distract us from our meager means. He wanted us to cling to that sense of honor, even if it only formed a sheer curtain over our poverty.

The memory of him remained vivid and comforting. His throaty, yet warm hymns filled my ears, their gentle strains cutting through the obtrusive sound of the ocean.

I pushed back the kickstand with the toe of my boot and started the bike. The motion of my foot on the metal and the bitter electric buzz focused me and masked a coaxing melodious hum that threatened to take over my brain.

The short ride with the speed of electricity would be plenty of time for the wind to dry Evie's wet curls and the boys would be none the wiser of our little escapade. I gave the throttle a twist before whipping around in the gravel to face the setting sun.

The Naming Tradition of Sertoda:

In Sertoda, the creation of a new surname is not a mere formality, but a deep-seated symbolic act that intertwines tradition with renewal. Unlike other territories where family names are inherited, Sertoda's approach reflects their emphasis on partnership and equality. By blending the first syllables of each partner's name, a new identity is forged—one that is neither rooted in the past nor dominated by one lineage over another.

This tradition, known poetically as 'casting their names upon the sea', illustrates Sertoda's connection to the ocean as a source of life and continuity. Just as the sea is ever-changing yet constant, so too is the evolving nature of family and community. It is a reminder that names, like the tides, can shift, but always carry with them the essence of their origin.

Sertoda's culture of naming teaches us that identity is not something rigidly inherited, but something that can be shaped and reshaped, in harmony with others. In a world where borders often define and divide, Sertoda's names are a quiet rebellion—blending the past to create a shared future.

In pursuit of truth and understanding,
—H. Wilhoph

Chapter Three

BETTA

Two sharp raps echoed from my living quarter's door, startling me.

"Mutta, you ready?" Draven Ballister's gravel-laden voice grumbled from the other side of the metal. It surprised me the Noble Warrior bothered to knock, considering his usual lack of tact.

Glancing over my shoulder into the sleek vanity mirror, I watched as my silky black hair cascaded down to the small of my back. Five years had passed since I let anyone near it with scissors—a clear marker of the deep-seated mistrust forged within me by my Brawn bloodline. Trusting someone to cut my hair felt like handing over the key to a locked vault or leaving a loaded gun unattended. The very thought of someone wielding scissors so close to me... well, that remained an advantage I refused to give.

Brawn heritage dominated my features. Deep down, I knew I could never pass for a Sertoda woman. My caramel complexion, straight onyx hair, and sharp jawline and nose betrayed my mixed lineage. My mother, with her fair skin, curly hair, and round, wholesome appearance, embodied Sertoda's traits. Even as I represented Sertoda, chosen by my people, I still shouldered the burden of my unwanted background. Even more so when Draven insisted on bringing it to my attention with his adolescent pet name.

Picking up the charcoal pencil, I turned to perfect the eyeliner I'd applied, deliberately ignoring the door. If he believed a few hurried knocks would drag me out of my sanctuary, he underestimated my skill at tuning out annoying distractions. *Let him stew while I finish my masterpiece.*

My silence seemed to push the door to slide open faster, as if Draven's impatience sped up the mechanics. I caught his reflection in the mirror—trimmed dark beard, fresh shaved head, and a look that carried both playful confidence and unwavering seriousness.

"After all this time, you still haven't grasped that I don't find your demeaning nickname endearing?" I snapped, my focus fixed on the mirror as I continued to apply my makeup. "Seriously, are you trying to irritate the hell out of me? Because if so, congratulations, you're doing great."

The room oozed modern elegance, its smooth surfaces gleaming under the soft glow of recessed lights. A prominent chandelier cast muted reflections off the dark, heavy wood furniture, lending an air of sophistication to the space. I hadn't minded the quiet, until it shattered with Draven's boots scuffing the marble floor.

Draven strode toward me, his towering six-foot-four frame crowding out what little light existed. I rarely saw him in the Noble Warrior's formal uniform, but the effect remained undeniable. The dark, fitted leather hugged his broad shoulders, emphasizing every muscular inch of him. Silver accents pinned at his neckline, displaying his military rank, caught the light, gleaming against the room's shadows. He looked every bit the hero, and, for a brief moment, I felt a slight tension inside me loosen.

His calloused fingertips grazed the bare skin of my shoulder, followed by his deep bronze arm brushing past. Our skin tones might have complemented each other—*the only compliment happening here*—but I still flinched at the touch and turned to face him.

"And after all this time, you haven't figured out that I'd never hurt you?" Draven purred, flipping the toggle on the light switch. The crystal chandelier above us blazed to life, expelling the calming glow of the room.

I shot him a glare, my patience wearing thin. "Is there something you need, or are you just here to mess with my light settings and my mood?" I swatted his hand away and turned the switch back down to the dim, sultry glow I preferred.

"I've come to retrieve you for the reading of the election results. You do remember that's tonight, don't you?" Draven's voice carried an exaggerated lilt of mock concern, his eyes flicking toward me in the mirror. He adjusted the straps of the tactical plate carrier over his fitted black leather suit, his movements slow and deliberate. "Or is all that makeup for some other grand occasion?"

He smirked, his tone teetering on teasing. "Not that I'm complaining, of course. You're making it very hard for me to focus on politics."

The Noble Warrior's formal attire seemed almost too inviting. Between the karambit at his waist and pistol strapped to his thigh, only a Cird or something with grit would try their luck. If he kept teasing me, I might be tempted to show him just how easily I could take them—and him—apart.

Meanwhile, they expected me to slip into a gauzy white frock they delivered to my room earlier that day. Nothing screams "divine" like a dress that barely offers as much protection as a piece of tissue paper. A relic that emulated goddesses and angels. Sandric predecessors must believe celestials needed to freeze their asses off in the name of presentation. I couldn't decide whether to snicker or spit at the absurdity.

The Cird launched no significant attacks since that night five years ago. Among the three current Sandric leaders, my firsthand experience during that terrorist assault had secured my election as a representative. Sertoda honored my bravery by thrusting me into this position. *Funny how doing the right thing led me into all the wrong places.*

I clenched my jaw. Memories flooded back with haunting clarity: children's piercing screams mingled with the crackling flames that lit the night sky. A night of desperation and fear. Yet despite the chaos surrounding me, an undeniable pull urged me to run toward the danger rather than away from it.

I glanced at Draven. His background in the Brawn military meant combat experience with the Cird. Did he understand that pull, that instinct to face the chaos head-on?

Sandric's reports painted the Cird as inhumane. Their devastating terrorist act a century ago had sent shockwaves across the world. After claiming countless lives, the Sanctioned's decree called for the Cird's eradication. Half of their society perished while the remaining members established a hidden community beneath the surface, known unofficially as The Depths. They remained out of sight from Sandric's citizens, for the most part.

The Cird inspired fear and fascination, their existence veiled in myth and propaganda. Stories cast them as reclusive enemies wielding advanced technology that ensured their survival in the dark Depths after exile. Whispers of their influence over Sandric persisted, though details remained elusive.

My attention snapped from the eerie memories of my past as Draven surveyed me—our taunting dance of cat and mouse leaving me unsettled. His eyes traced the sheer material wrapping around my slender neck, following the draping panels to the high slit right below my waist, revealing far too much of my hip's curve.

"Doesn't leave much to the imagination, does it?" he remarked, amusement flickering in his eyes.

"Trust me, there's plenty left for you to imagine," I asserted, standing and pushing past him. My shoulder brushed against his hulking presence, the unwelcome intrusion into my personal space sent an unexpected shiver through my body.

"Oh, don't worry, I'm great with fantasizing," he said, a playful smirk curling his lips. "But sometimes reality is far more intriguing."

"Keep dreaming, Draven. Reality has never been your strong suit."

Five years of enduring proximity to a man from a territory I despised drained my spirit. Brawn men were brutish—abusers of women, ruthless in their methods. They bred virile machines under the guise of men. Their war tactics might justify their position in Sandric's bureaucracy, but their barbaric ways made them intolerable. As the singular force against the Cird, they'd erected military barracks throughout Sandric, a new one for each discovered subterranean entrance. No other territories matched their militant culture and strategies in keeping the Cird subdued.

Their largest assembly occupied the desert town called The Mouth. My mother fled from there after my birth. It was never home. I knew it well from her cautionary tales. Located in a small cavern notorious for its unassuming craggy terrain lay the largest entrance to The Depths—the source of all Sandric problems.

Draven never feared displaying his aggression in front of an audience. A guard had dared break protocol and sneered at me during a briefing.

What would she know about leading? he taunted.

Draven seized the guard's arm and twisted.

Snap!

The sharp crack of bone echoed through the room. *Next time you think to disrespect a Sanctioned, remember this,* he had growled. The guard gasped, eyes wide with fear, while I had stood frozen, torn between gratitude for Draven's defense and horror at his brutality.

Each term, a decorated soldier from Brawn invariably occupied the Noble Warrior position. Captain Draven Ballister proved no exception.

The other territories sent inferior representatives time and again, and I cringed at the thought of who would arrive in the next few days. Who would take his place tormenting the next group of representatives?

His smirks and taunts wore down my defenses. "Betta, you wouldn't be the first woman I've had from The Mouth. Maybe before we part ways, I'll finally persuade you to use your mouth on me." Draven winked at me through the mirror—looking quite pleased with his crude remark.

It pained me to respond to such provocation, but it would pain me more to let Draven leave my quarters thinking he held the upper hand. I closed the distance between us, letting my golden eyes meet his reflected in the mirror. I held his stare. Slipping my hand around to his chest, I slid it under the armored plate, running my fingers with deft speed over the curves of muscle. The scent of crisp leather enveloped me, earthy and robust, mingling with the faintest hint of mint.

I pressed my body close to his so he could feel my warmth through his suit. My hand drifted down his taut stomach as he relaxed into my touch. I rested my chin on his shoulder—my tall frame allowing me reach—so I could catch any change of expression in the mirror. A smirk spread across his face. My hand roamed under the waistband of his leather pants, grasping exactly what he wanted my mouth on.

"I'm not from The Mouth, my love," I whispered into his ear, letting my top lip graze his earlobe. He began to stiffen under my touch, and as I wrapped my fingers around his girth, I squeezed tight until all four digits met my thumb. He tensed under the firm pressure. I bared my teeth at him and growled, "I'm from The Divide of Sertoda... and I've had bigger."

I shoved him away, removing myself from his pants and the room.

Lyonal Crestmore stood in the marble foyer, the sleek surfaces gleaming under the warm artificial lights that illuminated the grand space. Massive iron doors loomed at the far end of the room, designed with ornate patterns that hinted at the power and authority they guarded. Tall windows framed the foyer, revealing a view of the towering city buildings that rose against the evening sky. Lyonal's hands rested in the pockets of his tailored black slacks, the attire sharp and structured against his lean frame.

As I descended the staircase, his scrutinizing blue eyes, partially obscured by the rims of his tortoiseshell frames, locked onto mine with piercing intensity. His expression didn't suggest confidence; it boldly asserted his belief in his superiority over both Draven and me.

A flicker of amusement danced in the corner of his thin lips, curling upward into the briefest of smiles, as if he relished the power play within the distance between us.

"You look remarkable as always, Betta," Lyonal observed, his pale hand reaching out to take mine as he assisted me down the last few steps. His lips twisted into a grimace, revealing his discomfort. Gray hair peeked more prominently above the arms of his glasses—a sign of his copious stress since our anointment.

"And you are so handsome, Lyonal," I replied, grasping the lapels of his jacket and kissing his right cheek. Glancing down at my barely-there dress, I added, "I'll give your regards to whoever decided that less fabric equals more elegance."

I fixed a long stare on Draven, a mischievous smile tugging at my lips as he bounded down the stairs two at a time, reaching us with speed.

"The people are waiting. They cannot start without us." Lyonal reminded, playing the stern father role as if he saw right through the two children and their games. He brushed my hands off his suit jacket, compressing the creases my grip attempted to make.

Draven shot me a sidelong glance as he shuffled by.

I leaned back, crossing my arms with a smirk. "All this will be over soon, Lyonal. What are you gonna do with all that free time? Twiddle your thumbs instead of breathing down our necks?" I clicked my tongue, the mockery clear. "Bet you'll miss it."

Lyonal leaned in close to my ear, lowering his voice so only I could bear witness to his threat. "We still have duties, Elisabetta," he whispered through gritted teeth. "Those will be upheld with honor until our servitude is fully relinquished to the incoming representatives. I cannot risk the repercussions of your careless actions."

His words sent a wave of unease through me, setting every nerve on edge.

He ran an index finger down my forearm, wrapped his firm hand around my wrist, and applied pressure. Lyonal yanked me further into his atmosphere. My breath caught in the back of my throat. "I expect you to conduct yourself with utmost professionalism this evening. Follow these orders to the letter, or you'll find out how far their threats can reach. Don't test them, Betta. My livelihood depends on your compliance."

Lyonal hailed from the esteemed region of Trunta, renowned for its populace's staggering intellect, pushing the boundaries of genius. In this part of our world, innovation thrived in a way I only read about in textbooks.

Trunta stood as a bustling metropolis of modernization. They devoted every inch of land to technology and ingenious solutions aimed at enhancing daily life. Little room existed for agriculture amidst the sprawling advancements, as the focus remained steadfast on generating power and pioneering new scientific breakthroughs. Beyond the towering walls of

Trunta lay the epicenter of Sandric's wealth, and Lyonal's conglomerate wielded significant influence over its vast resources.

As Draven reached the iron doors, he halted, his posture tense and predatory. The moment his focus locked onto Lyonal's hand encircling my wrist, a feral intensity ignited in his eyes, transforming his usual calm demeanor into a storm of barely contained fury. We exchanged a knowing look—a silent acknowledgment that reverberated with unspoken truths.

Draven's warrior-like presence seemed to swell, radiating a dangerous energy as he took three powerful strides toward us. Without a word, he seized Lyonal by the shoulder, yanking him back and gripping a fistful of his shirt. He pulled him close, their faces inches apart, his glare cutting like warm steel on flesh. "If I ever see you touch her again, Lyonal," he growled, his voice dripping with venom, "I'll peel your fingertips off with a dull blade. One... by... one."

The perverse nature behind Draven's threat hung in the air like a chilling mist, evoking vivid images of pain that sent a shiver through me. *The brutality of his words.*

Lyonal met his glare with a defiant smirk, the corner of his mouth twisting as if he relished the challenge. "I'd like to see you try," he taunted.

The guards, usually steadfast and resolute, shifted uneasy in their places.

Fear of the impending violence, an odd protectiveness toward Draven, and a simmering anger at Lyonal's audacity all surged within me. I found myself caught in the crossfire of their game of power and pride.

As Draven released him, Lyonal straightened his shirt with a quick, dismissive tug. "Shall we?" he said coolly, brushing past Draven without a second glance. With a slight nod, he signaled to the two soldiers flanking the doors that we were ready to proceed with the events of the evening.

Only a little while longer and I'd be free of not just the brute, but also the asshole.

The Cird and Their Fall:

Once, the Cird roamed above ground, revered for their deep connection to Sandric's sacred lands. Their unparalleled knowledge of the elements allowed them to live in harmony with the world around them. However, as dominant populations expanded, driven by greed and fear, they were unjustly labeled as terrorists—a narrative that oversimplifies their complex history.

Pushed into the shadows, their vibrant culture faded, obscured by the very fear that fueled their downfall. They are not mere victims; their story compels us to interrogate the origins of such labels and the narratives that shape our understanding of history.

As I reflect on their legacy, I want to challenge my students to consider: What assumptions do we hold about those we deem different, and how can history's misinterpretations inform our view of cultural identity today?

In pursuit of truth and understanding,
—H. Wilhoph

Chapter Four

LEVITY

"Cirds-damnation, this is hot!" Triad pulled the wooden spoon back from his mouth and winced. He peered down at the cast iron pot simmering on the wood-burning stove with some worry.

"You know Pop wouldn't approve of that language. It's disrespectful to talk about the Cird like that." I raised an eyebrow at him. "Is it hot in temperature or just spicy?" I asked, barreling into the kitchen with the grocery bags.

My appearance brought a look of relief to Triad's face.

My eyes flitted to the corner where the patched-up floorboards bore the scars of a past we rarely spoke of. The faint scent of charred wood hung in the air, a ghostly reminder of a fire that once threatened to engulf more than just our home. I crinkled my nose, turning my attention to Triad's response, his words a brief respite from the uneasy memory.

"Spicy. Blue will never eat this if we don't fix it."

"We would be lucky if Blue graces us with her presence at all this evening. If she doesn't appreciate the warm meal, the little mouse will find something else to nibble on. She won't allow herself to go hungry for long." I pushed the canvas bags into the middle of the old oak table our father had crafted for Mama, and started to remove the items. Blue wasn't developing as fast as Sprout and I worried the culprit to be her distaste for everything in life. "Add a bit of sugar and a cup or two more of the stock. It should knock the spice down a notch."

Evie, who had followed close behind me made a quick turn, heading for our shared sleeping quarters, no doubt where Blue already lounged reading another book about a far off land she dreamed of escaping to.

"Tell your sister we are sitting down for supper in twenty minutes. I expect you both to set the table and light the candles this evening."

Smirking, Evie clasped her hands together, bowed her head, and scampered off to find Blue.

Triad scurried over to the monarch blue cabinets in search of the sugar. Born identical in nearly every way, Triad and Tivian became increasingly harder to tell apart with each new day, *and taller!* With responsibilities that most boys their age had yet to face, their intelligence matured far beyond their sixteen years. The distinguishing factor between the two being their personalities: Triad possessed a sweet nature, while Tivian embodied wildness and freedom. Triad thought about others, while Tivian thought about himself.

"Why isn't your brother helping?" I asked, not looking up from the drawer where I arranged the large, dirt dusted potatoes. I'd clean them tomorrow before using them.

Triad's hand stopped fiddling through the array of provisions, abandoning his search for the sugar. I heard a deep exhale release from his lungs.

I looked up at Triad as frustration began to wash over me. I could feel the tension of a headache building in my temples. "Where is he?"

"Um… He made a quick trip into the city," he stuttered, pushing a chestnut curl behind his ear; a little bit shaggier than I liked to see his hair, but only I could be blamed. I pushed off giving them a trim for weeks now.

"Why?"

"They are announcing the results of the elections today," Triad uttered a hair above inaudibly. He clasped the wood counter with both hands as he turned to look at me.

How could I forget about the elections? And that's when it shot to the forefront of my mind: I hadn't cast a ballot for our family, which meant we'd be fined at least twenty-five kilos. The five years since the last elections blew by right before my eyes. As if just yesterday, at nineteen years old, I again wrote down the names of my neighborhood acquaintances as my candidates of choice for the three coveted Sanctioned positions.

I didn't see any point in repeating history this election season. I couldn't offer an informed decision, rather I checked the box of a citizen obligation I wanted nothing to do with. They could have their kilos.

Sandric people fought hard for democracy. I understood the honor of selecting our best people to represent us as a collective group. However, I had long since lost faith in our aloof bureaucracy. The way they handled my parents' deaths—with indifference and inefficiency—left a bitter taste in my mouth. I didn't believe my assistance warranted any need in the matter. By the look on Triad's face, he didn't know if he should continue on the subject.

"Stir, or it will burn." I nodded at the pot.

As I finished separating the groceries, I glanced over at the stove where Triad swirled the hearty stew. The rich aroma of simmering vegetables and spices filled the kitchen, blending with the nutty scent of fresh bread I prepared that morning. I placed the remaining groceries in our small refrigerator.

The rhythmic clinking of the faucet as I turned on the water provided a momentary distraction. I scrubbed the dirt from my hands, watching as the dark, gritty water swirled down the drain. The repetitive motion provided a soothing effect, though my body and mind remained far from calm. Perhaps the ever-growing list of responsibilities weighed on me. Every decision felt like a stone I struggled to lift, threatening to crush any remnants of desire left in me. Or perhaps it stemmed from the elections—or anything related to our people—that stirred up unresolved resentment from the day of our parents' deaths.

I grabbed a towel and dried my hands, casting another glance at the pot on the stove, where Triad added the final touches. The idea of a new group of people representing us felt like a humorless joke. Taking a freshly baked loaf from the cooling rack, I sliced through the crust and the soft center. The bread exuded warmth, its yeasty scent wafted up, mingling with the stew's savory notes. Each cut provided a small respite from my racing thoughts. I placed the slices on a wooden board, their golden-brown surfaces reflecting the kitchen light.

The separation between Sertoda people grew wider by the day. Traditionalists lived simple lives minimally influenced by the authorities. Our meager existence kept us poor and our monthly wattage low. Then there were the city folk who had the wattage for shiny electric vehicles. I'd see them speed past The Divide on their way to the beach, where they'd lounge like lazy seahorses, indifferent to the sea's deeper significance.

As I set the bread beside the stew, my thoughts turned to those who managed to live without relying on energy and light. Our lives seemed far freer from the grasp of unjust regulations. The management over power allowed officials to manipulate the populace with ease, using energy as both a carrot and a stick. For those living outside this control, embracing a simpler, self-sufficient life became a quiet rebellion—a rare sense of volition masked by poverty.

"I assume Tivian thinks he'll be the next Noble Warrior?" I questioned with an indiscernible chuckle, trying to make Triad feel more at ease with broaching the subject of politics.

"He has been practicing hand-to-hand combat, but he lacks any notoriety. I doubt many would cast their vote for him." Triad finished cleaning up the leftover spices. "Thomas is the sure pick. People still haven't stopped talking about the size of the Tuna he caught last summer. Nobody in this whole region is as strong or hard-working as him. He'll be sent to Mass to represent us."

Mass. The central city bordered all territories. My Pop, from an early age, passed down to me the lore of our first city. Before bed each night, he'd read detailed pages from dusty history books as if describing a Princess' fairytale domain.

"Thomas will have a tough time in The Sanctioning, but at least he'd be a good representative to sit on the council," Triad continued.

Not much was known about The Sanctioning. One of Sandric's oldest traditions and yet what transpired within Mass's walls remained an enigma. The glimpses we received came from cryptic accounts in the media, but even the articles were shrouded in layers of mystery.

Some speculated the representatives were forced to confront their deepest fears and darkest secrets. Others believed they engaged in ancient rites, invoking the spirits of our ancestors to guide them.

Upon the representatives' return, they upheld a sworn secrecy, and no matter how reporters probed, the details never leaked. The solemn oaths they took bound them tighter than any chains, ensuring the true details of The Sanctioning remained hidden.

As I finished preparing some loose-leaf tea for our dinner, I rolled my shoulders to relieve the strain from my long bike ride. I glanced over at Triad, who stood sorting through a stack of papers on the kitchen table. The teapot clicked against the cups, the only sound that filled the moment. I poured the steaming liquid, trying to find some comfort in the routine.

Triad looked up, eyeing the papers now in his hands. "You know, Lev, all the chatter around town about The Sanctioning has me wondering what it is like. A few of the older Samsal boys told me it's like navigating through a maze of nightmares, and no one really knows what happens in there."

I set the teapot down and handed him a cup. "Yeah, the secrecy is part of the intimidation. It's all a big game of keeping us on our toes."

Triad took a sip of his tea. "If the Noble Warriors are tested in strength and combat skills, I'm sure Brawn will dominate that position, given their fierce reputation. But what about the Perpetual Sense? They're all about intellect and strategy. It could be anyone." Triad continued, leaning back against the counter, "It sounds like the most important job to me."

I shrugged with exaggerated nonchalance, lifting my hands in mock surrender. "I can't help but imagine their Sanctioning is a real drag," I said, rolling my eyes. I leaned forward, tracing an imaginary line in the air like a presenter. "Picture this—a marathon of debate," I announced as if delivering breaking news, "where they're trapped in a room surrounded by endless charts and graphs." I spread my hands wide, miming stacks of invisible data. "They're just trying to solve all the world's problems while the clock ticks louder... and louder." I tapped an invisible watch, voice lowered in mock horror. "If that doesn't drive someone crazy, I don't know what will."

Triad chuckled, shaking his head. "Yeah, that does sound like a nightmare. Maybe they throw in a few extra challenges for good measure, like having to endure the world's worst coffee or eat the most of the government's *special* lab-grown food while they're at it."

I laughed. "Exactly! Just some sort of *sinister* endurance test. If you can survive all that and still have your sanity intact, you've earned your spot."

As we shared the laughter, I felt a rush of affection for my younger brother. These moments of lightness reminded me of the bond we shared. Triad had matured before my eyes, revealing the man he would become. But he would always remain my little brother—someone I could laugh and confide in.

I smiled, my heart swelling with pride. "Well, whatever The Sanctioning holds, I'm glad we can still find something to laugh about," I said softly. "You're growing up so fast, Triad. I just hope you never lose this sense of humor."

Triad grinned, looking over to me and letting his youthful exuberance escape. "I'll try not to, Lev."

Before I could add more, Evie burst into the kitchen, her doe eyes wide with urgency. "Levity, Triad, you need to see this! Blue's made a complete mess of the sleeping quarters!"

I kept a straight face though amusement tugged the corners of my mouth. "Oh, great. What has she done now?"

Evie's eyebrows scrunched together, her lips twitching as she fought to hide a smile that threatened to break through her frustration. "She's turned the entire room into a pillow fort. There's a mountain of blankets and cushions everywhere! She's even using the laundry basket as a secret passage."

Triad chuckled, shaking his head. "Blue and her creative chaos. She's got more imagination than sense sometimes."

I set my teacup down with a soft clink and headed toward the sleeping quarters, shaking my head with a bemused smile. Upon my arrival, Blue occupied the center of her "fort," draped in a makeshift cape and wielding a plastic sword with exaggerated flair.

She mirrored her little sister Evie, slightly taller, with a face reflecting a seriousness no ten-year-old should possess. A faint, jagged burn marred the left side of her face, though it did nothing to diminish her confidence or imaginary heroics. Her familiar brown curls hung a little straighter around her shoulders, but those striking blue eyes—Mama's eyes—sparkled with mischief as soon as she saw me.

"Hey, Levity," Blue said with a sly grin, shuffling over to lean against the doorframe, blocking my path. "This is the '*Castle of Fun*,' and, uh, you're not exactly on the guest list."

I crossed my arms, stifling my laughter. "I hope all this castle building will not leave you too tired to set the table. If so, I may just have to move your bedtime up an hour to get you the rest you need." I jutted my chin to the fort. "Clean up this mess."

Blue pouted. "Okay, okay. I'll clean up. See, you're no fun."

I turned back to the kitchen, the sounds of my siblings filling the air. My mind drifted to the impending election reading—and, more importantly, to our current Surviving Aide, Elisabetta Rahmani.

Betta, as everyone called her. She was two grades ahead of me in school, already poised to handle whatever life threw her way. At just twenty-one, she earned election to her role, a leader even then. It had made sense to vote for her; she embodied everything I wasn't.

I'd seen her in passing, but we never spoke. I didn't need to know her well to see how strong she was. Everyone in The Divide admired her, and now, here I stood amidst the daily chaos of my family's home, torn between awe and guilt. The responsibility thrust upon her felt almost cruel, considering the part I played in her path to leadership.

She pulled my siblings from a fate nearly irreversible. The darkest thoughts from that night flickered through my mind causing a shudder.

I owed her more than thanks. I owed her everything.

I glanced over at my siblings again. Evie let out a delighted shriek as she grabbed a stray pillow and whopped Triad over the head, sending him sprawling with a dramatic groan. A pang struck deep in my chest. They were safe because of Betta.

The Rise of The Sanctioning:

The Sanctioning was originally conceived as a vital rite of passage within Sandric, designed to test the mettle of emerging leaders. Rooted in the belief that true leadership emerges through adversity, these challenges sought to reveal character, resilience, and the capacity for growth. In their early years, The Sanctioning was a public celebration, drawing communities together to witness the unveiling of potential leaders and the forging of bonds among the participants.

However, in the past decade, The Sanctioning has become shrouded in secrecy, veiled in mystery. All details and accounts kept from the very communities they were intended to serve.

Why might this shift toward secrecy have occurred? What impact does this level of concealment have on our culture and understanding of leadership? As my students reflect on these questions, I want them to consider the ramifications of removing transparency from such a pivotal cultural tradition. What does it suggest about our values and the trust we place in our leaders?

In pursuit of truth and understanding,
—H. Wilhoph

Chapter Five

BETTA

The labyrinthine tunnels of Mass were like veins coursing beneath a city that thrived on secrets. The cool, damp air clung to the gauzy white fabric of my dress. With each step, the garment rustled, its delicate fabric standing out against the utilitarian uniforms of the soldiers escorting us. Their heavy boots echoed against the stone walls, a rhythmic reminder of our constrained freedom.

Draven, the embodiment of casual contempt, met my glower with a roguish smile as if we shared a secret. The low light of the tunnel highlighted his sharp jawline as he spoke, "You know, if these tunnels are meant to serve as a fortress, Sandric has missed the mark. They feel more like a glorified maze, built to confuse us rather than protect us."

I shot him a sideways grin, tugging at the flimsy dress in a feeble attempt to ward off the cold. "Maybe it's just one more trick up their sleeve—keep us off balance, make sure we never know what direction we are heading in."

Lyonal walked in apathetic silence, his presence a counterpoint to my irreverence.

The air grew denser as we descended deeper into the ground. The tunnels were a legacy of a forgotten age. Narrow and irregular, their ceilings were uneven and just high enough to avoid feeling claustrophobic,

I traced the rough iron and copper deposits that streaked the stone. Their course texture greeted my fingers, their existence from a long-buried world.

When we stepped into the ancient auditorium, the transformation felt like slipping into another realm. The vast space stretched endlessly, carved out from rust-colored quartzite. Steep walls towered above us, etched with the marks of tools long disused. The stone gleamed in the low light, reflecting deep, reddish hues that bathed the room in a fiery glow, as though the quartz still carried the memory of molten rock. The ceiling soared overhead, disappearing into shadow, while the smooth quartz beneath our feet felt slick with polish, deeply contrasting the rugged tunnels behind us.

The auditorium exhaled a cool, musty breath, the scent of ancient stone mingling with the faint, sterile tang of modern machinery.

The space stood as a monument to time, grandeur arising from nature's raw power and the hands that shaped it. I stood still, overwhelmed by the stark contrast between past beauty and future brilliance.

The room burst with a cacophony of motion and sound. Reporters thronged the space, their cameras and recorders reminding me of a swarm of metallic insects. This space and ceremonial arena were the only areas of Mass legally allowed to be recorded. The clatter of equipment and the murmur of voices created a low, constant hum. The sleek lines of the polished stage jutted out from the natural rock as if the two were locked in a centuries-old conversation—man and nature, ancient and advanced, woven together. Five large screens projected live feeds from each Sandric territory, images shifting with the crowd's pulse. Holograms danced above, displaying intricate maps and charts flickering with futuristic light.

Draven's voice cut through the noise, laced with a hint of sarcasm. "Quite the spectacle they've set up."

I glanced up at him, a smile tugging the corner of my mouth as I adjusted the slit in my dress. "It's a damn show for the world, and a slap in the face for us—just their way of making sure we know our role: smile, look pretty, and keep the hell out of the way while they run their little circus."

Lyonal remained focused, surveying the room with the precision of a seasoned strategist. The media's excitement seemed to intensify the seriousness of his demeanor.

My line of sight followed his to the screens. The first to draw me in showed holm oaks twinkling with lights, framing city streets with their dark, glossy leaves. The soft, radiant glow of the ocean sparkled in the distance. The Sertoda crowd stretched like a sea of smiling faces, their joy radiating through the monitor, their laughter echoing memories of simpler times.

Brawn on the other hand…

The setting sun cast long shadows across the rugged mountains in the distance. The desert landscape stretched out in a barren expanse, bathed in the warm, fading light of dusk. Dusty winds swept through the rocky terrain, blowing the headscarves of the very few women in attendance. *Three, four… maybe seven total?* Brawn's people stared with stoicism; lines of endurance etched deep on their weather-beaten expressions.

Draven's earlier playfulness evaporated, replaced by a tautness that spoke louder than words as he fixed his focus on his territory's screen. His posture bristled with a subtle tension, revealing a simmering agitation beneath the surface.

"Ease up on those eyebrows, Draven. You're going to give yourself a migraine if you keep glaring like that," I said, my lips barely moving as I caught the prying eyes of the media starting to drift our way.

He grunted, rugged features tightening with a flash of annoyance, as he shifted his gaze from the Brawn screen to the reporters. His eyes swept the room like I'd seen him do hundreds of times. One hoped he was doing his Noble duties, while I wondered if he was searching for the next poor soul to accompany him into his bed. The soldiers assigned to protect him, despite their formal roles, paled next to his own honed instincts. Draven's presence radiated a security that transcended mere physical protection; he stood as a steadfast guardian, establishing authority in the tense atmosphere.

He would be a good Noble Warrior—if he had any real say in the decisions.

The thought warmed me more than I cared to admit, and I flushed, disgusted at myself for thinking so highly of him.

Seriously, Betta, when was the last time you got laid? Clearly, it's been too long. You feel a man's dick one time—

The same blonde from the conference room just days ago approached me. Her ill-fitting suit jacket rode up her too short torso as she pressed envelopes into my hand.

"You will read the results of Brawn first. We want to move swiftly away from their reactions if a choice is deemed unfavorable. They are on a five second delay. Don't forget." She coached. Her eyes never met mine, glancing around as if accessing her next task. "Sertoda is last. I don't care if it's your mom getting elected. We want no personal reaction from you. Are we clear?"

"*Of course!* Why the hell would anyone care what I think?" I mocked, rolling my eyes as I looked down at her. "I'm just here to be the pretty face of Sandric, the awe-inspiring Surviving—"

A hand shot up inches from my face. "Whatever gets you through the evening, darling. Just remember to pay attention to the directions I feed you through your earpiece." I couldn't help but think that the media aides must be raking in good wattage to have so much nerve. Unlike my fellow council members, they weren't devoid of emotion; they followed orders with an unsettling vigor.

I forced a smile, one so blatantly insincere only a gullible twit like her would believe I was receptive to her commands.

Satisfied, she scurried back to whatever dark corner behind the stage she crawled out of. A young man ambled over next, fumbling with the earpiece as he attached it to me without a word, treating me like a lifeless mannequin in a store window. His hands brushed against me without so much as a hint of asking for permission, like my consent didn't even matter.

Lyonal moved to the side of the stage, weaving through the crowd with the calculated precision that seemed as natural to him as breathing. I watched as he leaned in to exchange words with a few Trunta representatives, his demeanor cold yet flawlessly controlled. *'Calculated' might as well be his middle name*, I thought, as I followed a few steps behind, keeping my distance. While his title was Perpetual Sense, I'd rarely seen him apply his talents in a way that seemed useful to anyone but himself. Draven maintained his position nearby, shadowing my every move with an unobtrusive vigilance.

I drew a slow breath through my parted lips, held it for five seconds, then pushed off the heel of my right stiletto, reaching for the railing of the stage stairs. With each step, I fixed my expression, ensuring my face exuded the perfect blend of confidence and empathy. This was a persona I flawlessly honed over my five-year term. A front masking my true feelings and projecting the unwavering loyalty Sandric expected from its mouthpiece.

As I ascended the stairs, the blinding stage lights came into view, casting their harsh glow over the podium where I would soon stand. The crowd's murmur drifted, fading beneath the steady rhythm of my heartbeat. I straightened my posture, lifted my chin, and allowed a composed smile to settle on my lips. This marked my moment to deliver the results of the Sandric preliminary elections, reassuring the public that their voices were heard, even if the truth proved far more complicated.

Approaching the platform's centermost area, I felt Draven and Lyonal take their places behind me, their presence a mere formality to represent their respective positions and the unity of the Sanctioned. They flanked my blind spots like silent sentinels, their faces impassive as they waited for the proceedings to begin. I felt the weight of the envelopes in my hand, each one containing the fate of a region, and fiddled with them to calm my nerves.

A voice in my earpiece began the countdown. "Five, four, three, two…"

I stepped up to the podium, the microphone amplifying my measured breaths, and began to regurgitate the speech planned for me.

"People of Sandric. We gather here today not only to reveal Sandric's preliminary election results but also to honor a profound milestone—the hundred-year mark since the historic decree that safeguarded Sandric by eliminating the Cird from our lands. We remember the lives lost during the devastating attack on Trunta, the memories of whom echo as a solemn reminder of the sacrifices made to secure peace." The people in attendance and on the monitors bowed their heads. "In remembrance of those who fell and with gratitude for the vision of our forebears, we salute this day, a testament to our resilience and unity in the face of chaos.

"Welcome," I paused, spreading my lips for a full tooth smile, "to the reading of the Sandric preliminary election results," I began, my voice composed. "These results are a direct reflection of the people's choices in each region to fill the three coveted positions in Sandric leadership. While all elected representatives will serve on the Sandric council for the next five years,"—*and let's be real; it's not the prize it seems*—"only three will be promoted to the highest authoritative positions, becoming the official Sandric Noble Warrior, Perpetual Sense, and Surviving Aide. Officially Sanctioned.

"Once the results are read, the representatives will meet in Mass for

The Sanctioning to determine who among them will prevail and secure their prestigious role in history." I let my opening statements' settle—the confidentiality of The Sanctioning hanging in the air.

With a nod to the cameras, I carefully opened the first envelope, the one labeled Brawn, and began the ceremonious reading of the results.

"The results of Brawn: Ashar Needle elected Surviving Aide representative," I announced. "Naeem Veeder elected Perpetual Sense representative."

A rumbling erupted from the sullen crowd on the television screen broadcasting the live shot of the people of Brawn. I couldn't tell if the choice sparked a positive or negative reaction, and a flicker of nervousness ignited within me, evident in the slight twitch of my wrist.

"Quick!" The blonde barked in my ear.

As I read the next name off the card—"Lieutenant Dorian Ballister elected Noble Warrior"—a jolt of surprise shot through me.

Dorian Ballister.

Draven's younger brother.

I repeated the name aloud, the words tasting bitter on my tongue.

My eyes flickered to Draven, whose expression was a flawless mask of neutrality. The only sign of any recognition came from a minuscule shift in his stance that betrayed his awareness.

The aide's voice crackled in my earpiece, sharp and urgent. "Betta, stay focused. We need to keep this moving."

Ignoring the sharpness in her tone, my focus continued to linger on Draven. Despite my efforts to maintain my composure, I locked eyes with Draven unable to shake the nagging concern for how he might be grappling with the news of his brother's fate. The Brawn representative historically triumphed in The Sanctioning. But Draven knew better than anyone what awaited his brother—the danger, the risks, the possibility of a finality that no one could predict.

The aide's impatient hiss erupted in my earpiece once again. "Ms. Rahmani, we don't have all night!"

A pang of empathy tapped against the wall I'd built. With only my mother left as family, I couldn't fathom the bond between brothers—especially in Brawn, where discipline shaped men. Draven displayed the cocky confidence and strength of a Noble Warrior, yet I wondered if beneath it lay a vulnerability, stirred now that his brother faced such a grim future.

Draven stepped a foot closer to me and whispered, "Continue, Betta."

I glanced back at the podium, tucking my hair behind my ear, and forcing myself to move forward. I shuffled to the next envelope with a slight tremble in my hands as I prepared to reveal the next territory's fate.

"Now for the Trunta results: Zal Korbin elected Surviving Aide representative, Saria Meeth elected Perpetual Sense representative, and Joran Wexler elected Noble Warrior." The cheers from Trunta's crowd were immediate and enthusiastic, their jubilation unmistakable. I could feel the excitement reverberating through the broadcast, a reminder of the hope and expectations each region placed on their chosen representatives.

"Lizon results: Geraldine Sato elected Surviving Aide representative, Tama Li elected Perpetual Sense representative, and Kolvin Nakamura elected Noble Warrior." Again, the broadcasted crowd erupted in celebration, a seamless transition of joy.

Next came Dobia's results—the cold, sparsely populated region. On screen, bundled figures emerged, light eyes peering from beneath hoods and scarves. "Dobia results: Reika Vance elected Surviving Aide representative, Garon Fiore elected Perpetual Sense representative, and Roderick Thorne elected Noble Warrior." The crowd's reaction remained muted, lacking enthusiasm. Dobia had never seen a representative rise to Sanctioned; their members served on councils but wielded little real influence—unaware none of us did.

Yet Garon's ascension might change that. His name carried weight and admiration, and if anyone could calm Dobia's turbulent waters, it would be him.

The crowd maintained its somber silence, reflecting their long struggle and cautious survival in the harsh, mountainous land. I guess Shen's conspiracy didn't hold water after all. Yet their muted response hinted they were biding their time, waiting for the next step—The Sanctioning and it's outcomes.

Finally, I flipped to the envelope bearing Sertoda's name—*my home*. The paper slipped between my fingertips, slick with sweat that gathered despite my best efforts to remain composed. A shiver ran up my arm as I clutched the envelope–pride and anxiety creating an almost unbearable tension. My heart pounded, each beat resonating in my ears.

I buried these tumultuous emotions beneath a practiced smile. As I peeled open the envelope with the edge of a pointed nail, the rustle of the paper seemed to reverberate the significance of the moment.

Noticing the order of the names, I swallowed a scoff. Of course, they saved the Surviving Aide elect for last—nothing like a little dramatic flair to hammer home their self-serving spectacle.

I read the results for Perpetual Sense first. "Marmarie Pendavi elected Perpetual Sense representative," I announced, my voice steady. Marmarie was an Elder, well known for her sharp intellect and unwavering persistence.

I knew the next name would be a popular one too. "Thomas Ravleon, elected Noble Warrior." Thomas worked as a beloved fisherman in The Divide before moving to the city. He understood the dangers of the sea and the deadliness of the catch. I had heard he transitioned away from hands-on work to become a restaurateur in the city. It was challenging to envision him holding his own against Brawn in The Sanctioning. I feared for him, remembering him as tender-hearted and kind to all, often helping the Elders carry their heavy nets and baskets at the docks. His soft-hearted nature might not serve him well in the brutal test ahead, but the tight-lipped nature of The Sanctioning would leave him in the dark until far too late to prepare.

The irritatingly shrill voice of the blonde aide crackled in my earpiece. "Now we are going to say a few encouraging words to the incoming Surviving Aide representative. I want to feel your sincerity," she snarked, her tone grating on my nerves.

If I were to say what I mean…

I would tell them to run.

Don't answer the door when they come to collect you.

Avoid the train to Mass at all costs.

Instead, I slipped the mask remained and echoed the lines fed into my earpiece. "I want to take a moment to congratulate our new Sertoda Surviving Aide representative. I have faith in your fortitude and dedication. Your courage will inspire us all. I look forward to seeing the great things you will accomplish." The words felt meaningless as they left my lips, a rehearsed line veiling the harsh truth.

One deep breath and I let the name fall from my exhale.

"Levity Wilhoph elected Surviving Aide representative."

Invisible chains clamped around me, binding me to her, to this moment. Levity Wilhoph—the eldest daughter of the family I saved years ago during the Cird attack. While every name tightened the chokehold of secrets gurgling inside my throat, hers was a hammer that nailed me deeper to a future I didn't want to face.

I kept my smile in place, a mask honed through years of practice, perfected under the pressure of constant scrutiny and threat. No one cared about the thoughts I dared not speak. I'd learned that lesson long ago. But at this moment, the irony was laid on thick, a bitter sludge I couldn't choke down.

Years ago, Levity faced her worst nightmare that nearly tore her apart. She almost lost her entire family. And now, that same girl, so fragile beneath her quiet strength, would be forced to confront those fears once more.

Only this time, I wasn't sure she'd survive it.

The sudden urge to protect her—like I once did for her siblings—set my pulse racing.

But how could I shield her from the darkness that lurked ahead?

There it was; the grim reality of it all. The price of this battle. The stakes. Levity's future, her life, could very well be in my hands, but I wasn't certain I had what it would take to come to the rescue again.

I ended the reading with a curt: "Sanctioned. United. One."

Fucking bullshit.

The Creation of the Leadership Roles:

When Sandric's territories first united, three leadership roles were established to ensure balance: the Noble Warrior, the Perpetual Sense, and the Surviving Aide.

The Noble Warrior protected the land, standing as a symbol of strength. The Perpetual Sense offered wisdom, guiding decisions with reason and foresight. The Surviving Aide safeguarded the well-being of the people, ensuring that none were forgotten.

These roles were meant to work in harmony, each balancing the others' influence—strength tempered by wisdom, wisdom softened by compassion, compassion empowered by strength.

This system operated on ideals.... but ideals are fragile things.

In pursuit of truth and understanding,

—H. Wilhoph

Chapter Six

LEVITY

The evening sun cast long shadows across the worn wooden table as I fidgeted with the frayed hem of my mother's favorite tablecloth. The scent of stew lingered in the air, though it did little to mask the familiar bitterness of charred wood—an irritating reminder that surfaced when my patience wore thin. My eyes flicked between the idle twirling of a fresh parsley sprig in Evie's fingers and the untouched meal. It should have been comforting, gathered with most of my siblings at the family table. But the empty chair and waiting on Tivian soured the moment.

"Tivian should have been back by now," I muttered, brow furrowed.

Triad glanced up from his bowl, expression calm as if to reassure me his twin would be home soon. "He'll be here, Lev. Probably got caught up in all the excitement."

Blue, who managed to emerge out of the sleep quarters in time to set the last place setting, rolled her eyes in my direction. "Or maybe he got lost on purpose to avoid coming home to this boring meal."

I shot Blue a sharp glare, but the front door creaked open, cutting me off. Tivian sauntered in with a smug air of exaggerated importance, his chestnut hair tousled from what must've been a rushed bike ride back to The Divide. In his hand, he waved a crumpled piece of parchment like a victory banner, mouth tugged upward in a self-satisfied grin.

"I come bearing news from the city!" Tivian announced with dramatic flair, a mischievous twinkle in his dark brown eyes.

A heavy sigh escaped my lips, my patience waning. "Don't tell me, Tiv. You've been elected as the Noble Warrior, haven't you?"

Tivian's grin widened, as he thrust the parchment toward me. "In fact, I have! Can you believe it? Your own brother, destined for greatness!"

I stared at the document, my heart sinking. "But... that can't be right. You're not... I mean, you've never even..."

Triad leaned over the table to examine the official results printed on the sheet dangling from my hand. His forehead tensed in concentration as he scanned the lines of the neat script. "Tiv, this isn't for the Noble Warrior. It says here... Levity Wilhoph," the look of disbelief lifting to meet my eyes, "it's you. You've been chosen as the Surviving Aide representative for Sertoda."

The words rattled my brain, and for a moment, I couldn't breathe. This couldn't possibly be one of Tivian's jokes. I turned the paper over in my hands, trying to discern the legitimacy of the stationary. "Me?" I whispered, rolling my shoulders forward and sinking further into my chair.

Tivian's cocky demeanor faltered as he slipped into his empty seat across the table. "Yeah, Lev. It's you," he declared with softness, his eyes reflecting pride rather than the teasing I expected from the jokester.

Blue scoffed, breaking the tense silence. "Surviving Aide? You? Please."

I clenched my fists, fighting back the tears that threatened to spill. I knew Blue's sharp words were just her age talking, but the doubt still grated on me. What if she was right? Why me? My attention locked onto the flickering candlelight as inadequacy bore down on me. Each passing second deepened the chasm of guilt within me. I felt small, fragile—far from the strength expected of such an important role. How could I, still haunted by my own darkest moments, be trusted to lead others through theirs?

"I won't go. I can't leave you all here, not with... with everything that's happened. I could never..."

Triad placed a reassuring hand on my shoulder. "You don't have a choice, Lev. If you turn down the position, you'll be jailed."

Evie cleared her throat, having watched with innocent eyes. "Lev," she started, "you're the best person for the job."

Looking at Evie and Blue, my resolve wavered. My focus bounced between the two little girls sitting before me. "What about you two? What about our home, and..."

My siblings' needs squeezed my throat, stealing my words. I could feel my heartbeat quickening and my palms beginning to moisten. My mind raced with the implications. What I needed to do.

No. What I was being forced to do.

Evie tugged at my sleeve. "You always help us with our lessons, and you're the best at cleaning cuts and scrapes." She began listing all the qualities she admired in me, her voice full of genuine affection.

My face softened as a smile tugged at my lips. My little Sprout, perhaps the wisest among us all. Evie didn't understand the full extent to what being the Surviving Aide meant, but her pure words struck a chord deep within me. It wasn't just about being helpful or responsible—I would be the one expected to endure when others fell, to remain strong when the world came crashing down. It meant confronting horrors I hadn't yet faced myself, and worse, carrying the burden of others' lives in my hands.

The title wasn't a badge of honor, but a promise—a promise to survive, no matter the cost.

Evie smiled back, amusement dancing in her eyes. "You worry too much about us. We'll manage just fine."

The breath I held captive in my throat eased out. "I don't know, Evie. It's just..."

Evie's eyes searched mine, wide with concern. "Just what, Lev? You deserve this."

I shook my head, doubts suffocating my senses. "No one knows me. I've done nothing to warrant this position. Surviving Aide? It's a title meant for someone who has made a real difference, someone important. The only thing I've ever done is take care of our family."

Triad frowned, hands gripping the table's edge. "Taking care of our family is everything, sis. You've kept us all together. That's important."

I sighed, my eyes drifting to the charred branding on the floorboards, scars of the past etched into the wood like a reminder of what I'd tried desperately to leave behind. The conversation lingered in the air, sinking into me like the remnants of smoke still clinging to the walls. "Taking care of our family—it had to be done. It still has to be done. I don't understand what there is to admire. It's... just life. And I'm not even good at it."

I pushed out of my chair, steadying myself against the rough grain of the wood, and wandered toward the kitchen window. Mama's garden stretched out before me, a patchwork of vivid greens and soft blossoms, each plant precisely tended. Rows of pale blue *serenith* stood still, delicate petals catching my attention, reminding me of their soothing nature. Bright marigold with sunny yellow tips and vibrant orange centers attracted bees and butterflies. The dianthus stood elegantly among the blooms, pink petals edged in deep magenta unfolding like a tiny, ruffled fan. Together, they framed the deep, lush beds of ripening tomatoes and leafy greens. Everything existed in perfect harmony—each sprout, each bloom thriving in its intended place, flourishing under careful supervision.

But as I stared at the quiet beauty before me, the chaos inside only intensified. The neatly arranged garden, a portrait of order, contrasted sharply with the storm churning inside me. How could everything outside be so composed, while within me, nothing seemed to fit, nothing made sense?

Triad shifted in his seat, fingers drumming on the table. The dark apprehension in his eyes spoke volumes as he glanced at me. "Levity, there's something we should talk about. It might help explain why you feel the way you do about this position."

I swallowed hard, the familiar ache of dread settled in my chest. "What is it, Triad?"

Before Triad could respond, Tivian interjected. "We know a lot more about Mama and Pop's deaths than you think. We know Sertoda officials initially declared their deaths an accident, saying the boat capsized due to unforeseen circumstances and their bodies ended up with the wreckage. And we know that when you brought up the evidence that suggested it wasn't just an accident—that the hull had been punctured from the inside—the officials changed their story. They claimed it was a Cird attack, citing recent sightings as an excuse to avoid further investigation. Triad and I looked it all up in the public records files at the library in the city."

As Tivian spoke, Blue and Evie began to serve themselves from the pot of stew on the table. The clinking of utensils and the murmur of small talk filled the kitchen, buffering the gravity of the conversation. My gaze flitted between the two younger siblings, their innocent chatter and eager eating a jarring backdrop to the heavy discussion.

Triad leaned forward, his voice low but unwavering. "We both saw that the initial explanation didn't add up. They wanted to close the case, using the Cird as a convenient scapegoat." He paused, eyes narrowing with suspicion. "They've never attacked at sea. Every reported Cird assault we found has involved setting fires—always on land. Most of them were government facilities—armories, research labs, even a few supply depots. And yeah, there were some residential hits," I caught the slightest shift in his eyes toward the burnt edges of the floor, "but nothing like this. Nothing off the coast, and definitely nothing that fits the story they tried to sell."

A pang of grief tightened my chest as memories of that night surged up, unbidden. I pictured myself in the kitchen, watching Mama and Pop prepare for their rare overnight getaway. They'd saved for weeks, planning a special evening—a small luxury to escape the daily grind and reconnect. Pop arranged everything, giving Mama a well-deserved break from her usual duties.

Even now, the strangeness of Pop's goodbye lingered. His farewell had felt overly sentimental, almost as if he sensed he wouldn't return. That uneasy feeling as they left had refused to fade. One question haunted me still: why did he take Mama out on the boat at night? Pop, an expert on the water, made the idea of an accident feel like a cruel dismissal of our loss.

I walked back to the table. The stew had cooled to an unsettling lukewarm. I ladled some into my bowl, the rich aroma of the meal providing a fleeting comfort.

Settling back at the table, I took a deep breath, trying to steady myself. The normalcy of serving dinner warmed my chilling thoughts. Each movement, each bite, offered a small reprieve, even as the shadows of the past lingered nearby.

The clatter of a dropped spoon snapped me back to the present. Evie looked up, eyes wide and curious. I took in another deep breath. "They used the Cird as a cover-up," I said quietly, more to myself than to anyone, "because we weren't worth it."

I forced a smile and turned to my siblings, voice balanced. "We need to focus on the present," I said, pushing my own emotions aside. "We've got enough to deal with right now with these silly election results. Why dwell on the past?"

Triad offered a reassuring nod, seeing through my brave face. His eyes remained shadowed with sadness. Tivian's expression turned serious, concern evident in his grimace. The conversation felt far from over.

Triad spoke, voice firm. "It's not just about how the authorities handled everything. It's about finding out what really happened."

My stomach churned. "So, what, Triad? What are you saying? What does this have to do with becoming a representative?"

I glanced at Evie and Blue. Evie's face showed confusion at my volume, while Blue focused on her stew.

Triad didn't waver. "We have to keep pushing. We can't let them silence us. We owe it to Mama and Pop."

Tivian nodded, face softening as he tore off a piece of bread and stuffed it in his mouth. "Levity, you've done so much for our family," he remarked between bites. "And maybe this position is a chance to make a difference from within, to push for the truth."

I felt a surge of anger and helplessness. The memory of the officials' indifference and their refusal to investigate properly reignited the frustration I had buried deep. My fingers clenched around the metal spoon as I fought to maintain composure. I met Tivian's dark brown eyes—so much like Pop's—feeling the sincerity of my brothers' words. The room fell silent, except for the soft clinking of utensils.

"I'll think about it." I conceded with a deep breath. But their words ignited a quiet spark of determination within me. "And you're right. We can't let this go. We have to find the truth, no matter what it takes. And perhaps this is the way to do it."

Evie finished her food while Blue pushed around the stew in her bowl.

Tivian nodded, eyes filled with empathy. "You never gave up. You fought for the truth, even when no one would listen. And now, you have a chance to do more. To make sure the same thing doesn't happen to someone else. To hold those in power accountable."

I looked at them, their faces so young and eager. "You think I can make a difference?"

Triad smiled. "We know you can."

Tivian reached across the table and squeezed my hand.

Triad glanced at Tivian. A silent exchange passed between them before he turned back to me. "Levity, there's something else we need to tell you."

I raised an eyebrow. "I'm not sure I can handle much more. What is it?"

Tivian took a deep breath, a small smile playing on his lips. "We've been campaigning for you. Leading up to the ballot casting, we reached out to everyone we could. Elders, Mama's friends, Pop's colleagues at the college."

Evie piped up, her innocent voice cutting through the air. "I helped too! I talked to all the neighbors, especially the ones who have pets! And Blue helped me."

I blinked in surprise, glancing at Blue who shrugged and continued focusing on her food. "You did?"

She nodded.

"Yes! We told them how you always take care of us and how you would make things better," Evie squealed, face lighting up.

"Oh? And what exactly did you say?"

Evie bounced in her seat, her enthusiasm barely contained. "I told them how you always make sure we have everything we need, like that time you fixed my favorite dress even though you were busy with other things. And remember when Blue lost her favorite doll? You found it for her, hidden under the couch cushions!"

Blue looked up, cheeks flushed. "I don't play with dolls!"

I couldn't help but smile at their earnest praise. The mention of those small moments, the everyday acts of care and kindness, touched something deep inside me.

Tivian chuckled, ruffling Evie's dark curls. "She's right, sis. We all worked together. We campaigned on the promise you would bring change, you would hold the Sandric government accountable. People remember what happened to Mama and Pop. They remember how you fought for them, even when no one would listen."

Triad added, "And it's not only about us. There are so many people, especially in The Divide, affected by authority. By the power system in play. People are tired of being ignored, of being mistreated. They want someone who understands their struggles, who will fight for them."

Tivian nodded. "Many of the neighbors have offered to help out in any way they can while you're away at Mass. They know how important this is and want to support you."

I looked at each of them, my heart swelling with emotion. "I had no idea."

Evie beamed up at me. "Everyone believes in you, Lev! They know you can make things better."

As their words settled over me, I felt a swirl of emotions I couldn't quite untangle. My siblings began helping to clean up the table, their small gestures grounding me in the simplicity of the moment.

Triad cleared the dishes, his movements methodical as he stacked them in the sink. Tivian wiped down the table with focused precision, while Blue and Evie picked up stray utensils and crumbs.

I moved to the sink, washing the bowls with quick, firm motions. My mind wandered back to the days and nights after Mama and Pop's deaths, which had merged into a haze of grief and anxiety. At sixteen, I found myself thrust into adulthood, suddenly responsible for two eight-year-old boys, a toddler, and a newborn baby. I had fumbled through those early days, riddled with anxiety when the house filled with the silence of our parents' absence.

The nights were the hardest. I lay awake in the dark, feeling the pressure to be strong, even though I felt far from it. The fear of failing them tightened around me as I cried into my pillow, trying not to disturb the little ones who needed me to be their pillar of strength.

Every decision seemed monumental; each choice heavy with the fear of making mistakes. Could I truly fill the void our parents had left? Could I protect them from a world that had already taken so much from us? The doubts swarmed, leaving me paralyzed.

No one knew the full extent of my struggles; how close I came to losing myself.

But now, perhaps, was my chance for redemption. If I could fight for others, bring about the change we needed, maybe I could begin to forgive myself. The thought of standing up for those failed by the system kindled a small flame of hope. Through this role, I could transform my past pain into a force for good, not just for my family, but for everyone who had suffered.

As I scrubbed the last dish, I felt a new determination forming within me. I took a deep breath, letting the cold air clear the fog of doubt in my mind.

I knew this was my path, my chance to turn the darkness into light. I would not falter again.

Not now.

Not ever.

The Core of Civilization:

As a young world, still finding its footing, Sandric relies heavily on fifteen nuclear power plants fueled by the uranium-rich mountains of Dobia. These plants generate the electricity that powers nearly a million lives, yet even with this impressive infrastructure, energy use is carefully restricted—a stark reminder of how progress comes with limits.

Consider the plants near The Divide, perched precariously close to the ocean for cooling. They stand as symbols of melioration, but their location invites unease. One storm, one miscalculation, and the Divide becomes its namesake in the worst sense.

Nuclear power brings undeniable benefits: jobs that stabilize communities, technological innovation, and the foundation of Sandric's growing network. Yet the specter of waste management hangs over these achievements. The byproducts, stored in closely monitored facilities, remain a lingering threat.

From a cultural lens, energy is more than power; it's a reflection of Sandric's ambitions and vulnerabilities. In this fledgling world, decisions about allocation, safety, and waste shape not only daily lives but the identity of its people. How long can Sandric sustain its dependence on a resource that carries such risk, and at what cost will we learn to adapt?

In pursuit of truth and understanding,

—H. Wilhoph

Chapter Seven

BETTA

The living quarters in Mass made the tiny city apartment I shared with my mother in Sertoda feel like a shoebox. Here, everything exuded modernity. The room gleamed with polished surfaces and angular furniture, a far cry from the cozy clutter of our homey abode. *Just an uninspired attempt at covering up the shit show.* I kept the lights dim, hoping the shadows would obscure any telltale signs of my unease.

Five years in this prison had taught me caution. The powers above us had hidden their little spies: listening devices, cameras, whatever they needed to track my every move. I stood at the window, smoothing the gauzy fabric of my dress, feeling it cling to my skin. I clenched my fists, the cool material of the skirt bunching up in my hands as I stared out into the night. My teeth ground together as the anger simmered inside me. This whole position, this charade I'd been forced into, made my skin crawl. *Keep it together*, I reminded myself, but the bitterness felt impossible to shake.

I let go of my dress and started pacing the room. My fingers trailed over the polished desk where my personal laptop sat, the smooth surface cold against my skin. The cameras were certainly recording every move I made. *Relax. Don't let them see you break.* I knew they kept more than eyes on me: sensors to track my heartbeat, temperature, and who knows what else. One unfavorable mood swing and they'd lock the doors, cut the lights, and I'd be trapped in the dark.

I crossed my arms, feeling the delicate fabric pull tight against my body as I walked. Replaying the election results in my mind, my faculties swarmed with heat. The new representatives were probably celebrating right now, still buzzing with excitement, believing they had some say in their future. *Poor fools.* They had no idea what awaited them.

Stopping by the mirror where I prepared myself a few short hours ago, I caught a glimpse of my appearance. The pale dress clung to me like cobwebs. I could take the damn thing off, but the sensation of it would never leave. And for a moment, I questioned my identity. On the surface, I looked calm, but the tension hummed beneath my skin, and beads of sweat collected at my hairline. I swung my arms and fanned my face, hoping the movement might help settle my nerves.

It didn't.

The Sanctioning was coming for them, the same hellish experience I endured. They thought they were walking into power—into control. But once they crossed into Mass, they'd be swallowed whole by a machine designed to break them down, piece by piece. Torture, dressed up as tests of willpower and strength.

I should know; I survived it.

Barely.

Some may not.

I turned away from the mirror, crossing the room again, each step purposeful. My heels clicked in a manner that annoyed the shit out of me. Lyonal, Draven, and I were nothing more than pawns in a much larger game. *Our power is an illusion.* It pissed me off. Orders came from higher up, from people—or forces—we couldn't even name. Every move was surveilled. I felt like a performer in a show, acting out a role, waiting dotingly for my lines.

I stopped near the bed, gripping the corner post tight in my hand. I could still feel the effects of my own experience in The Sanctioning, the memories of how they manipulated my mind, how they pushed me to the edge. No, they weren't physical tests, like everyone thought—they were nightmares designed to break you from the inside out. And if you talked about them? Your family, your friends, and anyone you cared about would be the ones to pay the price.

I dug pointed nails deep into the wood, thinking of my mother and what they threatened to do to her. The fear that they'd hurt her—use her against me scratched like gnarled fingers at the back of my mind. A constant threat, even after all these years. I kicked at the bedpost.

The control, the manipulation—each element formed an impenetrable system that felt impossible to unravel. But that didn't mean I wouldn't try given the opportunity. *Don't lose your shit, Betta.* The truth had to be out there. And when I found it, I wouldn't let them bury me with it.

More thoughts of my mother drifted into my mind amidst the paranoia that clung to me like a second skin. I plunked down on the bed's edge, my heels slipping off with a muted thud as I kicked them aside. The coolness of the floor against my bare feet offered an odd, soothing sensation, and a small comfort. I leaned back against the headboard, tucking one leg close and leaving the other on the floor to steady me.

The isolation here was unbearable, a cruel irony given how often I yearned for solitude back in Sertoda. During my term, I had seen my mother only twice—fleeting, monitored visits that never allowed for a private word. I heard her voice in my mind, asking if I felt okay, sensing the dangers lurking in this labyrinth of deceit. I clenched my jaw, trying to shake the thought. I knew that even the slightest slip during our time together could raise red flags. Could put her in danger.

My mother, a resilient woman from Sertoda, served as my anchor. I absentmindedly traced the pattern of the bedspread with my fingers, lost in thought. Born in the harsh Divide, where survival meant fighting daily battles, she joined the military as a medic, just out of her teens. She escaped poverty and took up station in Brawn at The Mouth, where she met my father—a man whose domineering presence left scars that never healed.

I drew my legs up to my chest, hugging them tight as his memory surfaced.

Growing up with a mother who endured constant abuse marked my early years. As a baby, she escaped with me. Running from my father's cruelty. Taking refuge in a rundown house back in The Divide. Cold nights and relentless labor etched into my mind. Even now, I could almost feel the biting chill of those adolescent years as I curled up on my bed, drawing my body close in search of any comfort I could find.

My mother protected me from the worst despite the hardships. Her stories of Sertoda's vibrant festivals and its strong community were like a promise of a better future, contrasting our grim reality.

An unbreakable bond connected us. My confidant, my guide through every storm. We found solace in each other, even though our new life brought its own set of challenges. My mother worked herself to the bone to provide—mending clothes, cleaning houses—anything to scrape together enough wattage to keep us going. I could picture her, exhausted but unwavering, her hands deftly working as she sewed neighbors' worn garments for anything extra they could spare.

I uncurled myself and slid my legs off the bed. Taking a deep breath, I walked back toward the window. The city lights of Mass stretched out in the distance, mocking me with their silence. Thinking back on the fire incident that brought me recognition and offered a glimpse of Sertoda's much more humble city lights evoked bittersweet feelings. It changed everything—our ticket to a better life, allowing us to move to the city and away from The Divide. I could still see my mother's relieved smile, a rare glimpse of peace after all the suffering we had faced.

I longed to see her, to confide in her, to seek her advice. But exposing my truth carried too many risks. I missed our late-night talks, her comforting presence, and her uncanny ability to know what I needed without words. I worried about her, alone and vulnerable.

Lost in my thoughts, I was startled as the door to my quarters slid open with an audible hiss. I tensed, expecting guards.

Draven slipped into the dim room. His sudden appearance was like a crack of lightning in a quiet sky, sending a shiver down my spine.

I turned away from the window, my heart pounding as he emerged from the shadows.

"What are you doing here?" I whispered, the sound barely reaching my ears, tinged with surprise and caution.

Draven's finger lifted to his full lips in a sharp, silent gesture. He swept the room with meticulous intensity, scanning every corner and crevice as if he could sense hidden eyes watching us. The faint hum of the air conditioning seemed to grow louder in the tense silence.

"We need to talk," he said in a hushed tone. The seriousness in his eyes marked a sharp departure from our usual taunting exchanges.

"About what?" I asked, wary of the omnipresent surveillance that might be capturing this.

Draven's expression shifted. His movements were smooth, deliberate—too calm for the storm brewing behind those eyes. Without a word, he made a subtle movement, two fingers curling and brushing lightly against the fabric of his pants—a small, familiar gesture. He was signaling me to follow. It was a code we'd used before, one that only needed the slightest motion to convey the message.

Of course, like a dumbass, I trailed after him.

I hesitated, glancing back at the door to my quarters as we exited. "Where are my guards? They're always stationed here. Who's watching over me?"

Draven stopped, turning just enough for me to catch the corner of his smirk. "I sent them off. Gave them a little mission to investigate one of the council members."

That answer made my stomach tighten. "What? Which council member?" I demanded, my tone sharper than intended. "You've got to be kidding me, Draven. You'll get them in trouble. You know how they react to that sort of—"

"Relax," he interrupted, waving a dismissive hand as he resumed walking. I followed, the soft padding of my feet against the polished floor amplifying the growing tension. He fell back, aligning his strides with mine as we traveled through the building, his voice dropping to a whisper. "It's a wild goose chase. I threw them off with a mix of names: I gave them the first name of one council member, the last name of another, and a third territory that doesn't match either. They'll be too busy scrambling, trying to figure out who I meant, all the while terrified they've already messed it up."

A part of me was amused, picturing them chasing their tails, too one-track-minded to see through the misdirection. But another part of me made my pulse quicken. "You're playing a dangerous game," I muttered, the edge in my voice betraying my concern. I slowed my pace. "And what happens when they figure it out?"

Draven's eyes gleamed with a dark amusement. "They won't. By the time they start questioning the names, I'll have a new lie ready to throw them off balance again. You don't need to worry about them."

I crossed my arms, feeling the cold air of the corridor sink into my skin. "I don't like you moving my people without telling me," I said, my voice low but firm.

As we walked deeper into the building, my mind raced with questions. What could Draven need to discuss that required such secrecy? Despite my apprehension, I followed, keeping a cautious distance, unsure if anything beneath his warrior facade could lead to a favorable interaction.

"Are you going to kill me?"

Watching the Watchers:

New surveillance technology is steadily being integrated into each territory. Drones with enhanced optics, capable of tracking movement across vast distances, have become commonplace. These drones are officially hailed as necessary to monitor the subterranean entrances and prevent any possible incursions from the Cird, who are often painted as the real threat to Sandric's fragile peace. The reports assure us that this technology ensures safety, especially with the rise in rumors of Cird activity near The Divide.

In theory, these measures could stop hostile forces before they breach our little community. However, the question lingers: what defines a "breach" in the eyes of the government? At what point does safety become an excuse to monitor not only potential invaders but also dissenters, anyone whose actions might question the system?

The public view is clear: drones are the shield we need, keeping us safe. But there's an unsettling thought I can't shake. What happens when "security" extends beyond the enemy? When the tech that promises protection starts tracking everyday citizens?

There's no way of knowing who decides where safety ends and control begins. And that, I suspect, is the real purpose of these systems.

In pursuit of truth and understanding,

—H. Wilhoph

Chapter Eight

LEVITY

My retrieval for Mass promised to be swift, but the exact time remained a mystery. The night felt both endless and fleeting, like a dream just beyond my grasp. Each familiar task grew increasingly difficult to finish. A tangled list of things still needing attention with the thought of leaving had me dazed. The potatoes from the market sat untouched, waiting to be peeled and washed. Had it only been this afternoon since I got them? The trip felt like a lifetime ago. So much had changed since the morning sun warmed our little house.

I glanced around at the echoes of our past. The place struggled in Pop's absence. Small cracks lined the plaster walls, and the floorboards groaned underfoot. After the fire, neighbors had chipped in, helping us rebuild what we could, but the singed signs still lingered. Especially in the kitchen. Charred edges showed faintly beneath a coat of mismatched paint. Crooked cabinet doors hung from warped hinges. Tivian finally patched the leaky roof after years of growing, unattended holes.

Walking toward our sleeping quarters, I grazed my fingers across the lopsided shelves Pop built and Mama's well-used rocking chair. This house thrived on their memories but barely held together without consistent repairs. The paint on the doorframes had started to peel, and small chips were gathering on the floor below. I should've taken care of it last summer. I should've fixed a lot of things.

Evie and Blue were already lying in bed, but it felt too soon for goodbyes. There was so much left to say. So much I needed them to understand.

"Are you sure you've packed everything?" Evie asked, her wide eyes peeking from beneath the sheet as I tucked it around her.

Taking Mama's worn quilt draped at the foot of the bed, I laid it across the two. I prayed its thickness could soften the cold that crept through the slits between our bowed window frames.

"I have everything I need. You just focus on being good while I'm gone," I said, patting her curly hair that tangled like mine after a long day. "I'll be back before you know it."

Blue rolled away from me, pulling her thin blanket over her shoulder. My throat tightened as the bed creaked beneath her small frame and the distance she placed between us.

"I love you two so much," I said, my voice low and soft, trying to hide its tremble. "Your brothers will take such good care of you while I'm gone. Time will pass faster than you can even imagine."

Blue didn't stir. She remained stubborn and silent, even when I sensed her desire to speak. Her body curled tighter, a wall of quiet defiance.

"I love you, Levity," Evie spoke with a lilt in her voice that soothed the sharp edges of my heart.

"I love you too, Sprout," I whispered back, my fingers rubbing the fraying edges of the bedding. I stayed until Evie's eyes closed. Stayed watching her breaths even out as sleep overtook her. Stayed memorizing the way her chest rose and fell under Mama's patchwork quilt. Her innocent, peaceful face as she slept only made it harder to imagine being absent from her life during such an important time.

Forcing myself to stand, I moved quietly through the house. The rhythmic crash of the ocean waves could be heard from our open windows. I closed my eyes and memorized their music, not knowing when I'd hear them again. So much remained to be done. The kitchen table, scarred with knife marks and worn from years of use, sat in the center of the kitchen like a silent witness to our lives. I made my way over to the drawer with the arranged potatoes. I grabbed the old paring knife from the counter and started on the first one, the scrape of the blade against the skin grounding me, if only for a moment.

I ran through all the little things I needed to do before leaving again: make sure Tivian and Triad knew where the extra blankets were stored in case the nights got cold; leave a list of chores by the stove; remind them t check the firewood so they wouldn't run out like last winter. My hands moved on autopilot as I peeled potato after potato, the growing pile of skins matching the height of my worry.

A soft creak made me glance over my shoulder. Blue stood in the doorway; her small frame illuminated by the faint glow of a candle.

"You're really going, aren't you?" she asked, her voice small, hesitant.

I set down the knife, wiping my hands on a towel. "Yeah, I am."

Her eyes flicked to the half-peeled potatoes on the counter. "What about... me?"

I knelt, pulling her into a hug, even though she resisted for a second. "You'll be okay. You have Tivian, Triad, and Evie."

Blue's arms wrapped around me. She smelled like fresh air and wood smoke from the fire we'd lit earlier, the scent clinging to her clothes.

"I'll come back," I said, looking her in the eyes as I pulled away to make that promise. My gaze drifted to the faint burn mark on her face—its jagged edges still so visible, a scar she wore with quiet strength. Without thinking, I traced its outline with my fingertip. My heart ached at the memory of the pain she'd endured. I leaned in and pressed a soft kiss to the mark, my lips lingering there for a moment longer than I intended, before pulling my little sister into my arms once more.

"I don't want you to go," she murmured into my shoulder.

"I know," I whispered back. "I love you."

She lingered in my embrace for a moment longer, then pulled away and turned back toward the bed. I followed her back into the sleeping quarters and watched Blue disappear under the covers, her back to me again.

I tucked the corners of their blankets and placed a few of Evie's toys—her favorite worn-out doll and the little wooden horse Pop carved—within arm's reach. I brushed Evie's dark curls from her forehead, her hair soft as silk between my fingers. The thought of her growing older, turning thirteen without me here to guide her twisted painfully in my chest.

And then there was Blue—her fiery attitude would push the boys to their limits in no time. She tested boundaries and challenged every rule just to see if it would bend. The boys wouldn't stand a chance. Neither of them possessed the tools to handle Blue's stubbornness. Or maybe they'd have her strung up by her toes if she didn't mind them. I almost smiled at the thought.

I remained in the center of the room for a moment, feeling the enormity of what lay ahead settle over me and the ones I loved. The world outside these walls grew harsher with each passing day and leaving them behind—even to fight for a position I knew to be crucial—filled me with angst. What would they do without me here? Without my voice to guide them, to pull them back when the world got too close?

Trudging one foot in front of the other, I made my way to the small bed I called my own and sat on the edge. The mattress sagged beneath me, the springs groaning softly in the quiet. My mind raced through what I still needed to pack. The duffel bag I'd started filling sat open on the floor, hardly enough for a trip that would stretch to five years.

I surveyed the room, my eyes landing on the few trinkets that stared back as reminders of a paused, suspended life. One of the only possessions of real meaning I owned remained the pendant Mama gave me on my sixteenth birthday before she died. I picked it up from the small table next to my bed, running my thumb over the worn, familiar shape of the wave pressed into the silver.

I clasped it around my neck, the cool metal pressing against my skin like a promise. It kept me present, reminding me that my actions were for my family and the people of Sertoda.

Lost in thought, a knock at the door jolted me from my reverie. I looked over at Evie, her delicate features serene. She looked so fragile, like a doll carefully snuggled in for the night. Blue lay motionless next to her, pretending to sleep or maybe already lost in her own wild dreams.

"Yes?" I called softly, trying not to disturb the girls.

The door to the sleeping quarters creaked open, and Triad poked his head in. His face tensed, eyes darting with nerves as he whispered, "An official has arrived."

My eyelids fluttered shut for a moment, disbelief settling in. "Now?" A wave of anxiety surged through me, and my palms slicked with sweat. I wiped them on the worn pants I'd yet to change out of since returning from the beach, the faint grit of sand clinging to the fabric and my skin.

An official now stood on our doorstep, an abrupt reminder that the time for reflection had ended. No more waiting, no more delaying. With one last look at Evie's delicate face and Blue's back, I stood, my hand gripping the strap of the far-too-light duffel for the journey ahead.

I walked into the common area where Tivian and Triad were waiting, both stiffening when they saw me, trying to hold in the emotions I saw playing across their young faces.

Tivian's jaw tightened, the pride in his eyes unmistakable, but I saw the worry he tried to hide. Triad looked down, lips pressed into a thin line as though attempting to swallow the words he wanted to say.

The water flooding my eyes betrayed the confidence I wanted to show them. A single tear slipped down my cheek before I could stop it. "Look after Evie. Be patient with Blue," I choked out, my throat knotting tighter with every word. Even for a cause we believed in, the thought of leaving them was unbearable. How could I leave the four people who meant everything to me? For five long years?

I turned to Tivian first, gripping his broadening shoulders. He'd grown significantly over the past year, but the softness of his face still reflected his youth. "Promise me you'll be good," I said, my shaky voice opposing my grasp's firmness.

He nodded, yet I knew the look that flickered in his eyes—an uncertainty about meeting the expectations placed on him.

I reached out, pulling Triad into the embrace, wrapping my arms around them both. "Don't worry too much," I said, my voice quieter now. "I'll be back before you know it."

Their arms tightened around me in a way that made it impossible to hold back more tears. Our embrace lingered with me, its warmth holding off the ache of separation for a little while longer.

When I finally pulled back, wiping the stray tears from my cheeks, I peered at the front door. The official stood just inside, watching us with a stiff, unreadable expression. He wore the typical uniform of Sandric officers—a crisp black suit with silver accents, every inch of fabric perfectly pressed. His hands were clasped behind him, eyes scanning the room as if checking off an invisible list. The candlelight cast a sharp, pale glow on his face. An air of detachment surrounded him as if he grew accustomed to walking into homes like ours, indifferent to the lives disrupted by his presence.

The man broke the moment with his gruff tone, "Leave all personal communication and recording devices behind. You will be issued new devices when the time is appropriate."

"I don't have any," I responded.

The official pursed his lips.

With a final glance at the boys, I took a deep breath and nodded to my escort. He stepped aside, and as I crossed the threshold, the sensation of leaving an entire lifetime behind enveloped me. Each step forward pulled me further from the world I knew, from the only version of myself I'd ever been.

Now, I would leave it all behind.

The Eyes Among Us:

Officials. A word that carries more weight than it should. In most territories, the role of "official" isn't clearly defined; it's as if the title itself is a patchwork of vague responsibilities—a badge that can mean anything from a peacekeeper to an enforcer. These officials aren't local. They are almost always outsiders, implants from other territories, sent to keep the peace, or so it's said. But peace isn't their only job.

Officially, they patrol the streets, enforce local laws, ensure order is maintained in places where tensions run high. They act as a constant presence in the public's daily life, but there is always something about them that feels wrong.

In cultural studies, we often talk about the roles institutions play in shaping social order. The military may be tasked with the external defense of Sandric, but these officials represent the internal. Their presence is a reminder that authority doesn't always come in the form of soldiers in uniform—it can be a stranger who walks among us, observing and reporting.

We've been conditioned to accept their gaze as part of our everyday landscape. How easy it is to think of them as a safety net, when in truth, they might be the net keeping us contained.

In pursuit of truth and understanding,

—H. Wilhoph

Chapter Nine

BETTA

"What?" Draven spun around.

"Are. You. Going. To. Kill. Me?" I prodded. "I mean Cirds-damnation, Draven. What is this all about?"

He scoffed, grabbing my hand and tugging me along.

Draven led me through the dimly lit hallways, his familiarity with the layout clear. Unadorned corridors were devoid of the sleek, modern amenities that defined the public areas of Mass. I couldn't shake the feeling that we were slipping into a forgotten part of the center city. Surely, they documented every corner of this place. It reminded me of the dank tunnels the guards used to ferry us from one area to another.

The further we ventured, the more primitive our surroundings became. A musty smell clung to the air, mingling with the faint scent of rust and something else—a hint of mold, perhaps, or the ghosts of long-forgotten conversations. My body came to a sudden stop in the clandestine enclave known only to him, or so I surmised.

The silence hung between us, pregnant with anticipation, and I felt a shiver run down my spine as I realized just how vulnerable this place made me feel.

I shot a glance at Draven, his expression a puzzle in the subdued light. Despite the confusion swirling in my mind, I felt a flicker of security with him; if Draven dared to drag me into this secretive place, it meant he valued my presence. I thought of his brother, Dorian—his name hovering like a storm cloud. Should I even bring it up if he didn't? It felt like playing with fire, and I questioned whether I wanted to get burned in a place where no one could hear me scream.

Finally, we slipped into a secluded alcove where a single lit sconce danced in hypnotic patterns against the walls. I glanced down to my bare feet, noticing I now stood on packed dirt.

Draven turned to face me.

"I found this place during my night rounds," he explained, his regard flickering around the obscured alcove. "I've been testing the security measures, searching for blind spots where we can talk without setting off alarms and face repercussions."

"What's so urgent that it requires dragging me into this fresh hell?" I shot back, voicing skepticism and wariness.

The lack of light accentuated the harsh lines on his face. "We've never spoken a word about our Sanctioning," he started with some reluctance. "The shit they've put us through is a blackened spot on my soul I've buried deep. But I can't carry this alone anymore. I need someone who gets it—someone who can understand the hell I've been through. And right now, that someone is you."

He searched my face for a reaction. The cavern's ancient walls echoed our unspoken fears. His request demanded a promise of intimacy. It made my skin prickle. The thought of getting close to him, this man I at most tolerated and whose heritage entwined with the suffering of my past, felt impossible. Yet here he stood, ready to drag out the details of our shared trauma, and I needed to decide if I would let him.

"Why?" The word fell like a knife, sharp off my tongue.

Draven filled his chest with stifled air. He crouched, sliding down the wall next to me, sitting back onto his bottom, and resting his heavily muscled back against the stone. I'd never seen him assume such a subordinate position.

I looked down my nose at him. "Now's a hell of a time to dredge up the mess from five years ago. What is the point? Why do you need this so bad?"

"It's not about me and what I need, Betta. It's about my brother. He's not cut out for this. He won't make it through The Sanctioning. He might d—" His voice wavered, a flicker of agony crossing his face. "If he breaks, he'll end up just another brainwashed cog on the council, stripped of every bit of will and identity."

I arched an eyebrow, a sardonic smile curling my lips. "And you think you're any different? We're all just cogs in this screwed-up machine, whether we're in the spotlight or not. At least they get to hang onto a sliver of dignity while we're paraded around like animals."

Draven's expression darkened as he stared up at me. His voice dropped an octave. "From the intel I've gathered, council members don't just lose their trial. It's worse than that. They're subjected to something akin to a mind-sweep. That's why they always seem so removed. This isn't about ensuring compliance; it's about reshaping them, making an example of what happens when you show weakness. They're under constant threat like the rest of us, but I suspect what goes on behind the scenes is even more chilling. You must have noticed."

I felt the air hit my throat like a fist, and I struggled to keep my voice calm. "*By the Cird's breath,* just one more fun little detail." I shook my head, my frustration palpable. "I've noticed. Like a fucking factory reset. Empty shells after The Sanctioning. I thought it stemmed from the stress or the fear of—"

Draven cut in, his posture unflinching. "It's more than stress. And whatever they're doing to them, it's not just once. I think they're being... reprogrammed or some shit. Over and over, until they're completely removed from their former selves. The fire, the ambition they came to Mass with, it's erased, making them more pliable."

I nodded, my thoughts drifting back to the briefings with my team. I replayed the exchanges, trying to piece together anything that might shed light on the situation. Their eyes, once sharp and alive, now flat. The way they moved, spoke—they'd lost their spark, their will.

"Why are you telling me this now?" I demanded, suspicion coating every word. "You've never been this open about your thoughts on this nightmare of a system with me. You've been a jerk. Taunting me every chance you get. Are you setting me up? Is this some kind of trap? Gonna feed me to Lyonal or expose me in some sadistic loyalty test?"

Draven cracked his knuckles with loud synchronized pops, but I didn't flinch. "Think about it, Betta," he snapped back. "If I wanted to screw you over, I'd have done it by now. Why the hell would I need to set up an elaborate trap? I'd just do it." He let out an exasperated sigh, then ran his tongue over his teeth as if attempting to erase a bitter taste. "I don't trust anyone with ease. Least of all Lyonal. But you outlasted your trial like I did, and that means something. My brother, Dorian, doesn't have the same qualities we have. He's… softer." The word passed through his lips as if a Brawn man never used such vocabulary.

He was wavering, a rare crack in his otherwise aloof demeanor. "Growing up in Brawn, the expectations were brutal. You've met my father, General Ballister."

I recalled the man in vivid detail. During an official summit, I brought up concerns about civilian casualties in one of Brawn's more ruthless campaigns. Leaning back in his chair, he narrowed his eyes at me, conveying the impression that I represented an inconvenience.

Civilians? Casualties happen. Maybe if they fought like men instead of running like rats, they'd earn a little respect. His words pierced as sharp and unfeeling as the cold ammunition he worshiped, the disdain in his voice lingering long after the conversation ended.

Draven continued. "He's relentless. From the moment we could walk, the General demanded we become warriors. Pain persisted, discipline remained harsh, and any sign of weakness faced swift eradication. In my trial, they used that upbringing against me, tearing open wounds that never healed." His expression softened as he thought of his brother. "Dorian is different. More sensitive, more thoughtful. He never embraced the violence. He's not built the same."

I nodded, my thoughts flickering back to General Ballister's barbarity. "You're afraid for him."

"Yes," Draven whispered his admittance. "The mental torment they inflict here... I barely held onto my own sanity. This term, from what I've seen, they've pushed the limits even further. They dragged out my worst fears, twisting my mind until I couldn't tell reality from hallucination.

"And it's so much worse now—something new. I intercepted a communication being passed to the engineers. They're using... They called it *Quantum Projection Technology*." He frowned, struggling to explain. "It manipulates particles, controls them somehow, so the simulations are no longer in your head. They make everything feel real—*physically real.* The system creates objects you can see, touch, even the ground beneath your feet. It's formed from molecular structures. It's a living nightmare. Every inch of it."

I took a deep breath, placing my hand on the wall to balance myself as I absorbed his words. The Sanctioning was heinous, engineered to crush the mind and spirit into oblivion. My own nightmare served as a stark reminder of their sadistic nature, with the memory clinging to me like a contagion with no cure.

He paused, his face darkening. "I don't know all the details but from what I gathered it is no longer the old Sanctionings where the torment is solely in our minds. Now, your body will believe it's real, too. Whatever they show you, your senses will tell you it's happening. I barely survived the old system. And we know not all of us did."

Edward.

The Perpetual Sense elect from my home. My friend. The closest thing to a father I'd ever known. Gone. He was Jenalyne's dad, my best friend back in school, and our neighbor. He treated me like family, guiding me through the years, shielding Jena and I from the only real dangers we knew—hormonal boys and the occasional wild night.

And now, he was gone from our lives. Jenalyne likely remained unaware, living in a world of half-truths, wrapped in the comfort that he held a position on the small council after not winning a seat as a Sanctioned.

Draven's head fell. "Dorian… he's not prepared for that. I'm not prepared for that. If they force him into one of those projections, it'll break him."

To feel it…

I shuddered, reliving the torment. They broadcasted the scene around me—my mother, bound and beaten by a faceless Brawn enforcer, each agonizing detail magnified and replayed over and over. Her screams were unending, echoing in my ears like the relentless pounding of a storm on a window.

My hands trembled, grasping the stone wall, feeling the rough texture prime my nerves. I closed my eyes, trying to push away the vivid images that flashed before me—her eyes wide with terror, her body a canvas of suffering.

I forced myself to focus, drawing on the memories that anchored me. Waves crashed against our homeland's cliffs, their roar a brutal yet comforting reminder of my mother's resilience. Each wave had its rhythm, a callous cadence that mirrored the torment they forced me to witness. Yet the water bound us together—mother and daughter forged through the tempestuous seas of life's challenges.

I pressed my forehead against the cool stone, the chill of the wall soothing the heat rising. The waves, implacable and powerful, pushed me back to shore, a persistent force that reminded me of my identity even in the darkest depths of my trial.

Silence weighed heavily as I pulled back from the edge, battling the visceral shudders threatening to overtake me.

"What do you expect me to do?" I whispered. "I can't change the system."

"I don't know," Draven admitted, his voice thick with worry as he watched me unravel and then piece myself together. "If there's any chance you can help him—maybe talk to my brother when he arrives, share how you managed… anything to ease the blow or prepare him…" His voice faltered, a tremor betraying his usual composure. "I can't lose him, Betta. Not like this."

Seeing Draven so stripped of his usual strength and control rattled me in ways I hadn't anticipated. His vulnerability resembled an exposed, jagged wound. The fear he harbored for his brother, the desperation etched into his features tugged at something deep inside me.

I struggled with the irony of the situation. Here was a Brawn man—one of the very agents of the system that tormented my mother—now showing a level of genuine concern that both surprised and infuriated me. The same people who inflicted unimaginable suffering now pleaded for help. I clenched my fists, memories of my torment flashing behind my eyes once again—those faceless enforcers, the relentless malice. The scars could not be removed.

The idea of aiding Dorian, of extending a hand to someone tied to the very source of my anguish, was a bitter pill to swallow. I felt pulled in two directions—the desire to lash at everything Brawn represented and the nagging hope that maybe, just maybe, helping Dorian could make a dent in the monstrous machinery that almost broke me.

Perhaps this represented a form of justice, or maybe a desperate attempt to find some semblance of redemption for my own suffering.

But a noxious suspicion churned in my gut. "So that's it, huh? Just a heartfelt plea for your brother? Or is there something else you're hiding?" My voice danced on a razor's edge. "Something reeks, like you're trying to rope me into backing him for the Noble Warrior seat. I'm supposed to buy into this act of desperation while you play me?"

Draven's face tightened as he shook his head. Rising from the floor, he moved with a predatory grace, drew his knife—the blade catching light like a malevolent star. My skin prickled. The air thickened. He held the curved blade's sharp edge between us.

"Would you like me to evoke the Rite of the Bound Warrior?" he asked with an unsettling calm as he regarded me. He held his palm out. "It's a sacred act in Brawn—a bond forged through pain and truth."

My breath hitched. Fear clawed my insides. His words, the knife, pulsed with the gravity of what he proposed. *What wouldn't he do to prove his sincerity?*

"Draven, put the knife away," I choked out, heart racing. "This isn't the way to prove anything."

He hesitated, his grip on the knife steady as he searched my eyes. The tension began to ease in his shoulders, and he sheathed the blade with a definitive snap.

"It's not about securing a position," he resumed, his voice now firm. "If Dorian wins, he'll be trapped in the same system, subjected to the same brutality we are. I want to help him survive, not just win. His election stemmed from our father's ruthless schemes, I'm sure of it—he's a brutal man who commands respect through fear. He served as a Noble Warrior, and his methods of ensuring Dorian's election I'm certain were anything but honorable. He exploits and threatens people."

I frowned, struggling to digest the revelation as my mind raced. "So, your father rigged the election for him?" *Why am I not surprised?*

"He used his influence to sway the votes, thinking it would toughen Dorian up, make him into the warrior he never wanted to be." Draven crouched once more. His shoulders slumped as he buried his face in his large palms. "This will destroy him."

A moment of silence passed.

I stared down at him, my arms crossing my chest. "Why didn't they wipe us? You, me, Lyonal have been through worse. We've proven we're a hell of a lot stronger than those poor bastards on the council. So why leave us with our minds intact if they want us all to fall in line?"

Draven ran a hand over the smooth dark skin of his head, frustration etched into every line of his face. "It's control, Betta. The mind-swept ones are expendable. But us? They need our minds sharp enough to serve, dull enough to obey. They don't want sheep—they want wolves with leashes."

I scoffed. "Wolves? So, we're free to run, but only as far as the leash lets us? That's the game? They think they can hold us back and still expect us to fight their wars?"

"Exactly," he said, voice thinly veiled with anger. "They need us dangerous, but predictable. Controlled chaos. And they think they've got us so wrapped up in their system that we'll never see the leash for what it is."

I tilted my head. "And you're just okay putting your brother in the same position?"

Draven's lips curled into a bitter smile. "I've never been okay with it. But what the hell do you think I've been doing all these years? Playing along, waiting for the moment they loosen that reins just enough for me to turn around and bite back."

I held his stare, feeling around his words, searching for a hole I couldn't find. "Fair enough," I muttered, though doubt still lingered. "But don't think for a second I'll let you get the jump on me if you decide to take a bite. The real question: how the hell do we blow this corrupt clusterfuck wide open and expose what's really going on?"

I dropped down beside Draven, tugging at my dress to ensure it covered important things. "Because right now, you might be worried about your brother, but there is a whole world of people out there that have no fucking clue what is going on behind the closed doors in Mass."

"That's exactly it," he said raising his head to look at me. The despair now replaced with a fierce determination. "I've been mulling this over for a while. If Dorian makes it into a leadership position, it won't just be about him. We can use that role to expose the system from within."

I flicked a lock of my long black hair back with a dismissive gesture, my tone dripping with skepticism. "Sanctioned, huh? And how is sitting at the top of the food chain going to be any more beneficial for him than it's been for us? Because from where I'm sitting, it looks like the view's just as grim."

Draven adjusted the straps of his armored plate vest, his focus sharpening as the seriousness sank in. "I've been trying to figure out who's behind all this," he said, his voice low and intense. "The operative, the real power behind the scenes. But with our term ending, I've run out of time. I still don't have all the pieces of the puzzle."

He rubbed his temples. "I suspect that with the new representatives coming in, we'll have access to areas we've never seen before. We'll find the right information we need and expose the system."

A cynical laugh escaped me, half amusement, half disbelief. "So, you're planning to tear the whole damn thing down from the inside." My lips curled, but my tone stayed sharp, a challenge in every word. "Bold."

Draven's eyes blazed with fervor. "Yes. If Dorian can cling to even a scrap of sanity, we can leverage his position to expose the corruption I've been hunting. Uncovering every lie and secret might finally make this system's house of cards come crashing down. It's a gamble, but it's our shot to ignite a rebellion against this oppressive hell. I've been battling this nightmare on my own for too damn long. I need him in this fight, I need him to stay strong, but I also need you—your fire, your grit. We can't do this half-assed. We need to burn this whole corrupt mess to the ground."

"But how exactly am I supposed to help?" I shot back, my eyebrows arched in disbelief. "Sure, I can explain how I survived my trial to your little brother, but let's not pretend that even just sharing those details with him won't put me at risk with consequences from Sandric. I suppose that's just another day in our lives, right?" I shook my head, soaking in the absurdity of the situation. "Seriously, though, I'm all ears for your master plan, but you'd better have more in mind than just turning me into your brother's personal survival coach."

Draven leaned in. "You can help me dig up the dirt," he proposed, rubbing his meaty hands together. "We need to watch every shadow, listen to every whisper. Use every resource at our disposal to unbury the truth. Someone—maybe a whole damn cabal—is pulling the strings behind the scenes. We've got to sniff out who they are and their motive. Only then can we even think about exposing this whole poisonous system."

As Draven laid out his plan, a storm of doubts gathered over me. An uprising emerged, led by him and potentially his brother—both hailing from Brawn, a territory notorious for its cutthroat military tactics and relentless ambition. Could I believe that a revolution spearheaded by them aimed at genuine liberation? Or did this represent yet another power grab, cloaked in the pretense of freedom?

I studied Draven, his determination palpable and fierce. He had waged this fight alone. Now, he needed help. But what if his vision of Sandric didn't align with mine? What if his revolution amounted to nothing more than trading one tyrant for another? Could I trust him—or his brother—to lead a movement that would dismantle the system rather than just rearrange its pieces?

I hesitated, feeling the weight of the task settle on me like a leaden blanket. But something about Draven's drive ignited a spark in me—a spark that made me want to dive headfirst into the mess and blow it all up. "I'll see what I can do," I said. "But don't think you're off the hook just yet."

He raised an eyebrow. "Oh?"

"You need to be straight with me. No more of that smug, taunting bullshit. If we don't want to end up as collateral damage, we need trust."

Draven's dark eyes locked onto mine, and for a moment, the air between us crackled with something more than tension.

"Fair enough," he said, his voice softening. "But for the record, I've always trusted you, Betta. The truth is, I push you to see how far I can go; I want to provoke a reaction. In a world filled with battles, your moments of defiance remind me there's still fire in you. Beneath your tough exterior, I can see resilience and warmth—qualities I trust more than anything else."

"That's... weirdly sweet." My heart stuttered and I blinked, sideswiped by the unexpected sincerity. "Don't push it," I warned, trying to conceal a grin behind my hand. "But fine. We're on the same page now."

Draven gave a crooked smile of his own, showing off his beautiful white teeth, his eyes still warm. "No more games. Just the truth."

"Good."

As we stood, the significance of our pact washed over me. For the first time in five years of servitude, a chance to influence Sandric's fate existed. The opportunity to change the course of our future lived and breathed, and I wouldn't let it slip away.

Every decision from this point could lead to either redemption or ruin. With a sullen sneer, Draven whispered, "I know where we need to start."

Brawn's Military Might:

Brawn, once a land of sustenance, underwent a profound transformation fueled by desperation and ambition. Scarcity bred a survival mentality, compelling the populace to turn to militarization as a means of security. This shift has stifled the vibrant culture that once flourished, leaving behind an environment where strength is idolized above all else. The scars of this transformation run deep; fear and aggression have replaced the warmth of community.

In exploring this phenomenon, we must consider several key questions: What cultural narratives support the militarization of a society? How does fear shape identity and community bonds? What are the long-term implications of prioritizing strength over compassion in governance?

As we delve into the complexities of Brawn's evolution, I want students to reflect on the role of resource scarcity in shaping political landscapes. How do historical precedents inform the current state of militarization? And in what ways might this trajectory affect inter-territorial relations within Sandric?

This examination urges students to analyze the delicate balance between security and freedom. Can a culture founded on militarization ever return to its roots of provision, or has that path been irrevocably altered? Let us engage in these inquiries to foster a deeper understanding of the forces shaping our world today.

In pursuit of truth and understanding,

—H. Wilhoph

Chapter Ten

LEVITY

I arrived at the train station just after ten, the car ride from The Divide was brief but jarring. The city loomed ahead, with the platform alive in a haze of motion and light. Though deep blue of night crept across the sky, the station buzzed, glowing under a sea of electric lamps and the occasional flare from passing trains. My ears were overstimulated. Voices echoed through the cool air. Heels clacked against the polished floors. The low whine of motors accelerating and decelerating filled the space. It was all so different from the quiet isolation of our simple life.

The platform itself felt like a world apart from what I knew, a modern marvel standing in sharp contrast to the dust-covered roads and worn-down bikes of The Divide. The sleek metal of the tracks caught the light, casting sharp reflections, as trains sat gleaming like polished machinery waiting to whisk us away. I rarely encountered so much light, so much power and luxury beyond anything I could have imagined. The hum of energy pulsed through the station.

Then, through the blur of motion, I saw them—Thomas and Marmarie, standing just off to the side—a little island of calm amid the storm.

Thomas, with his strong, solid frame, looked like he belonged here. His fitted cotton t-shirt, the color of sand, clung to his chest, complementing the dark navy denim jeans that hugged athletic legs. His dark brown hair, slightly wavy and longer but cut just above his ears, framed his face in effortless, tousled strands. Olive skin accentuated brown eyes with a quiet intensity, hinting at the seriousness of what lay ahead yet radiating a warmth I knew capable of melting me.

Marmarie stood beside him with the kind of grace that could only come from experience. Her small, wiry frame seemed almost out of place in such a grand setting, but the lines on her face and the wisdom in her sincere gaze made it clear she belonged. The basic ash-colored linen dress she wore flowed against her form, matching the soft waves of her short, gray hair. Though petite, a steeliness defined her posture.

As I approached, anxiety knifed and twisted in my stomach. Thomas, the Noble Warrior elect, and Marmarie, the Perpetual Sense elect, exuded confidence and experience. Meanwhile, I felt like a child stumbling through a world meant for people like them. With no real reputation or accomplishments, what could I possibly offer that would compare? Their certainty only deepened the insecurities churning inside me.

I tentatively smiled, greeting them. "I'm Levity Wilhoph. I'll be traveling with you to Mass."

"Of course, my dear. I know who you are." Marmarie embraced me warmly. "I'm Elder Marmarie Pendavi."

I held my breath, searching Thomas's face. I wondered if he'd remember me from that one night we'd spent together, both too intoxicated for it to possibly mean much to him.

I'd slipped out in the early hours, certain he wouldn't recall my name in the light of day and unwilling to risk him waking with an expression of regret plastered on his face. But he looked at me now with the same polite warmth I'd seen him show someone on the streets, no hint of recognition in his eyes.

Thomas stood a step behind Marmarie, his bulky duffel slung over one shoulder. "Nice to meet you," he said smoothly, nodding. "Thomas

Ravleon."

I swallowed, feeling foolish.

I'd quietly admired him from afar as a girl at the fish market, drawn to his presence. He moved with a quiet authority, speaking to vendors like old friends. Tall. Self-assured. He belonged in a world far beyond the dusty paths and noise of that place.

Those moments, and the memory of our night together, had likely faded in his mind since he moved to the city. But they left an indelible mark on me, carving out a place in my thoughts long before the night we shared.

A sleek, silver bullet train shot into the station, its polished surface reflecting the station lights like liquid metal. The air buzzed with energy as the train came to a smooth halt just a few feet from us. Its electric doors slid open with an exaggerated hiss, as if the train exhaled a breath of relief.

"Can I take your bag?" Thomas asked, his hand extended toward the floppy duffel I held. In his other hand, he balanced Marmarie's large trunk effortlessly.

I clutched my bag closer, feeling the weight of home within its worn fabric. "Oh, no thank you. I can manage," I replied, offering a small smile as I pushed a lock of my unruly curls away from my face.

Thomas gave a brief nod and stepped onto the train, followed by Marmarie, whose graceful movements only made my awkwardness more apparent.

I lingered on the platform, my eyes scanning Sertoda. The salty air filled my lungs, mingling with the fading scent of fish and seaweed. The sea whispered against the distant shore; a sound I took for granted all my life. This would be the last time I heard it for a long while.

Forcing my feet to move, I stepped off the platform and into the sleek, metallic world of the train.

A *new* world.

The interior of the train struck me with awe. The air inside felt cooler, crisper—almost as if it filtered out the chaos of warm bodies lurking just outside. The official who escorted me from my home gestured for us to follow, leading us through narrow hallways lined with polished wood and steel accents. We moved toward our private car, and with every step, the sense of grandeur grew.

"Have you ever been on one of these before?" Thomas asked beside me, his voice almost drowned out by the hum of the train's systems.

"Never," I admitted, my eyes widening. "It's like something out of a story book."

The official opened a door to our quarters, and my breath caught at the sight. The room, though small, featured meticulous design elements. Dark wood paneling lined the walls, lending an air of sophistication. A soft, cream-colored carpet padded the floor underfoot. The common area featured four large, deep-cushioned leather seats, grouped in duos and a polished brass lamp cast a warm glow over the room, giving the space an almost cozy feel, despite its modern elegance.

"This will be your private lounge," the official said, his tone professional yet polite. He gestured toward another door at the far end of the car. "And through here is your sleeping area."

I stepped through, my eyes scanning the compact sleeping quarters. Four beds, two stacked on each side of the narrow room, were built into the walls, each made up with crisp white linens and dark woolen blankets. The beds appeared inviting, yet the narrow space between them offered only enough room to pass shoulder to shoulder.

To the left, a small door led to a bathroom. A sink and compact shower gleamed with chrome fixtures, spotless and polished.

"Not bad," Thomas said, setting down Marmarie's trunk on one of the beds. "I've seen worse accommodations."

I nodded, though words seemed to escape me as I took it all in. This was very fair in my eyes. The jolt of the train beneath my feet startled me. I lost my footing and stumbled into Thomas.

"I got you," he said, steadying me.

My face flushed as I quickly straightened.

We made our way back out to the lounge, now moving, gliding away from Sertoda and toward the unknown.

Marmarie settled into one of the lounge's deep leather chairs, her gaze gentle yet perceptive as it landed on the pendant at my neck and the small wave etched into the metal. I took the seat across from her.

Thomas settled into the seat beside me, close enough that his hand nearly brushed mine on the armrest. His nearness sparked a rush of memories I couldn't ignore—memories he clearly didn't share, judging by his relaxed, oblivious expression. A pang of insecurity welled up in me, but I pushed it down.

"That's a beautiful necklace, Levity," Marmarie said, her voice low and thoughtful. Something in her tone hinted at a deeper awareness, as though she sensed how much it meant to me.

My fingers curled around the cool metal and a small blush crept up my cheeks. "Thank you," I replied softly, my voice barely above a whisper. "My mother gave it to me."

Marmarie's thoughtful gaze stayed on me, then she looked back at the necklace. "The wave; it's a symbol of resilience." She paused for a moment before adding, "A reminder of Sertoda's strength, our civilization's hidden depths and… secrets."

A ripple of unease flickered in my chest. As an Elder, Marmarie held a place of reverence within Sertoda; Elders carried not just wisdom but an almost sacred authority. They embodied Sertoda's history and traditions, and they were respected. Trusted. Marmarie's presence alone commanded that trust, and her words carried the weight of her lifetime, well-rooted in the values and truths that formed the backbone of Sertoda.

So when she spoke with heed, it was worth paying attention.

I adjusted in my chair, my hand grazing the seam of the leather cushion.

"Secrets?" Thomas's voice held genuine curiosity as he looked to her.

Her expression eased into something almost reminiscent, like an Elder recalling a story she'd told many times before. Her eyes drifted toward the window, as if seeing through layers of history and tradition.

"You know," she began, "In the old days, we looked to the land for everything—the herbs, the plants, the seasons all had their place in our lives. Each remedy, each tradition held meaning, carried down from one generation to the next. There's a wisdom in that kind of knowing, don't you think?"

I was drawn in, almost as if she'd wrapped us in the comfort of her memory. Thomas leaned forward, his attention captured, though I noticed skepticism hadn't completely left his expression.

Marmarie continued with surety. "Over time, though, things shift. New laws are made, sometimes without clear reasons. Rules arise that don't seem to fit the way we've always lived." Her fingers traced an invisible path along the arm of the chair. "Take the law they're trying to pass on our herbal remedies," Marmarie's tone changed to one almost conspiratorial. "They claim it's for safety, but those of us who know these plants… we understand these traditions run as deep as Sertoda's own roots. They've sustained our people through hardships for generations. And now, suddenly, they're talking about restrictions." She paused, pursing her lips and narrowing her eyes, as if considering her next words with care. "One must wonder—why would something so harmless, so interwoven with who we are, need regulation? And who stands to gain from it?"

Silence filled the space, her question settling in the air between us. her gaze fixed on the necklace around my neck. "Think of it like the ocean, Thomas. On the surface, the waves move and ripple, giving life to what we see. But beneath the waves lies a different world, deeper currents that don't show themselves. Forces at work that are less obvious."

My heart beat a little faster, her words inviting an unease that was familiar and unnerving. Thomas shifted in his seat, his focus still enraptured by the conversation.

Marmarie relaxed her shoulders. She reminded me of an old teacher of mine and the way he'd cock his head just before throwing a challenge my way. "It's a powerful question worth asking. Who benefits? Sometimes, the changes serve a purpose beyond what we're told. Like the ocean and what lies beneath, our world has layers we can't see without peeling back the surface."

I glanced toward Thomas, noticing a frown pulling at his brows. Was he struggling with all of this as much as I was? Or perhaps, was he resisting an idea that rattled his own certainty about the world as I had since my parents' deaths?

"So... you're talking hidden agendas?" he asked, the words slipping out reluctantly, his voice lower than before.

Ignoring the question, she looked again toward my necklace. Her voice softened as if talking about something half in memory. "Currents are curious things. Sometimes they're gentle, guiding us, supporting us. But other times... other times, they carry a force behind them. They press and pull, steering us in ways we don't always see. And yet, we follow the flow, don't we?" She gave a small, knowing smile, one that didn't quite reach her eyes.

Marmarie leaned forward, her expression resting somewhere between caution and invitation. "Another question worth asking yourself, though—who or what sets those currents in motion?"

The thought settled in my mind like a quiet, unshakable truth. I looked to Thomas, finding his frown deepening and his mouth set in a firm line.

"Sertoda has always been a land of opportunity and freedom," he remarked.

"That's how the stories go," she replied with a long sigh. "But with freedom comes responsibility. And sometimes, those with responsibility twist it for their own purposes."

I mulled over Marmarie's words, my thoughts a bridge between doubt and agreement. "I've seen enough injustice to know there's truth in what you're saying, Marmarie," I finally said before I glanced out the window, my reflection barely visible against the blackness of the passing night and the soft glow in our train car.

Marmarie sat up straighter, her eyes sharp with sympathy and conviction. "Exactly." She patted my knee.

The rhythmic clatter of the train filled the silence that settled between us. The soft hum of the tracks beneath our feet pulsed in sync with the jitters building in my chest. I shifted in my seat. It agitated me, this talk of manipulation, and yet—it felt like a necessary conversation seeing what we were barreling into at breakneck speeds.

The leather beneath Thomas groaned as he leaned forward, his hands resting on his knees. "I get what you're wanting us to question, Marmarie," he said respectfully. "But I can't help seeing The Sanctioning as an opportunity. If we succeed, we could prove ourselves as brave, bold people of Sertoda—show that we have the strength to change things. The Sanctioning might give us the leverage we need to fix what's broken."

He spoke with a quiet conviction that matched his stature, and for a moment, his optimism felt contagious. But Marmarie's hardened sigh cut, her stern regard showing the years of lived experience.

"I admire your optimism, Thomas," she said gently. "It's a strength you'll need, no doubt. But we can't afford to be naive. We don't know what's waiting for us in Mass, and that uncertainty demands vigilance."

I glanced between them—Thomas, with his determined vision of change, and Marmarie, her wisdom etched into every line of her face.

They were right in their own way. But as I looked out into the dark of nightfall, I couldn't shake the feeling that none of us truly understood what awaited us in The Sanctioning.

"What do you expect Mass to be like?" I asked the two of them inquisitively. Pop extolled its majestic virtues and yet I struggled with my own skepticism, grappling with the limitations of my knowledge.

"I imagine it's a place of grandeur and authority," Thomas responded, his dark, inviting eyes brightening with jubilation. "A city where we can learn and grow. Where our contributions will be valued."

Marmarie's expression grew serious. "In the past twenty years," she said, her voice low as if someone might overhear, "Mass has changed. I've heard stories—stories from sources I trust—that paint a much different picture. We must be ready, for things are not as they seem, and the currents there can shift in ways we can't predict."

I hesitated, thinking back to the stories Pop used to tell me as a child. His voice would grow soft, almost reverent, when he spoke of Mass. "Pop always described Mass as a kingdom of sorts, emerging as if from magic. The stones, each one mined from different regions of our world, were not just ordinary rocks. They symbolized unity, strength—each carrying the essence of its homeland, telling stories of distant mountains, vast deserts, and deep forests. It's hard to imagine those ideas, the beautiful structures just crumbling away."

Thomas looked intrigued, his earlier excitement not yet dampened by Marmarie's words. "I've heard about the stones too—how they were gathered from all over Sandric."

I nodded. "Yes. According to Pop, each region sent its finest artisans and materials to build the city. The walls were adorned with intricate carvings, legends of our people etched into the stone. The idea of its beauty always left me in awe as a child. That is what I'm expecting to be met with."

Marmarie's serious expression didn't soften, but I could tell she listened intently. "That sounds... idyllic."

"Of course," I agreed, as my cheeks flushed. "Pop said to even set eyes on it in person is a privilege few ever get."

Marmarie glanced at us with a new curiosity. With head cocked to the side she asked, "And The Sanctioning... what do you think it will involve?"

Thomas shrugged. "Physical challenges, perhaps, or tests of our knowledge and leadership skills. Whatever it is, I'm ready to face it head-on. I've been preparing for this my whole life."

I looked at him, my own curiosity piqued.

"What drives you, Thomas? Why did you want to become a representative?" Marmarie inquired.

A shadow flickered across Thomas's face, a momentary lapse in his usual confidence. "I grew up in The Divide," he said slowly, his voice tangled with a quiet regret. "Opportunities were... limited, to say the least."

I understood his words all too well. His focus wandered, and I imagined he was lost in memories of dusty streets where the scent of salt and sweat clung to everything.

"My parents worked hard," he continued, his tone resolute. "They drilled the importance of conviction and perseverance into me. I remember watching my father as a small child. He'd work long hours at the docks, hands cracked and bleeding, just to keep food on the table. Each day brought its own struggles, and each night I vowed to discover a way to improve our situation. Not just for my family, but for everyone who lived like us."

Everyone... like me.

His voice carried a rawness I didn't expect. I imagined him as a little boy, standing at the edge of the docks, watching his father labor. The picture he painted felt so vivid—the hunger, the toil, the relentless grind of life in The Divide. I knew it all too well.

"Becoming a representative," Thomas added with a deep sincerity, "seemed like the only way to create real change. To give people like my father a reason to hope."

He looked at me then. And for the first time, I understood the drive behind his calm exterior. It transcended mere ambition or duty; a deeper motivation emerged, shaped by the harsh realities of a life he could never forget.

Marmarie nodded thoughtfully, her stare fixed on Thomas. "Your dedication is admirable, Thomas. Not everyone from The Divide sees beyond their immediate circumstances."

Thomas smiled, his eyes reflecting a warmth of pride and humility. "Thank you, Marmarie. I believe in the potential of Sertoda and its people. We have the steadfast mindset to overcome any obstacle, even The Sanctioning."

His sincerity radiated, tugging my heart. I didn't just represent myself. I represented my homeland. I might not feel strong, but accepting help might prove essential for surviving The Sanctioning. Although it conflicted with my pride, now wasn't the time for such concerns.

And for a moment, envy crept in as I admired the certainty and purpose guiding him. "It is admirable," I said, trying to keep my voice balanced. My thoughts darkened once more. "But what if The Sanctioning is something designed to… break us?"

Marmarie placed her hand on my arm, her touch warm and grounding. "That's exactly why we need to stick together," she said softly. "We'll face whatever comes by supporting each other. No matter what The Sanctioning throws at us, we stand a better chance as one."

We were an unlikely trio—Thomas, with his unwavering optimism; Marmarie, with her cautious wisdom; and me, still searching for my place in all of this. Yet, if we maintained our connection amid the unpredictability, we could confront whatever lay ahead together and emerge on the other side unscathed. At least, I hoped.

I nodded, though the knot in my stomach tightened. What if sticking together wasn't an option? What if they separated us, forcing us to face whatever awaited in Mass alone? I took a deep breath, trying and failing to calm my racing mind. The thought of isolation—being on my own—sent a tremor of fear through me.

I glanced out the window again. Sertoda's city lights faded into the distance as the train cut through the night. I often felt trapped within the borders of my own existence, the world's vastness beyond my everyday experiences both tantalizing and terrifying. As the landscape outside grew unfamiliar, the blur of fleeting images made me realize how little I truly knew about the land I called home.

What lay ahead? Possible scenarios raced through my mind, and none of them seemed favorable.

I needed a plan. Something—anything—to hold onto when we stepped off the train.

I turned back to Marmarie and Thomas, who seemed calm on the surface. "What if... what if we're separated the moment we arrive?" I asked, my voice quieter now, almost as if speaking the fear out loud would make it real. "What if we don't have the chance to stick together?"

Thomas spoke, his voice serious. "If we can't rely on each other physically, we need to remember the things we've talked about. The things that matter. We need to stay focused, keep our wits about us. No matter what happens."

Marmarie's warm voice broke through the swell of dark water preparing to drown my thoughts. "A good friend of mine, Edward Hilmat, sits on the small council," Marmarie said, a hint of a smile playing on her lips. "He served as Sertoda's Perpetual Sense representative last term, if you remember. I'm looking forward to seeing him again—it's been far too long since we last connected." She excused herself, heading toward the restroom, likely preparing for a restless night ahead on the train. As the door clicked shut behind her, the quiet settled over the compartment like a soft blanket.

I swallowed, facing the confident man next to me and forcing a smile. Thomas was right. If we were split up, I needed to rely on more than just the idea of companionship. I needed to trust my own instincts. But what would my instincts tell me? Would they lie to me? Take me back to the dark corner of my mind I didn't dare go? What strength did I really possess on my own?

Doubt grew, rising like an unexpected shift in the tide.▫

The Pathways of Power:

Transportation in Sandric reveals not only the practical needs of its territories but the cultural philosophies driving them. All systems rely on electricity, the invisible current tying Sandric together, yet each territory uses it in ways that reflect their values and challenges.

Trunta's bullet trains, swift and efficient, embody the territory's devotion to progress and technological supremacy. Time is a commodity, and Trunta ensures none is wasted. Lizon, however, remains deeply rooted in tradition, favoring slower trams and cable cars. These modes may lack speed but remind their people of the balance between modernity and heritage.

Dobia's mountainous isolation demands ingenuity. Their electric snow crawlers and trains conquer harsh winters, a testament to resilience. Sertoda, ever practical, blends electric buses for its cities with smaller trains for rural areas, bridging tradition and modernity seamlessly.

Brawn's approach is distinct. Its desert expanse is navigated by electric hovercrafts and solar-powered vehicles, perfectly adapted to the region's harsh climate. Notably, their military is the only force in Sandric authorized to utilize solar energy on a large scale. A subtle yet undeniable assertion of their significance to Sandric.

As a cultural exercise, I might ask my students to imagine the world without the grid. If each territory were stripped of its electricity and forced to rely only on its natural landscape and inherent skills, what would survive? What traditions would reemerge? Would they rebuild as one—or drift further apart? Such questions reveal as much about our dependence as they do about our collective identity.

In pursuit of truth and understanding,
—H. Wilhoph

Chapter Eleven

LEVITY

His breath warmed the curve of my neck, dropping slowly and dangerously close to the overly sensitive spot where it would meet my collarbone. A touch that could tease me into delicious surrender. The rough scrape of his stubble followed, dragging over my skin, leaving a trail of sensation in its wake. When his lips skimmed lower down the center of my chest, an involuntary gasp tumbled past my lips.

The train quaked as we rounded a bend in the tracks. My chest rose sharply, and reality came crashing back in like a bolder dropping from a cliff. My heart pounded against my ribs as I glanced around, half-expecting him to be standing right in front of me.

He wasn't.

Of course, he wasn't.

Thomas was probably asleep in the cramped bunks down the hall—just like Marmarie.

I cursed under my breath, forcing myself to steady my breathing. It had been one night. One reckless, stupid night I couldn't seem to forget, no matter how many times I tried.

And now, here we were, trapped in the same space, the memory of his touch far too vivid and far too enticing to shake. The thought of those narrow beds made my stomach twist with unease. The idea of being so close to Thomas, just a thin space to walk between us, unsettled me more than I wanted to admit.

"Levity."

I startled.

Thomas emerged out of the fog clouding my mind, returning to his seat next to me. He shifted closer, the usual lightheartedness replaced with a more meaningful tone. He seemed eager for conversation. "We covered a lot of ground but not so much about you. Earlier, you mentioned your mom's pendant and Pop's stories from Mass. What did they think about your election?"

A familiar tightness seized my chest, and I took a slow breath, tracing a finger along the edge of the chair to gather my thoughts. "It's... They... I try not to mention them,"—the right words were stuck—"They died when I was sixteen."

Thomas's expression softened, and he leaned forward slightly, his voice low with concern. "Oh... I'm sorry. I can't imagine what that must've been like for you. That had to have been... really hard." He hesitated as if he wanted to say more but wasn't sure he should.

"It was," I said, my voice trailing off as my old friend uncertainty crept in. The words hovered over my tongue. I thought it might be best to keep it all buried, but the weight of the tragedy was too much to hold in. "At first, they called it a boat accident. They were out at sea, and a storm capsized their boat. But I've never been able to shake the feeling that there was more to it. And then the rumors started... whispers about the Cird being involved that night. The officials jumped on that as the cause, but... nothing ever really added up."

Thomas's brow furrowed, studying me. His thoughtful gaze almost made it seem like he could see the faint thread connecting this story to an old memory—matching the face in front of him now with the tear-streaked one that had confessed it all to him that night. "Wait... I remember hearing about that. So much talk surrounded the tragedy—how sudden it felt—but I never realized it involved…"—He paused, his focus sharpening as though reaching back to a place he hadn't visited in some time—"Actually… have we met before?"

I hesitated and allowed a faint smile to tug at my lips. "Yes, we did. Just before you moved to the city. I'd been having a… rough night, drowning my sorrows at the Shorebreak—the little oceanside place down by the cliffs. You were celebrating something, I think. Maybe leaving," I let out a short, awkward laugh. "We were both pretty… out of it."

He leaned back, blinking as realization washed over his face. "The Shorebreak," he murmured. "That was you?"

I nodded, my cheeks warming as I recalled that hazy night when I'd shared my heartbreak over my parents through tears, hiccups, and eventually even laughter. He listened then just as intently as he listened now.

His cheeks flushed as he looked down at his lap, clearly unsettled. "I can't believe I didn't remember."

"Really, it's fine," I said quickly, hoping to ease his discomfort. "I'm… pretty unmemorable." I let out an awkward chuckle, shrugging. "And we'd both had more than a few drinks. You were… kind to me that night. That's what mattered."

But he shook his head, remorse etched in his expression. "No, that's no excuse. I should have remembered." He sighed, his gaze drifting to my eyes. "I… I'm really sorry, Levity. That was thoughtless of me."

"Don't worry about it." I pushed a curl behind my ear. "I had to get home to take care of my siblings. It was… no big deal."

I paused, taking a deep breath. The familiar pull to talk about the part of my family that still thrived cause to continue. "I have four younger siblings. Triad and Tivian are twins, sixteen now. They're tough kids, strong and resourceful. Tivian, though," I let out a small, bittersweet laugh, "he's got this cocky streak, always trying to prove something. He thinks he's invincible.

"There was this one time—Tivian decided he was going to climb this huge tree in our yard to show off. Halfway up, a branch snapped, and he ended up dangling upside down, screaming for us not to tell anyone while begging for help." I giggled at the memory, tucking my leg under me in the chair. "He made us swear to secrecy, but the moment he got down, he strutted around like nothing happened." I shook my head, embarrassed by the outburst but smiling all the same. "That's Tivian for you. Always acting tough, even when he's in over his head."

Thomas chuckled, leaning back with an amused look. "Sounds like Tivian's got a lot of personality, huh? Bet he's a handful. Must keep you on your toes."

"He does," I agreed. "Triad's his opposite. He's calm and keeps his nose clean. He's the one holding everything together when Tivian's off causing chaos."

"Quite the pair." A magnetic smile played on Thomas's lips, drawing one from my own.

"They are," I said, my cheeks growing warm under his gaze. "Then there's Blue; she's ten. Snarky and full of life, but sometimes… her age shows through, and I realize she is still a little girl just trying to figure it all out." I let out a sigh, as if just the thought of her exhausted me. "And, finally, Evie, the youngest. She's eight, sweet and innocent. A little ray of sunshine, always finding joy in the smallest things." My gaze drifted to the dim light of the lamp, a wistful warmth filling my chest. "Watching her discover the world with such wonder… it's like finding a bit of peace that I can't find anywhere else. Evie has this way of making me laugh on the days that feel the heaviest."

Thomas's eyes held a gentle caress that made my heart skip. "You must've carried so much after your parents passed… Taking care of four kids at just sixteen?" He shook his head, letting out a quiet, impressed whistle. "That's a lot. It says so much about you."

"It's not always easy," I admitted, a hint of vulnerability slipping into my voice. "There are days when it feels like too much, when I'm not sure if I have anything left to give. But then I think of them—Tivian, Triad, Blue, and Evie—and somehow, I find the strength. They're the reason I keep pushing forward, even when it feels impossible. They give me purpose, you know? A reason to believe that there's still something worth fighting for."

As I spoke, the words felt false. I hadn't always felt this way. In the darkest moments after my parents' death, I resented the responsibility. It crushed me. There were times I wanted to escape, to run away from it all.

Thomas caught my reluctance. "Hey..." His hand brushed mine, setting my nerves alight. "It's okay to feel conflicted. No one's expecting it to have been easy. But look at you—you're here, making them proud. *All* of them. That takes a lot of strength. I understand more than you know. We're in this together."

His words touched something deep within me, a shared sense of vulnerability. I looked over at him, letting my guard slip. "Honestly, Thomas, I don't remember everything about that night either. We'd both drank quite a bit." I chuckled, hoping to ease any lingering tension. "It's a bit fuzzy for me too."

He gave a small, relieved laugh, his embarrassment easing. "Guess we were both having one of those nights," he said, a sheepish smile breaking through.

I exhaled slowly. I hadn't planned on leaving the kids with the neighbor that evening. But after all the stress, I needed time to breathe—to not be Levity the Caretaker for just a few hours. The quiet of that evening had offered me a brief departure, and in the midst of it, I ended up stumbling into a night that I never fully understood till now.

"Yeah," I said, a bit more serious now. "I guess we were both looking for an escape."

I hesitated, studying him before I spoke again. "I was thinking… you mentioned earlier that your father worked hard to provide for you. But what about your mom?" I couldn't recall if I'd known this part of his story.

His expression shifted, a somber look replacing the warmth. "My mother… now she was amazing. Kind. Nurturing…" He glanced out the window into the dark. "She passed away just before I turned twelve. Her illness came on so quickly. One moment, she was with us, and the next… she slipped away. Just like that."

"I'm so sorry."

He nodded, becoming distant as he continued. "My father… he was never the same after. I watched him struggle every day, falling into this deep despair. Some days, he couldn't even get out of bed. He tried to keep it together for me, but I saw the pain."

"You must've gone through so much," I said, sensing the depth of the unspoken pain.

"Yeah," Thomas said hoarsely. "It was just the two of us. No siblings, no one else. The silence in the house… it was unbearable sometimes. There were days when it felt like the loneliness would swallow me whole. I thought I couldn't handle it. But I had no choice but to be the steady hand. For us."

His vulnerability stirred something deep within me. I hesitated, unsure if the simple act of touch would feel too close, too exposed. But when I looked into his eyes, I saw his unspoken plea for security, and my doubts melted away. I reached out and placed my hand on his arm. My heart leapt at the warmth of his skin. A nervousness that felt familiar, and it wasn't unwelcomed. I gently squeezed, pouring in my sincerity that I hoped he felt.

"You're not alone anymore, Thomas," I murmured, my voice softer than I meant it to be.

He looked at me, his lips curving into a faint, poignant smile. Gratitude flickered in his gentle eyes, mingling with the sadness that couldn't quite leave them. "Thank you. Talking about it… it helps. More than I thought it would." He pushed a few fallen wavy locks away from his face.

I nodded, feeling the growing bond between us, a quiet understanding forming. "We all carry our pasts with us. It shapes us, but it doesn't have to define us. We can choose to be stronger because of it." I chuckled, trying to lift the mood a little. "Honestly, I have to remind myself of that every day."

He let out a hefty breath. "You're right. And I choose to be stronger too—for those I care about, but for myself now more than anything." His voice was more grounded now as though my words had helped calm his frayed nerves.

We sat in a comfortable silence, yet the stillness amplified the tension building inside me. I turned toward the window, hoping to find solace in the hum of the train, but my thoughts swirled like the dark landscape outside. From the window's reflection, Thomas's focus, contemplative, lingered on me for a moment before he whispered, "Happiness."

I looked at him, puzzled. "What's that?"

He smiled gently, his eyes reflecting a depth of emotion I hadn't fully understood before. "Your name. Levity. It's a feeling of lightness, calm… happiness."

A soft surge of comfort spread through me. His words, simple yet profound, embraced me, easing the tightness in my chest. For a moment, all other concerns faded, leaving only the warmth of his gaze and the quiet, genuine connection between us.

But reality had a way of seeping back in as I settled deeper into my chair. Each jolt marked time, a subtle reminder of The Sanctioning, an unknown that loomed closer with every mile. Thomas had stayed in the lounge, quietly thumbing through a book while I waited for sleep. The familiarity of the position wasn't lost on me. I spent countless nights curled up like this in mama's old wooden rocking chair, soothing Blue or Evie when they were sick. My body remembered the ache of those nights, the stiffness in my neck, and the way I fought sleep, trying to stay awake while they dozed in my arms.

I ran my fingers over the smooth surface of my pendant. The memory of my parents grounded me. *What would you think of all this?*

A subtle shift of Thomas's posture drew my attention. His head dipped lower, his breathing deepening, steady and rhythmic.

He fell asleep.

Sitting up.

For a few moments, I watched him. His face was relaxed now, the prior tension and worry had melted into a stillness that felt almost fragile. Strange how quickly we'd fallen into this easy, quiet rhythm, as though the little spark from that night long ago had never really gone out. We'd barely known each other then, and yet, here we were—connected in a way that didn't quite feel like strangers anymore.

I closed my eyes. Thoughts swirled, catching between the journey behind us and the mystery ahead. Eventually, fatigue won out, and I let myself drift, the familiar ache of the chair beneath me pulling me into a restless sleep.

In the early morning hours, I pulled myself from sleep and slipped away to the restroom–trying not to disturb the fragile peace of the car. I splashed cold water against my face, the chill refreshing me just enough to push back the exhaustion. I took a moment to stare at my reflection, surprised by the weariness etched into my features. Dark shadows clung beneath my eyes. My skin was pale, the sharpness of my cheekbones more pronounced in the dim, sterile light of the small bathroom.

A fleeting temptation arose to find my mother's face in mine, to search for any familiar softness or strength. I leaned in closer, noticing my once-vibrant hair had dulled and curls hung limp around my face. I barely recognized myself. The person staring back at me looked older, worn—not the girl from Sertoda, full of purpose and hope I wanted to project.

I ran my fingers through my hair, twirling and reshaping my curls though the effort didn't help much. The confrontation of fatigue, the pressure of the future, and echoes of my past clung too tightly.

I sighed, lowering my hands and taking a step back. No point in trying to fix it now. This reflection represented the truth—unvarnished, hardened by loss and responsibility, and weary, yet still standing.

When I returned to the lounge, Thomas hadn't moved much. I settled back into my chair, trying not to think about the closeness. As I began to relax, he stirred, murmuring something under his breath.

He shimmied closer, and before I could react, his head was resting against my shoulder. I tensed, unsure how to embrace the intimacy of the moment. His soft brown hair brushed my collarbone. The warm, unexpected contact sent a shiver through me.

His breathing fell into a balanced rhythm, lulling me back into a fragile sense of calm. The tension melted away in the quiet of dawn, replaced by something softer, something real.

A faint smile tugged at my lips as I let my eyes close again. For now, in this fleeting moment of peace, I found solace in his nearness; his presence helping to quiet the chaos inside my mind. Worrying about whatever

awaited us in Mass could be put on pause.
Only this existed—simple and enough.

The Dominance Struggle:

The conflict among the five territories of Sandric extends far beyond territorial claims; it embodies a profound struggle for cultural dominance. Each region vies for recognition and authority, seeking to define what it means to be Sandric. Yet, in this competition, there lies a risk of erasing the rich tapestry of identities that together form our society.

In today's lecture, I will guide my students through this intricate landscape of cultural contention. We will examine how each territory's unique customs and beliefs contribute to the broader narrative of Sandric identity, while also recognizing the potential for conflict that arises from these differences.

I'll present historical examples of cultural exchanges and conflicts among the territories, highlighting how the pursuit of dominance has often led to misunderstandings and strife. To make this tangible, I'll divide the class into groups, each representing one of the territories. Each group will then role-play how their territory would approach settling its differences with the others—mocking the negotiation tactics, the posturing, and the blatant power plays.

I will encourage students to consider the implications of this cultural struggle. By reflecting on the narratives that emerge from each territory, we can better understand the importance of inclusivity and dialogue in shaping a collective identity.

In pursuit of truth and understanding,
—H. Wilhoph

Chapter Twelve

BETTA

Council members and representatives from different territories mingled around Mass's meeting hall. Colorful attire caught my attention as I entered the hall escorted by a contingent of soldiers. Symbols. Insignias. Bursts of tech embedded into their fabric. Each electee stood out, carrying an air of purpose and authority. On the other hand, their expressions ranged from stoic determination to cautious curiosity.

I surveyed the tall windows lining the walls, allowing streams of natural light to flood the space, a stark contrast to the sleek, artificial glow of the massive chandeliers above. The contemporary architecture radiated innovation, with towering walls displaying holograms of breaking news and leadership forecasts, casting vivid colors over the assembled representatives. A multitude of speculations ran rampant for a race in which no media personality truly knew what they were betting on.

The soldiers who had escorted me dispersed and took their positions along the perimeter, blending into the room's rigid structure. As I attempted to immerse myself in the throngs of people, my attire—chosen not for its practicality but for meeting expectations, *of course*—drew more attention than I wanted. The dress, a blend of regal, elegant, sleek lines and strategic, provocative cut, was better suited for a gala than this political luncheon. I begrudgingly complied, assuming looking like some ethereal goddess draped in flowing, muted-colored fabric was their absurd requirement to be the so-called savior of Sandric.

The looming Sanctioning cast a dark pall over the bustling hall's discussions. Low conversations hinted at covert plans and emerging loyalties, and while current council members kept their words bland and vague, the new representatives eagerly sought to learn what lay ahead.

I cringed, watching the small council. Their nods and smiles. Their appropriate interjections seemed rehearsed; each gesture calculated to show unwavering allegiance. Would the electees notice anything amiss? ⊡

Sertoda, the last territory to arrive, would complete the assembly of representatives and set the stage for The Sanctioning. A formal lunch in their honor would precede an escort to their new living quarters. Unbeknownst to most—except those familiar with the schedule from first-hand experience—this brief introduction to Mass marked the beginning of an indeterminable amount of time that would define their lives as representative elects.

My thoughts drifted back to my own trial—a relentless, three-week mental gauntlet. I emerged as the unexpected victor while other Surviving Aides crumbled. Four from my term stood in the room now, shadows of their former selves, carrying invisible scars from their ordeals. Yet my ordeal paled next to Draven's two months of daily torment—the longest endured by any of the three positions.

I scanned the room for Draven, unease settling in after our clandestine meeting the night before. He believed everything traced back to Trunta, who held the Sanctioned Perpetual Sense seat for as long as records showed. Their control over technological advances and the Sandric power structure strengthened his argument, suggesting they might be manipulating events from behind the scenes for their benefit. Such prolonged influence made it plausible that they were central to a larger conspiracy. I understood Draven's suspicions and had to admit they did seem logical.

Yet, from all appearances, Lyonal endured the same torture and threats that Draven and I faced.

How would I approach him? March over, grab him by the collar, and shake the answers out of him, or just sit here stewing in my own rage?

To gauge his knowledge or involvement felt impossible. Lyonal moved with an air of guarded composure, his level-headed behavior betraying little of his thoughts or intentions.

Draven's instructions echoed in my mind: listen and observe. Playing the wallflower while I hunted for the unusual in what everyone else mistook for ordinary, I kept my mouth shut and my eyes wide open. Any of these mundane interactions could be hiding the juiciest fucking secrets waiting to be uncovered.

The atmosphere buzzed with anticipation. Blending into the background, I tried to remain inconspicuous as the representatives mingled and exchanged pleasantries. A merciful task with the dress I wore, designed more to draw attention than deflect it.

I drifted closer to a couple discussing the recent energy regulations, situating myself within earshot while I feigned interest in a lesser conversation between two council members. An athletic man about my height, wearing a fitted gray jumpsuit that zipped at a diagonal across his lean chest, began with a booming voice, "These new blackout regulations on power consumption are crippling our efforts to sustain the food production we've worked so hard to cultivate." He shook his head, clearly frustrated. "With innovation like what we have in the food sector, we cannot afford to be stifled."

Another delegate, a woman with striking green eyes and rich, earthy brown skin as though painted by sun and soil, nodded slightly. Her full lips pressed into a line. Her steady gaze spoke volumes as her eyebrows arched slightly, conveying a message words could not. "I don't think I'll ever get used to the idea of lab-grown food." She sighed and continued, "I heard whispers that the regulations are all a ploy to keep the traditionalists from gaining too much influence." She cast a quick glance over her shoulder. "It's harder for them to spread their ideals when they're not allowed to gather in any capacity, not even virtually."

The man, who I now could assume to be from Trunta, nodded in appreciation, a smirk playing at the corner of his mouth. "Well, if they can't gather, they can't strategize. And if they can't strategize, they can't challenge the status quo. It's efficient, in a way," he admitted with an edge of distaste.

The woman rubbed her temple. "In Lizon, we barely feel the effects of the blackouts. Simple lives, low energy usage. The restrictions seem more a nuisance than anything." She paused, casting a cautious look his way. "But in high-consumption territories like Trunta, I can understand the struggle."

The man scoffed, his eyes narrowing. "If your territory is so keen on simplicity, maybe all the traditionalists should return to Lizon or Sertoda. Or, for all I care, go freeze to death in the mountains of Dobia and stay away from places like Trunta. All they do is preach against our progress."

The woman shrugged, clearly not offended. "Maybe they just can't stomach the idea of their hamburger being born from a machine and not a cow." I covered my mouth, stifling my giggle. "Some of them believe they're preserving history. There's something to be said for tradition. Clever with technology and innovation doesn't mean understanding how to wisely use—or respect—the land in which we stand on."

Feigning interest in the hem of my sleeve, I listened closely, catching the tension threaded through her words. Sertoda, the heart of heritage, held a reputation for quiet, untouched landscapes—a living reminder of our history. Lizon reflected a simpler, pragmatic life; its people were skilled in the efficient use of verdant soils. Both regions bore the sympathizer label, allies in the traditionalists' struggle. Trunta had sacrificed its land for towering skyscrapers and relentless technological growth, and now everyone felt the consequences. A touch more sympathy for tradition might have served them well.

Just as I was about to turn away, the Trunta man lowered his voice and said, "Between these blackouts and the rationing measures, we're giving up so much in the name of resource distribution. That's all I'm saying. They say it's necessary, but it feels like a leash." He turned with an exasperated wave. "When does it stop? Without Trunta's food innovations, territories like Lizon won't keep up with demand. What then?"

Feeling the pressure to embody my Sanctioned role and steer the conversation, I forced myself to casually insert, "The regulations are challenging, but they're meant to ensure fair distribution of resources. It's about maintaining balance and preventing any one group from monopolizing power."

Even as the words left my mouth, the mask I wore felt increasingly suffocating.

The man nodded reluctantly. "True. But if they really are to suppress the traditionalists, how long can we maintain these restrictions? I know we need to regulate food rations carefully, but it feels more like a stranglehold. Our lab-grown foods are crucial; they could help solve the food rationing issue. But to produce enough to move the needle, we need more power. Without it, we're only prolonging the inevitable." His expression turned serious. "We must find a balance between control and support, or we'll be left with nothing but the skeletal remains of our society."

His grim words twisted my stomach, conjuring images of a society stretched thin by Trunta's endless pursuit of power, masked as progress. For years, people in The Divide had endured starvation, scraping by while Trunta bloomed with luxury and innovation. The thought of sacrificing more—our principles, our very humanity—for another round of technological gains felt like swallowing poison. I bit back a sarcastic retort, knowing it would only fuel his resolve. With a heavy sigh, I excused myself, feeling claustrophobic by the weight of his ambitions.

I moved toward another cluster of representatives, eager to eavesdrop on anything that would bring me solid evidence for our cause.

Melding into this new group of representatives, a fair-haired gentleman challenged an older woman beside him: "I'm curious about The Sanctioning." His sharp features and sun-kissed cheeks contrasted with his dark, authoritative Brawn military suit. "They say no one really knows what to expect—guess that means most of you won't make it."

The older woman replied with a knowing smile, "That's the point, isn't it? To keep us on edge, guessing."

I stepped closer and added, "The unpredictability of The Sanctioning is designed to test our physical stamina, mental endurance, and adaptability. It's a way to measure our resilience under constant pressure. The secrecy ensures that every representative is equally prepared—or unprepared, as the case may be." *Or so I'd been coached to say.*

The woman tilted her head, her wrinkles showing intrigue in my offering. "And what of your first-hand experience?"

I met her cool blue eyes. "Let's just say I understand the importance of preparation and the necessity of these measures. They weed out the weak and ensure that only the most adaptable and resilient lead." Inside, that knot of disgust further tightened in my stomach.

Excusing myself, I slipped away and finally spotted Draven. His hulking frame, dressed in all black, only served to emphasize his intimidating presence. There he stood, the perfect blend of beauty and danger—those chiseled features and piercing eyes practically screamed: approach at your own risk.

Next to him, I assumed, was his younger brother, Dorian. Smaller in stature, but he had a striking resemblance to Draven. His longer hair on top and close-shaved sides framed his beautiful, bronzed skin like artwork. No hugs or slaps on the back passed between the two men, but the way Draven looked at Dorian revealed a depth of care I hadn't been privy to.

I approached the two men, trying to maintain an air of casualness. "Draven," I greeted softly.

He nodded, eyes scanning the room. He placed a hand on the small of my back, and my stomach flipped from the sudden contact, his warmth sending a roll through my core. He led me away from his brother before a proper introduction. "Betta. Anything of note?"

I paused, feeling Draven's fingers tense against the thin material of my dress. "Is that him?" I asked quietly, shifting my attention to Dorian.

Draven's posture softened just a fraction, betraying his pride and showing his worry. "Yes. That's Dorian."

I scrutinized him like a hawk sizing up its prey. Draven painted his brother as some delicate flower, unprepared for the brutality of The Sanctioning, but I wasn't buying it just yet. I needed to determine whether that assessment held any merit or served merely as a clever disguise for something far more dangerous. No way would I let my guard slip.

The subtle stiffness in his shoulders, outside of his overall relaxed posture, was the only sign of his discomfort in the crowded room. His military-inspired attire hugged his frame, a blend of formality and practicality that seemed to clash with the tense atmosphere. His hands fidgeted, fingers brushing against his black trousers as if searching for something hiding in a pocket. When our gaze locked, things began to click. He lacked that piercing intensity of Draven's. Instead, his eyes held a softer warmth that felt oddly out of place in an environment dominated by cold calculation.

Between the smile he carried that hinted at an underlying wariness and the gentleness in his demeanor, it reinforced Draven's concerns. A rock fell in the pit of my stomach. The hard edge The Sanctioning demanded was absent in Dorian. He seemed almost out of place, like a lamb among wolves.

As I studied him, I noticed the tension in his jaw. He shifted his weight, and his eyes darted around the room as if searching for an escape. And yet beneath his discomfort lay a quiet determination. Despite the odds stacked against him, I hoped he would remain resolved to face them.

"Dorian," Draven called, his voice balanced with an undertone of something protective—almost tender.

Dorian turned toward us, his expression softening as he approached. "You must be Betta," he said, extending a hand. His grip felt steady yet gentle, conveying a sense of connection rather than dominance. "I've heard a lot about you."

The sincerity caught me off guard. Dorian's words were coated in a genuineness that was almost disarming. No hint of manipulation or power plays surfaced, a refreshing change from what I'd come to expect.

"Likewise," I replied, forcing a smile.

Draven placed a hand on Dorian's shoulder. "I need to speak with an official," he said, glancing at me. "Keep an eye on him, will you?"

"Of course," I replied, taking in a breath and watching Draven weave through the crowd.

With a smirk, I leaned in closer to Dorian, my voice laced with sarcasm. "So, the General couldn't make time to escort his son to Mass? What's he off doing, banning empathy from the military?"

Dorian snorted, shaking his head. "Pretty much. Either that, or he's busy making sure no woman ever gets the chance to serve as a soldier. Apparently, that would spell disaster for everything he's worked for."

I raised an eyebrow. "Ah, yes, the real threat to society: competent women in combat."

"Exactly," Dorian muttered, his tone biting. "Priorities, right?"

"Of course," I said dryly, rolling my eyes. "Because nothing says strength like keeping people oppressed just to protect your own fragile ego."

Dorian let out a small chuckle, the tension between us easing as we shared a brief, sardonic smile.

I quickly glanced around, making sure no one would overhear my next words and leaned in. "Dorian, listen. There's something you need to know. I'm here to help you, but we've got to be discreet."

His expression grew more serious, concern flickering in his eyes. "What are you talking about?"

"We're about to go to lunch," I said quietly, urgency creeping into my voice. "I can't say for sure, but the food or drink—it might be drugged. When you wake up, it's not just going to *feel* like your worst nightmare. You'll be in it."

Dorian's eyes widened. "What do you mean?" He took a small step back, worry creeping into his expression. "Are you sure?"

I stepped closer, lowering my voice even further, mindful of the representatives milling nearby and the soldiers lining the walls. "It's the beginning of your trial, and you have to ground yourself. Draw on something real—an item, a safe place, or a connection. It will get intense, and you need something to hold on to."

Dorian fidgeted with the hem of his jacket, seeking solace in the fabric's familiar texture. "What kind of connection? I don't... I don't understand."

"It could be anything, something that reminds you of who you are, what you love," I said, willing him to see the gravity of my words. "Trust me, you'll need it. You need to remember that it exists outside the nightmare."

He hesitated, his focus dropping to the floor as if searching for an answer in the polished tiles. "What if I can't find it?"

"Then you fight," I replied firmly. "You have to fight to remember."

A moment of silence passed between us, charged with unspoken fears. Dorian looked up, his expression suddenly vulnerable. "I have… someone back in Brawn. His name is Hector."

My heart sank as I recognized the depth of his admission. "Is he…?" I let the implication hang in the air.

"Yeah, but it's complicated," he said, a tremor in his voice betrayed his attempt to steady himself. "Men like me… we can't really be open about it. It's not accepted."

I reached out, gently squeezing his arm. "Dorian, that kind of love is powerful. It's your truth, and it matters. Hold onto it. No matter what they throw at you in The Sanctioning, that connection is your anchor."

He met my gaze, a mixture of relief and fear swirling in his eyes. "You really think so?"

"Absolutely," I said, my tone softening.

Dorian nodded slowly, digesting my words, his expression shifting to one of quiet determination. "He's everything to me," he admitted, a spark of defiance igniting in his voice. "But it's not just about me. If they found out…"

"I know," I replied, my heart aching. "Just remember, they can't take away what's in your heart. It's yours to keep."

He took a deep breath, visibly steeling himself as if preparing for an unseen battle. "Thanks, Betta. I appreciate it."

Before I could respond, a group of representatives burst into laughter, snapping my attention. Their boisterous voices rose above the ambient noise of the gathering. My stomach tightened. "We should be careful. Let's not draw attention."

"Right," he said, his shoulders caving as if trying to make himself smaller. "I'll remember what you said. I just… I hope I can do this."

"You will. Just keep your head down and don't let them break you," I assured him with a fierce conviction, stepping back as the sound of approaching footsteps drew near.

"We need to speak privately," Draven said as he came up beside me. His look held an urgency that didn't escape my notice.

As Draven led me away, the image of Dorian's earnest gaze lingered in my mind, his wordless entreaty for understanding resonating deeply. One thing remained certain: Beneath Dorian's military-inspired exterior lay a man with quiet strength, grappling with expectations and the burden of secrets.

Dorian would either crumble under pressure or rise as a promise of a better future. I couldn't help but wonder which side of him would emerge in The Sanctioning.

Draven furrowed his brow as he watched Dorian from a distance. "What do you make of him?" he asked, his tone measured yet probing.

I hesitated, weighing my words carefully. "He seems… genuine. Not quite the warrior your father envisioned." I opted to keep Dorian's secret close, not wanting to risk Draven's protective instincts. "I helped the best I could."

Draven nodded, his attention lingering on Dorian before shifting back to me. "What have you picked up on? Any odd conversations to note?"

I shook my head, pushing aside the swirl of thoughts in my mind. "Just the usual complaints and speculation."

"Good. Stay sharp," he replied, his expression sharpening into something fierce as if bracing for battle. "We need to focus on Lyonal. He's our key to unraveling this mess."

Draven blended back into the crowd, and I couldn't shake the urge to keep a watchful eye on Dorian. I hoped that whatever guidance I had offered would be enough to help him navigate the storm ahead.

Lyonal stood near the back of the room, engaged in an intense conversation with one of the Trunta representatives. Small in stature yet radiating an undeniable presence, she boasted stunning red hair cascading in waves that framed a face dominated by vivid blue eyes—the exact hue of azureth, the guardian's blossom, in full bloom. Their body language hinted at an intimacy that felt almost conspiratorial.

A holographic screen flickered to life to my right, throwing splashes of shifting color across the room as it displayed projections of the latest results from the Perpetual Sense evaluations. I leaned closer, my pulse quickening as I scanned the names scrolling past. Garon, the Dobian tech phenom's name stood out, far ahead in the rankings, and a mixture of admiration and apprehension bubbled within me.

I shifted slightly, letting the kaleidoscope of light from the monitors ripple over the dress I despised. *At least it was good for something.* I blended into the background while I kept a sharp eye on Lyonal, careful not to draw his attention. My heart raced as I listened intently, straining to catch every word of their conversation while keeping my own presence masked.

The Trunta representative leaned in, her posture stiff.

The woman's striking eyes flicked around the room, a furtive sweep that conveyed a deep awareness of the stakes. Satisfied that their corner remained unobserved, she lowered her voice, each word dripping with intent. "Our preparations must guarantee that the outcome favors the right candidates."

Lyonal set his jaw; his focus locked onto her with an intensity that made the hair on my neck stand up. "I have measures in place to ensure that outcome," he replied with a methodical tone as if outlining a strategy in a game of chess. "But it will require careful manipulation of the variables. Do not underestimate the consequences of failure. We can't let emotions or morals interfere."

"Morals?" the woman scoffed, a smirk creeping onto her lips. "In this game? Spare me. If that means sacrificing a few... so be it."

The room felt charged, the very air thick with tension as they exchanged calculated glances, a tacit agreement hanging between them like a noose. I scooted closer to the screen, my heart pounding in my chest, desperate to absorb every word, every hint of their scheme.

"What happens if the wrong people make it through?" the representative challenged.

Lyonal's usual detached authority transformed into something darker, a frigid calculation that set my nerves on edge. He drew forward, his voice a menacing whisper. "If the wrong people make it through, it won't just be The Sanctioning at stake. It will be everything. The balance of power depends on us."

The woman's stare turned icy, her voice dripping with haughty resolve. "Then they will fucking fall. I'll make damn sure I'm the last one standing, no matter what kind of bloodbath it takes."

The Technological Cleansing of Trunta:

Trunta, once intertwined with nature, has undergone one of the most radical transformations in Sandric's history. Its shift toward technology has reshaped its landscape and the very soul of its people. What served as a haven for thriving ecosystems now embodies a sterile environment—a monument to human ingenuity and human hubris.

The cleansing of Trunta from its organic roots raises questions about the costs of progress. While the advancements made within its borders impress—leading in innovation, from infrastructures to governance—we must ask ourselves: At what cost? The removal of natural landscapes in favor of artificial environments strips more than just flora and fauna. It severs a connection to the world that civilizations have relied on for cultural and spiritual balance.

As I reflect on Trunta's path, technological advancement must be weighed against the loss of what makes us human—our connection to the world, understanding of ecosystems, and rhythms of nature. Can a society truly thrive if untethered from these roots? Or does the sacrifice of nature, in pursuit of progress, sow the seeds of instability and cultural loss?

In pursuit of truth and understanding,
—H. Wilhoph

Chapter Thirteen

BETTA

Lyonal and the Trunta representative's exchange hit me like jamming a knife into an electrical socket. My mind was reeling. That discussion transcended strategy. It was a chilling orchestration of control; a crafted manipulation. The precision of their dialogue and the subtlety of their interaction all pointed to a premeditated effort to bend the will of The Sanctioning.

Draven's suspicions no longer seemed like the paranoid ramblings of a man burdened by too many secrets; they were a foundation to build upon. The intricate web of deceit was unraveling before my eyes, and I knew I needed to be vigilant.

I steeled myself, conviction tightening across my chest like armor.

Fine. If they wanted to play dirty, I'd dig deeper—peel back every rotten layer of this conspiracy until the truth screamed for air. Lyonal and that Trunta snake weren't just playing a dangerous game. No, they acted as puppet masters.

But here's the thing about puppet masters: They're only untouchable until someone cuts the strings.

I watched Lyonal and the rep split, their conversation still burning in the back of my mind, when something caught my eye.

Not something.

Someone.

A new figure moved into my line of sight with an effortless swagger that turned heads. He owned the room the moment he stepped in; his muscular frame was impossible to ignore. For a second, I almost pegged him as one of the Noble Warrior reps, but the sharp cut of his clothes and his confident posture suggested otherwise. He embodied something far more dangerous.

The man exuded an undeniable presence, a dynamism that radiated with every step. His long, almost silver hair was pulled back into intricate braids with shiny beads woven in, while the sides of his head were buzzed close to the scalp. Early thirties, I surmised. The faint lines around his eyes and mouth gave him a seasoned edge. His fair skin, far from sickly, caught my attention, and his piercing blue eyes scanned the room with a mix of curiosity and precision before finally landing on me.

Garon Fiore. Dobia's rising tech entrepreneur was the so-called genius making waves in every media outlet. They called him the next big innovator, some even whispering that he might reshape Dobia's entire tech industry if given the chance. That kind of attention didn't come easy, and it sure as hell didn't come without a few well-hidden knives.

Muted clothing clung to his body that showcased practicality edged with menace. He donned a long-sleeved cotton shirt that was pushed up his forearms, revealing sharp and intricate tattoos that wound around his skin. The shirt was tucked neatly into heavy, cream-colored utility pants, while sturdy boots hinted at someone accustomed to navigating Dobia's harsh forests and snowy landscapes. It dawned on me that he was not only dressed for the occasion, he was prepared for battle.

As he made his way toward me, his eyes held an intensity that sent an uneven pulse thrumming through my body. A hint of a smile played at his lips, carrying just enough mischief to make my thighs clench together. "Elisabetta Rahmani, I presume," he said, his voice deep, rich,

141

and resonant, like someone who knew exactly how much power he wielded. "I've heard quite a bit about you."

"Betta." I arched a brow, matching his energy with a coy smile of my own. "All bad things, I hope?"

His eyes flashed a playful glint. A shrug rolled off his broad shoulders. "Mostly," he played back. "Garon Fiore. It's a pleasure to finally meet you in person."

"The pleasure's mine," I replied, inclining my head just slightly. "Dobia's Perpetual Sense representative, if I'm not mistaken?"

"Correct." His attention remained on me as he steered the conversation. "Mass is... quite the contrast to Dobia. The architecture and atmosphere are mesmerizing. But you might agree, it's the things people don't see that are the most fascinating."

I chuckled softly. "Yes, Mass… it radiates *charm*. I imagine Dobia's forests and snowy mountains hold their own beauty and hidden *secrets*."

"They do, and I'll miss not seeing them for the term," he replied, his eyes narrowing in what I could only read as fascination. "But there is plenty of beauty here I'd like to explore." He drew his attention away from my face and focused on the screens around us. "Mass hums with life and technology. You can feel it, can't you? The systems running beneath the surface, the constant exchange of data, like the city itself is breathing."

"I think I did hear somewhere you have an eye for tech."

He chuckled, which sounded more like a low growl that lacked any casualness. His icy blue eyes roamed the room, dissecting every detail. "It's hard not to notice the nuances when you're wired for it. Take these holographic screens, for instance"—he nodded toward the glowing panels scattered throughout the space—"they're layered with infrared proximity sensors and adaptive light emitters, which sync with the city's grid in real-time. But what's really clever is how they've incorporated biometrics into the airflow system." His eyes darted to the ceiling as if mapping out something only he could see. "Most people wouldn't catch it, but you can feel how the air adjusts depending on who's in the room. It's all tied to individual heat signatures, real high-end tech—probably Trunta's doing."

I blinked, taking a moment to digest his rapid-fire analysis. "You picked all that up in the short time you've been here?"

Garon raised a muscled shoulder, clearly enjoying my awe. "Let's just say I've got a real interest in the mechanization of infrastructure. Dobia might be all snow and grit, but we also know how to make systems hum." The word vibrated low in my core, the way a promise could. "Just in... subtler ways." His gaze darted between my eyes and lips, and I couldn't help but wonder exactly what those *subtle* ways might entail. Whatever they were, it surprised me how willing I was to find out.

"Well, you've certainly got me beat," I admitted, the corners of my mouth lifting. Years in Mass passed without a second thought about the air or the screens, yet he rattled off the details as if reading the room's code. *And made it sound damn sexy.* "It's almost like you can see the city's pulse."

He gave me a knowing look. "That's exactly it. Every city has a pulse—some just beat louder than others."

I couldn't help but wonder what else he'd noticed that I hadn't, what other layers of control were woven into the very fabric of this place, unnoticed by most but fully understood by someone like him.

I raised an eyebrow, caught off guard by his observations. "I must admit, I didn't expect Dobia's representative to have such a... commanding presence," I teased, letting my eyes flick over his solid frame.

"Appearances can be deceiving, Betta. I might look like a Noble Warrior, but I assure you, my skills lie more in technology, diplomacy, and strategy than relying only on what I can do with my bare hands."

I leaned in slightly, lowering my voice to a conspiratorial whisper. "A man of many talents, then?"

His eyes sparkled with amusement. "You could say that. And what about you, *Dark Siren*? What hidden layers do you possess?"

I ran my fingers through my long black hair, flipping it coyly over my bare shoulder. "Oh, I have my fair share. Revealing them all at once would ruin the mystery, wouldn't it?"

Garon's laughter filled the space between us, a deep, rich sound this time that sent pleasant tingles through my mostly naked limbs. "Indeed, it would." He paused, stepping in closer, his voice dropping an octave as he studied me. "And while I look forward to discovering them all, taking my time could be very enjoyable."

My lips pressed together in a smirk. "So, what is it about me that makes you call me '*Dark Siren*,' Garon? You think I'm dangerous?"

He leaned his full lips toward my ear. My pulse quickened. He regarded me with such intensity that it felt almost predatorial. "It's not just danger," he purred. "There's something almost magnetic about you. Like how sirens lure sailors to their doom. You don't even have to sing; one glance, one breath. You could make someone risk everything—ruin themselves completely—just for the chance to get closer."

I met his gaze, surprised by such an overt omission. "I do love a little risk," I murmured, my voice laced with intrigue.

His lips curled into a smile, his eyes darkening. "I'd expect nothing less from a dark siren."

Our conversation continued, and I found myself enjoying the flirtatious ardor of this little dance. He faintly probed for more information while maintaining the playfulness of the banter. His presence offered a welcome distraction from the pressure of my responsibilities and the looming trouble of The Sanctioning.

Garon and I exchanged a few more light-hearted barbs, his sharp wit matching mine with surprising ease.

Just as I found myself genuinely hooked on his company, a familiar presence interrupted us. Draven appeared at my side, casting a long shadow over our conversation. His narrowed eyes took in Garon with a scrutiny that bordered on territorial.

I could practically feel the temperature plummet.

"Something I'm missing here?" Draven's voice dropped to a low growl, his energy crackling like thunder before a storm. No hint of curiosity. He demanded an answer.

Garon confronted Draven with his dazzling white grin. Yet now it held an unapologetic edge. "We were just getting acquainted," he said with unflinching confidence. "Funny how the representatives of Sertoda and Dobia can find common ground so easily. Guess it's a rare talent... knowing how to read a room."

Draven's lips pressed into a thin line, his jaw tightening like a coiled spring ready to snap. "Common ground," he repeated, his voice dripping with cold skepticism. "An interesting choice of words. Sandric tends to prefer its representatives to be more... focused on their own territory's affairs. Keeps things from getting messy."

Garon chuckled, unfazed by Draven's stately demeanor. "I've heard Brawn men are known for their aggressive nature. It's refreshing to see it in person."

I leaned back slightly, crossing my arms as I took in the brewing tension between them. *Cirds-damnation, if this wasn't a front-row seat to the best kind of conflict. Who knew political standoffs could be this entertaining?*

Draven took a step closer, his posture stiff and challenging. "And I've heard Dobia's representatives are more adept at diplomacy than confrontation. Perhaps you should stick to what you know."

The shades of blue in Garon's eyes seemed to sparkle at his words. "Oh, I'm quite adept at both, I assure you. I've always believed that true strength lies in knowing when to use which skill."

The atmosphere around us grew heavier, the surrounding delegates sensing the sizzling conflict. A few curious onlookers began to creep closer.

Garon continued, keeping his tone light but with an undercurrent of defiance. He closed the space between them. "Tell me, *Captain* Ballister, is it the policy of Brawn to always meet diplomacy with hostility? Or is it just your personal approach?"

Draven's hand hovered above the knife at his side, playing with the clip. "We believe action speaks the truth because words can be twisted."

Garon's smile widened, though his brows began to furrow. "Actions certainly have their place. A wise leader knows that a balance of both is essential."

Keeping these two testosterone-fueled idiots from tearing each other apart, I interjected. "Gentlemen, perhaps we can agree that both strength and diplomacy have their merits. Our territories benefit most when we find ways to complement each other."

Draven casually stroked the hair on his jaw, a hint of arrogance in his posture. "Betta's right. There's no need to waste our energy on this."

The holographic screens lining the walls flashed an update that captured my attention before Garon could give his retort: SERTODA REPRESENTATIVES ARRIVING AT THE NEXUS TERMINAL OF MASS. The buzz in the room intensified, pulling everyone's focus.

I seized the moment. "Well, I'd hate to miss the grand entrance of my people," I said, dipping my chin and tucking a strand of loose hair behind my ear. "Gentlemen, behave."

The Stripping of Sandric History:

Mass is a prime example of how history can be erased while leaving most citizens oblivious to the depths of the manipulation. Narratives are being rewritten to obscure the Cird's vital contributions, transforming our rich cultural tapestry into propaganda that serves only those in power.

This insidious process reveals itself in our schools, where pivotal events are omitted, and influential figures are relegated to footnotes. Sandric's vibrant stories have been replaced by a homogenized version that fosters ignorance and conformity, ensuring that citizens remain docile and unquestioning.

As all educators, I too wrestle with the implications of this reality. We bear the responsibility to unearth and share the truth when those who govern us stifle our freedom to do so.

How do we awaken minds dulled by complacency? How do we reclaim a history that has been systematically stripped from us?

Our very identity hangs in the balance but is continuously manipulated by those who fear the power of knowledge.

In quiet moments, I ponder the ramifications of this historical amnesia. What will it take to reignite the curiosity that once drove our pursuit of truth?

We must challenge the prevailing narratives and expose the conspiracy behind our erasure before we lose ourselves completely. Only by reclaiming our past can we hope to forge a future that honors the complexities of our heritage.

In pursuit of truth and understanding,
—H. Wilhoph

Chapter Fourteen

LEVITY

My dozing body jolted forward in my seat. I blinked my groggy eyes open, making out a muted screech. The blurry land out the window slowly became focused as the train slowed. Thomas stirred beside me, lifting his head from my shoulder with a sleepy grumble. The depths of his golden-brown eyes met mine.

He straightened, ran a hand through the strands of his sleep-mussed hair, and offered a shy, almost apologetic smile. "Sorry about that. I guess I was more tired than I thought."

A warmth spread through me, chasing away the remnants of sleep. "It's okay," I replied, my voice softer than intended. "You seemed peaceful."

The train came to a complete stop, and I took a deep breath, steeling myself for what lay beyond the platform. The doors to the sleep quarters slid open with a mechanical hiss, and Marmarie emerged, looking refreshed but with narrowed brows as if bracing for battle. Thomas picked up his bag and, once again, helped to gather Marmarie's trunk.

Mass's overwhelming resonance engulfed me like a dense fog when I stepped off the train. The city buzzed with a vibrant energy that excited and terrified me. My heart pounded in my chest as I moved through the bustling station, taking in the scene; my growing anxiety echoed with each beat. The towering buildings, the hordes of people, and the sounds of urban life pressed in on me from all sides.

This could not be Mass.

There didn't appear to be an ounce of resemblance to what Pop described. His stories painted Mass as a primitive, almost mythical, revered place filled with quaint charm and rustic simplicity. Instead, my eyes were assaulted by sprawling monstrosities of technology and concrete.

Mountainous skyscrapers loomed overhead. Their glass facades reflected the harsh LED lights that seemed to pulse with an artificial life of their own. The air thickened with the hum of machinery. The chatter of countless voices. All of it created a discord that threatened to drown my thoughts.

Thomas seemed to sense my unease. He tugged on the collar of his shirt, adjusting it as if it were an armored shield. "We'll make it through this," he said softly, his tone secure.

Marmarie approached, her smile tight with her own nerves. "We need to stay united," she urged.

A knot tightened in my stomach as I compared this reality to the fairytale I once imagined. Pop told me of a city that felt like stepping back in time, where nature and civilization could coexist in harmony. Here, only occasional patches of synthetic grass or carefully placed trees struggled to survive amidst the concrete jungle.

Holographic displays hovered above. Pink. Blue. Yellow. Zig Zags. Flashing. The colors and patterns made me dizzy. My attention darted to the automated drones buzzing overhead, their lifeless eyes scanning the crowd. Cool sweat prickled the nape of my neck. I dug my fingernails into my palms.

I couldn't help feeling a sense of betrayal. Mass offered no sanctuary from the chaos of the world. I felt anything but safe. My lungs fought against the air I breathed, and I fought to keep my rising panic at bay.

I clutched my small duffel tighter on my shoulder, its modest weight doing its best to keep me centered as I faced my surroundings. Pop often spoke of our heritage, tales of unification, and culture that celebrated the human spirit. This was supposed to be the epicenter for those ideals.

Now, I stood in a place that felt suffocating. Indifferent even. How could I navigate this alien landscape? How could I find my place here? I wiped the sweat from my hands on my pants.

I would be here for five years, whether I liked it or not.

A transport vehicle wasted no time delivering the three of us to the meeting hall in Mass. As we stepped off, attendants collected our luggage and whisked it away to wherever we would be staying. I felt grateful for the moment I took on the train to freshen up, but a lingering fear persisted that I would stand out no matter what I did.

I glanced down at my attire, swallowing the urge to hide away. Where sleek outfits announced pristine purpose, my worn cargo pants from countless adventures and hard work screamed dirt. My cream-colored button-down blouse clung to my frame, thin and threadbare in places. Despite my efforts to clean up, my trusty, cracked and weathered boots still adorned my feet.

"We're ready for this," Thomas murmured assurance as we neared the towering doors of the meeting hall.

"Ready or not, we don't have a choice," I replied, though the attempt to sound confident fell flat. My stomach churned with nerves, and I absently rubbed my arm, trying to ease the apprehension building inside me.

Marmarie straightened the hem of her simple blue dress, a pattern of white flowers blooming along the fabric. In Sertoda, it would have been perfect for a formal gathering, but here, it felt woefully out of place. She glanced at me, her eyes unwavering. "They can judge our appearance all they want. It's our actions that matter."

"Surviving Aide elect, please step forward," a gruff soldier called out.

I nodded, forcing a smile as I pushed a curl from my face and took my place in front of the other two. My heart pounded louder as I looked over my shoulder at Thomas and Marmarie. They offered encouraging smiles, but I recognized the same unease behind their eyes.

Before me stood doors carved from dark wood, inlaid with intricate designs that shimmered in the light. They were unlike anything I'd seen in Sertoda, symbolizing wealth and power. With a resounding creak, they swung open.

The room's grandeur hit me all at once: soaring ceilings adorned with crystal chandeliers, gleaming marble floors that seemed to stretch forever, and walls lined with interactive displays pulsed with more vibrant colors. My eyes snapped to the sea of people before me—possibly a hundred, maybe more. Conversation, laughter, and the rustle of opulent garments filled the air as people interacted.

I forced myself to step forward, feeling the cool draft from the hall brush my face as if beckoning me inside.

As I observed the diverse assembly, exuding a unique aura of power and tradition, I felt like an outsider peering into a world where every thread and stitch carried significance. The room buzzed with various dialects, the rich tapestry of our language creating a symphony that echoed through the grand hall.

Would I be seen as a worthy representative among them, or would my differences set me apart?

The delegates from Brawn strode through the crowd, their immaculate uniforms were adorned with gleaming medals and intricate insignias that told tales of valor and conquest. I tucked my bottom lip under my teeth, feeling small in the face of their imposing presence. The dark-as-night jackets and tailored trousers hinted at a society soaked in discipline and authority. And a rush of heat crept up my neck, comparing their poised forms to my fidgeting fingers.

Across the hall stood Lizon's representatives, dressed in simple, utilitarian outfits that revealed their agrarian roots. Their modest clothing, made from rough-spun fabrics, held patches and wear that spoke of hard work. I couldn't help but feel a pang of admiration for their quiet dignity. I instinctively clasped my hands together and held them to my chest, willing my heartbeat to slow.

"I feel like we've walked into another world," Thomas whispered, his eyes wide. I followed his gaze to Trunta's representatives, who were dressed in futuristic garments shimmering with embedded technology.

My breath caught, mesmerized by how their fabric shifted colors with their confident movements. I instinctively adjusted the hem of my own outfit, wishing it weren't so plain.

Breaking my attention away, I noticed Marmarie studying the representatives clad in neutral-toned attire, practical yet subtly stylish. Dobia. Their utility vests and cargo pants spoke of resourcefulness, each pocket and strap serving a purpose. I, too, found myself studying the craftsmanship, momentarily distracted from my unease as I admired the way they carried themselves.

"Now, this is more like what Pop described," I whispered to myself, awestruck by the scene before me. He always said our strength lay in our differences, a living mosaic of a sunset blending into one another. The opulence before me felt almost surreal, a breathtaking display of heritage and innovation that made my own attire a wasteful worry. I belonged in this sunset just as much as anyone else in this room. I spoke of Sertoda—of The Divide.

"We're here to make a difference." Thomas embraced my shoulder, easing a bit of my tension with a squeeze, but replacing it with a charge that ran straight to my core.

Every eye in the room settled on me as my scuffed boots echoed too loudly on the polished marble floors. Sprout's encouraging words tickled the back of my brain... *you're the best person for the job.*

Pushing my shoulders back, I straightened my body, holding my head a little higher. I needed to make the most of this opportunity.

"Just remember," Marmarie whispered, "no one can intimidate us unless we let them."

As I nodded, absorbing the supportive moment passing between us, a svelte figure approached, ready to challenge that statement. Her golden eyes gleamed against her keen, elegant features.

Every detail of Betta seemed to warp the space around her, drawing everyone's attention like a magnet. Her dress, a cascading waterfall of pristine white silk over her long, lean body, shimmered with movement. Its delicate fabric caught the light and transformed into a halo of ethereal brilliance. The train of her dress flowed behind her like a whisper of luxury. Evie wouldn't know what to do with herself. The gown's high collar framed her slender neck with grace, while the intricate embroidery along the bodice glistened with threads of gold and silver, holding my eyes captive.

I felt that familiar pang of intimidation mingled with a healthy dose of envy as I observed her.

A harsh realization hit me: winning my trial and reaching her level felt impossible. Her effortless superiority exacerbated how much I still needed to grow. With each clack of her heels, the idea of ever measuring up seemed more unlikely.

"Levity," she said, her voice calm and confident. "I don't believe we've ever officially met. I'm Elisabetta Rahmani, but please call me Betta."

A rush of nerves surged through me. I recognized her, of course—the woman who saved my family years ago. Memories flooded back, and I swallowed hard, glancing at Thomas and Marmarie for support before meeting her warm, honey gaze. "Yes, I know," I said, my voice steadier than I felt. "These are my fellow Sertoda representatives, Thomas Ravleon and Marmarie Pendavi."

They both approached my sides, nodding and giving a brief hello.

Betta slipped a genuine smile between her lips, lighting up her face. "Welcome to Mass. I hope your journey here wasn't too taxing. That train ride can be a real bore."

I shook my head, though my mind wandered back to the train and the city's stark contrasts. "It was… eye-opening," I admitted. "Mass isn't at all what I anticipated."

Betta's smile widened, raising her cheeks sky-high. "It tends to have that effect. It's a city of contradictions, where the old and new clash… and yet coexist."

"It's a lot to absorb," Thomas said, glancing around the bustling hall.

"We'll need to find our place here," I added.

"Speaking of finding our place. If you'll excuse me, I'm going to track down my friend Edward." Marmarie smiled at Betta and then funneled into the throngs of people.

A fleeting shadow of what appeared to be pain crossed Betta's face. *Odd.*

"Well, you're not alone," Betta reassured me with a composed but soft voice. "Everyone here will need to adapt at some point. The key is to stay focused on your purpose. Keep yourself anchored to reality."

She kept her gaze trained on me. I felt a twinge of understanding pass between us, fragile but undoubtedly present. "Thank you," I murmured, the weight of her words sinking in. Something about her steadiness made me want to believe it. "We'll do our best."

Betta's eyes softened, the armor around her slipping just enough for me to see a flicker of something more—empathy, perhaps, or something more profound. "If you need anything, don't hesitate to reach out," she said, her voice almost a whisper now like she was offering me a lifeline. "We're all here to support each other, even when it feels like we're not."

She reached out, her fingers brushing gently against my arm. Though brief, I felt a connection at that moment—raw, unspoken, but undeniable.

Before I could respond, a loud chime reverberated through the hall, signaling the start of whatever proceeded this initial meet-and-greet. Betta nodded to us and gracefully navigated herself back into the crowd.

The Agricultural Heart of Sandric (A Living Mosaic):

Sandric's agricultural landscape is a living mosaic, with each territory contributing its own unique hues to the sunset of sustenance and survival. Lizon, often regarded as the agricultural heart, flourishes with fertile fields that seem to embody the nurturing spirit of Sandric. But this mosaic extends far beyond Lizon: Brawn's arid stretches, Sertoda's lush valleys, and even Dobia's mountainous terrain each add their essential pieces to the greater whole.

Farmers in Lizon work tirelessly, adapting to the seasonal rhythms and striving for sustainability. Yet, their reliance on neighboring territories for resources is an ever-present challenge, made more precarious as scarcity looms and governmental pressures mount.

This raises vital questions: How does this interdependence affect the relationships between territories? Can food security be ensured when each territory relies on the others for survival? And as policies threaten Lizon's way of life, will its people unite with their neighbors to preserve their agricultural heritage, or will divisions fracture the mosaic?

For my students, these questions underscore the importance of understanding how each piece fits into Sandric's broader tapestry—and what is at risk if the threads begin to fray.

In pursuit of truth and understanding,

—H. Wilhoph

Chapter Fifteen

LEVITY

Teams of attendants ushered the representatives into the grand hall. Tables draped with crisp white linens gleamed under the soft, radiant glow of the crystal chandeliers, which dripped like frozen waterfalls of light from the ceiling. The air brimmed with the enticing aroma of gourmet dishes, each meticulously arranged and steaming. Waitstaff glided across the polished marble floor, bearing platters of culinary masterpieces.

I took my seat. Sitting in front of me were piles of marbled crimson fruit that glistened in decorative crystal bowls, bursting with strange, fragrant juices that spilled over the rims. Peering across from me, Trunta's Perpetual Sense representative settled into her seat. Her fiery red hair cascaded in luxurious waves over her shoulders, a vivid contrast to her composed, aloof demeanor. Her name tag dangled from a delicate gold chain, the sole marker of her identity. Saria Meeth. Her calm eyes surveyed the room with an air of detached curiosity. Her mouth clasped.

I caught sight of Marmarie farther down the table, engaged in conversation with an older man who seemed to be from Lizon by his own humble attire. The three Sanctioned, Betta, Lyonal Crestmore, and Captain Draven Ballister, occupied the head of the long table. I wasn't the only one who felt drawn to their commanding presence. Representatives across the room peeked in their direction. To my left, Thomas immersed himself in the banquet details, his trained restaurateur eyes scanning the array of dishes with professional appreciation and personal curiosity. Noting the empty seat to my right, I brought my attention back to Thomas.

A large, tiered platter displayed piles of chilled sea blossoms, a local delicacy to Sertoda I hadn't tasted since my mother last made them. Their translucent, petal-like shells were filled with a pale gold paste, lightly salted with hints of ocean brine. Further down, beyond Thomas, I caught a glimpse of what could only be Trunta's famed smoked *elyn* plant. This rare and flavorful green was preserved under glass domes to keep it from wilting, its pale green leaves shimmering as if lightly glazed.

Thomas turned to me, drumming his fingers on the table. "You know, being here reminds me of when I first came to the city from The Divide," he said, his voice uncertain. He held a miniature pastry layered in whisper-thin sheets of crust and stuffed with some sort of violet cream I'd never seen before. "I worked the docks in Sertoda for a while—though, of course, you probably already know that." He gave a small, apologetic smile. "It's... kind of surreal, honestly. I've dreamed of sitting in this seat, making it to Mass—but I never thought it would actually happen."

I grazed my fingers over my lavish goblet filled with sparkling nectar, flecked with edible silver. "I'm not used to anything like this. The details are incredible. All this food. After living with rations for so long, it feels... too much." I glanced around, still taking in the grandeur, before tilting my head to him, overwhelmed if not a bit embarrassed myself. "But tell me, what was it like for you? Moving into the city in Sertoda, I want to hear."

Thomas looked past me, his gaze distant, as if seeing a memory just out of reach. "Leaving The Divide for the city felt like an impossible leap. The Divide has its beauty and simplicity that's comforting, I suppose. But when I stepped into places like this for the first time, surrounded by all this brilliance, it felt like a different world altogether, full of possibilities I didn't even know existed." He paused, contemplating his next words. "It's unsettling at first, but you start to realize—you're capable of more than you ever thought. And maybe that's worth the risk of leaving behind what's familiar."

He gestured to the lavish banquet spread before us, his professional eye trained on the array of exotic meats nestled in beds of charred herbs, each cut roasted to deep, succulent shades and topped with an array of sauces. "Now, seeing this level of precision and artistry, it's like living a dream. The balance of flavors and presentation is all executed with such finesse. Even in Sertoda, you wouldn't see this kind of detail."

"Moving to the city must've been a huge change," I said, leaning in a bit. I felt a flush of shame color my cheeks. "I mean, I've never quite fit in back home, but I still love it… in my own way. What surprised you the most about city life?"

As Thomas spoke, a pang of envy tightened in my chest. I admired his ability to leave behind The Divide and carve out a new life in the city with what seemed like relative ease. The transition appeared so seamless for him. Moving to the city had always felt like a fantasy meant for someone else. Not for people like my family and me. But here I was, in Mass, on the brink of becoming a council member at the very least. Maybe that could be enough to turn things around. Enough to finally lift us out of The Divide. The idea felt surreal, almost too much to hope for, but for the first time, I could imagine it: a new life in the city, a fresh start I never thought could be ours.

A smile played on Thomas's mouth as he crossed his arms on the table. "I always hoped I'd make it here. Now that I'm actually sitting at this table… feels unreal." He shook his head, chuckling more to himself than me.

I was charmed by his excitement, but my attention was soon stolen by a voice cutting in.

"While the aesthetics are impressive, one has to wonder what's being concealed behind all this extravagance."

Smooth and measured.

A kiss of breath to my ear alone.

A stranger sat down on the empty seat to my right. I closed my gaping mouth in awe of his long, silver hair flowing over his shoulders in varying braids. Light danced across it, giving him an almost otherworldly quality. Unlike me, he was relaxed, comfortable even.

"You, um, must have a critical eye," I stammered, fumbling to lift my name tag into his line of sight. "I'm Levity."

His face remained casual but inquisitive. "Levity. It's a pleasure. Garon Fiore of Dobia." He raised his name tag and let it drop back onto his solid chest. "This place certainly is overwhelming. It's not what I expected from Mass."

I let out a nervous laugh. "Yeah, it's… it's quite a spectacle. I'm still trying to wrap my head around everything. It feels so far removed from what I'm used to."

Garon nodded thoughtfully. "Adapting to such a drastic change will be difficult. It's hard to leave behind everything you know and embrace something so unfamiliar, though your friend would have you believe otherwise." He nodded towards Thomas with a smile, then added, "That's the thing about the Noble Warriors—they make it look easy. It's not just bravery; it's the image of it. Even when they're terrified inside, projecting strength is as much a part of their role as wielding a blade."

I smiled faintly, feeling myself relax just a little. "It definitely is."

He leaned forward to reread my name tag. "You're here from Sertoda. What position have you been elected to, exactly?"

The question took me by surprise; it marked my first real step toward embracing my new role. I carried the title for less than twenty-four hours but saying it out loud made it feel real in a way that it hadn't before. "I'm Sertoda's Surviving Aide lect."

Garon's eyes narrowed as if he was auditing me. "Surviving Aide? That's a significant role. Why do you think your people chose you for it?"

I hesitated, fidgeting with the edge of my sleeve as I searched for the right words. "It's hard to say," I muttered, unable to hold his gaze. I took a shaky breath, gathering thoughts of my past. "I think it might have something to do with my life experiences. After my parents died, I... I took on responsibilities far beyond my years." I glanced at Garon, then quickly looked down at my hands. "I have four younger siblings. Maybe my people saw something in me that made them believe I could handle this role if I could handle taking care of them on my own..." My voice trailed off.

Garon's expression dissolved into what I could only discern as compassion. "That sounds incredibly challenging. Managing a family while dealing with personal loss—it must have shaped you in ways that others might not fully understand or appreciate."

"It did shape me," I admitted, my voice wavering. "But I never really wanted to be in this role. *Surviving Aide*. It just... happened." I fiddled with the fork in front of me, searching for the right words. "There's a lot about this position and the situation we're all in that feels off. It's like something's not quite right, but I can't put my finger on it." Heat rose in my cheeks. "I'm just trying to figure things out... to understand why things are the way they are. I want to help, even if it's not the path I would have chosen."

Garon inched forward, an elbow now on the table to turn in my direction. "What do you mean by 'not quite right?'"

I took a shaky breath, struggling to find the courage to voice my thoughts. "Well, it's... about my parents. It might be hard to understand, but their deaths have always felt... I don't know, suspicious? *Officially*, they were killed by the Cird, but I've never really believed that."

Garon's piercing blue eyes widened as he tipped back in his chair. "The Cird? That's serious. You doubt that?"

I hesitated, my heart racing as I looked away, feeling exposed. "I don't know. This probably isn't the right forum for this—"

"No, please, I'm interested to hear your thoughts. That's the Perpetual Sense in me." He gave a sly but reassuring smile.

"It just never added up, you know? They were good people, dedicated to our community and family. My father always said that the Cird were painted in a harsh light, misunderstood by those in power. He believed history often distorted their actions into villainy, making them convenient scapegoats for the government's failures." I took a breath, lowered my voice, and tried to pace myself. "It feels like there's more to it, like my parents might have stumbled upon something that made them a threat. But it's so hard to think that way. I don't want to believe they were caught in something sinister. But I thought... coming here, I might learn... more..." My voice trailed off, unsure of how much more to share with this man I barely knew. Something about him though, his eyes perhaps? There was a familiarity in them that cracked me right open.

Garon asked, "Were your loved ones traditionalists?"

I reached for my water glass, taking a quick sip before responding. "Yes, in a sense. They believed in the old ways but never imposed those beliefs on anyone else." I tried to distance them from any hint of extremism. "Why do you ask?"

Garon scratched the back of his neck and then leaned deeper into my personal space. "In Dobia, there are whispers—rumors, really—that traditionalists are more than just nostalgic for the past. Some people claim they're a threat to the current government, that they're involved in some kind of underground resistance."

"Resistance?" I echoed, the word feeling foreign and wrong when associated with my parents. I fidgeted in my seat, looking around to make sure those around us were still busy with other conversations.

Garon nodded, his expression serious. "There have been mysterious deaths in Dobia, all linked to people rumored to be traditionalists. The official word is that they were accidents or natural causes, but... I've heard different accounts. Some say these people were silenced because they knew too much or were too vocal about the government's failings."

A chill ran through me. "You're saying my parents could have been targeted?"

"It's possible," Garon replied, dropping his voice even lower that I bent at the hip to hear him. "The officials in Dobia have been spreading lies, painting traditionalists as radicals."

"But my parents were just trying to keep the old traditions alive, to remember where we came from..."

"*Ciridis*," he whispered, his voice taking on the most subtle accent.

"*Keer-i-dis?*" I asked, sounding it out slowly as though I was learning the right way to say it.

"The Cird."

I stared at him, trying to grasp the significance. Once I made sure Thomas was deep in his own conversation with a representative to his left, I turned my body to face him more.

Garon's whole demeanor seemed to harden into ice. "Ancient lore, if you believe in that sort of thing, speaks of them rising from the sea, claiming to be the very architects of our world. The name Ciridis combines *keer,* rooted in the ancient word for 'to grow,' and *idis*, meaning 'from God.' Their powers are said to have come as a gift from an unnamed God before Sandric even existed."

The air seemed to thicken, making it hard to breathe. Every word mirrored the lessons of my Pop. The words my Mama sang. Goose bumps

163

raced across my arms.

"*The Light of God*." I breathed out, a memory released.

Garon's gaze locked onto mine. "Gods. Banished to The Depths like fallen kings and queens, their power buried with them. Myths, disgraced, forgotten—except when we spit their names in anger and damnation. To think that they were systematically erased from history by the *Ordinis*. The ordinary. It's unfathomable." He rolled his eyes, grabbing a glass of bubbling burgundy liquid in front of him.

His words struck something deep that I didn't want to acknowledge, something deep within the wreckage of my heart, igniting a fire that still smoldered. My parents were far more than I ever imagined, more than the simple lives they led. They were part of something larger, something I had barely begun to understand.

"They knew. They knew they were gods," I declared, stunned by my own conviction. The shock only intensified the determination surging through me. "I will uncover the truth. Their sacrifice won't be in vain."

The ice in Garon's eyes melted. "I hope you do. It's a big task, but I can see you've got a strong sense of justice driving you. That's admirable. It's what makes a great leader. If you're ready to challenge the status quo and look beneath the surface, you might find allies where you least expect." He raised his glass with a slight nod.

The opulent feast before us seemed almost inconsequential compared to my conversation with Garon. While luxurious, the effervescent beverages and fine wines paled against the more pressing matters at hand.

With Garon's revelations settling into a thoughtful silence, the atmosphere changed. My focus drifted across the table to Saria, who observed us with a contemplative air.

As the meal continued, I spoke with Thomas more, talking of my siblings and their constant shenanigans.

"Blue," I grinned, "the second youngest, is a little troublemaker. Just the other day, she decided our neighbor's dog needed some fresh air. The poor thing had been cooped up all day, so Blue, in all her ten years of wisdom, snatched him from their yard, tossed him in the basket of her bike, and went tearing down the street. She was pedaling like a maniac, saying she was just 'taking him for a ride'—like it was completely normal to steal a dog for an impromptu adventure. The neighbor was outside shouting for the dog, but Blue just zoomed by, waving like she hadn't stolen him. When I asked her what she thought she was doing, she just shrugged and said, 'He looked bored.'"

Thomas laughed, shaking his head. And across the table, I caught the slightest shift in Saria's expression—like she wasn't expecting that. It was funny how the antics of a little kid could soften even the hardest of faces.

"Do you have a family?" I asked, inviting her to join in.

Her voice, tinged with a quiet melancholy, carried unspoken burdens. "My husband. Yes—" she paused, her gaze distant as if she caught herself and began choosing her words wisely. "Adjusting to my absence will be a challenge for him. Five years feels like an eternity when I think too much about it."

I nodded, feeling a pang of empathy. "Balancing duty and personal life is going to be incredibly demanding. My siblings will be all but grown by the time I return. Just the thought of it makes me sad."

Saria's sharp eyes met mine. "It's a sacrifice we make for a greater cause, I suppose. But it doesn't make it any easier."

I sensed a shared recognition of the personal costs of our roles. "No, it doesn't. But knowing that others understand the gravity of these sacrifices makes it a bit more bearable."

Saria managed a faint smile. "Indeed."

Conversations changed to the exquisite dishes before us. Each bite revealed layers of flavors. The ambiance hummed with the clink of silverware and the murmur of diplomatic discourse, blending into a harmonious backdrop.

As the luncheon drew to a close, Lyonal, whom I recognized from seeing in the news over his term, rose from his seat, commanding attention. His smooth and resonant voice carried through the hall, addressing the assembled dignitaries.

"Esteemed representatives, welcome to Mass," Lyonal began, his eyes scanning the room with a keen intensity. "In the coming days, you will face trials of endurance, intellect, and diplomacy. These trials will test each of you, pushing you beyond your limits. Through this crucible, we will discover who among you possesses the strength and vision to lead Sandric forward. Who will prove themselves worthy of becoming Sanctioned."

A ripple of murmurs and nods followed his words, acknowledging the gravity of the challenge ahead. I glanced at Saria as she observed Lyonal intently.

"As we adjourn, please follow our soldiers to your designated living quarters," he continued, his tone decisive yet welcoming. "Rest well, for tomorrow marks the beginning of our journey together—a journey that will demand not only your skills but your unwavering commitment to the ideals we hold dear. Remember, the choices you make during this Sanctioning will echo far beyond these walls and into the future of our territories.

"Sanctioned. United. One." Lyonal ended with a casual raise of his fist in salute.

Suddenly, the heavy doors swung open, and a bevy of soldiers clad in black swept into the room, their presence dominating and unsettling.

I stiffened in my seat, my heart racing, and a knot of fear twisted in my stomach. What purpose did this display serve? Why did the soldiers' arrival feel so ominous? My mind raced through possibilities—were they here to enforce order or to intimidate us? I glanced at Thomas, who wore a mask of calm. Under the table, he grasped my hand and squeezed, giving me pause.

The soldiers moved with confidence, their disciplined strides echoing in the spacious hall. They formed a line, blocking all exits.

I forced myself to look around the table, scanning for familiar faces. Marmarie's brow furrowed, a layer of anxiety coating her features. I tried to find comfort in her presence, but the growing sense of foreboding wrapped around me and tugged.

Rooted in place, I felt an undeniable sense that this marked only the beginning of my fear. My instincts screamed for me to flee, to escape the room's suffocating tension.

I held onto Thomas's hand tighter as I forced myself to stay put and face whatever came next.

The Truth Behind the Cird Eradication:

Almost a century ago, the Cird became the scapegoats for a devastating attack that resulted in countless lives lost, leading to their systematic eradication. Official narratives branded them as terrorists, but this portrayal obscures the more complex truths surrounding that tragic time.

In the years leading up to the attack, the Cird vocally opposed Brawn's expanding influence, whose military ambitions threatened to dominate the five territories of Sandric. On the day of the attack, the Cird gathered peacefully to protest, seeking dialogue and understanding, entirely unaware that they were being drawn into a precarious situation.

The explosion that ripped through Trunta's capital marked a turning point, but its origins remain skeptical. While many narratives suggested that the Cird were responsible, others hint at a more complicated reality: implications pointing at Brawn elements, or opportunistic factions within Trunta may have orchestrated the chaos to serve their own agendas. Whether planned or merely exploited, this explosion provided a pretext for the brutal crackdown that followed.

In pursuit of truth and understanding,

—H. Wilhoph

Chapter Sixteen

LEVITY

The windowless corridors of Mass stretched endlessly, wide enough for Marmarie, Thomas, and me to walk side by side. The lack of natural light made my other senses prickle to life. Each turn blended into the next, creating an intricate entanglement that further disoriented me. The walls, smooth and metallic, reflected the dim light from embedded pulsating fixtures, casting an eerie glow that seemed to dance along the surface, matching the smell. Sterile.

The soldiers escorting us from where we had dined dwindled to only two as we reached this part of the building we now passed through. The fifteen representatives, each grouped by their territories, moved in tight clusters. Our two black-suited guides, their hands firmly grasping the guns at their hips, moved with practiced precision. Their mechanical demeanors were devoid of warmth—*forget reassurance.*

With each step, my sense of direction faltered. The air pressure and the dense, cool atmosphere that enveloped us changed. The faint slopes in the floor heightened an unsettling thought. Were we descending?

The soft hum of machinery filled the air. After so long living by candlelight, I could hardly comprehend the wattage needed to power a place like this. Maybe a megawatt. I ran the tip of my finger along the wall. The very surface vibrated.

As we continued, our quarters came into view.

The two soldiers began to parse the representatives off toward their respective accommodations, directing us down separate corridors marked by featureless doors that slid open silently. Marmarie, Thomas, and I remained together as the guards flanked us from behind.

Curiosity flickered in Marmarie's eyes, but I could still see the worry in her pursed lips. She glanced around, absent-mindedly. "I tried looking for Edward during the luncheon, you know, my friend from the council. I couldn't find him anywhere," she said with a slight furrow in her brow. "I'm starting to wonder if he's gone ill or something. Not that he's as old as me, but he's a bit... well, full around the middle. Loves his cakes too much." She chuckled lightly, though the humor didn't quite reach her eyes.

Ever the optimist, Thomas flashed a reassuring smile, trying to lift the anxious mood that seemed to cling to the space.

"I hope we're getting close to our rooms," he said, his voice firm against the echoing silence of the polished marble as he looked back over his shoulder. "I hardly remember how we got here."

I nodded, still uneasy. A nagging feeling of being watched clung at the edges of my mind, like an invisible weight pressing down on me.

At a junction, one soldier tipped their head to Marmarie. She turned to us with a determined expression and straightened her back. "I think this is where our paths diverge," she said, inhaling deeply and reaching out to brush my arm. "We should settle in before The Sanctioning begins."

I asked the soldiers about our schedule, but they remained silent. As if I never spoke. I searched for a reaction to my words, but nothing existed beyond the hard lines of their impassiveness.

Thomas and I branched off from Marmarie and after another disorienting set of twists and turns, the soldiers fell back, pointing us toward our rooms conveniently across from each other at the end of a long corridor lit by a single sconce.

"Well, looks like we're neighbors," Thomas said with a playful grin as we approached our rooms. His tone was casual, but there was a little something more in the way his eyes lingered on mine.

My pulse quickened at his proximity to me. A nervous excitement stirred beneath my skin, like a charge in the air that hadn't been there moments before. "We've always been neighbors," I replied with a quieter smile, my gaze dropping, only to flicker back up at him. "You just... didn't remember me."

His smile softened, and there was something apologetic in the way he looked at me. "Guess life has a way of keeping us distracted sometimes," he said, his voice dipping a little lower as though the words were meant only for him. "But it's not that you were forgettable." He paused, his gaze unflinching, almost searching. "I just didn't see you the way I do now."

I felt a sharp pull in my chest. My mind wandered to the warmth of his body against mine during that one night—his lips on my neck, his large hands on my waist. The way the tips of his fingers made me forget the world around me.

I blinked, forcing myself back to the present.

Those same fingers brushed my chin, lifting it gently, and the intimacy in the gesture froze me. "I didn't forget you, Levity," he whispered, his voice thick with sincerity. "Not for a second."

My breath caught in my throat, and I was acutely aware of the heat building between us, of how close we now stood. "Thank you," I managed, my voice a little shaky, my heart pounding louder than I could ignore. "That means a lot."

He parted his lips as if to say something else, but his eyes seemed to settle on searching mine instead. It felt like there was so much left to explore, more than either of us was willing to voice just yet.

After a beat, I forced a playful smile, trying to break the tension.

"Maybe you can share a few survival tips with me before The Sanctioning starts," I suggested, trying to ease the sudden intensity I felt rising.

Thomas gave a half-laugh, but there was a quiet hunger in how his eyes raked over me. "I'll definitely help you with that," he said, running a hand through his chestnut hair. My stomach flipped. His hand fell to the sleeve of my blouse fiddling with the hem at my wrist. "But I bet you've got a few tricks up your sleeve yourself."

The thought of him learning from me felt absurd. I couldn't imagine how anything I knew would be of much use to him, but the idea of him being this close—his curiosity, his interest in me—stirred a yearning I'd never felt with anyone else. Heat bloomed at my core.

"I'd like to talk about The Divide," he said, his voice low, with that same warm, genuine interest. "I'd really like to hear what it's been like for you. See it through your eyes."

Addressing my life in The Divide sent a flicker of unease through me, but I nodded all the same. "Yeah," I said, my voice quiet, "That would be nice." My gaze lingered on him, memorizing the way the light played in his dark eyes. "Thanks," I whispered, feeling the heat rise in my face again. "For being... so kind."

"Anytime," he said, his voice thick with meaning.

He chuckled, but it was rougher. It was like he was trying to ease some tension that neither of us had fully acknowledged. *Was Thomas... nervous?*

He cleared his throat. "First, though," he said, looking toward our rooms, "let's figure out these doors."

Diverting my eyes away from him, I stepped closer to my room. The door opened with a sudden whoosh, stealing my breath.

"Easy enough," I murmured, my mind already spinning with thoughts of what might happen next—how much longer we could keep pretending we weren't already falling into something far more precarious than we anticipated.

I bid Thomas goodbye, and even as I turned toward my room and entered my living quarters, I could still feel the heat of his gaze, like a whisper against my skin.

Brilliant lights illuminated the room's elegant furnishings—a blend of Sandric craftsmanship and modern conveniences. The subtle scent of herbs added a familiar touch to the atmosphere.

I glanced around, absorbing the spacious and surprisingly comfortable arrangement. A large window revealed a panoramic view of Mass's skyline, its glittering towers glowing against the vibrant hues of the setting sun. The bustling streets below felt worlds away, and I couldn't shake the peculiar dissonance of my experience.

I distinctly felt like we were going underground, descending deeper into the world, yet here I stood, staring out at this breathtaking view. It made no sense.

Maybe I needed to sit down.

The bed, draped in rich textiles, beckoned me. After sixteen years of either sharing a bed with a growing sibling or contorting myself on the small cot I'd claimed in the sleeping quarters, this felt like a luxury I could hardly comprehend.

Despite the plush surroundings, I couldn't shake the knot in my stomach that had only grown thrice its size since departing Sertoda. The day's events and the fear of the impending Sanctioning left me unsettled. I kicked off my boots and socks, feeling the coolness of the polished floor beneath my feet, and walked back to the window.

Outside, Mass was alive with activity. The city's incessant motion seemed to mock the stillness I craved. As I peered out, my mind replayed the revelations from Garon—the real history of the Cird and the government's efforts to squash traditionalists shook the foundation of everything I thought I believed.

How could I even begin to face The Sanctioning when my parents could have been punished for defying the government? For living a truth that they believed in? Could I really be part of a system that might have taken them from me? Or, at the very least, covered up something more sinuous?

I turned away from the window and sank onto the edge of the bed. The room seemed to spin, a dizzying reminder of the challenges awaiting me. Closing my eyes, I took a deep breath to calm the storm of emotions.

Lying back on the bed, exhaustion washed over me. I closed my heavy eyelids. My thoughts swirled in a disorienting haze, and a profound lethargy settled deep into my bones. The familiar call of darkness pulled me down into its ominous embrace. And before I could resist, I succumbed to its enveloping grasp, slipping into unconsciousness.

The Fight to Preserve Our Heritage:

By definition, Traditionalists are those who cling to the customs and values of the past, seeking to preserve what they perceive as the essence of our culture. In Sandric, these groups have emerged in secret, rallying around the idea that modern society has lost its way. They argue that our rapid technological, political, and social advancements have cost us our heritage, our sense of community, and our moral compass.

Critics often miss the deep sense of loss that fuels this movement. Traditionalists, do not resist change simply out of fear or ignorance but out of a profound respect for the wisdom of our ancestors. In the traditions we fight to preserve, there is a balance—a harmony between people and the natural world, between ambition and responsibility.

Yet, I recognize the tension. Many argue that Traditionalists threaten societal cohesion, that by holding on to the past, we foster division and prevent necessary growth. I understand this perspective, but it is misguided. We do not reject progress outright; we seek a path that honors our origins. Change is inevitable, but progress without roots is dangerous.

The real question is: Can we integrate the lessons of the past into the solutions of the future? Or will we allow the rush toward modernity to strip away everything that once gave us strength?

In pursuit of truth and understanding,

—H. Wilhoph

Chapter Seventeen

BETTA

I shifted in my seat. My mind fell back into my own nightmare room, buried somewhere in this part of Mass. The flickering screen in front of us cast its dull glow across the sturdy metal table. Behind us, the control room and the infirmary—places designed to monitor, manipulate, and mend whatever The Sanctioning broke. I'd been to the recovery chamber as well. The dumping ground for the representatives that '*won*,' dragging them back to a fraction of who they once were. Like tending to livestock—patch them up and sending them back out just to eventually be slaughtered.

It felt like a tomb in here, with its low ceilings and stale air. Although connected to the primary residence for the Sanctioned, this space held an entirely different purpose. We were deep underground, where most didn't even know existed.

This was the site of The Sanctioning. Far away from the world above, where the Sanctioned enjoyed their comforts. We sat where every thread of control converged. From this room, they orchestrated everything—the simulations, the surveillance, and the systematic dismantling of each representative's psyche.

Now the three of us were on the other side of it all—congregating in the so-called '*Leadership Room*'. I let out a short, bitter laugh. *We lead nothing.*

The hallways branching out from this room offered nothing better. With meager lighting, I could only see a few steps ahead. Likely a tactic to keep us from memorizing the pathways. The guards that typically shadowed our every move remained behind in our living quarters; I assumed fewer guards meant fewer witnesses—an intentional choice to keep the darker truths hidden from even the most loyal of the regime's forces.

Now, we waited. Waited for The Sanctioning to be fully underway. Then the lights would go out. It would swallow us all in that darkness I knew too well—disorienting and absolute. The kind of black that left you stumbling in circles, not knowing which way led to safety or straight back into the abyss.

A barrage of data flashed before us—each representative's starting vitals, graphs, and numbers that spun in dizzying patterns. None of it meant much to me. It was clinical and cold. I was waiting. Waiting for the screen in front of us to deliver the next phase of our *instructions.*

Did I expect the truth?

Maybe some.

But they sure as hell weren't spilling the details of the schemes I'd kill to get my hands on.

Levity's pale and wide-eyed face crossed my thoughts. She had walked into the grand meeting hall with no idea what she'd been elected to. And how would she know? How would she know The Sanctioning would tear her apart soon enough, just like it did all of us.

No one came out of this place the same. Not even me.

I looked at Draven, who sat beside me. His expression was unreadable as he studied the rotating images on the screen.

I studied Lyonal next, who sat across from us, searching for any sign of the duplicity I suspected. His ocean-blue eyes, hidden behind the frames of his glasses, locked on the large digital screen lining the wall ahead of us, a slight smirk playing on his lips. His recent interaction with Saria Meeth, the redhead from Trunta, replayed in my head. Their whispered words alone jarred me enough, but something about overhearing that conversation emboldened me with the urge to dig deeper.

"Lyonal," I drawled, my voice coated with faux innocence, "you honestly believe these representatives will handle their little nightmares well? I mean, have you seen them? They look like they're one strong breeze away from crumbling. Especially that redhead. She's all bravado. I doubt she could handle a simple power outage without panicking."

He didn't even look at me, his eyes still fixed on the screen. "It's too early to tell. But they'll manage…or they won't. That's the point, isn't it?"

Choosing my words carefully, I leaned forward, pressing further. "And speaking of that redhead, did Saria's input influence your thoughts on possible outcomes?"

Frustration began to simmer under his careful surface, as he ran his fingers through his graying hair. "What are you implying, Betta?"

I crossed my arms tightly, flexing as tension built within the fibers of my muscles. "You seemed very close in the meeting hall. Just wondering if you're planning on giving her a little… advantage."

I watched as Lyonal wiggled his fingers on the table. "You're walking on thin ice."

Draven's jaw tightened, and he ran a hand over the stubble of his trimmed beard, a sign of his own agitation flaring.

I knew to be cautious around Lyonal, but I couldn't help myself. "Just trying to understand the game, Mr. Crestmore. We're all on the same team, aren't we?"

He shot up, his chair scraping loudly against the floor. In a few swift steps, he rounded the table and towered over me. His aging hand shot out.

Gripping my arm with a bruising force I hadn't known he could exert; he extracted me from my seat. "This is not a game. You don't know what you're talking about."

Pain shot through my arm, but I didn't back down. "Then enlighten me." I spat back.

Before he could react further, Draven moved so swiftly in the weak light that I hardly registered him prying Lyonal's hand off me. He stepped in between us. He loomed over Lyonal, his presence a solid wall of intimidation. "Back off, Lyonal," he snarled, a cruel smile twisting his lips. He drew his knife, the blade glinting menacingly in the dim light. "Want to find out what happens when you push me? I'd be happy to carve a reminder into your skin so you won't forget."

Lyonal's eyes widened with fear and just as much anger. Reluctantly, he took a step back. "Keep your nose out of things you don't understand, Betta. For the good of everyone."

"I'll add your threat to the growing pile."

Draven didn't move; his predatory glare fixed on Lyonal until the man turned and stormed out of the room. Only then did Draven turn to me, concern softening the aggressive edge in his features, and sheathing his knife. "Are you okay?"

I rubbed my arm, nodding. "I'm fine. Just frustrated."

The small space felt more intimate with just the two of us standing so close. "Let's talk," he said, his voice gentle but firm.

I sat back down in my chair, still rubbing my arm. Draven pulled his chair closer, spreading his legs so my knees were between them. His posture seemed relaxed, but the concern in his eyes deceived him.

"Thank you, Draven," I said quietly, "for looking out for me."

He gave a small smile, but it didn't reach his eyes. "It's what friends do."

I hesitated. "Are we friends?"

Draven leaned in. His overwhelming presence made breathing difficult, and it only became harder when his heavy hands settled on my knees. The warmth of his palms seeped through the thin fabric, but the slow, deliberate graze of his thumbs against the sensitive spot on my inner knees sent a jolt through my chest.

His voice dropped to a low growl, raw and unfiltered. "You think you know what I am." His grip tightened ever so slightly, anchoring me as though he was afraid I'd pull away.

I wanted to look anywhere but at him, to break the intensity of his gaze, but I couldn't. The sincerity in his words pinned me more effectively than his hands ever could.

"I can't shake all the preconceived notions you have," he continued, his thumbs brushing against my legs again, sending heat coursing through me. "But I deserve a chance to prove I'm better than them. I need you to see me for who I really am."

I blinked, unprepared for how he hovered in front of me, his body swallowing up the space between us. "You can't possibly understand—the agony of watching the woman I love more than anything in this life, plead for release from the relentless torment she endured. Seeing her haunted by memories of having to willingly separate from my father, with his child, knowing that the fear of keeping me around him posed greater dangers than the pain of growing up without him." My tone grew despondent, the emotion choking the words as I fought against the vulnerability his intensity stirred within me. "It's a torment that tears at the very fabric of my soul, leaving wounds that will never truly heal."

"I do get it—there's a history with my people, a lingering distrust that's impossible to dismiss." Draven's hands slipped from my knees. His warmth was replaced by the room's chill. He leaned back, dropping his gaze to his fingers twisting together in his lap. He looked almost unsure as if the words he needed were balancing precariously on the edge of his lips.

"But in the midst of all this," he continued, his voice quieter now, "I've come to see more than just the surface." His dark gaze lifted, locking onto mine with an intensity that made the air feel thinner. My breath caught, shallow and uneven, as he leaned forward again, closer this time, his hands bracing against the chair's edge beside my thighs. "I see you—not just as a representative from a rival region—"

Before I could process his words, firm hands pulled me toward him in one deliberate motion. The scrape of the chair legs on the floor sharp against the room's silence. I gasped. He was so close. His breath feathered against my ear, sending a shiver through me. "I see you—your strength, your fear, and everything you try to hide from the rest of the world." His warmth kissed the side of my face, his lips so close they could've brushed my skin if I leaned in even the slightest bit.

Draven hesitated, then leaned back. He took me in and gently brushed a strand of hair from my face. His fingertips lingered against my cheek, a whisper of contact that raised goose bumps. "Maybe it's reckless, maybe it's foolish," he continued, his voice hoarse, "but I care for you more than you might realize."

His hand dropped to mine, his fingers brushing over my knuckles.

My heart stumbled as his thumb traced slow, soothing circles against the skin, a touch that felt both steadying and undoing all at once. "And despite everything," he murmured, "I'd like to think you *could* care for me, just a little, even if at times it's hard to."

Draven stayed there, inches away, his hand still resting on mine, waiting for me to meet him in the fragile space he'd dared to open between us.

I couldn't move, couldn't speak. The heat of his breath on my skin blurred every rational thought I tried to hold onto. He had pulled me so close, unraveled me wholly, that I wasn't sure I could put myself back together. My chest tightened as I searched for the right words, something to fill the charged silence that fell between us.

Finally, I whispered, "You make it sound so simple, like caring is easy… but it's not." My fingers curled slightly under his touch, my heart pounding in my ears. "This world, what we've been forced to do—it doesn't leave room for things like this. For feelings." I shook my head, the words tasting foreign on my tongue. "And yet, you're here, saying things I don't know if I deserve to hear."

The corners of his mouth twitched as if he was holding back a response, but he stayed silent, letting me spill the chaos that had been brewing inside me before I even realized it was there.

"Draven, I don't know how to do this. To trust, to hope… to feel like this isn't going to break me in the end." I finally lifted my eyes to his, finding the steady, unrelenting gaze that had the power to ground me and shake me all at once. "But you make me want to try." My voice broke on the last word.

He sank into his seat, his voice tinged with vulnerability. "You know, in the meeting hall, I talked to Dorian."

I tilted my head. "What did you tell him?"

Draven's focus drifted as if lost in the memory of the conversation. "I told him to stay true to himself, no matter what comes next. To hold on to why he's here and who he's fighting for. Not what our father expects but what he wants for himself. It's all too easy to get lost in The Sanctioning and become someone you're not. I just don't want that for him."

"He's lucky to have you as his brother."

Draven shrugged, a morose look in his eyes. "I just hope it's enough. This Sanctioning…"

I reached out, placing my hand on his forearm. "We won't let them break him, Draven. We'll see to it he makes it through."

He covered my hand with his own, nearly twice the size of mine, giving it a reassuring squeeze. "Yeah, we will."

We sat in silence for a moment. Despite the unknown, I found comfort in knowing we watched each other's backs.

"Draven," I said, breaking the silence, letting a sliver of my heart underneath its guard peek through. "If you're going to say things like that, you'd better promise me one thing." My voice wavered, but I pressed on. "Don't hurt me. I've got far too many wounds to allow one more."

He slid his hand over the smoothness of his head, licking his lips before he spoke. "This world throws shadows at us, and the fight is tough. But know this: I'll stand by your side, no matter what. I promise to protect you from harm—be it enemies or the fears that haunt us." He leaned closer. "I'll be your shield against the darkness and your strength when you feel weak. I don't ever want to be the cause of your pain." His voice carried a lightness that made his promise resonate. "I am committed to honor the trust you've shown me."

I was caught in the warmth of his words, the way they seeped into the cracks of the fortress that was my heart. Then I found my voice again, my lips quirking into a faint smile. "Good," I said, "I've got a sharp tongue, Draven, and I'm not afraid to use it."

He chuckled, the sound curling around me like heady smoke. "Oh, I wouldn't mind seeing you use that sharp tongue," he said, his flirtatious smirk making a fleeting return.

"There he is," I laughed.

But before I could add to my retort, his voice softened again, the sincerity cutting through the teasing. "Just not against me—not like that. I'd rather be the reason you smile, not the reason you have to fight."

The door swished open, and we immediately broke away. I swiveled to fully face the screen before Lyonal reentered. He approached the displays, which still laid out an array of detailed diagrams and statistics.

Suddenly, the screen buzzed and flashed to white, making my eyes strain to adjust. My attention snapped to the fifteen new images.

Levity's name appeared first on the screen.

Speculation on the Underground Network of Mass:

A complex network of tunnels remains largely unexplored and mysterious beneath Mass's city. As a cultural studies professor, I find it intriguing and concerning that such a significant aspect of our urban landscape has been overlooked.

Some speculate these tunnels serve as escape routes for dissidents fleeing the oppressive regime, while others believe they may host clandestine meetings of those who seek to challenge the status quo.

The tunnels may also carry remnants of the Cird's legacy.

Moreover, the speculation around these tunnels raises critical questions about power dynamics in Sandric. What does it mean for a society to harbor such concealed structures? How does this secrecy impact our cultural identity and the narratives we create?

The ambiguous nature surrounding the tunnels invites us to examine our beliefs and biases, prompting us to question what lies hidden beneath the surface of our daily lives.

In pursuit of truth and understanding,
—H. Wilhoph

Chapter Eighteen

LEVITY

The acrid stench of charred wood and a sourness pierced my senses, wrenching me from a foggy sleep.

My eyes flew open.

The world blurred.

A brutal assault of smells stung the back of my throat. Everything felt wrong. A suffocating haze of smoldering ash replaced my plush surroundings. I blinked rapidly. But my vision remained hazy. Shadows flickered. Sputtering light seemed to come from nowhere and everywhere at once.

I was paralyzed. Disorientation gripped me in its cold, staunch fist. My heart hammered against my ribs, a relentless beat reverberating in my ears.

How did I get here?

The bed felt wrong. The sheets were rough, unlike the soft textiles when I laid down. They crunched under my movement. Panic crushed my chest. Poisonous smoke seared my throat and lungs.

Move.

As I tried to shift, my limbs felt submerged in tar, heavy and unresponsive. The room around me was a nightmare made into flesh. A layer of soot covered every surface.

A fire?

My eyes shifted to the faint light from what I vaguely recalled as the bathroom door.

Following its glow, my gaze landed on the far side of the bed, where a small, charred figure lay beneath a ragged ashen sheet. My breath caught in my throat. Icy fingers of dread wrapped around my bones.

A scream threatened to claw its way out of my chest, but all that emerged was a strangled gasp. I stumbled to my feet. The floor shifted beneath me. Fear gripped me, primal and unrelenting. Unsteady, I lurched forward. This couldn't be real, but the terror corroding my soul told me otherwise.

Who is this?

Is this…?

"No," I whispered, my voice drowned by the roaring in my ears. My pulse hammered in my veins as I took a hesitant step closer. "No, no, no..."

The figure was a grotesque parody of innocence frozen in time. It clutched a doll in its tiny, blackened hands. Thoughts tumbled over one another in a chaotic frenzy.

A child?

What happened here?

How did I not wake up sooner?

My hands quivered uncontrollably. Tremors coursed through me like the onset of a fever. As I reached out, I also longed to pull back. My fingers stiffened with dread, wanting to shield myself from the truth I knew lurked beneath that blanket. The air thickened with every breath, turning to sludge in my lungs.

I needed to get out.

I needed to breathe.

Spinning away from the charred figure,I bolted for the bathroom. The crackling of my footsteps on the gritty surface of the floor filled the eerie silence. The partially opened metal door slid back in full with a sharp hiss, and a sudden wave of cool air crashed over me as I stumbled in. My senses were shocked by the sensation after having been plowed over by heat and pungent smoke. The chill enveloped me, seeping into my bones, momentarily freezing the terror masticating the edges of my sanity.

A massive marble tub gleamed under the harsh light in the center of the room. Its surreal surface remained pristine, untouched by the chaos outside. It was filled with stagnant water that acted as a dark mirror. The room's illumination gleamed across its surface, hinting at something deeper that whispered safety—a refuge from the nightmare lurking beyond the door.

Gripping the tub's edge, knuckles white, I leaned over, staring into the liquid. My gaunt and haggard reflection stared back at me, sunken eyes and skin stretched tight with exhaustion. The water called to me, a silent promise of solace and escape. I felt an overwhelming urge to submerge myself, to wash away the grime and fear clinging to me. My breaths came in shallow, ragged gasps. Tears blurred my vision. The events of the past hours—*or was it days?*—pressed down on me.

I shook my head, my attention shifting back to the tub. I gripped my palms harder against the white marble, trying to keep myself grounded.

The water remained still as night. But then, there were their faces. Triad and Tivian, just eight years old, their sleeping expressions so peaceful and unaware of the chaos that would soon surround them. I watched the rise and fall of their chests, their small bodies wrapped in blankets, innocent and trusting.

Then I turned and left them.

Alone.

The brisk air bit at my skin, the sand pulling at my feet, dragging me toward the shore. Each step felt heavier than the last. The waves, dark and relentless, seemed to promise a way out from the guilt that weighed me down. The ocean's call tempting me... pulling me toward its depths.

But I found myself unfairly yanked back from that edge, pulled from the torrent of the sea just seconds before surrendering to the euphoria of drowning. The bitter irony lingered: someone rescued me that night, yet I would never know who they were before leaving me on that beach.

The burning pain in my chest flared anew at the memory of the accusations that the Cird kidnapped me. How easy it became to cast them as the villains of my own story, pointing fingers at shadows while ignoring my own darkness. I let those claims stand, wrapping myself in their false security. The truth proved far more terrifying. I was the architect of my own suffering. My despair fueled the fire, and my choices led to that night of horror. Yet, I couldn't bring myself to admit it. Guilt settled like ash in my lungs, choking me with the realization that the true monster always resided within me.

I was drowning in my regret, and that felt more insidious than the water that once threatened to consume me.

I failed to escape this world, a bitter poison that coursed through my veins. I only wanted to silence the voices that whispered my worthlessness. I begged to find peace in the cold, dark depths.

The water below me rippled like a mocking mirror, its surface eerily calm. It contorted my reflection into something malformed and unrecognizable.

My heart pounded in my ears, each beat a harsh reminder of my existence. I remained here, alive and haunted by my demons of desperation. I felt as if I were being pulled apart from within, torn between the suffocating guilt of my failed escape and the paralyzing fear of what awaited me outside the door.

I forced myself back into the bedroom, and the sight of the scorched remains struck me in the gut. Too small to be the boys. Too small to be

Blue…

Evie.

My baby sister.

My world shattered. A wave of nausea washed over me.

The room spun. My vision blurred until I spotted a discarded matchbox and an accelerant container at the foot of the bed. I trembled as I raised my hands to my face. The noxious odor clung to my skin like a curse.

"This can't be," I whispered, repeating the words until they felt like a chant. My knees buckled, and I crashed to the floor. "No, no, no." Sobs tore through my chest, desperate cries for answers. *How could this have happened? How could I have let this happen?*

I failed. Failed to end my torment. Failed to protect those I loved most. Despair surged through me like a storm, leaving me trembling and weak. I staggered to my feet, muscles quaking, and stumbled toward the bathroom once more.

My eyes were drawn to the verdant greenery covering the base of the tub that hadn't been there before. *Or had it?* The pale blue blooms stood out against the sterile white of the room. *Serenith.* The sturdy clusters of flowers insulting my deep-seated agony.

My mother taught me that serenith carried Sertoda's essence and grew in our land's sun-soaked hills. A powerful, sacred herb. Its minty scent warded off evil and symbolized hope and defense.

But I had seized the serenith not as protection but as a last, frantic measure to shield my siblings. With trembling hands, I had crushed its petals and leaves and brewed them into a elixir I hoped would numb their senses and consciousness.

The haunting image of the charred figure returned to the forefront of my mind. The fragility of life became a truth I could no longer ignore. The darkness I fought to keep at bay finally caught up to me, swallowing me whole—

You're the best person for the job, Sprout's voice echoed in my head.

I choked on my tears as an image of Evie's tangled curls and Blue's back as she slept stumbled into my thoughts.

"They're alive… This isn't real." I shook my head violently.

This is a nightmare.

A serrated thought pierced through the fog: *This is Mass. They created this.*

I needed to understand why. Why I was here.

What it all meant. What dark purpose lay behind this terrifying recreation of my past.

They want to break me. No, I would not survive by giving in to terror.

Steeling myself, I reached for strength I didn't know existed. Falling to my knees, I plunged my hands into the flowers and began pulling the serenith.

This plant in my hand was real. But how?

It didn't matter. I could use it.

I would face the nightmare head-on.

I would survive.

I must.

The truths I sought lay within these walls, buried beneath layers of deception and terror. I would tear them free, no matter the cost.

Closing my eyes, I thought back to my mother's lessons. *Sertodan Balm can be used as a calming remedy* she had said as she ran her soft fingers along its leaves. *Its pale blue blossoms sharpen focus and fortify the spirit in times of crisis if chewed.*

Now, clutching a handful of its sprigs, I felt their delicate leaves brush against my skin. I needed their power. Clarity. And strength to soothe my anxieties in a way nothing else could. My eyes sprung open.

I crushed the flowers between my fingers, releasing their essence, and shoved the broken plant into my mouth. The bitter taste nearly made me gag, its sharpness like a slap across the face. Yet, that same bitterness jolted me awake, grounding me in reality.

As the pungent taste lingered on my tongue, I recalled my mother's rituals to invoke inner fortitude. "Strength flows through me like the ocean's tide," I murmured, echoing her words.

I pushed sweat-soaked curls from my face. If I couldn't wake from Mass's make-shift nightmare, I needed to face it with every ounce of strength I could summon. Serenith would no longer serve as a reminder of my past failures. It was calling me to action.

I refused to succumb to my surroundings. My family would be my guiding light.

Tivian.

Triad.

Blue.

Evie.

I repeated their names like a mantra.

I would not be a passive victim of my circumstances.

The Rite of Silent Strength
(A Sertodan Tradition):

In the fertile and sea-kissed lands of Sertoda, the Rite of Silent Strength remains a deeply revered tradition rooted in the people's connection to the sea and their ancestors. Surrounded by bountiful waters and lush soil, Sertodans have long understood that true strength comes not from dominating the land but from living in harmony with its rhythms.

The Rite of Silent Strength takes place during the calmest week of the year: when the tides are low and the seas offer a rare moment of tranquility. During this time, the people of Sertoda retreat to the shore, each standing alone in the sand facing the horizon. For three days, they maintain a vow of silence, listening only to the sounds of the ocean and their thoughts.

The silence, like the ebb and flow of the tides, teaches patience and flexibility. Participants are encouraged to reflect on the balance of life, the give-and-take of the sea, and their inner depths. The quiet allows them to confront their fears, doubts, and weaknesses, and through this introspection, they discover their personal reserves of strength.

Sertodans believe that just as the sea sustains life through its calm and its storms, so too must individuals find strength in both peace and adversity. The rite is a reminder that silence is not a weakness but a source of power—a way to connect with the strength within that can endure any challenge.

In pursuit of truth and understanding,
—H. Wilhoph

Chapter Nineteen

BETTA

A charred figure lay motionless on the bed, barely recognizable as an adolescent. The sheets that failed to protect them from the flames now cradled their remains. My heart clenched with recognition. Levity's nightmare.

The scars on my hands burned with the memory of that harrowing night, when I'd fought through a similar inferno. Smoke suffocating. Ash stung my eyes. Heat sapping my strength. I remembered my heart's frantic beat as I dragged terrified children from their beds, their tiny hands clutching mine with a trust that both empowered and shattered me. Their panicked cries still echoed in my ears. Those innocent faces haunted me still.

This struck too close.

A fisherman had found her body along the ocean shore after the Cird's attack. They'd set the fire that burned parts of her home, leaving her younger siblings to perish. The wreckage she faced now was more than a simulation—it echoed her deepest traumas. They were making her relive the agony of nearly losing everything: her family, her home, her very identity.

The screen shifted, plunging us into Dorian's nightmare.

Draven stepped closer to the screen.

A harsh, brutal desert landscape replaced the room. The sun blazed with a fury that cracked the very ground, casting tangled scars across the barren terrain. Sandstorms raged without mercy, their swirling clouds turning the world into a blinding void. Heat pounded down like a hammer on flesh and bone as Dorian stumbled through this hellscape; visible pools of sweat soaking his clothes.

His movements were sluggish, each step a monumental effort against the desert's might. The simulation showed his skin beginning to blister and tear from sun exposure. His chapped lips bled as dehydration threatened to set in.

Draven's hands balled into tight fists. He forced a slow, deep breath, trying to calm the tremor in his fingers.

Several other representatives' nightmares played out on the screens. Each one more horrifying than the last. Their suffering bore down on me. It suffocated. But I refused to buckle. I'd breathe through it. I'd think my way out. I wouldn't freeze. Each scenario revealed a personal hell, crafted with precision to target their fears, weaknesses, most intimate terrors.

It wasn't until Saria's scenario emerged on the screen that I noticed a subtle shift in Lyonal's demeanor—a tightening jaw, tension in his stance.

Her torment was different. The simulation trapped her in a tech-driven labyrinth of holographic projections and shifting data. Screens flashed relentless information. Numbers and images assaulted her with false alarms and dire warnings until she could no longer distinguish truth from illusion. Her mind unraveled under the constant barrage. A slow, creeping dread wrapped around her like a boa constrictor, squeezing the sanity from her thoughts.

The live feeds painted a haunting portrait of psychological warfare. Each scene hit me like a punch to the head, making it crystal clear how deep we were in this perverse system. We weren't just spectators—we were complicit if we didn't intervene. That realization boiled my blood. If we didn't fight back, we'd be no better than the bastards who orchestrated this Cird-forsaken hell.

The room fell silent, a familiar tension hung in the air between the three of us. The AI voice sliced through the stillness with its cold, clinical tone—the same soulless voice we endured in all our briefings:

```
Your roles in The Sanctioning require
active participation in the strategically
deployed tactics. Elisabetta Rahmani and
Captain Draven Ballister, you will over-
see the simulation environments, directly
escalating the representatives' psycho-
logical states. Your involvement must be
hands-on and absolute. Specifics have been
sent to your personal devices. Failure
to meet these expectations will result in
immediate and severe consequences.
```

This voice—devoid of empathy or life—echoed our grim reality. We were expected to engage in the torment we witnessed, to twist the screws tighter until our targets broke. Anger simmered beneath my skin.

The mechanical voice continued, cold and indifferent:

```
Lyonal Crestmore, you will now handle
simulation adjustments utilizing quantum
projection technology developed by Crest-
more Industries. Your role ensures envi-
ronments exacerbate fears and anxieties to
breaking points. This technology, a deriv-
```

```
ative of your own work, must be deployed
with precision. Any lapse will have dire
consequences.
```

The news landed like a slap to the face. Draven went rigid, his knuckles white against the table's edge. I pressed my palms against the cold metal, my jaw clenched. "Crestmore Industries," I murmured, the name a bitter taste on my tongue. Draven released a slow, deliberate breath, his silence speaking volumes.

Lyonal's fingers tapped once, twice against the table. He stared blankly at a spot beyond the room as his family's legacy emerged as the weapon breaking minds.

```
Failure to comply will lead to catastrophic
outcomes. Suffering is ensured for disobe-
dience. Should you falter, there will not
be hesitation to act with brutality.
```

The voice finished with the final word:

```
Obedience above all.
Sanctioned. United. One.
```

The reality of our directives crashed against us. Stakes were rising. Moral lines were blurring. Every wrong move could bring unimaginable consequences.

How could I be a part of this torture? The thought festered in my brain. As Sandric's mouthpiece, I'd believed my words only swayed and influenced—never harmed. I advocated for the policies set by the invisible hand and crafted justifications for regulations whether I agreed with them or not.

Indifference came easy when I stood at a distance. I could stand before crowds, speaking of stringent security measures or economic reforms, light-heartedly believing in the abstract good they represented. I never saw the shopkeepers who lost everything, the families struggling under new tax burdens. That distance between my words and their impact shielded me from their reality.

Now, they shoved a knife into my hand, demanding I wield it—or else. Anger burned deep. At the system. At myself. At my own helplessness. I would become their weapon against Sandric citizens. And worse, I knew the pain I would inflict because I'd endured it.

That thin shield between myself and the horrors? It crumbled under the blow of what I would be forced to do.

Draven's expertise suddenly felt vital—his war tactics no longer repulsive but necessary. We needed his instincts to play our part while gutting the system from within. His knack for navigating conflict and turning dire situations into leverage might be our only lifeline.

The screen outlined Lyonal's task in terrifying detail. He controlled the web of technology latched onto the minds of the representatives, weaving nightmares that manipulated their deepest fears with accuracy. Each adjustment could escalate the suffering, push them past breaking points. His influence could dial up their torment with a few change in settings.

I couldn't stomach it. Lyonal sitting there, hands on the controls, cranking up the agony like some sick experiment. Disgust rose in my throat. I leaned back, my thoughts churning. The more I uncovered, the more convinced I became—Trunta orchestrated this through him.

We needed to outplay him. Every move just as precise, just as cold. We needed to do this with a different goal—dismantling his influence and exposing the conspiracy. Not easy, but I sure as hell wouldn't sit idle and let this stand.

I glared across at him, the screen's flicker casting harsh shadows on his face. "How the hell can you sit there and do this?" My voice dripped venom. "You built a system to break people—to torture them. For what? All so Trunta can sink their claws deeper?

The next words burst from me. "Edward was a Perpetual Sense, just like you. He died during our Sanctioning. And now you've made it worse? Created a killing machine—and you don't even care. Hell, maybe you even like it."

Lyonal remained unfazed. His voice was cool as ever. "It was a heart attack," he said flatly, treating a council member's death like a statistic. "Unseen. A casualty of the system."

"A casualty of the system..." The words echoed—too familiar. General Ballister's voice rang in my ears. I shook my head, fresh anger rising, but I didn't wait for his hollow justifications.

My mind raced, trying to calculate our next steps. I was done playing by their rules. Done pretending we lacked power to fight back. Between Draven's expertise in war, my own buried strength...

We'd find a way to twist this back on them.

The Perils of Technological Advancement
(A Cautionary Reflection):

As we navigate an era of rapid technological advancement, I feel compelled to examine the benefits and the hidden dangers that accompany such progress.

In our pursuit of efficiency and connectivity, we risk surrendering our humanity. The allure of smart devices and artificial intelligence is tempting, yet it often comes at the cost of authentic human interaction. Each swipe on our screens fosters a growing isolation, where virtual relationships replace genuine connections.

Moreover, I cannot ignore the motives behind these technological trends. The alignment of new advancements with the interests of those in power raises unsettling questions. As algorithms dictate our information consumption, we may unwittingly become passive recipients of a manufactured reality.

With the imminent arrival of surveillance technologies masquerading as safety measures, we must remain vigilant. The commodification of personal data threatens our autonomy and calls for ethical scrutiny. It is our responsibility as scholars to advocate for transparency and accountability in the face of these changes.

Let us not allow the seductive promise of progress to overshadow the dangers lurking beneath the surface.

In pursuit of truth and understanding,
—H. Wilhoph

Chapter Twenty

BETTA

Deep into the night, silence stretched thin with expectation. I'd managed to slip out of my room unnoticed, leaving behind an array of sensory decoys that would fool the guards stationed outside my door. A coin-sized device emitted subtle heat signatures, mimicking my breathing beneath the blankets. A thin strip of reflective film near the window cast shadows to fool the cameras. Draven slipped them to me after our briefing with a smirk and a whispered word to use them tonight.

But it wasn't just the devices that got me out. A concealed vent panel offered just enough space to crawl through. While the guards stood stationed at the door, I slipped into the vent and dropped silently down into a maintenance corridor.

Draven would do the same. This meeting needed to stay hidden.

I stepped into the alcove and the air felt colder than I remembered, the stone alive with some eerie, unspoken awareness. Draven leaned against the wall, arms crossed, his focus on me the second I arrived. Though still, his stance held a readiness to spring.

"Betta," he greeted, his voice barely breaking the quiet. He motioned for me to sit, but I remained standing.

I began, wasting no time, "It's all connected—the plotting with Saria, Crestmore Industries, the tech in The Sanctioning, everything."

A sharp acknowledgment flickered in Draven's eyes. He straightened from his position against the wall, stepping closer to me. "I knew it. Trunta pulls the strings. Lyonal is in deeper than I thought."

"Worse," I said, frustration rising like the tide. "They've built this nightmare. This system. If his company developed it, he's in complete control."

Draven began to pace, his hands curling into fists. "He made the tool to destroy minds, and he'll wield it like it's nothing."

I swallowed hard, feeling the heat of anger prick at the edges of my control. "We have to stop him. We can't just play along. We need proof tying Trunta and Lyonal to this mess. Something we can expose. If we don't, countless people will suffer."

Draven turned back to me, determination hardening his features. "We will. But we have to be smart about it. One wrong move exposes us as traitors."

My pulse raced with the urgency as Draven extended his hand, palm open—a silent offer of solidarity. His eyes bore into mine, searching for any sign of doubt. "Are you with me, Betta? If we take this on, I need to know you're all in. There's no turning back once we start."

"I'm with you," I said, the words becoming a vow to myself as much as to him. I grasped his outstretched hand in mine. "Whatever Lyonal or Trunta throws at us."

Standing before him, I recognized this had become my battle too. Ready or not, I'd been drawn into the heart of a revolution.

His dark eyes held mine with an intensity that sent a shiver through me. "Trunta's grip on the system is ironclad, but even iron shatters if you strike right. When Dorian takes his seat as Noble Warrior, we can use his position to bring everything into the light."

"Guess your intel was spot-on after all. This term's Sanctioning is pure hell," I said, releasing his hand and crossing my arms. "Those simulations... they're beyond anything we imagined."

Draven ran a hand over his head, his silence an admission in its own right.

My thoughts flashed to Levity's room. The smoke. The flames. "It's brutal, and I'm sick knowing I haven't done a damn thing to stop it yet."

Draven glanced at me, eyes sharp. "There's no pretending, Betta. This is real."

I scoffed, fists clenching. "And Lyonal's pulling the strings. We've got to find proof, something inside the control room maybe?"

Draven folded muscled arms across his broad chest. "Lyonal's been set up as the key player. If they put him in charge of the simulations, it's because they trust him. They control The Sanctioning through him."

Inspiration struck me like a bolt of lightning. "Garon."

Draven's expression flickered, the barest hint of hesitation before his face hardened again. "Garon?" He questioned.

"Yeah. Garon," I leaned forward, voice brightening. "He's not just another representative, Draven. He's Dobia's prodigy—a genius. Media's top tech pick for a reason. No one understands systems like he does. He'll crack it wide open in half the time anyone else would need."

Draven shifted, eyes narrowing as he looked away. For a second, he appeared jealous, but I didn't have time for ego.

"He's the best shot we've got," I pressed. "You know it. He understands these systems, the tech, the code—all of it. We need him."

A muscle ticked in his jaw. His hands flexed, then relaxed. Finally, he nodded. "Alright. You're right. It's a smart move."

I could see him recalculating, weighing the options. The initial flash of jealousy faded into a more tactical resolve.

"It's a good idea, Betta." He exhaled, the tension in his shoulders easing as he looked back at me, this time with a glimmer of respect. "Garon's got the skills. If we're going to pull this off, we'll need every advantage we can get. He can help us lessen the effects of the simulations and search for the communications we need." Draven spoke now through gritted teeth, his words clipped but resolute. "Setting aside personal differences, I can recognize who will optimize our efforts."

I felt certain Garon possessed the skill to hack the system. And with the unrest in his territory, I could also assume he'd be on our side. That made the plan all the more tempting.

Draven reached into his cargo pocket, pulling out a synthetic material rolled and tied with a thin cord. "I've been working on this for weeks," he muttered, spreading a detailed map on the packed dirt between us, smoothing the rolled edges. "Swiped it during one of the briefings. No one's noticed it's missing yet."

We crouched together, studying the intricate blueprint sketched in dark ink.

"The layout's complex," he traced a path with his finger. "Representatives' rooms here, Leadership Room adjacent, and the control room—where Lyonal monitors everything." His finger moved with purpose. "But here's what's interesting: The simulations drain an obscene amount of energy. That's the real reason the halls go dark once The Sanctioning starts—they can't light them and run the simulations at full capacity. They made darkness part of their design, keeping representatives stumbling both literally and figuratively."

I nodded, understanding the cruel logic. "And the guards?"

"Only two allowed in at a time. Surveillance is sparse—they must've figured the simulations, the darkness, and the maze-like design would be enough to prevent any real escape attempts. Only the highest-level security personnel, like Lyonal, sees all the feeds. Guards work blind most of the time."

Draven's finger lingered over the control room. "So that's our opportunity. If we can get in here and tap into their systems, we might find what we are looking for."

I nodded, absorbing the details. The proximity of the rooms to each other made our plan more dangerous than first anticipated. "And this section?" I asked, pointing toward a corridor snaking to the right.

"That leads to the backside of the recovery room. Beyond that," he moved to the lower corner, "the tunnel system connecting to our living quarters and this alcove."

I shot him a challenging look. "And what about Lyonal? How the hell do we lure that bastard out of the control room without him catching on?"

Draven's stare intensified. He rubbed the coarse hair on his chin. "We need to orchestrate a diversion that's both significant and subtle. Compelling enough to draw him away without raising suspicion. Your role will be to handle that aspect."

Dread surged through me. The thought of leveraging Lyonal made my skin crawl. Every method that flashed through my mind clashed with my sense of morality. This wasn't just strategy anymore—it was a storm of conflicting emotions and dirty decisions.

"With Garon, managing the tech, we can find the evidence. But you need to keep Lyonal distracted. As long as we avoid the marked areas," he motioned to red x's scattered across the map, "we should be able to execute our plan without detection."

The alcove's shadows pulsed with each flicker of the sconce, as if the old world itself were casting its approval. Cool air, heavy with the scent of damp stone and soil, filled my lungs.

"First and foremost we'll need to extract Garon from The Sanctioning without raising suspicion."

I nodded, the strain evident in my voice. "How do we create a story that will keep any guards from questioning Garon's sudden absence from his simulation?"

A thin smile curved Draven's lips, revealing a confidence that never seemed to waver. "Our public disturbance in the meeting hall earlier will play nicely into that."

Unease knotted in my chest. The testosterone-fueled standoff before the luncheon—sharp words, tension brimming beneath the surface. Draven had held his ground unshaken, but that volatile moment still prickled at my nerves. I didn't know what he might have in mind now, but I hoped it wouldn't lead to a unfavorable or even dangerous altercation.

I squared my shoulders, determination igniting in my chest. "I'll keep the asshole's attention," I declared with a wide grin. "I think I might have an idea on how to do that."

Draven's jaw tightened, concern breaking his hard exterior. "Good. We need to move fast. Dorian enduring another damn minute at the hands of Lyonal…" His voice roughened. "It's unacceptable."

The alcove's dim glow flickered across Draven's face, revealing tension etched beneath his projected confidence. His shoulders rounded slightly as if shielding himself from his own worry.

I bit my lip, studying him as he rolled the map. The silence stretched, thick with unspoken fears. Unable to hold back my concern any longer, I asked, "Draven, how do you… cope with knowing Dorian is trapped in that torment? Being left in the desert–"

His hands froze, eyes finding real estate on the ground. "It's a battle." His voice barely rose above a whisper. "He's forced to relive our father's harshest tests. The desert almost broke him. Seeing him struggle again, knowing I can't intervene…" His mask slipped, revealing something raw beneath. He spread one leg and then the other out and leaned back against the wall. His lips pressed into a thin, trembling line, as if holding back words or maybe even tears.

The sight pierced through me. My chest tightened as his eyes, shadowed and distant, fought against visible anguish. Previous judgments faded as I truly saw him.

I scooted my body over and sat next to him against the wall, leaning my head against his rigid shoulder. "I can't imagine the torment—for him inside, and you out here."

Draven turned his body to face me; his almost-black eyes filled with a storm of conflict. The vulnerability struck me deeply, the honesty of his emotions creating a profound sense of intimacy.

Without allowing myself to overthink, I reached out, fingers brushing the supple leather covering his chest. The gentle touch felt charged with electricity. Draven watched my hand travel until I stopped just above his heart.

His breath caught as his stare fell to my lips.

Draven lifted a calloused hand to my cheek. His featherlight touch sent a ripple of sensation through me. We seemed caught in a shared orbit of emotions.

"Betta," he murmured, his voice low and aching. "I…" His voice trailed off, leaving the words pregnant with meaning.

Do I want this closeness? The thought both terrified me and stirred something tantalizing deep. My hand twitched against his chest, torn.

His thumb brushed my cheek with a tenderness I didn't know he was capable of. Draven's brow softened, yet the intensity of the moment remained, as if he grappled with the implications too.

"What are we doing?" I whispered, trying hard to hide the tremble.

Draven's hand trailed from my face down my neck to my shoulder. Then my arm. Each new spot ignited a heat that seared through my skin straight to my core. The world narrowed to just us, leaving only my thundering heartbeat matching the energy crackling between us.

"I don't know," Draven admitted, his voice almost broken. "But I can't ignore how deeply connected I feel to you."

I searched his face, tracing the sharp lines of his jaw and the curve of his full lips, so agonizingly close. Every inch between us pulsed with possibility, as my chest tightened, caught in the war between caution and desire.

His hand returned to my face and thumb brushed the corner of my mouth. I leaned into his touch, unable to resist the pull any longer.

"I feel it too," I breathed, watching as resolve hardened in his eyes—the same resolve that saw him through every battle.

He leaned in slowly, his breath mingling with mine. The first brush of his lips felt tentative; a question. The second—ah, the second ignited like fire, consuming the confusion and hesitation in its wake.

His kiss both demanded and promised; fierce, yet tender. My hand fisted the leather beneath it, pulling him closer. His arm wrapped around my waist, pressing me against him with a possessive intensity that sent a current through my system.

The world ceased to exist; the only reality lay in the press of his lips against mine and how our bodies fit together like two pieces of the same puzzle. Every touch, every caress stoked the fire between us. There was no going back.

When we finally broke apart, breathless and reeling, I kept my eyes shut for a heartbeat longer, savoring the sensation of his lips on mine, his warmth, and the scent of leather and mint. The alcove charged with new tension—no longer about survival or strategy, but something deeper that thrilled and terrified me.

My lashes fluttered open to find him watching me, his gaze as vulnerable as I felt. I licked my bottom lip, still tasting his kiss. Despite everything, I allowed myself to feel something I'd been resisting for a long time.

Hope.

Draven released a heavy breath. "Betta." My name left his lips like a desperate request, cut short as he claimed my mouth again. This time, I didn't shut the world from my view. I drank him in as I opened myself to him. He took the invitation like a hungry beast. He grabbed my waist and pulled me onto his lap.

Our lips moved with the need to escape, to forget the perilous path ahead. His hand at the nape of my neck sent a thrill through me as he traced his mouth over my jawline. Every touch held a promise of what could be if we allowed ourselves this brief moment of reprieve.

But even as the heat built between us, reality clawed at my mind. The connection I craved felt right, yet fraught with complications I couldn't ignore. Still, I pressed closer, feeling the wild thrum of his heartbeat beneath my fingers.

I closed the space between us, my breasts meeting his chest. His arm tightened around my waist as if he feared I might slip away. The sensation of his strength, his warmth against me was intoxicating.

A thousand thoughts raced through my mind.

I jerked back.

The closeness was suddenly unbearable.

Images flooded in—Levity's and Dorian's torment. Disgust for Lyonal choked me.

I fought for a steady breath.

"I can't," I pressed my hands to his chest, regret heavy in the words. Pushing out of his embrace, I forced myself to erect the emotional walls that protected me for so long. "We need to stop. We need to focus."

Our intimacy dissolved as quickly as it came on, leaving only our plan and the world we fought. Draven's hands fell to stabilize himself on the ground, his expression shifting between understanding and hurt. Cold clarity of our reality replaced the heat between us.

My thoughts churned. Trust felt like navigating a minefield. My connection with Draven formed through shared danger and emotional upheaval—was that even healthy?

I stamped down the urge for his touch. This distraction could jeopardize everything. Drawing a deep breath, I centered myself. "We need to set up Lyonal. That's the priority. I'll create the diversion, and you'll extract Garon without raising any flags." As if it needed repeating.

Draven nodded. "We'll make it work. I'll have Garon ready."

With a final glance at Draven, I pushed to my feet and walked away, leaving our shared moment in the secret stone alcove.

The Transformation of Dobia
(A Cultural Reflection on Technological Intrusion):

Dobia, the snow-clad mountainous territory of Sandric, has long stood as a bastion of rustic beauty and ancient traditions. Its dense forests and secret cave systems nurture a culture intimately connected to the rhythms of nature. However, the recent infusion of technology raises questions about the motives behind this shift and its implications for the future.

As Dobia begins to adopt advancements once confined to Trunta, I can't help but speculate. The pressure to modernize may stem from a desire to escape historical marginalization. For too long, Dobia has been overshadowed by the more technologically advanced territories, often viewed as an underdeveloped outlier. In their quest for recognition and equality, the Dobians might believe that embracing technology is the key to elevating their status.

However, such aspirations come with potential risks. The introduction of modern tools could inadvertently erode the cultural foundations that have defined Dobia for generations. The balance between progress and preservation hangs precariously in the air. Moreover, the increase in technological presence may reflect external pressures, perhaps even orchestrated by neighboring territories that view Dobia's rugged breath as a threat.

As we observe this unfolding narrative, we must ask: Will Dobia rise to meet the challenge of modernization while safeguarding its cultural identity? The choices made today will shape the legacy of this resilient territory for generations to come.

In pursuit of truth and understanding,

—H. Wilhoph

Chapter Twenty-One

LEVITY

I dug my fingers into my palms. The small pain sharpened my focus for what felt like the millionth time. It had become harder to recognize how long I'd been awake or how long I'd spent in the bathroom, trying to piece myself back together. My body ached. My mind was sluggish from the broken rhythm of sleep, no longer discerning the patterns it once followed.

As I walked out of the bathroom, careful where I stepped, the charred remains lay before me like a haunting specter. The smoldered walls, blackened and scarred, still radiated heat, an echo of the fire's wrath. Smoke lingered in the air, thick and suffocating.

I rubbed my eyes, desperate to shake off the surreal haze that clung to my mind.

This isn't a dream.

There is no waking up.

It was a nightmare that refused to fade. The pain in my throat burned with every breath, the gritty taste of soot coating my tongue. Fear blistered through my veins like poison.

"Tivian. Triad. Blue. Evie." I repeated to myself.

I grabbed my boots from the bedside, wiping my feet clean and stuffing them back on. I approached the door that led back into the hallway, my heart pounding. Stepping in front of the metal like I did just the day before…

Had it been the day before?

How many days have passed? Or was it only hours?

Before my thoughts spiraled, I shook my head. I sucked on the Sertodan Balm in the back of my mouth, doing my best to keep my grasp on the small amount of clarity I retained. The door didn't budge. With no handle, I couldn't simply release myself from the confines of this Cird-forsaken room. My heart pounded with new vigor. Exasperated, I turned, placing my back against the warm metal, and sunk to the floor.

I was trapped.

Trapped in my nightmare.

Trapped in The Sanctioning.

I scanned the room again, focusing on every corner as I sought evidence that might justify the nightmare unfolding wasn't real. The air thickened with the pungent scent of burnt remnants. My attention fell upon the small form lying motionless in the bed. Each heartbeat that echoed in the silence of my mind urged me to turn away, yet something compelled me to confront the horror.

Rising unsteadily to my feet, I leaned against the wall for support as I navigated the debris scattered across the floor. The crunch of shattered glass and brittle fragments underfoot bounced through the air like a discordant symphony to the horror that awaited me. Each step felt heavy. The gloom deepened as I approached the bed. My breath came in labored pants. My heart raced.

Crouching beside the remains, I peeled away the blackened sheets that clung to the body. I barely stifled a gasp, bile rising in my throat as the last singed threads pulled away. I pressed my fingers to my lips, trembling against the visceral revulsion that threatened to come out of me.

What remained formed a dismal canvas of melted skin and exposed bone. The eye sockets gaped like sinister voids. Ragged strips of flesh hung limply, leaving behind a grotesque corpse that bore witness to unimaginable suffering.

The chilling scene whispered a haunting truth. This was my fault. My legs buckled from under me, and I collapsed onto my knees, the rough debris tearing my pants and biting into my skin.

I reached out with shaky hands, desperately trying to connect with the remains before me. My voice, raw and choked with emotion, broke the silence. "I didn't mean for any of this," I cried out. "I swear, I didn't mean for this to happen. I was so weak… so lost. I didn't know what I was doing."

My hands, slick with sweat, pressed against my face as I sobbed. "I wasn't okay," I continued, my voice a desperate plea for absolution. "I thought I was strong enough to handle it, but I was wrong. I didn't know… I didn't know how to stop the thoughts."

Tivian. Triad. Blue. Evie.

Their names echoed in my mind.

They are alive.

Tears streamed down my face, mingling with the grime and ash that coated my skin. Each breath felt like a jagged knife, cutting through the suffocating guilt that bound me. "I'm so grateful," I whispered hoarsely. "I'm so thankful you were saved."

The suffocating atmosphere of the room seemed to pulse with my despair, but amidst the haze of grief and confusion, a flicker of clarity pierced through the darkness. Evie's missing incisor. I forced myself to breathe deeply, dragging my focus back to the present. It had fallen out a few days before my departure for Mass. If the teeth did not match, this wasn't real; it amounted to nothing more than an elaborate fabrication. If Evie truly lay before me, this offered a means to identify her.

I leaned in, squinting through my tear-blurred vision. I carefully pried open the mouth, dreading what I might find. I pulled down the flesh that had once been their lips. The warm texture under my frightened fingers slid as I pushed aside the charred remnants.

No sign of the missing bottom incisor. My body quaked as the real-ization sank in—

"You are not my Sprout."

The missing tooth, the small yet significant detail, granted me a lifeline of hope. A tooth remained.

The deception of this simulation laid bare before me, and with it came a surge of fierce doggedness like I'd never experienced before. I wiped away the vestiges of my anguish, my resolve hardening as I dragged myself upright from the floor.

Each step toward the door became a reclaiming of hidden strength. I pushed through the debris, every footfall filled with purpose. This nightmare would not claim me any longer.

As I approached the mechanical door, I recalled Tivian's makeshift lessons on mechanical systems. Once, he rigged our house's pantry lock using a spoon and a bit of wire. The troublemaker grinned as the door popped open to reveal my hidden stash of sweets. Simple objects, he'd said, could sometimes trick sensors into activating mechanisms that otherwise seemed impenetrable.

I scanned the floor, spotting a shard from a broken mirror glittering menacingly. I ripped the sleeve off my blouse, wrapping the fabric around my hand. Then, carefully, I picked up the shard, trying not to cut myself.

My heart pounded in my chest as I maneuvered the piece of mirror, positioning it strategically between the door and its frame. Maybe insert-ing it at the right angle would trick the sensor into thinking the door was misaligned. Would it open or set off alarms?

Unsure but unwilling to stay a second longer, I wedged the shard in place, bracing myself as I adjusted it with painstaking precision. The glass slipped in my grip, and I hissed, afraid I might have cut myself.

I jumped back when a hum filled the silence.

Perspiration dampened my forehead, and I pushed my curls away from my face. I stood back and watched with bated anticipation. For a moment, the world seemed to freeze as the door's sensors processed the interference.

Then, with a mechanical whirr and a faint gasp, the door slowly slid open. The sound of its movement became a victorious symphony to my ears. I felt a surge of relief and determination, knowing that each obstacle I overcame brought me closer to escaping this nightmare.

Relief washed over me, but I couldn't dwell on it. I slipped through the narrow gap and into the hallway, the inhuman quiet pressing down on me.

The hall was swallowed by a darkness that blotted out all traces of light. The hum of the facility vanished, replaced by a suffocating silence that pressed against my ears. My heart pounded as I moved cautiously toward the room across from mine, where Thomas entered what seemed like ages ago. We pledged to stick together, to guard each other against whatever horrors came our way. Now, more than ever, I needed someone.

I needed him.

I approached the door with my shard still firmly in my wrapped hand, ready to apply the same principles I had used before. With a steadier grip, I inserted the mirror into the narrow gap between the door and the frame. My fingers fumbled, working to align it with the latch mechanism. The darkness made every movement a challenge.

With my ear to the metal, I listened intently for any sound of movement within the room, my breath catching in my throat. The faintest click and the door gasped open a fraction, just enough to allow me entry. My pulse quickened. I crawled through.

"Thomas," I whispered.

No answer.

My footsteps echoed off the marble floor, fearing every shadow hid a new threat, every corner a potential trap.

The sight hit me hard. Light filtered through a cracked window, casting a sickly jaundiced glow.

Stained, tattered blankets were strewn over a sagging, filthy mattress. Years of dirt fused into every fiber, soaking the bed in misery.

The walls were worse. Streaked with grime, paint peeling to reveal the rotting structure. The stench of decay hung in the air, thick and suffocating. Each breath tasted like mold.

Thomas slumped against the wall, surrounded by rusted furniture like skeletal remains. A crooked chair. A battered crate serving as a makeshift table.

I weaved my way toward him, careful of scattered belongings and rancid food that clawed at my throat. The man in front of me no longer resembled the humble Thomas I said goodbye to. His clothes hung in tattered shreds as if the fabric itself gave up and surrendered to his suffering.

Nothing here looked like the world Thomas or even I knew. It wasn't a room—it was a prison, trapping Thomas in a nightmare of what I could only surmise to be the worst of a previous life. Or one he feared.

"Thomas," I said gently, kneeling beside him. "It's me, Levity. I'm here to help."

His hollow eyes barely reflected the dim light. When he looked up, the movement came slow and painful. His gaze remained unfocused, lost in confusion and fear. He stared at me with unfocused eyes as if he couldn't believe I existed—or, perhaps, wished I didn't.

He searched my face, and gradually, recognition set in. Then sheer bewilderment. "Levity?" he croaked.

Before he fully grasped the situation, his attention swept over his surroundings. His eyes widened, and he began trembling. Panic set in like a wild storm, his breaths coming in ragged gasps.

"No... no, this can't be real," he muttered, clutching his head. "This can't be happening. I've worked so hard."

I quickly reached into my pocket and pulled out a small amount of serenith blossoms. "Thomas, you need to calm down. Here, chew these." I opened my hand.

His trembling fingers reached out. "What are these?" he asked, his voice quaking.

"They're serenith blossoms," I explained, keeping my voice soothing as I placed the petals in his palm. "They'll help calm you and clear your mind. I use them to help my anxiety."

Thomas stared at me. "Where did you get this?"

"They are a part of my nightmare," I admitted.

Thomas hesitated, then, seeing no other option, he brought the pale blue petals to his mouth and began to chew.

Minutes ticked by as the flowers took effect. His breathing steadied. I sank beside him, placing a gentle hand on his forearm, trying to offer him reassurance.

"Thomas, we're in The Sanctioning. They're using our rooms to simulate our deepest fears." I softened my voice, channeling the many nights I calmed my siblings' worries while hiding my own fear.

Thomas's warm brown eyes, once determined, now held a dull, vacant glaze. His shoulders slumped under an invisible force. "They must have drugged us at the luncheon," I continued, barely whispering. "So, we wouldn't notice them creating these elaborate effects."

He stared at me, the flicker of panic hardening into something deeper. His jaw clenched. "This... this is my worst nightmare," his voice shook. "I've known poverty like a shadow. But this," he waved his hand across the room with trembling fingers, "this is failure. This is me crumbling into nothing, just like my father. It's the future I've fought to avoid."

His jaw set hard. Anger simmering beneath his next words. "I've spent my whole damn life pushing through. Every grueling day, every sacrifice, everything I gave up—led to this moment. I can't let it slip away. I won't." Resentment crept into his voice. "Do you know what it's like? Watching everything fall apart because the one person who's meant to hold it together—my father—couldn't. When my mom died, he just... he gave up. Disappeared. Let me wither. I was just a kid." He clenched his fists, "I don't have the luxury to fail."

Tears threatened to spill from his eyes. "I need this. I need to be someone. I need people to see that I matter—or what the hell was the point of everything?"

I breathed deep. His words hit so close to what could have been my siblings' reality. "You've always mattered, Thomas," I said, touching his chin to raise his eyes to mine. "Even if you didn't realize it."

He looked at me, expression unreadable. "What are you talking about?"

I hesitated, pulling my knees to my chest, eyes falling to my boots. The memory spilled out. "I remember watching you on the docks when I was fifteen. You were hauling crates, working yourself raw like you always did. Then, this old woman dropped her coin pouch. You stopped everything. Set down your load to help her search for it. You didn't care about how long it would take or what it would cost you. You ducked in and out of stalls. Asked other merchants if they'd seen it. That's who you are. Who you've always been."

His brow furrowed, and he gave a light scoff. "So what? Being decent doesn't pay the bills. Doesn't get recognition. I need more than that. I need this."

"Do you really?" I questioned. "Is this worth breaking yourself? Losing that person. This isn't a challenge—it's torture, Thomas. They're trying to destroy you, not test you. I know you're strong. But this... this isn't the way to prove anything."

He frowned. He sat rigid, knees bent, head low. "I have to see it through. If I don't, then what's left? Going back to nothing? To The Divide? To what?"

I exhaled slowly, composing the truest answer I could form. "The Divide doesn't have to be a place of sorrow or failure. It's where I laugh with my siblings, where we learn hard lessons, yes, but we come out stronger. We aren't weighed down by regulations, by the expectations of people who don't know us. We just live. And life there may be simple, but it's real. Filled with love... resilience. You don't have to fear that."

His jaw worked. "Maybe for you. But for me? It's empty. I've got no one waiting for me there. No family to fall back on. It'll just be... me."

"Then let me share mine." I said, gripping his hands. "My family would welcome you without a second thought. You don't have to prove your worth by surviving this nightmare, Thomas. You've already proven it in a hundred small ways you didn't even realize. You matter—whether you're holding the Noble Warrior position or carrying crates at the docks. You matter."

A faint smile touched his lips, some of the hardness in his expression easing.

"Evie would absolutely worship you," I went on, a warmth spread through my chest. "She'd mirror everything—your stance, your words. And Tivian..." I laughed softly. "He'd follow you everywhere, pestering you to show him every trick and skill you know, dying to measure up. He'd be right at your heels."

Thomas chuckled, a spark of hope in our darkness. For a precious moment, we shared that future where he belonged.

His eyes held mine. "And if I let this go? If I walk away?"

"It's not walking away." I leaned closer. "You are choosing better. You are choosing to end their game. The approval you need? It's been right in front you—in the people around you. You just need to see it."

He looked down, absorbing my words. "So… what do we do?"

"We get out of here. We find Marmarie and stick together like we promised." I huffed. "She knew something felt off about Mass. No wonder The Sanctioning stays secret. No one would accept this."

Thomas's shoulders loosened up, lifting his head, the hesitation still in his grip. "What if we're supposed to finish? What if this is part of the test?"

I glanced away, uncertain how to share my growing understanding. "I don't know. I don't think this proves anything good anymore." I paused. "I don't know what's waiting for us if we finish, but… can you really trust it? What if it only gets worse?"

He swallowed hard, attention dropping to the floor once more. "But how do we know leaving is better?"

I sighed, gripping his hand tight. "We don't. But look at what they've done. They made your deepest fear real, used it against you."

I opened up to him then—about my room's horrors. I spoke of the serenith I gave my siblings that night. About the fire that could have been. My baby sister's small lifeless body in the ashes. I shared it all. Guilt. Despair. How I'd hidden behind the lie of a Cird attack to escape the truth. I let him see it. The same way this system tore me open, I bore the worst of myself to him, but on my own terms.

When he finally spoke, his voice was steadier, reclaiming a lost conviction. "What you've carried… I can't even imagine that weight. You were just a child yourself, overwhelmed and desperate, who needed support. I know that better than anyone. I could have made a decision like that myself."

"We don't owe them this. We don't have to prove ourselves through torture." I hesitated, then added, "And honestly, if this is how they treat their own—what kind of system is that? Why would you want to be part of something that hides this from everyone?"

The decision pulled at and tensed his features. Years of work balanced on this moment. "*Walk away.*"

An alarm suddenly blared:

```
Attention, representatives. Return to your
rooms immediately. Non-compliance will re-
sult in restricted access to food and
basic necessities. Continued defiance will
escalate to imprisonment of loved ones.
This is your final directive. Obedience
above all.


Sanctioned. United. One.
```

We exchanged a look.

Words unnecessary.

Our hands locked together as we ran for the door.

The Unseen Strength of Partnership
(Reflections on Wilhelmina):

In life, strength often reveals itself in moments of quiet resilience. I have long studied the cultural bonds that unite people through adversity. Still, it was my own partnership with Wilhelmina that I have witnessed the most profound example of enduring strength. During the birth of our five children, she showed a fortitude that rose above any trial or hardship I've encountered.

Though deeply tied to Sertoda's fertile shores, her roots seem to reach even further back to a lineage older than many know. There is a quiet wisdom in her people, one that whispers of knowledge passed to every generation. I've often marveled at the way she moves through life with an awareness I struggle to fully understand—a connection to the terra, to the natural rhythms that govern not just the tides but life itself.

Partnerships like ours thrive when strength flows not from one but between both. There are moments when we must draw from the well of our own courage, and moments when we must draw on others we trust to provide the strength we lack.

Together, we stand not merely as individuals but as a testament to the power of unity.

In pursuit of truth and understanding,
—H. Wilhoph

Chapter
Twenty-Two

BETTA

Starlight cloaked the world outside. I had tossed and turned in my room, battling elusive sleep during the few moments I allowed myself to rest. Fatigue clung to me, settling in my bones and pounding in my head. That ache drove me forward. They'd been in their simulations for over twelve hours, cycling through the torment and fear just corridors away. Draven and I had agreed to enact our plan at dawn, hoping swift action might lessen the representatives' suffering—if that was even possible.

My hand hovered over a particular representative's room when an alarm pierced the hallway's silence. The shrill wail had me stumbling back, pulse racing.

Did I trigger this? The sound ricocheted down the hall, scattering my thoughts into chaos.

I froze before snapping back to focus. Draven's mission to retrieve Garon flashed in my mind. A representative left their room—that made more sense. If Garon was caught, everything would fall apart. No time to waste. I needed to distract Lyonal.

The cold, metallic door slid open at my touch with a soft hiss. Our titles granted us access to every room—a privilege that now felt as much a burden as a tool. Anyone watching the camera feed would see my actions as part of my directive, fulfilling my role in guiding the simulations from the ground level. Exactly as I intended. I wanted Lyonal glued to the monitors, locked on my every move.

I stepped into the tech storm fueling Saria's nightmare. Screens buzzed and glowed with eerie light, each displaying fragments of Saria's fears.

Wires snaked across the floor, some sparking, others hanging like mechanical vines from the ceiling. Burnt plastic and ozone filled my lungs. Servers hummed in tune with Saria's erratic breathing, creating a symphony of distress.

Blue light flashed across her face. Dark circles rimmed Saria's wide eyes, swollen veins pulsing around her irises as she fought the unfolding nightmare that refused her any rest. Her gaze darted, wild and frantic, between data streams as if desperately seeking an escape buried somewhere within the flashing code.

Her fingers hammered at the keyboard in fits of desperation. At any moment, one strike would shatter the plasticware. The faded keys creaked beneath her touch, worn from endless hours of use. Saria's shoulders hunched inward, body trembling. Sweat matted strands of fiery red hair to her brow as the screens cast sharp shadows against the angles of her face.

She wouldn't last much longer.

I moved closer. I needed to push her past panic, force Lyonal to intervene. I hated myself for what I was about to do but saw no other way. Draven and I chose to reveal the treachery. I needed to see this through.

"Saria," I called out softly over the cacophony of noise. She didn't respond. She stayed fixated on a horrifying projection. I took a deep breath and tried again, louder. "Saria! Look at me!"

Her head raised, strain creased her youthful face. I hesitated at the toll visible in her features, the words catching in my throat. But the thought of Dorian, of Levity, of all the others suffering in their own personal hells.

I had to act.

"This isn't real," I said, inching closer and injecting as much calm authority into my voice as I could muster. "None of this is real. You're in a simulation, Saria. They're using your deepest fears against you."

She shook her head violently, dried tears on her cheeks. "No, no, this is real. I can feel it. I can't escape."

I knelt beside her, placing a hand on her trembling shoulder. "Listen to me. I know it feels real, but it's all a manipulation. Lyonal is controlling this..." I trailed off as Saria's focus snapped to attention at his name. Something beyond fear crossed her features—anger, betrayal, a deep-seated pain. I wasn't sure. I decided to change my approach. I needed to exploit that reaction.

"Saria, think about it," I continued, voice firm. "Lyonal is torturing you with this illusion. He knows you the best, knows how to torment you. He's not on your side."

Confusion and suspicion clouded her face. "What are you talking about? He wouldn't... He's—"

"He's the problem," I cut in. "He doesn't care about you, Saria. Look around. Look what he's putting you through. Do you really think someone who cares would let you suffer like this?"

She glanced around the room, realization permeating.

"He's watching you, waiting for you to break," I pushed just enough, crouching closer. "He's pulling the strings. Can't you see? He's not your ally. He's your tormentor."

Her eyes darted to me, the initial suspicion giving way to doubt. I could see the wheels turning, the seeds of apprehension taking root. I pressed harder to drive the wedge between her and Lyonal deep.

"He's manipulating you, using your fears to break you down," I continued, coaxing. "Do you think he truly cares what happens to you? You're just another pawn in his game."

She shook her head, but her resistance wavered. "No, he... he wouldn't—"

"Yes, he would," I insisted, voice rising. "And he is. He's behind all of this. He's the one torturing you with these illusions. He's why you're suffering."

Tears welled as the reality sank in. Once more, she looked around her prison of screens, seeing the echoes of failure.

"You're lying," she whispered without conviction.

"I have no reason to lie," I said gently, seizing her vulnerability. "I know it's hard to believe, but Lyonal is not on your side. He's the enemy. He's the one you need to fight."

She searched my face for any sign of deceit. I held her focus, willing her to see the truth in my words. Finally, she nodded, the last vestiges of doubt crumbling away.

"What do I do?" her voice came small and fragile. "How do I get out of here?"

I edged into her space, my voice smooth as honey. The art of manipulation came naturally as Sandric's Surviving Aide—*sometimes I scared myself*. "There's a way, but not what you think. If you want to escape this hell, you need to quit. Stop fighting. Give in. Break. It's the only way to end your suffering."

Anguish contorted her face, body trembling. "But if I give up... what happens to me?"

"Quitting means freeing yourself from this torment," I lied. "Let the illusions wash over you. It might seem like surrender, but you'll escape. You can be part of the small council, free from Lyonal's clutches, and leave this hell behind."

This is what I needed to do—to save Levity, Dorian, even my mother. I knew the lies I spun. Quitting didn't end the nightmare; it replaced one kind of torment with another. The Sanctioning broke you either way, making surrender unbearable. If Saria gave up, she'd face an even darker fate. I convinced myself that this was the only way.

I could see her will crumbling, the internal battle of fight or surrender.

Time was of the essence. As soon as Lyonal saw how I twisted her thoughts, he'd rush to reach Saria before she could give in.

"Remember," I whispered, "surrendering now will bring relief. He'll only become more brutal if you keep fighting to succeed in this nightmare. Letting go might be your only chance to break free from his control."

Casting one last, deliberate look at Saria, I strode into the corridor. I veered away from the path to the control room Draven showed me. I couldn't risk an unexpected encounter with Lyonal. The hallway stretched before me like an endless expanse. My thoughts sharpened to a single point of focus: expose Trunta. If our scheme unfolded flawlessly, Lyonal's attention would shift to Saria, leaving the control room defenseless.

I turned a corner and collided with a solid form.

We sprawled onto the hard floor, the crash reverberated through the stillness. I scrambled to my feet, my heart pounding fiercely against my ribs. Through the darkness, a shape emerged—a glint of silver hair, pale skin, and sharp features caught the red emergency light.

"Garon!" I exclaimed, but my instant relief was fettered into the gravity that he was here, in front of me. "What happened?" I demanded, voice tight.

Garon's words came slow, his voice a fleeting hush. "In my room... a living nightmare. Pitch black that no light penetrates enveloped me. It was suffocating, invading my very being. I couldn't see anything, not even my hands." His voice faltered.

I grasped his arm with a delicate hand to comfort him, needing him to focus. *We don't have time for this.*

"My family, my nieces and nephews... babies. I saw them dying in that void. One by one, they... they screamed." He clutched his head as if trying to silence the memory. "Their cries crawled inside me. I couldn't save them."

Garon's hands shook violently. "Then Draven appeared. He didn't save me—he taunted me about you."

I blinked. *Me? Why would Draven use me?* But answers had to wait. Garon needed to pull himself together.

"I knocked him out, Betta," his voice cracked. "I didn't want to, but it was him or me. The door was open. I ran. I just... left him there. I don't know if he's ok."

I swallowed hard, my chest twisted to the ache in his voice. *Draven, you stupid ass.* He pushed too far, riding out his role as the aggressive Brawn man all the way to the end.

I knelt beside Garon as he sank to the floor. "Listen to me," I kept my voice steady, anchoring us both. "What you saw, what you felt—it's just tech, remember? What did Draven call it... quantum projection technology? Creates illusions so vivid your mind believes them. That's all this is—a nightmare built to break you." I gripped his shoulder, leaning in and keeping his eyes trained on me. "You're stronger than they ever counted on. I need you back, Garon. I need you to focus on what's real. I need you to help me."

"Quantum projection." He closed his eyelids, breath uneven.

Come on, Garon. We're running out of time.

I gripped Garon's arm and using all my strength, pulled him up off the floor. "I know you don't understand everything. Believe me, neither do I. But you do understand tech. If Lyonal is onto us—we have to move."

Garon followed without question, trusting me in the depths of darkness.

Each step felt agonizingly slow with him gathering himself, but fear of

Lyonal's wrath for my meddling with Saria drove me forward.

Then, the flicker of emergency light finally revealed the control room door.

The metal slid open with a hiss, and I pulled Garon inside. Screens and control panels cast lambent light across rows of consoles. I watched Garon's tech-savvy focus sharpen on the blinking displays showing the different nightmares currently in play.

"This is where it all unfolds," I murmured, my voice laden with urgency and dread. "I need your assistance making sense of this."

Though still visibly shaken, his breathing leveled out as he positioned himself at the console. Terror lingered in his tight jaw and twitching fingers, but practiced rigor took over. His movements grew sure with each passing second.

"What's happening here?" he demanded, his eyes darting between the equipment and my face.

I inhaled slowly, my chest tight as I prepared to unveil the chilling truth. I took my place in a chair near the control panel and turned to face him. "The Sanctioned in Sandric are… mere figureheads," my voice trembled as if the words themselves were wrapped in heavy chains around my throat. "The authority is an illusion, a carefully crafted front. We're not making the real decisions." I hesitated and drew in a deep breath. "Everything points to Trunta as the invisible hands behind the scenes."

"Listen carefully, Garon. Their manipulation undermines our society," I whispered as I laid it all bare. "We're already living in subjugation—monitored thoughts, false freedoms." Nothing but an illusion. I let out a sardonic chuckle. "The Sanctioning. The surveillance. The psychological warfare… These aren't just tools—they're weapons to crush spirits and silence our voices until we forget choice exists. I refuse to let that happen."

Garon's expression, already shadowed by his recent ordeal, darkened with a recognition that pierced deep. "I know oppression, Betta. I know the price of losing freedom," his voice raw, filled with fire. "My people have been forced into the shadows, suffocated by control. We've felt tyranny's cold grip tightening around us for generations. And we've fought tooth and nail to break free from it."

I knew he'd comply. Dobian's loathed the entire system. I leaned closer, my voice a fierce whisper. "Someone needs to grow a backbone and act. That's us. This isn't about surviving The Sanctioning; it's snatching back our right to shape our own damn destiny. If we sit on our hands, we shackle future generations to a life of fear. Change won't fall in our laps. We've got to be the change. And I need your help finding proof."

Garon's brows furrowed. "Trunta? I don't disagree, but what makes you so sure?"

My speculation had quickly built into a truth that couldn't be ignored. "Everything leads there," I said. "Their regulations and technological grip force dependency. Engineered energy shortages keep us reliant on their systems. Access to tech and services are reserved for those who can pay wattage through the nose. Now, they're garnering control with food from their lab-grown supplies. Our survival is becoming their leverage, to keep us under their thumb. And then there is *this* Cird-damned system."

"It doesn't surprise me," Garon replied. "The Perpetual Sense never leaves Trunta's hands. They control it for a reason." He wiped perspiring palms on his thighs, preparing to dive in.

I reached into the pocket of the white pants I wore and pulled out a flash drive. "We need evidence before Lyonal returns or soldiers realize you're gone—not to mention Draven. Find solid proof linking these practices directly to Trunta. This is our chance to expose them and turn the tides against them."

His fingers flew over the keyboard. He pulled up his room's surveillance and slid the video over to a monitor closer to me, revealing Draven still unconscious on the floor as two armed soldiers with infrared helmets stormed in to assist him.

"What's Draven's involvement in all this?" Garon asked, his irritation noticed in his furrowed brow. "His aggression toward me—there's got to be more to it."

Garon's jaw tightened as if recalling something that had bothered him. "He kept prodding me about you. Implying you were some reward I needed to earn, like he had claim over you." He exhaled sharply. "The shit he said... No one talks about a woman that way and expects me to fucking tolerate it. So... I shut him up."

His honesty stirred something unfamiliar in me, like warmth from embers thought to be dead.

"Draven's aggression was—unfortunately—part of the act," I said, watching the detestable scenes of the representatives' rooms scroll by. "We are working together and using our positions to gather intelligence. Disrupt from within." I smiled with a teasing glint. "Two men fighting over me? Guess my siren skills are more effective than I thought." I shrugged, feigning nonchalance.

Garon's lips curved dangerously in that playful smile I was coming to really enjoy. "Oh, believe me, it's not just your skills that have drawn me in," he said, his voice dropping an octave lower. His eyes never left the screens, but there was something far more mischievous in his gaze. "Though, if I had to compete for your adoration, I'd venture to say I could easily win." His grin softened enough to make my heart stutter. "But I'll let Draven think he stands a chance."

With an inconspicuous wink, he turned back to the monitors, playful tension lingering between us.

I cast my attention on the array of heartbreaking simulations once more.

One room showed an eerie forest where gnarled trees loomed like skeletal fingers clawing at the sky. An unnamed representative wandered through the dense underbrush, their face a mask of terror. The path shifted with each step, fog obscuring their vision while whispers taunted them. Every turn led to dead ends or horrifying illusions of lurking creatures, preying on their rising panic.⬚

"Can you bring up Saria's room?" I asked. "She's a Trunta representative. That's where we should find Lyonal."

He scanned screens until he found Saria's nightmare, sliding it over next to the surveillance of Draven. Lyonal sat on the floor beside the redhead, speaking with intimate reassurance, desperately undoing my manipulation.

"Look at them. Completely preoccupied." Feeling the pressure mounting, I continued, "Find anything yet?"

Garon worked with a frenetic intensity, slicing through files at dizzying pace. Each click and keystroke unraveled secrets at breakneck speed, his expertise both mesmerizing and nauseating, a testament to his skill as urgency escalated.

My concentration bounced between monitors. "And soldiers are heading here with Draven. If he can't stall them or throw them off your tracks, we'll need to think fast."

Sweat gathered on the nape of my neck with each second Garon navigated the system. This opportunity could not be manufactured twice. Failure was not an option.

"There," Garon said, his voice tense with excitement. He pointed to a folder labeled *'Confidential'* bearing Trunta's emblem. "This could be it."

Inside lay a trove: Regulations on energy consumption, surveillance protocols, and memos about maintaining compliance through technological dependency.

Perfect.

"Download and let's go." I shoved the drive into the panel. My heart pounded like war drums.

His movements were swift, initiating the download. The progress bar crawled, each pixel agonizingly slow. Every structural creak and distant murmur amplified in our heightened state of anxiety.

I could feel my pulse in my temples.

Fear throbbed in my veins.

The sensation of being on the precipice of discovery overwhelmed me.

Garon's fingers flew as the download bar completed. My hand shot out, snatching the drive and slipping it into my pocket. Our breaths came in shallow, hurried gasps as we prepared to leave.

"Hold up! We need to cut these simulations' impact," I snapped. "We can't just watch them suffer when we can actually help. Let's show them we won't let this continue!"

His hands moved across settings, reducing dials for each candidate while I watched with bated breath.

"Lyonal's still with Saria," I whispered, scanning feeds. I gasped. "The soldiers and Draven are nearly here." Then something else caught my eye. A surge of panic tightened my chest, making it hard to breathe. "What the hell? Levity and Thomas—their rooms are empty."

Garon frowned, quickly searching the other feeds. "Levity? The young dark-haired girl from Sertoda."

"We need to find them," I said, fear tightened my throat. "Escaping their rooms invites disaster."

"What kind of disaster?"

"If we don't get them—and you—back, you and your loved ones face worse threats than you can imagine. That nightmare you were in will become reality!" My voice trembled, each word carrying dread of what I knew to be true.

Garon's jaw set like iron. "I'm not going back to that room."

I pushed back my chair and locked eyes with Garon. "They won't hesitate." I touched the pocket I hid the drive in. "I don't know how this information changes things, but we need to be strategic. One misstep loses any advantage we currently hold. Please understand, we cannot give these monsters more leverage, Garon."

He checked the soldiers' positions. "I'm done. They've taken everything from my people already. There's nothing more they can do. I can help better out here, where I'm not shackled in their manipulation." I clenched and unclenched my hands. Time was up.

His words crackled with defiance as he tracked Levity's and Thomas's rooms. "I can find them, but we'll need to split up. Where can we meet?"

I detailed the alcove's location and which cameras to avoid. "The darkness isn't accidental. Without light, they strip our sense of direction, hope, will—binding us to their control."

Garon straightened, rolling his shoulders. "I have an idea." He grasped my hand, sending an unexpected flutter through me. My breath caught as he pulled me toward the door. "How good are you at improvising under pressure, Siren?"

I managed a wry smile despite the warmth pooling in my chest at his little nickname. "Surprisingly adept, given my role as Surviving Aide."

Garon's lips curved into a playful grin, eyes holding a dangerous promise. "Layers." The word felt like our secret as his thumb traced my hand before bringing it to his lips.

I blinked, disoriented. How could he find amusement now? How could I be intrigued?

Yet, something about the way he looked at me—those eyes, that smile—made me wonder if I was the one being played.

Garon positioned himself beside the door, a shield of calm amidst the chaos. He guided me behind him, hand protective on my lower back.

The metal door hissed opened. Two soldiers entered.

In a single heartbeat, Garon struck. His movements were fluid as he disarmed the first soldier, wrenching away the pistol.

Before I could process, he spun me flush against his chest, taking my breath away. His robust arm encircled me as the cold metal of the gun pressed against my temple.

The door opened once more. Draven stepped in, his face raw with aggression... and fear.

Real panic seized me. My heart thundered as I leaned into my role with intense vulnerability that nearly paralyzed me. Trusting Garon—his plan and instincts—was my only lifeline. The pistol's pressure marked the razor-thin line between life and death. This challenge extended beyond mere survival—I had to stay ahead of a system determined to crush us.

"Give me your helmet," Garon demanded the downed soldier.

The second soldier trained his pistol, calculating variables. Tension crackled in the air.

"Let her go." Draven's voice erupted. "She's not part of your scheme."

Garon's body tensed against mine, muscle coiled, as he secured his escape route.

The door shuddered opened once more. Lyonal entered, disbelief and alarm crossing his face as his gaze swept across the scene.

"What is going on here?" Lyonal's voice emerged as a strained whisper.

"Draven, please help me!" I pleaded with feigned anguish. "He's trying to gain an advantage for Dobia."

Garon dug the muzzle harder into the side of my head. "Keep that pretty mouth of yours shut." His breath hot and erratic against my skin. He jerked his head toward Lyonal. "You've failed my orders with your pathetic distraction. I needed him away longer. You're worthless."

His next words were a fierce declaration, filled with pure defiance. "I won't go back to that hellhole. I won't be tormented again."

His chest pressed against me like a wall of resistance, face hidden behind my shoulder.

Draven lunged, knife ready. The room erupted as he collided with Garon.

I clenched my eyelids shut.

A gunshot cracked—freezing time.

Primal fear paralyzed me.

Waiting.

I felt the sudden release of Garon's grip.

My body lurched free.

Eyes flew open.

A heavy thud shook the room.

A pained, guttural cry rang out.

Then suffocating silence filled the space.

The Conspiracies of
Sandric Governance:

The political landscape of Sandric has been increasingly shrouded in secrecy, prompting a rise in conspiracy theories that threaten our society's cultural fabric. As a professor of cultural studies, I find it crucial to address these changes and their implications for our communities.

The government's lack of transparency raises significant inquiries about its true intentions. What motivates recent policy movements? Such an obscure environment breeds distrust, compelling us to question authority and the narratives fed to us.

In light of these concerns, I plan to convene a meeting with my students to discuss their fears and perceptions regarding the current political climate. Encouraging dialogue will not only help illuminate these pressing issues but also empower us to reclaim our cultural identity amidst the shadows of governance. We must confront these challenges together, for understanding the forces shaping our society is the first step toward fostering a more informed and resilient community.

In pursuit of truth and understanding,

—H. Wilhoph

Chapter Twenty-Three

LEVITY

The alarm shrieked every three minutes, piercing the reticent domain and making me flinch. Thomas led us through the ink-black darkness, his hand gripping mine. My heart raced beneath heaving breaths. We moved erratically, neither of us remembering how we got to our rooms. Only instinct drove us forward.

A subtle tremor ran through Thomas's hand, revealing the worry he worked so hard to mask. He stayed resolute, posture tense but straight, projecting a calm resilience. But underneath, I sensed a current of fear. Even so, his grip remained firm and warm, anchoring me from slipping into despair. I squeezed my fingers, a silent promise we'd face whatever lay ahead together.

"We need to find Marmarie. We promised her we'd all stick together," I whispered, barely audible over my pounding pulse. My mind raced, trying to recall the layout of this nightmarish maze. "She went off to the left—or was it the right?"

Thomas's jaw tightened as he inhaled deeply, as if trying to recall a memory. "Let's go that way," he said, though his voice carried an unusual rigidity. "We can't afford to hesitate."

I nodded, and we moved forward. The faint red emergency light flickered in the distance, offering minimal guidance.

A guttural male scream ripped through the silence, muffled behind the door closest to my right.

Thomas's grip turned slick with sweat. "We'll find her," he said, his voice stayed firm despite the palpable fear in the air. "And then we'll get out. Figure the rest together. Maybe she'll have ideas."

Our arrival played in my mind like a distorted half-remembered dream—Marmarie bidding us farewell, her bright smile masking her worry. How foolish we'd been, blind to the lurking danger. I prayed we were heading in the right direction before this place devoured her too.

We approached a door at the end of the corridor. Hairs rose on the back of my neck as cold dread pooled in my stomach. Marmarie's room.

The alarm blared again, listing the consequences for disobedience.

Thomas and I exchanged tense looks. I reached out with trembling fingers, the door cool to the touch. Using the mirror shard like before, I heard the mechanism click and the door opened with a groan.

More darkness greeted us, swallowing even the hall's feeble light.

"Marmarie?" My voice quivered as it echoed back at me, distorted by the suffocating blackness.

No response.

Only quiet.

I forced air into my lungs.

She had to be here.

I hoped.

We stepped inside cautiously, afraid to leave the security of the open door. The darkness wrapped us like a living thing. Dense air carried a faint metallic tang that stung my nostrils and left a bitter taste in my mouth.

Then we saw her in the glow of a small lamp.

Marmarie slumped in a corner, her frail form draped over a metal chair like a discarded marionette. Gray hair hung limp around her weathered face. Her eyes, once sparkled with life, now cloudy and vacant. Her skin looked almost spectral, translucent, bluish veins visible beneath. A thin sheen of sweat glistened on her forehead. And her lips, once full of stories and wisdom were parted in a silent scream.

"Marmarie?" I whispered, taking a tentative step. Horror twisted my stomach at the sight. This was not our stoic Elder from the train who'd been ready to face whatever The Sanctioning threw at us. This was not Marmarie.

Thomas reached out to touch her shoulder but thought against it and dropped his hand to his side. He knelt beside her. "Marmarie, we are here. Levity and Thomas. We're here to help you."

No reaction. She just stared straight ahead into an abyss, unseeing and lost. Then, slowly, she turned her head almost robotically, stiff and unnatural. Her voice emerged detached, alien.

"Thhooommaas... Levvvvity..." She drew out our names slowly. She looked in our direction, but it was like she was looking right through us. "Why are you here?"

The government's monstrous capabilities slammed into me, drowning me in a flood of disbelief. I wrapped a hand around my pendant, the cold metal focusing me.

"What did they do to you?" Thomas asked, his voice cracking as he searched her blank face for any sign of her spirit.

She blinked slowly, processing the question. "They... helped me see the truth," Marmarie replied, her words slurred and mechanical. Her lashes fluttered, then they opened...

Still.

Void.

"There is no escape. No reason to fight. It's better this way... to surrender... to accept..."

Terror clenched my heart. *They broke her.* Whatever the method, they stripped away her will, her fight, her devotion. Only a shell remained—a grotesque mockery of who she'd been.

"They must've drugged her. They did something… I don't know. What could do this?" An unanswerable question.

Thomas's face contorted with rage, his hands fisting at his sides. "We have to get her out," he growled, a helplessness threading his voice that mirrored my own rising anxiety. "We can't leave her like this."

I reached out, brushing clammy skin. She flinched. "Marmarie, please… you have to fight," I begged. But her expression remained vacant, her gaze unfocused. "We're too late," I whispered. My eyes stung with unshed tears as I turned to Thomas who looked just as lost as I felt. "She's… she's gone, Thomas. They've taken everything from her."

For a moment, we let the silence exist between us, saturated with the bitter sting of failure. This is what breaking looked like—humanity stripped away, leaving behind the flesh of the human. A dagger of truth, laying bare the cost of weakness.

I couldn't even begin to grasp the dark reality of what awaited those who emerged victorious.

We needed to escape this nightmare. But how could we leave the others behind? How could we help them, trapped in this hell with us? We needed to find a way out for all of the representatives before it was too late

But first, we had to survive.

With Thomas's hand tight in mine, we stumbled back into the hall.

The alarm buzzed and the directive played once more. I raised a shoulder to my ear, my feeble attempt to block the noise.

"We have to get out of Mass," Thomas said suddenly, his voice cutting through the message. "If there's any chance your siblings are in danger from these threats, we need to reach them."

Tivian, Triad. Blue. Evie.

His words hit me like a punch. The thought of my siblings being dragged into this nightmare, subjected to this psychological torture, filled me with a cold dread that thwarted my body.

"Do you remember how we got here from the meeting hall?" I asked.

I tried to make out his face in the dark. "I was hoping you did."

I took a deep breath, pushing away the choking fear. I thought of my brothers' maturing faces. Blue's sass. And Evie... *My little Sprout.* As I tried to calm the frantic rhythm of my thoughts, an old memory surfaced—one of Pop's stories that stayed with me long after the storyteller went silent. He'd spoken of winding tunnels beneath Mass's sacred city, constructed long before the city was hidden beneath this modern veneer.

"My Pop used to tell me about tunnels," I began, the memory coming back with unexpected clarity. "Built ages ago. They stretched all throughout the city. It's how they brought the stones in from the different regions. There must be an exit."

Thomas's brows knitted together. "Tunnels? But this place—"

"It's an illusion," I interrupted, the cold realization hitting me like a winter wave. I placed my hands on Thomas's shoulders to draw him in closer to see him. "Think about it. The rooms, the view of the city—it's all projection, a trick. I felt like we were going down when they brought us here, even though we were supposed to be in a high-rise. It's all been a lie."

Thomas's mouth parted as understanding struck him. "So, we're underground?"

"Yes. If the tunnels are real, they're nearby. We just need to find our way through this darkness and follow any hint of light." Hope pounded in my chest, fragile but insistent. "It's our best chance."

Thomas's hands fell to my waist, grasping me tight. "But how can we be sure the tunnels still exist? The government has hidden so much."

I swallowed hard, acknowledging his uncertainty. "We don't know.

But it's better than staying here and ending up like Marmarie."

His grip tightened with resolve. "Then let's find those tunnels."

He leaned in, pressing warm lips to my cheek. In a soft, brief kiss.

Heat surged through me.

I nodded and took a deep breath; new determination rose as we moved away from Marmarie's door. The corridor's darkness seemed less like an impenetrable void and more like a path to freedom.

Rounding the corner, my breath caught in my throat. A silver light glowed at the corridor's end like a beacon.

"There," I said, my voice trembling with fear and relief. "That has to be the way."

The air grew cooler, damper as we advanced. We were going the right way. I fixed my attention on the faint glimmer ahead, clinging to the hope it marked escape.

But as we approached, I realized the silver light's origin gleamed from a figure blocking our path.

As the figure's features became clearer, Thomas and I stopped abruptly.

Garon stood ahead, a helmet tucked under one arm, and a gun pointed in our direction. The weapon jolted my frayed nerves.

"Whoa, whoa. Put the gun down." Thomas demanded. "We are no threat."

"I'm aware. We need to move," he murmured. He lowered the pistol.

"Where did you get a gun? And the helmet?"

"A guard." Garon tossed the helmet to Thomas. "It's infrared. I don't need it, but I didn't want them having an advantage at finding us. I see fine in the dark. No time to explain everything. Betta will be meeting us soon."

My heart sank at the name. "Betta?" I repeated, struggling to keep my voice composed. "The same Betta seated in Sandric leadership? A Sanctioned? Do you know what they've done to Marmarie? She's shattered,

Garon. Betta won't help us."

I wanted to trust her, the woman I looked up to. But she sat in a position of power. She was a stranger. How could I believe in someone who was part of this system? How could I trust a woman who clearly knew what we were headed into, yet still allowed it to unfold?

Garon turned in the opposite direction we came from, leading us down the hall. "There is a lot we need to figure out. Our best chance at securing answers is her."

Emotion swelled within me. "Thomas, no. We can't."

Thomas—who stood so sure of what needed to be done—glanced between Garon and me. He placed a hand gently on my shoulder. "I understand your fear," he said softly. "But right now, we don't have many options. We need to hear what Betta has to say before making any decisions about what we do next."

I wanted to believe him. I wanted to believe that Betta could be the answer, but how could I trust her after learning all this was going on behind closed doors? Could I really lay my hopes at her feet when the pain of betrayal was still so fresh, so raw? The ghosts of what she might have known—and what she might have chosen not to do—haunted me. But we were running out of time, and that truth left me no choice but to wonder: Could Betta still be the woman I remembered from Sertoda, or was she something else entirely?

Frustration and fear surged through me. My chin dropped. "I'm suffocating here. We just saw Marmarie hollowed out by The Sanctioning. What if Betta is the same? What if she's just another instrument for the government to wield, and Garon is leading us right to her?"

"I assure you that is not what is happening." Garon said over his shoulder. "She is going to find a way to help us."

Thomas turned my body to fully face him. "I'm scared too. But we have to at least listen. Garon likely knows something we don't, and he is one of us—a representative. Maybe she's not completely under their control."

I felt rooted to the spot, as if the ground had wrapped around my ankles, keeping me from moving forward. "And what if it's a trap?"

Garon's voice cut through the fog of my panic. "If she's under their control—and I don't believe she is—then yes, we would need to be careful. But we can't sit here in the dark and hope for a miracle. We have to take risks if we want to escape this nightmare."

Thomas stepped closer, his warmth pressing against me. "Levity, I know this is terrifying. But this might be the lifeline we need to get you back to your family."

Tivian. Triad. Blue. Evie.

I looked up to Thomas's face, seeing the same semblance of fear and determination reflecting back at me through the dark. My family needed me. I took a deep breath, fighting tears. "Alright," I said, my voice worn. "Take us to Betta."

Garon turned on his heel. "Follow me. I think we're close."

The Veil of Deception
(Observations on the Small Council):

As I delve into the actions and statements of the small council members, a troubling pattern emerges, shrouded in ambiguity and secrecy. The news reports, often laden with half-truths, reveal a striking contrast between the council's public demeanor and their private machinations. I question the intentions behind their polished speeches, which seem scripted as if crafted to pacify the masses while masking a deeper agenda.

In my recent analysis, I've noted subtle shifts in their body language—fleeting glances exchanged during discussions, an almost imperceptible tension that belies their carefully constructed masks. What truths lie beneath their polished presentations? Why do their proclamations of unity ring empty in light of the growing discontent among the populace?

Are we witnessing mere governance, or is there a deeper game at play? The conspiracy of silence that envelops them is palpable and suggests a deliberate manipulation of public perception.

I feel a duty, to my students, to uncover these layers of deceit, to question the narratives handed to us, and to encourage critical thinking in the face of such pervasive obscurity. As I sift through these layers, I urge all to remain vigilant.

There is more at play than meets the eye, and only by peeling back the layers can we hope to reclaim our understanding of Sandric's true political landscape.

In pursuit of truth and understanding,
—H. Wilhoph

Chapter Twenty-Four

BETTA

The overpowering scent of antiseptic hit me as if trying to scrub away the violence that just unfolded. My ears still rang from the gunshot, its echo lingering in the back of my mind as the muffled sound of the alarm pulsed through the halls.

Draven sat on the edge of the gurney in the infirmary. His face tight with pain, but alive. Lyonal had called in a medic when it was all over. He barely spent any time at the control panel before heading to the Sanctioned living quarters. I doubted he changed anything Garon had done... not yet, at least.

The medic worked quickly on Draven's arm; movements almost mechanical as if she'd done this a thousand times before. It made me think of my mother and all the soldiers she must have stitched up during her time in Brawn. His shirt lay discarded, but the coppery scent of blood remained.

I leaned against the doorframe, my heart racing from the frenzy. The adrenaline from Garon's escape began to wane, leaving behind fatigue. As the medic finished her work, she left us to speak in private.

Draven dropped his attention to his arm, irritation etched on his face. He tested the bandage, flexing his bicep and rotating his forearm with a wince. "Garon's escape was a little impromptu," he said, his voice dry and unamused. "Nonetheless, it worked."

Once the soldiers got Draven to the infirmary, he had barked an order as the Noble Warrior, sending them off in the opposite direction to track down Garon. As they disappeared down the hallway, unease coiled within me. With all the chaos surrounding Garon, I feared that the knowledge of Levity and Thomas's disappearance hadn't even risen to a head yet.

I closed the distance to where Draven sat bare chested in black tactile pants and boots. "Yeah, Garon is with us now. And before he left the control room, we got our hands on something. Something that might give us the answers we need."

Interest flared across Draven's features as he homed in on my hand in my pocket. "What did you manage to secure?"

I pulled out the flash drive and dropped it onto the small table beside him. "This," I said, keeping my voice balanced despite the adrenaline still thrumming through me, "is everything they didn't want us to see. Confidential files from Trunta. Garon downloaded it right before you showed up. We don't know what's on it yet, but I'm hoping for intel on their tech—and maybe their communication channels. A real game changer."

Draven's face registered surprise at first as he picked up the flash drive. Then his expression shifted from curiosity to focus. "This could be it; the leverage to expose everything."

I nodded, a feeling of relief edging up my back. "Exactly. But we need to handle this with care." I placed my hand on Draven's and plucked the drive from his palm. "It might reveal more than we expect, and if we're not cautious, we could walk straight into a trap."

Draven ran his fingers along his beard. "We'll review the files tonight, piece by piece. But we need to stay off their radar. We should figure out a time and place to go through the data. Then we plan our next move based on what we find."

I took a deep breath, preparing myself to deliver a new stumbling block. "Levity and Thomas are not in their rooms," I said. "Garon escaped to retrieve them. I'm to meet them in the alcove to discuss our next steps."

Behind his stoic mask, a storm rumbled. "We have to ensure my brother's path to the Noble Warrior position stays on track. The Sanctioning must unfold without interference. He secures that position, and we use the intel to bring this system down. We can't have mistakes like this."

His tone grated on me. "I get it, Draven. I know what's at risk. But we can't brush them aside. Levity and Thomas need to be back in their rooms, and Garon—he's refusing to return. We may have to force him, or worse... something I don't even want to think about." I paused, shaking away thoughts of more violence. "And what if a representative completely flees? What then?"

Draven's expression hardened, he clenched his jaw as he looked away. "These fucking Sanctionings are buried in so much secrecy. I wouldn't be surprised if no one even knows what happens if someone escapes. As far as I'm aware, no one's ever made it out. Every representative from our term finished The Sanctioning and made it to the small council... except for Edward." I shut my eyes at the mention of his name. "If anyone has disappeared it's well hidden. The Cird will live freely above ground before anyone dares find out what's really going on."

"We need a plan."

Draven's frustrated gaze met mine. "And we need to be more careful."

The silence was thick. Each thud of my pounding heart was a reminder of how precariously we stood on the edge of chaos.

Draven raised his hand to the back of his neck, rubbing it—a quiet, uneasy gesture that felt startlingly out of character for a man like him. "When I saw Garon holding that gun to your head..." His voice wavering, "I didn't know if he'd gone rogue or if he'd misunderstood me when I let him loose. For a moment, I was terrified he'd turned on us."

"Everything turned out fine. I mean, I was fine—"

Draven stood from the gurney with determined energy that belied his injury.

I stepped back but failed to restrain myself from what I feared... from what I wanted.

He grabbed my waist and pulled me to him. Draven wrapped hard arms around me, not caring about the bandage or injury, as he lifted me off the ground with ease.

Our lips crashed together in a fervor that took my breath away. I tasted mint as his tongue parted my mouth. Casting off the worry of what this could be, I kissed him back like my life depended on it. My legs wrapped around his body, hooking at the ankle. Glass bottles rattled as he pinned me against the shelves that lined the infirmary's wall.

He growled against me.

Draven spun us and rested on the counter's ledge. We lined up perfectly. I could feel him grow and harden against the apex between my legs, beneath the fabric that guarded our skin. Warmth and need grew between my legs. My body began to writhe under his hold, putting pressure and movement on all the parts that touched. His mouth moved against mine with a consuming hunger. His wild passion permeated our embrace, intensifying our bond.

Chaos.

Urgency.

The heat of our bodies.

The mingling of our breaths.

An intoxicating mix of desire and desperation filled the air. Nothing else mattered but the intense connection we shared.

Draven's lips traced a heated path down my neck, his touch both tender and fervent. His kisses lingered on my collarbone, brushing against the delicate fabric of my silk top. The material shifted under his lips, exposing more of my skin for him to touch.

"I want you, Draven." It escaped my lips, and I couldn't put it back.

My hands roamed over his bare back, the packed muscle beneath my fingertips taut and firm. The texture of his skin felt rough with old scars from combat. I felt the subtle tremors in his breathing against my palms. My nails dug in, scratching his back, tracing the contours of his shoulder blades, and sending shivers through us both.

As his lips continued exploring the curve of my breast under my shirt and then to the sensitive space between the two swells of flesh, a soft moan escaped my lips. Each kiss a plea for solace amidst the noise of our world. His injured arm tightened around me with a possessive strength that brought comfort and exhilaration. He thrust his hips, applying pressure to the sensitive bud swelling beneath my pants—his thickness straining to be released.

I reached a hand between our bodies in an attempt to find the button on his pants.

A warm trickle of liquid slid down my skin. I went rigid and broke away.

Why was I stopping?

Blood.

I unwrapped my legs from him, placing my feet back on solid ground. His confusion vivid on his face.

Without a word, I shuffled items around and grabbed a fresh roll of bandages. He didn't stop me when I gripped his bad arm. The bleeding had worsened. Blood soaked through the bandage. I slowly unwrapped the old gauze, tossing it aside as I grabbed the antiseptic cloth to clean away the streaks of red that clung to his skin.

"I could get used to you taking care of me, Betta," Draven said, a half-smile tugging at the corner of his swollen lips.

I scoffed, pressing a bit harder than necessary as I cleaned his arm. "Don't get too comfortable. I'm not going to play medic every time you play hero and wind up taking a bullet," I replied, voice laced with a bite of sarcasm. I kept my tone light, but my hands trembled as I began re-rolling his arm with fresh gauze, something akin to adrenaline still running through my veins.

As I worked, a sandstorm of thoughts swirled in my head. What was I doing with Draven? *Draven!* What was I letting happen? The intensity of our situation blurred the line between desperation and something I couldn't yet name. I'd spent years forcing myself to see the Brawn men as nothing more than tools for their aggressive agenda. But Draven... Draven was different, *wasn't he?* Or was it just the danger, the looming threat, and the constant need for escape that clouded my judgment?

I tied the bandage with a final, sharp tug. He winced, and I forced myself to meet his dark eyes again.

He really is beautiful.

"Thanks," he murmured, his voice sincere.

I stood and wiped my hands on my pants, smearing red streaks across the fabric, ignoring the tightness that gripped my chest. "Don't mention it," I said, stepping back, regrouping my thoughts.

"I'll meet Garon at the alcove," I said. "Hopefully, he's found Levity and Thomas. From there, I'll strategize how to get them back into their rooms. You should go throw the guards off some more so I can try to return them with as little interference as possible. Then we will look through the information on this flash drive." I patted the pocket the small lifeline lived in.

"Agreed. We'll meet up later tonight?"

"Of course." But who knew what later would hold for us.

I paused at the door, watching him tug at the bandage I'd tied a little too tight. "Stop messing with it," my voice steeped in biting sass. "You break that wrap, and your next injury will come from me."

Draven's brows lifted with defiance, as he reached a hand up to his arm and snapped the bandage.

I rolled my eyes and shot him a vulgar gesture.

His low chuckle followed me as I walked away from him… yet again.

As I neared the meeting point under our living quarters, I paused. Something nagged and tugged at my mind. It burned in my pocket. I pressed down on the fabric and a prickle of suspicion met my hand. Something felt off. That unease in my mind turned into a quiet voice insisting that I examine the contents before meeting Garon.

I pivoted, retracing my steps to the privacy of my room. I could use my personal device to quickly open the contents of the drive.

My normal two guards were nowhere to be found. They were probably out searching for the missing representatives. I needed to be fast. If Levity, Thomas, and Garon made it to the alcove, they'd be safe from being found, but if they hadn't… well, then time was running out.

Quickly, Betta.

Once inside my room, I retrieved my personal device from the desk. The screen hummed to life.

I hurried over to my bed and huddled close to the headboard, knees drawn up, computer balanced on top of my legs screening the display from prying eyes. The flash drive connected with a shiver of anticipation and trepidation in my hands as the files uploaded. I glanced toward the window where the first light of morning stretched over Mass's skyline, washing away the last traces of dawn's soft pinks and purples.

The drive's contents populated on screen with a far too cheerful pop.

With a trembling tap, I navigated through the encrypted directories, each click unveiling layers of hidden information.

The first file, 'OPERATIONAL DIRECTIVE - LEVEL 3', presented a tangled web of technical jargon that threatened to unravel my mind. Grappling with the context, its chilling mandate became clear: Brawn's military hierarchy imposed draconian controls over Trunta's technology, specifically targeting Crestmore Industries' innovations. The directive demanded their advanced technology be wielded with ruthless expertise—a weapon designed to inflict maximum psychological distress on The Sanctioning's participants while ensuring no external oversight could penetrate their operations. They wanted to ensure that the technology was ready to serve its greater purpose: to be wielded as a weapon of war.

As I delved deeper, I uncovered more grave revelations. 'POLICY AMENDMENTS - RESTRICTED ACCESS'. This was again Brawn's campaign to maintain control over the territories, ensuring no region could establish power independency. The orders were stark and foreboding:

```
In light of the increasing inefficiency of
the nuclear power plants and the signif-
icant depletion of uranium resources, the
following amendments are enacted to address
the ongoing crisis:


Energy Utilization Restrictions
Due to the inability of existing nuclear
power plants to meet the rising energy
demands, and the unsustainable rate at
which uranium is being mined, all energy
utilization across territories must be
```

meticulously monitored and strictly cur-
tailed. Any attempt to create or utilize
unauthorized power sources, including but
not limited to alternative energy generation, will be met with immediate and severe
punitive actions.

Increased Surveillance

To ensure total compliance with these new
energy restrictions, surveillance systems
will be expanded and recalibrated to cover
every inch of territory. All energy-related
activities will be under constant scrutiny,
and any deviation from the prescribed limits will be flagged in real-time. This will
include enhanced monitoring of private and
public energy usage, with operatives tasked
with the continuous surveillance of both
high-traffic areas and remote locations.

Enforcement and Punitive Measures

Operatives must maintain unwavering vigilance and will be held to the highest
standards of enforcement. Any failure to
report unauthorized energy activities will
result in immediate and harsh consequences.
This includes, but is not limited to,
termination of operatives found to be
negligent in their duties, as well as more
severe punitive measures for any acts of

```
collusion or tampering with the surveil-
lance systems.
```

Resource Management

```
Given the escalating shortage of uranium
and other critical resources, all mining
and resource extraction will be closely
monitored and subjected to government over-
sight. Unauthorized mining operations or
attempts to redirect resources for private
use will result in swift and extreme
measures taken against those responsible.
```

Each document I opened originated from a classified Brawn military official and addressed a redacted Trunta official.

As I sifted through file after file, I stumbled upon a header that read 'CONFIDENTIAL COMMUNICATION – LYONAL CRESTMORE & GENERAL BALLISTER'.

My heart seized.

This correspondence detailed explicit consequences from General Ballister directly to our Sanctioned counterpart:

```
Lyonal Crestmore,


I trust this message finds you well, though
I doubt it will offer much solace given the
circumstances. We observe the progress of
The Sanctioning with great interest, and it
has come to our attention that this term
```

the outcome for the Trunta Perpetual Sense may be in jeopardy.

You are well aware of the agreement we reached. The success of Trunta's representative in The Sanctioning is non-negotiable. Should the Perpetual Sense fail to secure their position, there will be severe consequences. I urge you to recall the terms of our accord. If you do not ensure the victory of your candidate, the ramifications will be dire.

To be explicit, should the Perpetual Sense fail, we will initiate a series of retaliatory measures:
1. Exposure of Sensitive Information: We have significant leverage over your administrative records and personal data. Failure to meet our demands will result in the public dissemination of this material, which would undoubtedly compromise your position and reputation beyond repair.
2. Operational Sabotage: We have access to key infrastructure that, if compromised, could disrupt your operations and create widespread instability. This sabotage would extend beyond mere inconvenience and could cripple your efforts in unforeseen ways.

3. Personnel Repercussions: Should our demands be unmet, we will not hesitate to employ additional pressure tactics on your associates and remaining family. The discomfort and distress caused to those closest to you should serve as a powerful motivator to ensure compliance.

Consider this a final notice. The successful outcome of the Perpetual Sense's Sanctioning is imperative. We expect you to act decisively and ensure the desired result. The balance of power is delicate, and our patience is wearing thin.

General Ballister

The impact of Draven's father's words constricted my breathing. These incriminating orders and the menacing threats against Lyonal laid bare the ugly truth of the conspiracy. Lyonal found himself caught in a much larger game of power and control beyond my comprehension. But what truly shook me was the revelation of Draven's father as the central architect of this nightmare. The acid in my stomach churned.

This situation was a stranglehold on power.

Trunta didn't cooperate willingly, they operated under threat.

General Ballister's involvement darkened everything Draven had ever said and done.

A chilling doubt infiltrated my mind like a parasite. Was Draven truly an ally in this fight?

Could he be using me to advance their agenda?

His easy agreement to utilize Garon could simply have been a tactic to neutralize a rival to the Perpetual Sense seat.

The thought that these enacted plans could be a part of some grander, more sinister plot, felt like Draven stabbing me and twisting a knife.

Was Draven's commitment to me genuine, or did he merely recite lines from a play for which only he held the script? If that were the case, who could I trust? The realization that Draven's father orchestrated this nightmare ignited a firestorm of betrayal within me.

I slammed my hand down on the table beside me, sending a glass tumbler crashing to the floor. The shattering glass echoed my fracturing understanding of our world—of Draven. I was caught between the warmth of Draven's touch and the cold reality of his bloodline. Treachery burned hotter than any fire, threatening to consume everything I thought I knew. Trust—that delicate construct—had been reduced to ash.

I needed to get to the alcove, regroup with Garon and, hopefully, Levity and Thomas. Yet the dread following me as I exited the room felt suffocating. Our enemies were far more cunning, more entrenched than I'd ever imagined.

Each step felt heavy with my newfound knowledge. I needed to focus on the task at hand. All I could do was brace myself for whatever came next.

And put on the brave face of a survivor.

The Hidden Tensions Between
Sandric Territories:

Recent investigations into the history of territorial conflicts in Sandric revealed a pattern of underlying tensions that suggest more than mere disagreements over land and resources. For example, the long-standing feud between Brawn and Dobia appears driven not only by military ambition but also by a desire to control the resources hidden within Dobia's ancient caves.

Similarly, the rivalry between Sertoda and Trunta hints at a desire to stifle Sertoda's cultural heritage in favor of Trunta's technological dominance. Reports indicate that Trunta actively promotes lab-grown fish, undermining Sertoda's traditional fishing practices and pressuring local communities to abandon their time-honored methods.

The feud between Trunta and Lizon intensifies as Trunta expands its server farms and nuclear power plant infrastructure, encroaching on Lizon territory. This relentless pursuit of advancement threatens to erase Lizon's unique cultural identity, raising alarms about the consequences of such ambition.

These conflicts, historically framed as isolated incidents, point to a coordinated effort to control territories deemed weaker. As I delve deeper into these findings, I cannot shake the feeling that we are only scratching the surface of a much darker conspiracy at play within our fractured society.

In pursuit of truth and understanding,
—H. Wilhoph

Chapter
Twenty-Five

LEVITY

The alcove formed a narrow pocket, intricately carved into the stone of the old world. Pop referred to the tunnels as the veins of the city, connecting the five territories—Brawn, Trunta, Dobia, Sertoda, and Lizon—like lifelines. This subterranean network fostered unity without the barriers that divided them above ground.

The air pulsed with history, carrying a musty scent that seeped through the walls. Ghosts of past scholars and leaders enveloped me, a familiar comfort that reminded me of my father's teachings. The very rocks embodied a vision of collaborative prosperity, where no single territory would dominate.

Pop often spoke of how the tunnels were integral to maintaining peace in those early years. Down here, they were simply people, working together to build something greater than themselves.

Standing in the alcove, I shifted my weight from hip to hip, fingers tapping the cold stone wall. My breaths were shallow, each one catching in my throat as I glanced at the empty passageway. Pop used to say the past always found a way of staying around, leaving traces in unexpected places. He was right. These tunnels weren't just old stone; they were a forgotten promise—buried but not broken.

I rubbed my hands together, fighting off the chill. The city of Mass had lost that promise, but the tunnels remained like a thread tying the city back to its original purpose. Could that vision of unity still survive in these abandoned paths?

Silence pressed in. The alarm's warning had faded, leaving only the anticipation of Betta's arrival.

Garon's posture was rigid as he kept watch. Thomas sat against the wall, fidgeting, one leg bouncing with nervous energy that frayed my nerves.

"Where is she?" I demanded from Garon.

"She will be here."

I crouched and leaned back against the wall. Thomas shifted beside me.

"What if something happened to her? What if—"

"Stop," Garon interrupted, his tone sharp but not unkind. "Worrying won't help us. Focus on what we can control."

I turned to Garon, my exasperation and agitation bubbling over. "And what exactly is that? Waiting in this dark, silent cavity feels like the worst kind of helplessness."

Garon's expression softened as he considered my frustration. "I know darkness can feel suffocating, but there are ways to deal with it. Back in Dobia, the caves seem foreboding, but there's beauty hidden in their depths."

"What are you talking about?" I asked, intrigued despite my impatience.

"There's a spot in the caverns we frequent, where the stones glisten like stars, even without light," he said, picking up a small pebble and turning it in his fingers. "When I close my eyes there, I allow myself to feel the cool stone against my skin. Nothing else. Then I open my eyes, and I see the stars above and let that image comfort me."

Thomas glanced at Garon, eyebrows raised. "That sounds... nice. But it doesn't really help us right now, does it?"

Garon shrugged, a slight grin breaking through his serious expression. "Maybe not, but it serves as a good reminder that even in darkness, beauty exists. It's about finding your calm amid what might feel scary. Focusing on and deciding how much power you let the rest have over you." He looked at me and nodded.

I took in a deep breath, trying to let his words settle me. "I'd trade any beauty for a way out of here."

"I get that," Garon replied. "But no matter how dark it seems, there's always light closer than you think waiting to break through. We have to be patient." He motioned to our surroundings. "Don't let this scare you, hone it."

It was a nice thought, as Thomas said.

And I wished I could believe it.

Where are you, Betta?

Time crept by, each moment stretching the shadows of doubt in my mind. This stitched-up plan felt fragile—threatening to unravel and expose us with each passing minute. I kept replaying Betta's few simple words from the meeting hall over and over, trying to find the sincerity, trying to convince myself that she would be on our side.

What if this was a trap? What if Betta was in on these horrors? The questions clung to me, refusing to release their grip. The more I attempted to dismiss them, the stronger they grew, until they appeared as the only truth I could glean.

I stole a glance at Garon, hoping to find reassurance. Instead, his tension mirrored my own. He vouched for Betta, but now, even he seemed to be questioning that belief. His clenched jaw spoke volumes—trust proved a dangerous and fragile luxury.

How little we truly knew about each other haunted me. Betta had appeared out of nowhere, extending help to him at his most desperate moment. But why? What drove her?

"What do you think, Garon?" I asked. "How much do we actually know about her?"

Garon's eyes flashed toward me. "Not much," he admitted. "Betta's been careful with what she shares. But..." He hesitated, and I caught the question in his unfinished sentence.

"Do you trust her?" I pressed. "Do you think she's really trying to take down The Sanctioning?"

Garon ran his index finger and thumb along his jaw. "I've wondered that myself. She helped me, but she also needed me. I don't know if she's using us or protecting herself."

My stomach churned, my instincts screaming with caution. "What if we're being manipulated?"

Thomas shifted toward me, his face pale in the dim light. "We don't know. But what choice do we have? We're stuck either way." He rose to his feet.

"We are not stuck," I whispered. "These tunnels lead out. We could—"

A soft scrape echoed from where we entered. My breath hitched and my heart lurched, as I whipped my head toward the sound. Movement flickered just beyond the dim light.

I tensed, ready to bolt, but Garon's hand gripped my arm. "Wait," he murmured and drew the gun up.

Thomas pulled me away from Garon and behind his body.

The figure slipped through the entrance, shadows clinging until she stepped into view.

"Betta," Garon said under his breath, lowering the gun.

I opened my mouth to demand answers, but Betta's curt voice cut through the silence first.

"You'll know everything soon enough," she said, her golden eyes pinning me with intent. "And if you want to survive, you'll have to trust me."

Her white blouse bore crimson stains, a stark contrast against her inky black hair and stone-carved features. She moved swiftly, her form merging with the dim light of the alcove as if she belonged to it. Despite her regal appearance, the exhaustion in her posture was unmistakable.

"You're late." I accused with clenched fists.

I watched her closely, searching for any sign of betrayal, anything that would confirm the doubt brewing inside of me.

She didn't speak. Placing a hand on her hip and using the other to cradle her brow, she stood contemplating something. Then she took a slow, deliberate step toward me, her voice low and earnest.

"Levity," she began, "I know you're scared. I know you have every reason to doubt me. But I swear to you, on everything that matters to me, I would never do anything to hurt you."

Her simple words soothed the raw edges of my anxiety, but something inside me screamed to stay on high alert.

"Why should I believe you?" I asked, my voice trembling despite my efforts to keep it steady.

She took another step closer, her eyes never leaving mine. "Because I saved your siblings," she said gently. "Because I've been where you are, surrounded by darkness, unsure of who to trust. And because I feel a connection to you. Something that goes beyond all of this." She gestured vaguely to the alcove, to The Sanctioning, to the very air that seemed heavy with our collective fear. "I don't know why, but I do. And I'm asking you to trust me, even if it's just the bare amount you can offer."

I wanted to push back, but my persistence wavered. She seemed so sincere, so… human. My shoulders relaxed, the tension slowly circling the drain.

Maybe she was telling the truth.

Garon's voice broke through the haze of my thoughts. "What took you so long?" he asked with concern.

Betta's attention flicked to him; her face shadowed by the dim light. "I found something," she said. Her voice carried a heaviness that set me back on edge. "The communications we secured—they weren't what we thought they were." Betta looked down toward her feet. "They are all coming from… Brawn. They've been manipulating everything. Trunta. The Sanctioning… all of it."

Brawn.

Brawn was west of Sertoda. Its militarized grip impossible to ignore.

Garon tilted his head. "How?"

Betta's shoulders sagged; the strength she showed moments ago began to fade. "Brawn is domineering all the regions, including Trunta and their technology. They're using Lyonal, forcing his hand to ensure the Trunta representative takes the Perpetual Sense position. I have reason to believe they are orchestrating each seat. It's the only way their imperceptible control can continue."

My thoughts turned over again and again, trying to make sense of this new information. Lyonal was being used? And the Perpetual Sense position—

She continued to tell us more details of what she learned in the directives.

"And Draven's involvement?" Garon cut in.

Betta's face darkened. "I believe he is working with his father to secure his brother reaching the Noble Warrior position."

The room spun, a sickening realization crept in. Everything I thought I understood, everything I thought I would fight for in Mass—we were nothing but collateral damage.

"And the Surviving Aide?" I forced myself to ask. "What are their plans for that position?"

Betta hesitated. A deep, painful shame crossed her features. "The Surviving Aide... doesn't matter," she admitted, voice thick with self-loathing. "They only need a pretty mouthpiece, who will blindly follow orders."

Her confession settled on me like a cloth pressed over my mouth. I looked at the woman who saved my siblings, who risked everything to stand with us now. Torment clouded her tired eyes. Guilt had been festering inside her for so long. Her body language spoke of her shame, being regarded as a tool, and the realization of her own powerlessness.

"Betta..." I started, but I didn't know what to say. What did I have to offer?

Thomas cut in; voice strained. "What's our next step?"

Betta's head snapped up as if an idea struck her. Her movements were quick and decisive.

"I need to take you back to your rooms," she pointed out. "I don't know what the consequences will be for being out this long, but maybe they'll chalk it up to a glitch in The Sanctioning. If I round you up and bring you back like I wasn't involved, it might be enough."

Garon frowned, his disapproval clear. "And then what? We just wait for them to break us?"

Betta shook her head, her features blazing with tenacity. "No. We play along, but on our terms," she snapped. "We've got what they need here—the Perpetual Sense, the Noble Warrior, the Surviving Aide. You win your Sanctionings, we don't just survive, we take control. We use these power positions and turn the tables on their game."

My heart raced. What she suggested felt reckless, a gamble. There had to be another way—something less dangerous. Less final.

"What if we lose?" Thomas whispered, fear lacing his words.

Betta stepped closer, her blood-stained blouse catching the faint light. She looked at Thomas, her voice resolute. "We won't lose," she said, a blaze of determination in her golden eyes. "We can't. This is our chance to break free, to expose what they've done, and take back our lives. But we have to be smart. We have to stay strong."

"There is not enough wattage in this world that would make me go back," I said, my voice trembling with anger. I couldn't just go along with it. "Not after what they've put us through."

"I know it's terrifying, Levity." Betta placed a gentle hand on my shoulder. "But if you try to escape, they'll come looking for you or worse... they'll use your family to flush you out. If you return, there's a chance we can outsmart them."

Garon stepped in. "Betta's right. We need to go back. But this time, we won't be alone. We'll have her on the outside, interrupting the simulations whenever she can. If we work together, we can stay ahead of them."

I studied Garon for any sign of doubt, but his expression stayed firm.

"So, what's the plan?" Thomas asked beside me. "How do we outsmart something that knows our deepest fears?"

"We use every resource we have," Betta stated. "I'll monitor your rooms. I'll let you know how many have dropped out, and I'll do whatever I can to interfere with the simulations to give you the edge you need to hold on."

"That won't be enough," I said, shaking my head. "We need something more, something that can counteract the effects of the nightmares, something to dull the edge."

Betta's lips pressed into a thin line, her expression intense and searching as she focused on me. "What are you thinking?" she asked.

I took a deep breath, reaching deep into the well of knowledge my mother passed down to me like a precious inheritance. She taught me about the natural world, the secrets hidden in the leaves, and roots of plants. Now, more than ever, I needed to draw on that wisdom.

"Serenith and... *nokara root,*" I said, my voice gaining strength.

"*Widow's Source,*" Garon mused.

"Yes, we need both. Serenith to calm our nerves, nokara root to help us sleep."

There had to be a medical supply area somewhere in this Cird-forsaken building. Serenith and nokara root were staples across all of Sandric. I knew it. They'd become woven into the fabric of every well-stocked medical room. They were so common that even this sterile, heartless place couldn't afford to overlook their importance.

Betta nodded, her expression serious. "Tell me what to do."

I closed my eyes, summoning the memory of my mother's hands, deft and sure as she worked with the flowers, her voice patient and gentle as she explained their properties. "Start with the serenith," I began, opening my eyes to meet Betta's gaze. "It needs to be handled carefully. The leaves are the key, and hopefully they are dry. Crush them into a fine powder. We can mix it with water or brew it into a tea if we are able to get hot water. It'll help soothe our nerves, keep us sedated."

Betta listened intently, nodding as I spoke. "I should be able to find this in the infirmary. There were various bottles of tonics and dried contents I believe the medic uses. What about the nokara root?"

"You'll recognize it by its strong, natural scent. It's more pungent than you'd expect, but that's how you know you've got the right plant. The roots will be thick, almost gnarled, with a light brown skin. It should be crushed into a powder. If it's not you need to grind it. We'll also need to steep in hot water. A small pinch will help us sleep. It's potent. Too much can leave us groggy, and we need to stay sharp."

Thomas and Garon took note of every word on how to use the herbs.

"We know the root well in Dobia." Garon grimaced. "Too much won't just leave us groggy. We could wind up dead. Be very cautious." He raked his eyes over Betta.

I paused, meeting Betta's gaze, trying to gauge her understanding. This knowledge, passed down through generations, carried more than just information; it served as a lifeline, a connection to my mother and those before her who endured harsh conditions with these very methods.

Now, I placed my trust in it to help us survive as well.

"I can do this. I'll get it," Betta said, determination hardening her features.

I bit down on my bottom lip as I thought it through. "If you can't find them both, even just one will help. I had serenith in my room, but who knows if it'll still be there when I return. We don't need much, just enough to take the edge off."

Betta nodded, her mind already calculating the next step, yet the tension in her jaw hinted at her doubt. I felt it too. But it remained our only option.

Thomas squeezed my shoulder. "It will help."

The herbs alone wouldn't save us. They might offer us a brief edge—a moment of clarity or relief in a trial built to shatter us. Delicate as it remained, hope lingered, and here, even a fragile hope proved worth holding onto.

Garon leaned in, his voice low and urgent, the intensity of the moment pressing down on us. "We have to make a pact right now," he said, features tightening with fierce determination. "No matter what happens in those rooms, we don't let them win. We don't give in."

His words settled like a thick fog, charged with the unspoken gravity of the promise we were about to seal. Fear coiled tight in my chest. But when I met Garon's cool blue eyes, a small flame gained strength with each breath of air I fed it.

"We fight," I said, my voice firmer than I expected. "We fight with everything we have."

I thought of my parents, of the countless lessons they imparted over my years with them—of strength, of resilience, of never backing down in the face of adversity. All of that—every ounce of wisdom and strength they imparted—bubbled up inside, a vivid reminder of who they raised.

I was Levity Wilhoph, daughter of Hophsted and Wilhelmina, two people who believed in a better world. And I refused to be used. Clarity washed over me.

I would make them proud.

I would carry them with me, using everything they taught me to guide my actions, to give me strength to face whatever came next.

"I won't forget who I am," I added softly, almost to myself.

But Garon heard me. He tilted his head, his brilliant blue eyes—that I now realized reminded me of my mother's—questioning.

"I'll honor them," I continued, the words coming more easily now. "I'll honor my parents and everything they stood for. I'll believe in myself the way they believed in me. And I won't let this place break me."

Thomas's voice was thick with apprehension. "And what if we can't? What if it's too much?" The tremor in his words struck a chord deep within me. This side of him scared me—his usual optimism now over-shadowed by doubt.

Betta placed a hand gently on his arm. "If it gets to that point, I'll be there. I'll do whatever I can to pull you back. But you have to trust me, Thomas. Trust all of us."

He nodded, swallowing hard. "Okay."

As I watched him, a swell of empathy and respect rose within me. True strength wasn't about being unshakable; it was about confronting fear and choosing to move forward despite it.

I realized that no matter how well we thought we understood those around us, there was always more to discover and connect with. That connection and trust would be our lifeline, keeping us fighting even when darkness threatened to engulf us.

"We'll all fight," Garon said, looking around at each of us. "This is our chance to take control, to stop them from doing this to anyone else. We have to make it count."

Betta glanced at the entrance to the alcove, as if expecting someone to emerge from the dark. "We don't have much time. We need to move."

With courage fueling our veins, we steeled ourselves to return to our rooms. The merciless Sanctioning awaited but fear no longer isolated us.

United by purpose, we transformed from mere survivors into a force ready to defy the odds. Though unpredictability obscured the path, one truth remained: we were prepared to fight back.

We would not break.

A Moment of Reckoning:

In my recent class on the cultural dynamics of Sandric, I was at a crossroads. A simple discussion on the historical manipulation of narratives turned into a deep dive into the socio-political implications of our current state. When a student questioned the integrity of the small council, I felt compelled to explore the topic.

Fueled by a sense of urgency, I introduced the concept of grassroots movements and their potential to effect change, suggesting that our voices could rise as one to challenge the status quo. I encouraged students to document their experiences and perceptions of government influence in their lives, creating a repository of testimonies that could shine a light on the hidden truths behind our fractured society.

As the conversation grew more impassioned, I could sense the unease among my colleagues. They whispered about the need to "stay in line," warning that our discussions might attract the wrong kind of attention. Ignoring their cautions, I pressed on, urging my students to think critically and question everything.

Now, I find myself contemplating the consequences of that class. Will the government view this as radicalization? Will my students' testimonies expose us to scrutiny? Perhaps this is the risk we must take.

In pursuit of truth and understanding,

—H. Wilhoph

Chapter
Twenty-Six

BETTA

Responsibility bore down on me as I led the representatives back into the black well of The Sanctioning. I battled to keep my expression stern, upholding the guise of authority expected of me. Yet inside, a storm raged—chaos, doubt, guilt—threatening to unravel me.

The alarm still buzzed and the brief flash of the red emergency lights remained the only illumination. I didn't have to look back to know they were following. I could feel them—Levity's barely restrained panic, Thomas's exhaustion battling with his will to survive, and Garon's simmering defiance. Each of them hesitated at every corner, their movements stilted as if expecting the walls to close in.

Levity broke the silence. "Aren't you afraid they're watching us?"

With an almost casual tone, Garon spoke for me. "When I was in the control room, I skimmed through Lyonal's unsecure files. There's a note buried in the data. Power usage from the simulations—and across all territories—is at an all-time high. Production can't keep up. The cameras…" His gaze flickered toward the ceiling. "They're supposed to be used minimally, not unless it's necessary. They are more concerned about what is going on in the rooms. Escape…" His words trailed off once more, his voice hardening. "They think it's impossible."

Thomas snorted a bitter laugh that bounced off the walls of the dark hall. "Impossible, huh?"

No one spoke for a long moment.

We reached the first door—Levity's—and I paused, turning to face her. I saw the doubt she tried so hard to hide. Her hands clenched at her sides, knuckles turning white as if bracing for what might await her.

The door slid open from my touch, revealing the stark interior of Levity's room. The scent of ozone and disinfectant wafted out, sharp and clinical.

Before Levity could step inside, Thomas reached out, wrapping a strong hand around her arm before embracing her. The gesture came quickly, brimming with unspoken emotions. Levity's shoulders relaxed as she leaned into him. They held each other tight afraid to let go as if the world would crumble if they did.

When they finally pulled apart, Levity turned to me. "Trust is a fragile thing, isn't it?" she whispered, her voice carrying a wisdom that belied her years. "It's the foundation of everything we hold dear, yet it's so easily shattered."

Her words struck a deep chord within me, resonating with the doubts and fears I'd tried to suppress. Trust. The word echoed in my mind, flooding me with shattered memories—Draven's reassuring smile, the quiet moments when I dared to believe in him and in us. Trust could be broken easily, torn apart by the vicious hands of betrayal. By the harsh reality of Brawn's involvement.

But the trust she spoke of existed between her and I.

I hesitated "Trust is... a risk, a wager," I replied, my voice quieter than I intended. "It's a choice to believe, in spite of everything."

Levity nodded, her focus unwavering. "Then I choose to trust, not because it's easy," she said, her voice quiet so the words would not be overheard. "I trust that you'll find a way to keep us safe. And I trust that when this is all over, we'll rebuild and make something better out of the ashes of what was."

I felt a swell of admiration for her—a young woman thrust into a nightmare, yet still choosing to believe in something greater than herself. "I will come back," I promised. "And I won't stop until we're free."

She gave me the best smile she could offer. Valor emerged in her as she straightened her spine and entered her room. Each step was a declaration of her defiance against the consuming fear.

I watched her until the door slid shut, sealing her once more in the cold, unfeeling light of the simulation.

Thomas was next. He stood pale, the dark circles under his eyes a stark contrast against his able-bodied stature. He resembled a man teetering on the brink, yet a glint in his taut features revealed a will to survive against all odds.

When the door gave its soft hiss as it opened, I leaned in close. "Thomas," I said softly, hoping my voice could be his lifeline in his sea of darkness. "You can do this. I'll bring you what you need—just hold on a little longer. I'll keep you updated on the others too." I motioned back to Levity's door. "So you know you're not alone in this."

His throat bobbed as he nodded. His hand brushed mine as he entered his room. The brief contact was my reminder of the human connection we all still clung to. He turned back to me, his voice low and urgent. "Betta, if I don't make it... if something happens to me, promise me you'll protect Levity. She's... she's stronger than she knows, but she'll need someone to watch over her."

The fear and sincerity in his voice struck me like a knife. "You're going to make it," I replied, my voice firmer than before. "I will look after her. You have my word."

"Thank you," he murmured. The door shut behind him with a finality that echoed in my ears.

Garon's room, a little further away, was the final stop. As I reached for the door, he studied me with that sharp, calculating focus of a Perpetual Sense—but more lay beneath it now. Something softer, more intent. I ignored the shift, brushing it off as his dedication to the mission.

The door slid open, and I leaned my hand to rest on the frame. Garon hesitated. He didn't speak, but I could feel the quiet concern. His icy blue eyes lingered longer than necessary, almost as if he could see the cracks beneath my steadfast façade... the one's Draven left behind.

I drew in a deep breath, forcing the thought of that bastard from my mind.

"I'll disrupt their hold whenever I can," I whispered, trying to move this process along. "But you'll need to stay vigilant. Trust your instincts—they've gotten you this far. And remember, you're not alone."

His hand enveloped my hand against the doorframe, igniting that surprising warmth beneath my skin. I nearly withdrew, but his grip trapped me in this moment. I glanced up at him. His strong, broad shoulders filled the space. His shirt in disarray revealed the inked lines that snaked across his muscled chest and down his forearms. He studied me with a fervor that felt electric.

"I won't forget," Garon said softly. "And Siren... you don't forget that either. You don't have to carry this alone."

For a moment, I almost let the sincerity blind me.

Almost.

I wanted to believe in Garon. I longed for a shred of loyalty I could rely on. But that sincerity I glimpsed... it wasn't enough. Not anymore.

"Yeah, well," I muttered, jaw tight as I slipped my hand out from underneath his and wrapped my arms tightly around my core, "I make better decisions alone."

He gave a tight nod, releasing the doorframe and walking away. Whatever he saw in me, whatever confusing feelings lay hidden underneath it all, would have to wait.

He stopped, his back to me. When he turned, his gaze locked onto mine—not with frustration, but with understanding, as if seeing through my walls. My well-constructed armor. His voice, when it broke the silence, was calm and unwavering, as though he'd already known that would be my answer, but he needed me to hear his next words.

"You think you're better off alone, Siren?" His words were measured, each chosen with care. "I get it. The world's been rough on you. On both of us for that matter." His gaze was disarmingly tender, stripped bare to reveal something achingly genuine. "Whether you are ready to hear it or not, you don't have to do it all by yourself anymore. I'm not just another player in this game, Betta. I'm something far different."

Garon closed the distance between us.

His hands cupped my neck with a surprising gentleness, his thumb brushing my pulse. The motion was slow, deliberate, feeling for the frantic rhythm of my heart and connecting my life to his. A warmth radiated from him, calming me, and I swore I sensed a faint glow around us.

His eyes flickered to mine, searching for something—permission, maybe. I wasn't sure.

"I know what it's like," he said, eyes never leaving mine, "to fight alone. To carry everything on your shoulders because you think it's easier. But I'm telling you right now—no one's built to carry all that weight. Not you. Not even me." His voice softened. "It's okay to need people. And it's okay to be scared of the kind of trust that requires."

His thumb pressed against my pulse point, and my breath caught. Every nerve screamed to surrender, to let myself fall into whatever he was offering.

But I fought it. I wasn't sure I could trust this—trust him.

I dropped my eyes to the ground.

He leaned in, and I held my breath. But instead of kissing me, he tilted my head, brushing back my hair. His lips pressed just beneath my ear, a caress that seared through me like fire.

"You're worth more than this fight, more than you even know. You're beauty in the darkness," he murmured against my neck and I could feel the quiver of his breath on my skin.

He pulled back, hands still cradling my face. His eyes held an emotion I couldn't quite name—affection, maybe, but also deep respect.

"I'm not going anywhere, Betta. You'll never have to fight this alone. Not as long as I'm breathing."

I watched his silver braids fade into the shadows, but his kiss and those words lingered long after the door hissed shut.

The alarm cut out. The red light blinked off, leaving a heavy, unsettling silence in its wake.

By the time I reached the doors leading into the Leadership Room, my heart pounded in my head, each beat a reminder of the truth I carried. I paused at the door, willing myself to steady my breath and fight the fatigue threatening to steal my resolve. There was no room for hesitation. Not now.

Inside, the overhead light glowed at it's lowest setting—their feeble attempt to conserve power. The polished marble floor seemed to mirror the tension, reflecting Lyonal's rigid stance as he stood near the center of the room, his tall frame taut with suppressed aggression. Behind his glasses, he assessed me with a predatory scrutiny.

Draven leaned back by the far wall, arms crossed. His bandaged gunshot wound on display as he now wore a simple black T-shirt. Though his expression remained neutral, tightness in his posture belied the calm front. His presence, once a source of reassurance, now fed my growing unease. *How had I missed it?*

"Betta," Lyonal's voice cut cold and clipped. "You've been busy."

I met his scowl with a calm expression. "The representatives needed to be returned to their rooms. *I* did that. *I* secured them."

"Secured," Lyonal repeated, the word dripping with suspicion. "Or reassured?"

Beneath my unflinching exterior, my pulse pounded relentlessly. "It's crucial they believe everything is proceeding with The Sanctioning as expected. If they suspect otherwise, we risk losing control."

Lyonal took a step closer. "And you're certain you haven't already lost control? Your recent... *activities* have raised concerns, Betta. Serious concerns."

The pressure built, his words a trap ready to snap shut around me. But I couldn't back down. Not to him. Not now. "I'm doing what needs to be done to ensure The Sanctioning proceeds smoothly. The representatives have returned to their rooms, none-the-wiser. My methods may be unconventional, but the results speak for themselves."

His gaze hardened. "What do you propose we do with Garon? He can't possibly continue this way. His behavior was... unacceptable."

I resisted the urge to roll my eyes. "He's fine," I said, brushing the matter off with practiced nonchalance. "Rough around the edges, but he'll fall in line. There's no need to worry about him."

Draven looked from Lyonal to me. Pinning me with concern.

Lyonal's voice tightened. "We can't afford disruption. We've worked too hard to—"

"We've worked too hard? You mean you?" I cut in. "To create a system that doesn't account for the simple fact that people—especially those like Garon—might resist? You didn't think your technology might encourage rebellion? Defiance? Violence? But of course not—your system was flawless."

I leaned in, letting the words land. "Garon shouldn't be punished for reacting to the manipulation. He's what your precious technology failed to predict. And now you're scrambling, wondering how to fix it. Maybe start by taking responsibility for creating the very fucking thing you can't control."

Lyonal's heated stare bore into me. "You're on dangerous ground, Betta—where missteps are unforgiving. You're far from ready for the fallout."

Doubt crept in, but I pushed it aside. I couldn't waver. Not with *him* watching.

Draven stepped forward, his voice a commanding rumble that cut through the tension. "Enough, Lyonal. Betta always acts in Sandric's best interest. You would do well to remember that."

The tension in the room spiked, Lyonal's attention snapping to Draven. For a moment, it felt like the room would explode from the force of their silent standoff. But then Lyonal took a step back from Draven. The suspicion in his eyes remained, now tinged with something I knew to be more personal.

"Just remember," he said, ice coating his warning. "There's more at stake here than you realize. Don't forget that. Some of those stakes are... closer to home than you think. Already being surveilled."

The implication hit like a blow. *My mother.* The last person I had, the one person I couldn't lose. Panic surged and I lunged, fist clenched.

"Don't you dare threaten her," I spat, my voice trembling with the anger.

Draven's hand shot out, grabbing my arm before I could take another step. "Betta, stop." His grip stayed firm, his voice too calm. "This isn't the way."

I jerked against his hold, but Draven held me in place. Lyonal's words tangled with the fire in my chest. How dare he. How dare he use my mother.

With the satisfying look of besting me, Lyonal turned sharply and stalked out of the space to return to the control room.

I released a breath I hadn't realized I held, my shoulders sagging with exhaustion as I exhaled the anger. But as the door closed behind Lyonal, another kind of lethargy settled on me—Draven. He moved closer, expression softening, but I could finally detect the calculation lurking beneath. Like fog lifting.

"Are you all right?" Draven asked, his voice quiet and carrying something that mimicked concern.

I nodded through spinning thoughts. "I'm fine. Just... trying to stay ahead of him."

Draven studied me as if trying to read between the lines. Then he nodded. "You're doing what you have to do. But be careful. Lyonal's not the only one watching."

His words struck a nerve, my suspicions about him flaring. What did he know? How much was he hiding? His access to *intel* seemed to be growing. Could he bring up the live surveillance feeds like Lyonal? I met his gaze, trying to gauge his meaning, but he turned toward the briefing console, activating the system with a swipe of his hand.

The cold, mechanical voice filled the room:

```
Current status of The Sanctioning: Surviv-
ing Aides remaining—Levity Wilhoph of Ser-
toda and Geraldine Sato of Lizon. Perpet-
ual Sense representatives remaining—Garon
Fiore of Dobia, Saria Meeth of Trunta,
and Naeem Weeder of Brawn. Noble Warrior
```

```
representatives remaining—Dorian Ballister
of Brawn, Thomas Ravleon of Sertoda, and
Kolvin Nakamura of Lizon.
```

My heart lurched at Levity, Thomas, and Garon's names. So many had fallen to The Sanctioning in less than twenty-four hours. I clenched my fists, fighting to keep my expression neutral. The briefing ended and the room fell into a painful silence as the voice faded.

Draven turned back to me. As he took a step closer, his voice dropped to a whisper. "Betta, about the flash drive—"

"I lost it." I dropped my eyes as I swallowed the lie. "It probably slipped out of my pocket on the way to the alcove. And the chances we'll find it in this Cird-forsaken darkness. I'll be damned if I don't stumble into a guard trying to retrace my steps. I've messed up everything." I bluffed.

Disappointment creased Draven's face, but then his expression hardened, becoming unreadable. He let out a long sigh. "We'll find another way to get the information we need," he said. "But we need to stay on course. Don't let Lyonal shake you."

I nodded while guilt wreaked havoc on me, intertwining with the suspicion taking root. Draven lingered as if he wanted to say something more but then turned to leave.

He paused at the door, his hand hovering just above the cold steel. He turned back to me, his stare locking onto mine with a seriousness that raised the flesh on my arms.

"Betta," he began, his voice measured, "Dorian... he's in a precarious position. The nightmare he is submerged in is harder than I even expected. We need him to succeed."

I swallowed, forcing myself to keep my expression neutral.

He ran a hand over his shaved head. "Dorian's strong in his own right, but the physical strain will wear on him. Lyonal's watching my every move. If I were to intervene, to go into his simulation, it would be too obvious, too risky. It has to be you."

"What do you need me to do?"

Draven continued, his tone growing more intense. "Dorian is being subjected to extreme heat, far beyond what the human body can endure for long. He's at risk of dehydration and heatstroke. You need to find a way to get him water and keep him hydrated. Anything you can do to lower his body temperature could save his life. A damp cloth, shade—anything."

I nodded. "I'll see what I can do." Unsure if even that were true.

"Good," he said, satisfied with my response. "Dorian's success is crucial. We can't afford to lose him now."

With that, he turned and exited the room, leaving me standing alone with his directive.

The door gasped shut, and I let out my own slow, controlled breath. The tightness in my chest loosened, though my mind was a storm of conflicting thoughts. I aimed to disregard Draven's orders completely. Manipulating The Sanctioning to favor Dorian went against everything I'd just learned about this corrupt system.

Yet, I couldn't afford to reveal my true intentions. Not yet.

I needed to maintain the charade, let Draven believe I was on his side while I maneuvered to undermine the very structure he sought to uphold. The time to act drew near, but I needed to mind my step.

I turned my attention inward, focusing on my next task; securing the herbs for Levity, Thomas, and Garon.

But my thoughts shifted to the other representatives, each trapped in their own personalized hell.

The ethical dilemma tore at me, pulling me in opposite directions. If I convinced the remaining representatives to quit, to end their suffering sooner, perhaps Levity, Thomas, and Garon wouldn't have to hold on as long. Fewer left standing, the sooner this nightmare could end for them. Was I truly prepared to push others toward that dark unknown, to sacrifice them in the hope of saving those fighting a common cause?

The very thought sent me teetering on the edge of an abyss, staring down into a void of my own making. Would I be any better than those who designed this perverse system if I interfered like that? Better than Lyonal or Draven as I fought for my own representatives to succeed?

A cold sweat broke out on my skin. The representatives were people, each with their own fears, their own lives beyond these walls. To guide them toward quitting, knowing what awaited them, would betray everything I believed in. But to do nothing... to do nothing felt like a betrayal of a different kind.

I was trapped between my desire to protect Levity and the others, and the crushing guilt of what it would take to do so. I saw no right answer. No clear path forward. Every choice led to suffering, to loss, to the degradation of my soul.

I would find another way—a way that didn't involve choosing who would suffer and who might survive.

But the longer I hesitated, more minds would be lost to this brutal, unforgiving machine.

Lyonal already held suspicions, and Draven's scrutiny felt sharper than ever.

I straightened myself, rolling back my shoulders.

Every small victory counted.

Each act of defiance marked a step toward unraveling this fucked up system.

Contemplating Defiance:

Today, an official sat in on my class, a stark reminder of the scrutiny that surrounds us. Their presence felt like a noose tightening around my words, yet it also ignited a spark of defiance within me. As I engaged my students in discussions about our shared histories and the importance of questioning authority, I sensed the official's intention to stifle any hint of dissent. But the whispers of discontent among my students grew louder, urging me to consider a more active role in challenging the oppressive structures governing our lives.

I find myself contemplating organizing a gathering to discuss the very real implications of our society's descent into silence. This would not only include traditionalists but open the discussion up to others as well. A forum for debate; it would serve as a rallying point for those who refuse to accept the narratives imposed upon us.

I know the risks. They watch closely, and their reach extends far beyond mere governance. But inaction feels like complicity. If I am to teach the value of truth and courage, I must embody those principles myself. Perhaps it is time to transform quiet reflection into a collective movement, to turn our thoughts into action.

~~In pursuit of truth and understanding,~~

From darkness, we rise. For light, we fight.

—H. Wilhoph

Chapter Twenty-Seven

LEVITY

Time became a nebulous concept, a formless entity that slipped through my fingers like sand. I no longer held understanding of its passage, no sense of how long I'd been here, locked away in this room.

I kept track of the days by counting the pathetic meals they brought me, a meager offering that amounted to three pitiful rations. Each meal consisted of a slice of stale bread slathered with some bland spread—peanut butter or a mushy avocado—along with a small portion of dry, flavorless chicken that seemed to have lost any semblance of seasoning or warmth.

At first, the meals were few and far between, designed to punish any urge to escape. Consequences. A single meal would stretch into an agonizing wait, leaving my stomach growling in protest. Each pang served as a reminder and the discomfort, a bitter taste that lingered long after I finished eating.

But as the days dragged on, the meals began to arrive more frequently, albeit with no increase in quantity or quality. The gnawing hunger never truly subsided, a constant reminder of my captivity.

The charred room that existed as my nightmare faded. Replacing it was a new horror that wrapped around me as I woke. No longer did I linger in the suffocating darkness of that burnt space, the scent of smoke and despair clinging to me like a second skin. Now, I found myself in a different torment, one that felt just as visceral and carried an entirely different meaning.

Instead of walls blackened by flames, I stood on the precipice of an endless abyss. Craggy and dark. I could hear the distant echoes of laughter—childlike and innocent—piercing through the silence, a haunting reminder of what I lost and couldn't get back to. The faces of my siblings fading in and out of view, their smiles twisting into expressions of fear and confusion. I reached for them, desperate to bridge the chasm that separated us, but the darkness swallowed my voice, rendering me mute and powerless.

Each time I leaned my worn-out body against a rock and dared to let my eyes close, I'd wake drenched in cold sweat, heart racing as if I sprinted through the very depths of my mind. I longed for the charred room to return, for its familiarity. The new nightmare reminded me of my failure to protect them—a punishment more severe than I felt I could bear.

"Levity," Betta's voice emerged as a whisper, soft as the rustle of fabric in the dimly lit room. She moved with a deliberate grace, her steps measured and quiet, as though every movement she had carefully choreographed like a delicate dance. "In moments like these, when everything feels overwhelming, finding your anchor is crucial."

I watched.

My heart ached under the burden of the situation. "My anchor?" I finally asked, my voice barely above a murmur. I tried to match her volume as my blurred vision focused on her. I sat on the cold and dusty ground. The grit of stone and pebbles still beneath my fingertips. She looked so out of place.

Betta nodded, her expression reflecting a depth of understanding. "Yes, your anchor. It's what keeps you grounded when the darkness threatens to swallow you whole. For me, it has always been my mother. Her voice, her strength—those memories helped me stay tethered, no matter how fierce the storm."

She moved through the sparse landscape, her white apparel casting a brightness that brought a touch of light to the room, transformed to resemble the outdoors. I stood to follow her as she guided me through the space still meant to be a void. The fissure in the earth that separated me from my siblings was still off in the distance.

"Find something that reminds you of your anchor, Levity. Let it be a source of strength. For you, it's your family, isn't it? The thought of seeing them again, of being reunited. Let that hope guide you." As she spoke, Betta's voice occasionally rose, sharp and commanding as she barked orders, creating the illusion of escalating my situation. "Come on, Levity! We need to focus!"

In her flurry of movement, Betta discreetly tucked a small pouch of herbs where it blended with the shadows and rock, yet remained easily accessible.

I watched her with apprehension and curiosity. "My family..." I began, attempting to grasp the essence of what she suggested. "My strength does come from them. But right now, it's so hard to think of them. These screams."

Just then another one of Evie's cries tore through the dark room.

Betta flinched.

Her hand rested gently on my shoulder as she guided me to a more shadowed and secluded part of the simulation. "Think about the moments you shared with them. The laughter, the love. Imagine their voices, their faces in good times. Let those memories fill the void. They are part of who you are and will give you the strength you need to get through this."

Betta's tone became forceful once more, her directives cutting through the room's tension. "We need to get this done! Move!" she commanded, her voice echoing off the walls, ensuring that any observers would focus on her doing "her job".

Betta's honey eyes met mine, filled with a quiet reassurance. "Hold onto that anchor, Levity. No matter how dark it gets, remember why you're fighting. You're not alone, and you have the strength to endure this. Hang in there. There's only one Surviving Aide representative left now, from Lizon. The horrors within that room are… beyond description, but you've made it this far."

Her words, though meant to inspire strength, only served to deepen my growing terror. The vague mention of the Lizon representative frayed my nerves. "What about Thomas?" I asked, the name escaping my lips in a breathless, desperate plea. "How's he holding up?"

Betta's posture, usually so erect, slumped forward. That meant something—fear, guilt, or maybe both. She hesitated, a painful silence stretching between us. "Thomas is... fighting," she finally said, her voice doddering. "It's not easy for any of you. But you need to focus on yourself. You need to keep going."

I closed my eyes tightly, wishing not to think of what might be happening to him.

When I opened them again, she was gone.

I visualized the faces of my siblings, the sound of their laughter. A fleeting comfort as it was often interrupted by their screams, but a comfort nonetheless. Betta's words, coupled with the subtle presence of the herbs she hid, began to weave a fragile thread of hope through my despair.

Tivian. Triad. Blue. Evie.

Tivian. Triad. Blue. Evie.

Tivian. Triad. Blue. Evie... Thomas

In this grim existence, I clung to the hot water they supplied with meals for making my own tea. The steam curled into the air, as I brewed the herbs Betta smuggled in. Each sip became a momentary escape—a taste of something that felt adjacent to freedom.

I closed my eyes, feeling the grip of my nightmare, and a memory emerged from the depths of my mind—one that once felt hopeless but now brought me the gift of warmth. I remembered the afternoon when sickness swept through our small home like a shadow, stealing our laughter and leaving only coughs and soft whimpers. I fell sick too, feverish and weary, but all I could focus on was my little sister, Evie. At only two-years-old then, she nestled against my side, her small frame shivering with chills. Her warm brown eyes, usually sparkling with liveliness, looked glassy and lost.

Blue, at four, sat in the corner, her cheeks flushed, hands wrapped around her knees, staring blankly at the wall. The mischief that usually radiated from her had dulled. Triad and Tivian, at ten-years-old, sprawled out on the floor, foreheads glistening with sweat. Tivian's voice had grown hoarse as he grumbled about how unfair it all was.

"Why do we have to be sick?" he complained, furrowing his brows in frustration. Triad, ever calm, could only manage a weak shrug, fatigue etched across his face.

I could feel the heaviness of my own fever and weakness, but something inside me stirred. I pushed myself upright, determined to bring a little light into our dim afternoon. Each step toward the back door felt like a battle, but I pushed on to our mother's garden.

The garden, though overgrown, burst with life; vibrant greens and colors stood in stark contrast to the dullness of that day. The soothing aroma of herbs enveloped me as I gathered handfuls of *citranelis, florabella,* and *mintara.* Each leaf, a lifeline, a promise of comfort that only nature could provide.

I brewed a warm tea, fingers trembling as I poured the steaming liquid into mismatched cups. Delicate scents wafted through the air, soothing and masking the tension curling in my chest. I handed each sibling a cup and settled down among them, tucking my legs beneath me. "Let's pretend we're explorers in a faraway land," I began, a hint of playfulness intertwined with the words. "We're searching for the rarest herbs to make the strongest potion."

Unbeknownst to them, I had tucked extra flowers and sprigs of foliage into the corners of the room—beneath the edge of a chair, behind the leg of the table, nestled into the folds of a cushion. The room became a secret landscape, brimming with hidden treasures waiting to be found. It was a simple touch, but I hoped it would give them a spark of joy.

Their skeptical expressions softened as I sang a simple tune our mother often hummed. The melody wrapped around us like a warm blanket, weaving comfort through the air.

Slowly, the tension in the room began to fade. Evie's eyes blossomed with curiosity, and Blue's lips curled into a faint smile. Tivian and Triad exchanged glances, their illness momentarily forgotten as they frolicked about the room searching for the herbs.

As we sat sharing the magic of simple things, I felt the healing power of togetherness. I gave them all a reprieve from their suffering, wrapping us in a cocoon of love and hope, even in the depths of despair.

Now, as I took another sip of my tea, that memory burned bright against the backdrop of my current darkness—a reminder that even in the bleakest times, I could find the strength within myself, just as I did back then.

Through barely cracked eyelids I watched the walls of my room ripple, their edges blurring as the air thickened. The familiar scent of salt hit my nose. I felt the ground quake beneath me and grains of sand shifted around my face and body. The colors of the space faded to muted grays and blues.

The beach.

Once a place where I sought solace, transformed into an expanse of desolation. The shore lay scattered with contorted, half-submerged wreckage and skeletal remains.

The waves crashed against the shore, tainted with a dark, oily sheen, as if they carried with them a dark forewarning of the death. The sea itself resembled a void, a black gorge that dragged the scent of decay and rot.

Screams rented the air. I recognized these voices. The torment of hearing them without seeing them felt like a sadistic mockery of my love.

Then, they washed up on the shore—my parents. My mother's broken neck and my father with an impalement wound to his side.

Their lifeless bodies lay at my feet. Their once vibrant faces were now a horrifying illustration, frozen in expressions of fear and pain. Their limbs were deformed, their bodies marred by the ravages of the sea. The waves continued to roll in, dragging their broken forms back and forth, underscoring their finality.

I sat in the sand, watching them.

I held the pendant between two fingers and I cried, letting my tears run down my face and back into the sea.

I lay in the cold sand, staring up at the sky, the heavy gray clouds hanging low as if they were deciding whether to let their fury loose. The air brimmed with the threat of rain, the kind that seeped through skin and chilled the bone. Maybe the storm would come, maybe it wouldn't—it didn't really matter.

The sand shifted beneath me as I focused on the wave's dull thrum, their endless rhythm a strange comfort. The salty breeze brushed my skin, carrying the ocean's familiar tang, but it didn't feel the same anymore. This beach felt unreal, a ghost of what was.

I let my lashes fall shut and somewhere deep within the chaos, my father's voice echoed, soft and distant, like a whisper carried by the wind.

Whispers of the Night...
In shadows deep, where silence sighs,
A flicker of light beneath dark skies.
Hold tight, dear heart, when fear takes flight,
For dawn shall break, bringing back the light.

I breathed in, willing myself to feel something, anything beyond this crushing sense of emptiness. I held his poems tight when the world felt too heavy. Now, it barely registered as a murmur, swallowed by the roar of the storm that always lurked just beyond the horizon.

> *The storms may roar, the winds may wail,*
> *But love's embrace will always prevail…*

The words were slipping away, like the sand running through my fingers. I wasn't sure if I was holding on anymore, or if I was letting go. The wind picked up, the sky darkening further as the first drops of rain fell, cold and sharp against my skin. Perhaps it proved better to yield to the storm, to let it envelop me like I once attempted with the ocean.

> *From darkness, we rise.*
> *For light, we fight.*

The final words lingered on my lips. I didn't know if I believed them but saying them kept me tethered to something… anything.

I sat on the icy wooden floor, my back pressed against the cold stone wall, the house around me barren and broken. The roof finally caved in, letting in the bitter chill of the elements. My home—once full of life—was now an empty shell, falling apart, just like me.

My mind, with nowhere left to go, drifted to the dark revelations Garon shared at our lunch so long ago now—his account of the Cird and their crucial role in Sandric's history. The government ruthlessly oppressed the Cird and their allies, including traditionalists like my Pop, resulting in hunting and murdering those who knew the truth about our past. This oppression illustrated the lengths to those in power would go to crush any threats to their dominance.

It all came back to the Cird. The civilization my father spoke of with awe and mystery. I recalled him saying they possessed a supernatural power of sorts, yet they had been driven underground. How could something so powerful be brought down by mere ordinaries? The question haunted me, tickling the edges of my sanity like a riddle that needed solving.

The answer became clear.

Power wasn't always physical.

The Cird fell not to force but to manipulation—subtle, insidious control that twisted their perceptions and broke their will. I could feel it happening to me, too. The cold seeped into my bones. Every nightmare, every fear they unleashed aimed not only to hurt but to transform me. To erase my identity. To shatter me, just as they shattered the Cird.

Power and manipulation. Two sides of the same coin.

The Sanctioning wasn't a test of strength.

It was a battle for my mind. And in this empty, broken house, I doubted my strength to keep fighting.

Twenty-four meals.

Eight to ten days in.

The Weight of Choice (A Conversation with Wilhelmina):

Today, Wilhelmina's concern about my growing defiance became evident. After the official attended my class, she sensed the shift in my demeanor and the mounting need to challenge the government's narrative.

Her intuitive nature often unsettles me, but it also provides clarity. As I contemplated my next steps, I recognized the gravity of my intentions. The potential repercussions for our family and the thought of exposing our children to danger weighed heavily on my conscience.

Yet, I am compelled by a sense of duty to confront the lies that have permeated our society. Remaining silent feels like complicity, and the idea of allowing fear to dictate our actions is intolerable. I reflected on the countless injustices I have witnessed and the lives affected.

In the depths of my contemplation, I grapple with the conflict between my resolve and the determination to protect my family. Wilhelmina's unwavering support anchors me, but her caution serves as a reminder of the risks involved. Each decision carries consequences that could ripple through our lives, and I cannot ignore that reality.

As I consider the path ahead, I realize that turning back is not an option. The fight for truth and justice must begin, no matter the cost.

From darkness, we rise. For light, we fight.

—H. Wilhoph

Chapter Twenty-Eight

BETTA

I pressed myself against the cold counter, reaching for the top shelf with shallow breaths. Nearly two weeks had come and gone. This marked my third attempt to gather what I needed. I dared not take too much each time, in case anyone checked inventory. The bottles dwindled with each visit, a small victory and curse all at once—they never received refills.

Close by, Lyonal likely lingered in the control room, intensifying the nightmare scenarios. Recent interaction with Levity, Thomas, and Garon revealed the brutality of their ever-shifting rooms, each change more ruthless than the last. I managed at least two visits with each, providing what little comfort I could. Guilt drove me to slip Dorian extra water once... though I refused to stay long. He wasn't doing well and though I didn't want it to, that knowledge tore at my soul.

My fingers grazed glass vials and containers as I hastily found what I needed. By now, the layout of these shelves was familiar. The sharp scent of antiseptic struck me, triggering an unwelcome flash of Draven—his hands braced on this counter, his warm body pressed against mine, his mouth carrying the taste of mint. I pressed my lips together, willing away the memory.

Since uncovering Draven's father as the suspected architect of Sandric's suffering, I avoided him at every turn. Most nights, I retreated early, seeking solitary refuge rather than confronting our unspoken truths. Conversations with him transformed into tightrope walks. My playful banter began to falter under the strain of my growing unease. We agreed to separate the representatives we interacted with, never crossing paths. He urged me to keep trying to find information, to devise a new plan, to help his brother... but I couldn't. So, I chose silence over words, evading the tension that threatened to unravel everything.

The thin sliver of light from the slightly ajar door reminded me to be swift. I grabbed a few small plastic bags I'd be able to discreetly hide in my pockets. Every sound felt amplified as I selected the herbs.

My heart raced, each beat pounding out the threat of being caught. *Just a few more moments*, I told myself, reaching for another vial with trembling fingers.

"Betta."

I froze, the blood draining from my face.

The calm measured voice carried the unmistakable authority of some-one not to be trifled with. I slowly turned, my hand gripping the counter as if it could fasten me in place.

Lyonal stood in the doorway, tall and imposing. The faint lines on his forehead and silver threads in his dark hair hinting at both age and influence. His blue eyes, normally sharp and focused behind his glasses, now seemed clouded with something that looked disturbingly like fatigue—perhaps even despair.

"What do you think you're doing?" he asked, his voice soft, yet hiding an undercurrent of steel. The question, while deceptively simple, existed between us as a command.

I straightened, trying to calm my rapid heartbeat, and casually pushed the bags behind my body. "I could ask you the same," I said, voice firm. I needed to buy time, to gauge how much he knew.

Lyonal narrowed his eyes on the counter, and he entered, the door hissing as he pushed it shut behind him. "You're in a restricted area, Betta," he said, his tone still maddeningly even. "I don't think you stumbled in here by accident. And I don't see any emergency needs." He scanned my body for injuries.

My palms became slick with sweat as he moved closer. His penetrating stare searched my face. I could feel the heat of his scrutiny like a physical touch. *Careful, Betta.*

"I needed something," I replied with indifference. "Something that could help the representatives."

"The representatives?" His voice carried a note of incredulity, as if the idea defied all logic. "And what exactly do you think you can accomplish with a few herbs? This isn't some minor ailment to treat."

I bristled at his condescension, but I couldn't afford to let my temper get the better of me. "I'm trying to keep them from losing their minds. From dying," I said, meeting his accusatory stare with as much defiance as I could muster. "Or don't you care about that?"

Something—guilt, perhaps?—passed over Lyonal's face, so fleeting I almost missed it. He adjusted his glasses, a small, habitual gesture that only emphasized his age and the weariness that clung to him. "You're playing a dangerous game, Betta," he said quietly, almost as if in warning rather than reprimand. "One you don't fully understand."

"Then help me understand," I pressed, taking a step away from the counter and closer to him. "You've been in this longer than I have. You know the stakes, the players. So, tell me. What's *really* going on here?"

Lyonal remained silent. He squinted, deliberating over his next words. There was an internal struggle playing out behind his astute blue eyes.

I pressed onward, determined to break through his defenses. "I know about Saria," I continued, the words tumbling from my mouth before I could second-guess myself. I noted the fear in his eyes—brief, but unmistakable. "I know about General Ballister and the threats he's been making."

His silence stretched on. Lyonal took a step closer, and I instinctively backed up, my fingers brushing against the countertop behind me. Cornered. Nowhere to go.

"You don't know what you're talking about," he said, his voice low and dangerous. A barely perceptible tremor in his tone revealed I hit the mark.

"I know a little bit," I countered, squaring my shoulders. "I've seen the communications, Lyonal. The General's orders. The threats. He's using you, using Trunta, and he's using Saria—"

"Enough!" Lyonal's shout echoed through the small room, startling me into silence. His composure cracked, just for a second, and I saw the man behind the mask—a desperate man caught in an impossible situation.

"Walk me through it," I urged, my voice softening with genuine concern. "Lyonal, if you tell me the truth, I can help you. I can help Saria."

His features iced over, and a sharp edge danced on his next words. "Help me? You, who barely knows the breadth of this world's darkness—how could you possibly help? You think you can wade into this mess and fix everything with a few snarky words and misplaced bravery?" He advanced, his anger palpable. "You're naive if you believe you can untangle what's been decades in the making with nothing but your idealism."

The accusation stung, but I held my ground. *I will break through your bitterness.* But as I stood there in defiance, the ice in his demeanor started to melt. The tension in his shoulders began to ease. He exhaled, the sound rife with grief.

Removing his glasses, he ran a hand down his face. He moved back toward the door. His tone darkened as he began. "You have no idea how fragile things are between the territories right now. The power struggle... It's more than just politics. It's life or death. If we go against Brawn, if we defy their hold, it could start a war between us and every other territory. And right now, Trunta doesn't stand a chance. We may have technology, sure, but Brawn? They have it, too, now. They have numbers. They have the military, the ammunition, the resources to crush us. They've been preparing for this day for years.

"Trunta's running on fumes, Betta. We can't even get a reliable energy supply across all the territories. Trunta can't afford to waste it on a battle we can't win. Brawn controls everything—every scrap of fuel, every weapon, every power source." His blue eyes hardened, his brows pinched. "They can afford to play the long game, waiting for us to make a wrong move. And we're too dependent on them. Too weak. You don't go up against Brawn unless you're ready to fight with everything you have. And even then, it's a gamble.

"That's why compliance is the only option. Trunta can't afford rebellion right now—not without destroying everything in the process." He paused, letting his words settle between us. "And we're all bound to their rules, even if we can't stand them. You've seen it. How their influence ripples through everything we do. It's not just business, Betta. It's survival."

He let out a strained sigh, looking away for a moment, as if seeking some semblance of clarity. Finally, his soft gaze met mine again, revealing a vulnerability that struck me to my core. "I don't just have a stake in this. I have something—someone—to protect. You've met her... Saria. She's my daughter."

Saria.

The Perpetual Sense elect.

The one who must win at all costs.

His daughter?

His voice revealed a father's love, overshadowed by a harsh reality. The pieces began to snap into place. The walls he built around himself crumbled, exposing a man driven by an all-consuming love and a desperate need to protect the one person who mattered most.

A wave of empathy washed over me, replacing my earlier anger with a deep, aching understanding.

"I had no idea," I whispered. "Lyonal, I... I'm so sorry." The simple apology was all I could offer.

He nodded, but I found no relief in his expression, only a deep, abiding pain. "General Ballister knew. He's always known. He's been holding her over my head since the beginning of my term. The threats began long before Saria entered The Sanctioning. They began when Crestmore Industries teetered on becoming the next major tech conglomerate. Ballister wanted control, and he made it clear that if I didn't play by his rules, my family would suffer.

"When I refused to bend to his demands for advanced technology and market share, the threats escalated. He manipulated positions within the government to control me, threatening my business, even my wife—though illness claimed her before the General ever could. And now, with Saria in The Sanctioning, he's tightened his grip. If she fails... if she doesn't win, he'll destroy my business, my daughter—everything."

I approached Lyonal, my anger now directed at the General who manipulated us all. "But why? Why is he so determined to see Saria win?"

Lyonal's face darkened, the bitterness in his tone deepening. "Power," he said. "You see, Trunta has always been a problem for Brawn. Our territory's technological advancements threaten their dominance. Where Brawn controls through brute strength and military might, Trunta offers innovation, a vision of the future that doesn't rely on force. But Brawn spent generations asserting their control over Sandric, forging alliances and crushing rebellions. Trunta lives in fear of that and Brawn thrives off it."

He paused, his focus distant as if he were seeing the machinations of Brawn play out before him. "The Sanctioning, Betta, is about maintaining that control. The Perpetual Sense is a tool for their end game. With Saria in that position, Ballister can ensure that Trunta remains under Brawn's thumb. She's still malleable at her age. Out of my reach, he will corrupt her, use her to quash any dissent and push Trunta's innovations to continue serving Brawn's interests."

"Why would Brawn care so much about Trunta's innovations?" I asked, trying to grasp the full scope of the situation.

"Because innovation is power," Lyonal shared, voice intensified. "And Brawn fears losing control. They fear a Sandric where power comes from harnessing technology, not army size. If Trunta advanced without Brawn's interference, we could create a society where knowledge and progress are the cornerstones of power, not fear and violence. But that threatens everything Brawn stands for. They can't face becoming obsolete."

He clenched his fists until his knuckles turned white. "Ballister sees Saria as the key to maintaining Brawn's control. But if she fails..." His voice broke.

"He'll ruin her," I finished. "He'll break her, just like he's broken so many others."

Lyonal's silence confirmed it. A deep, burning rage settled in the middle of my chest. This transcended Saria; it encompassed all of us. The Sanctioning, the representatives, the entire system—all mere facades, cruelly orchestrated by a man who saw us as nothing more than grunts.

But I refused to be a grunt.

"We can stop this," I said, my voice firm with conviction. "Lyonal, we can outmaneuver him. We can save Saria and expose Ballister."

Lyonal raked his hair as he released a deep scoff. Any hope he harbored remained tempered by years of caution. "How?"

"We won't just manipulate The Sanctioning," I declared, watching Lyonal's brow furrow. "We'll reshape the outcome. Saria will reach the final two, as Ballister expects."

Lyonal crossed his arms, the muscles in his jaw tightening.

"But instead of victory, she'll stumble—just a heartbeat, enough for the simulations to record failure. Yet it won't be real."

"And how do you propose to pull that off?" Frustration edged into his voice.

"Use that big brain of yours," I raised my hands. "With your help, Lyonal, we'll hack the system. Craft a seamless illusion of defeat that keeps her safe."

He leaned back against the wall near the door, contemplating, but I pressed on. "Saria stays protected from the small council's horrors. Meanwhile, Garon claims Perpetual Sense as the last one standing. His victory serves our purpose; it will ignite a media storm, marking Dobia's first seat and turning the tides."

"You think the media will just accept that?"

"I know what makes the media salivate," I said, my voice tightening with confidence. "The moment Garon's victory is televised, it'll send shockwaves through Sandric. Dobia's rising against all odds—the perfect underdog storyline.

"We'll release everything we've gathered at the Sanctioned induction ceremony—broadcasted for all of Sandric to see. We'll leak the files. We'll expose how Brawn controlled us, manipulated territories, and suppressed our right to thrive. The truth will spread like wildfire, from Dobia to Sertoda, Lizon, and Trunta."

Lyonal stared at me, calculating the possibilities. "And you're sure the other territories will follow?"

"The evidence leaves no choice." I smiled. "We'll rally them all. The truth will allow you to pull Trunta out of their silence. Compliance ends now, Lyonal. We're going to unite the territories under a banner of truth, not fear."

Lyonal's expression softened. "Losing isn't an option, Betta."

"Yes, I intend to win."

I paused, letting the impact of my proposal sink in. This represented a way to use our oppressors' own tools against them. "As The Sanctioning concludes and the induction ceremonies unfold, we'll be ready."

My voice dropped. "In the midst of that chaos, with the people rising and the system in disarray, you'll have cover to get Saria out. While our revelations distract, she slips free. Ballister will be too busy trying to salvage his crumbling power base to notice she's gone."

I met his gaze, my expression reflecting a mix of determination and empathy on his glasses. "I know what Brawn is capable of. I've seen it firsthand. Their system breeds men who use their power to dominate and destroy. I've witnessed the personal cost of that mercilessness, and it's driven me to fight against their tyranny. Draven, too, has played his part in this web of deceit—I can't ignore the possibility that he might be manipulating me. I'm wary of his loyalties, and you should be too. But I trust my instincts. I believe that Brawn's control sits at the heart of Sandric's struggle."

Lyonal stared into my soul, questioning every word that fell from my mouth. He stepped back against the infirmary's doorframe, decision pressed down on him. "And what makes you think I can trust you, Betta? How do I know this isn't just another tier of deceit? Another way to manipulate me, to use me like Ballister has?"

"You have every reason to doubt me, after everything. You're right to be cautious but think about what's at stake. Saria's fate, Trunta's independence, the very foundation of Sandric's future—it all hinges on what we do next. I'm asking you to trust that we both want the same thing: to protect the people we care about and to stop Ballister from continuing his reign of terror. No one should suffer like this."

He focused on a spot on the floor, wariness in every muscle. "You're asking me to risk everything," he murmured, almost to himself.

"I know," I said, drawing closer. "But we're already risking everything by staying silent. Now we have a choice—let Ballister keep manipulating us, subjecting Saria to horrific threats, or take control. And if we do this right, we save your daughter, expose Ballister, and ignite Sandric's rebellion. You will get to be on the right side of history."

I feared he might refuse, that his doubt would outweigh his desire for justice. Then, he let out a long, weary sigh. He looked up with resolve shining in his eyes.

"Alright," Lyonal said, his voice firm. "I'll help you. But know this, Betta—if you betray me, if this is all just another—"

"It's not," I interrupted, my tone leaving no room for doubt. "I won't betray you, Lyonal. We're in this together."

He nodded, the finality of the decision settling over both of us. "For Saria."

Wrestling with Action
(A Cultural Awakening):

As I sit here, a longing stirs within—a desire to resist, to awaken the minds around me. Yet, I find myself at a loss for how to begin.

I think of organizing small discussions on our hidden histories, perhaps focusing on the Cird and their legacy. Could that spark something larger? Maybe I could incorporate art, allowing people to express their dissent creatively. A collective effort might be our best chance to foster change, but how to unite my colleagues without raising suspicions?

Each idea flits through my mind, but the fear of repercussions finds me around every corner. I know I must act, yet the unknown keeps me anchored. The path ahead remains murky, but I feel hope—perhaps through education, we can reclaim our narrative.

From darkness, we rise. For light, we fight.

—H. Wilhoph

Chapter Twenty-Nine

LEVITY

The piercing buzz cut through the oppressive silence. I drew my hands to my ears and curled my body into a tight ball. The harsh, mechanical sound reverberated through my bones like an electric shock. The noise was jarring compared to the insidious whispers and echoes that lulled my mind into an eerie calm. *Another evil twist in the simulation? Another layer of torment designed to break me further?*

With a groan of effort, I forced myself to rise from the simulated darkness. My limbs felt heavy as though the very fabric of the nightmare weighed them down. My muscles ached with a profound fatigue. Sleep deprivation. Hunger. Every step felt like wading through an invisible quagmire.

A robotic voice crackled through a hidden speaker, its flatness intruding the haze of my disorientation:

```
End of simulation. Proceed to the recovery
chamber immediately.
```

No hint of empathy or relief, just a directive that mirrored the cold, mechanical precision of this hell.

I hesitated, my mind racing with conflicting emotions. Had I truly emerged out of this... *alive?* Doubt curled into a corner of my mind making itself right at home. The room, now stripped of my most recent nightmare, still lingered, neighboring that doubt.

I stumbled toward a door, my vision swimming in my haze of fatigue and apprehension. Not the door I knew to enter the hall, but a different door that only revealed itself now that the simulation ended.

When this door slid open, it revealed a stark, sterile light that seemed almost too harsh after the smothering darkness I came from. I shielded my eyes as they adjusted to the intensity. The moment felt surreal.

As I stepped into the hallway, the wall's radiant whiteness and the unyielding fluorescent lights above created a gaunt atmosphere. Yet, there was something different here. The air was no longer stagnant. Instead, I inhaled a strange, invigorating freshness that seemed too vivid to be real. The oxygen tasted artificially enhanced, forced into the room to jolt me awake and rejuvenate me.

Each step I took felt disjointed from my body. My movements bounced off the walls, producing a sound that felt strangely hollow and detached. Green directional lights on the floor guided me forward. The sensory overload—

A surge of emotions flooded through me in that moment—relief, exhaustion, and an almost overwhelming sense of triumph. I made it through The Sanctioning, a feat that seemed impossible only minutes... *hours... days before?* The thought of emerging from the dark, psychological labyrinth—of having survived the harrowing ordeal—filled a source of profound satisfaction. For the first time in what felt like the entirety of my life, I allowed myself a fleeting moment of pride. If I endured this, if I came out on the other side, then perhaps the chance existed—however slim—that I might see my family again.

The invigorating air, the stark brightness of the hallway, and the distant

311

hum of machinery all combined to create a new reality, one that both exhilarated and terrified me. Each breath felt like a victory, each step a testament to my resilience.

Another door opened to reveal a stark space that seemed part doctor's office, part utilitarian washroom. The entire space, from the spotless floor tiles to the gleaming fixtures, exuded a stark cleanliness that felt almost too perfect. Its purpose wasn't clear, but the rows of medical supplies and the faint scent of disinfectant hinted at a place meant for mending. A single chair, the kind you'd find in a medical examination room, sat at the center, surrounded by monitors and various machines. The cold steel of instruments gleamed in the overhead light, all laid out on sleek counters nearby.

A small bathing station came into view, complete with a low basin and a row of neatly arranged towels, merging the clinical feel with a hint of personal care.

Two attendants with faces covered by plain medical masks, entered the room and moved with disconcerting efficiency. They were impersonal and focused solely on their task: observation of my every move.

"Thank you," I replied as one of them handed me fresh folded undergarments and clothes. It felt odd to thank someone for finally treating me human.

They did not respond.

They guided me through a series of steps that felt both surreal and left me unnerved.

The cleansing process filled me with a strange mix of relief and discomfort. Warm water flowed over me, a stark contrast to the cold, harsh environment I just came from in my nightmare room. The soap, with its artificial lavender scent, seemed overly sweet. Any semblance of normalcy felt out of place.

As the attendants rinsed and dried me, I caught glimpses of my reflection in the mirrored surface above where the extra towels sat. My face appeared ghostly pale and thin. Wet dark brown curls dripped in tangled strands around my shoulders. Haunted eyes stared back, with dark circles beneath them the color of bruises.

Once the cleansing completed, I found myself enveloped in an all-white, flowing dress. The delicate fabric and ethereal beauty seemed almost mocking against my surroundings and extravagant against my worn body.

I missed my boots. They carried me through my darkest moments, and now their absence felt like a void. It disconnected me. I touched my mother's pendant that still hung at my neck, my only reminder.

In my mind, I could almost hear Evie's excited voice, envisioning her wide-eyed admiration as she would have gushed about how beautiful I looked. Her pure and innocent enthusiasm would have soothed my jaded spirit.

But any sense of comfort remained distant, until I knew whether Thomas and Garon were safe. Without that certainty, even the slightest glimpse of beauty felt meaningless, offering no real solace.

The Leadership Room as they called it, held a long, polished table at the center of the room. Its surface reflected the dim, ambient light that emanated from recessed fixtures overhead. Rows of high-backed chairs stood at attention, their dark leather upholstery as hard lined as the responsibilities that awaited me.

On the walls, digital screens flickered to life, casting an unsettling glow that bathed the room in a bluish light. The screens displayed lines of code, geographical maps, and a live feed of various locations around the building.

Betta stood at the head of the table, her angular white blazer and matching slacks cutting a sharp figure against the backdrop of data streams adorning the screens. She was the embodiment of composure. She stood rigid, and her face was an impenetrable mask of authority. As I entered, her golden eyes locked onto mine, brimming with a depth of emotion that contradicted the formal role she steadied herself to play.

"Levity," Betta began, her voice clear and authoritative, "as the newly appointed Sandric Surviving Aide, it is my duty to congratulate you on surviving The Sanctioning."

Her words carried an impact that went beyond mere formality.

I nodded in acknowledgment, the gesture small but meaningful.

Betta regarded me a moment longer, as if trying to convey something, but then she continued. "Now, that you have emerged as the Sanctioned Surviving Aide, you must understand the full gravity of your position." She began to pace, her steps measured, as if rehearsed. "Your role is not just an honor; it is a duty that demands unwavering compliance with the orders of the Sandric Sanctioned. Your actions from this point forward will be scrutinized at every level. Any deviation, any failure to meet the expectations set forth by your directives, will have dire consequences."

She paused, allowing her words to settle, ready to deliver her next injunction with a bit of hesitation. "Your family," she continued, her voice dropping an octave, "is now under the *protection* of Sandric. However, this protection is conditional. Should you fail to execute your duties as Surviving Aide, or if you show any signs of dissent, their safety cannot be guaranteed. They will be monitored, day and night, and any action you take that threatens the stability of our society will result in immediate retaliation."

As she spoke, the screens around us flickered to life, displaying images that made my breath catch in my throat.

My family.

Tivian and Triad, their faces set with the seriousness that only comes from experiencing more than children their age should have to; Blue, her eyes full of the mischief and curiosity that so often got her into trouble. But Evie's face hit me the hardest—her round cheeks flushed with innocence, her brown curls bouncing as she played, oblivious to the nightmare that had become her sister's reality.

The sight of them hit my gut with a force I'd not experienced before now. Data streamed next to their images—heart rates, locations, and other cold, impersonal statistics—reducing the people I loved most to mere numbers on a screen.

Evie's laugh echoed in my ears, a phantom sound conjured by the sight of her tiny body twirling in a blur of brown curls and pink ribbons. She looked so small, so fragile, her world still one of dolls and bedtime stories, blissfully unaware of the darkness that hovered just out of sight.

My fists clenched tight as I imagined what they could do to her, to all of them, if they caught on to our plan. The coldness of the screens turned my energy into something icy and infinite. They took the most precious parts of my life and turned them into weapons against me.

Betta continued with her directives, her voice steady—almost detached. "Should you even entertain the idea of defiance, these threats will be realized with swift and unforgiving repercussions."

Her words tightened like a noose around my neck. Yet, a slight hitch, a fleeting hesitation that could easily have been imagined, drew my attention to her more closely. The moment she mentioned the other's Sanctioning, a crack appeared in her composure.

"The Sanctioning for the Noble Warrior and Perpetual Sense positions continue," Betta stated, her voice firm. "You are the first to finish, but the others are still fighting their battles."

My mind raced, and I found it difficult to mask my growing unease. I

315

needed to know how Thomas fared. The thought of him still enduring the torment cracked my composure. I couldn't suppress the urgency in my voice. "How many Noble Warriors are still in The Sanctioning?"

My question came out sharper than intended, anxiety and frustration spilling over. No longer a participant in The Sanctioning, I acutely sensed the human cost. The thought of Thomas suffering while I stood in this unsettling semblance of freedom felt intolerable.

Betta measured her response, but the shifting from foot to foot betrayed her irritation. "The Sanctioning is ongoing. The exact number of remaining participants is not something I am at liberty to disclose. What matters now is your role as Surviving Aide." She placed her hands on the table in front of her and I noticed only two fingers spread before me.

Betta remained unflinching, her focus reflecting someone accustomed to delivering difficult truths. "Your role as Surviving Aide now holds paramount importance. You embody our society's resilience. The decisions you make will resonate far beyond your immediate sphere, affecting everyone connected to you."

She paused. "Compliance is not merely expected; it's essential. Sandric's stability hinges upon your unwavering adherence to your role. Every action and choice must align with this duty. Your role is critical to maintaining our society's fragile equilibrium."

As the briefing drew to a close, Betta's formal demeanor softened ever so slightly, though her words remained as resolute as ever. "Prepare yourself for your responsibilities. Further instructions will be provided shortly. From this point on, you hold the privileges of the Sanctioned. You'll be taken to your private quarters now, where you'll be free to move about the Sanctioned living space."

I nodded, absorbing the implications. She continued, her voice composed but with a hint of caution. "Your public relations training will begin soon. Aides will visit you regularly to help sharpen your skills of communication and media handling. You'll need to refine your ability to present yourself as a figure of authority while maintaining the public's trust. Until The Sanctioning concludes and the final two seats are determined, try and remain..." She stumbled to find the right word, *"composed."*

"Thank you," I managed to say, though the words felt empty and meaningless.

Betta gave a final nod, her honey-colored eyes conveying what words could not. Then, without another glance, she strode past me and exited the room, the door sliding shut with a quiet hiss. The images of my family lingered on the screens.

My heart clenched at the thought of how easily they could be harmed. Fear knocked at my mind, begging to be let in. But as I stared at Tivian, Triad, Blue and Evie... I realized something that strengthened my determination to revolt: They were already at risk. Compliance wouldn't guarantee their safety; it only prolonged the inevitable.

If I did nothing, they would remain in danger. The only way to truly protect them lay in the power I possessed to bring the hands of the invisible authority down.

As two guards escorted me from the Leadership Room, leading me to my living quarters, my resolve solidified. I would play the role of the Surviving Aide, while I prepared for the moment I could strike back.

For my family.

For their future.

I would find the strength to see this through.

Walking down the long corridors, I held onto that thought, letting it fuel the fire within me.

Welcoming the Call
(A Look into The Depths):

A recent revelation from one of my students has unearthed significant information about the Cird, the original guardians of Sandric's sacred lands. Their history is not merely one of loss; it is steeped in lore, rich with tales of terra illumination—powers that allowed them to manipulate the earth's energies for growth and healing.

As I delve deeper into their history, I find myself contemplating what life must be like in their underground realm. For over a century, they have navigated the shadows, creating a society that has persisted despite oppression. How have they structured their world? What customs, beliefs, and systems of governance have enabled them to thrive away from the surface? These questions intrigue me, as their resilience may hold invaluable lessons for us.

Imagining the possibilities, I've considered what it would mean for the Cird to return to the surface. Their reemergence could ignite a cultural renaissance, challenging the mechanized forces that threaten to consume our identities. Would they bring with them their ancient wisdom and powers, revitalizing our connection to the land? The potential for unity among the territories could redefine our society.

Would the Cird welcome our call?

From darkness, we rise. For light, we fight.

—H. Wilhoph

Chapter Thirty

BETTA

My pulse hammered in my ears as I stared at the screen, the sudden conclusion of the Noble Warrior Sanctioning hitting me like a kick to the stomach.

Dorian Ballister won—too swiftly, too conveniently.

Moments earlier, I had visited Thomas. I didn't expect him to hold it together for so long—he seemed fragile, vulnerable—but to my surprise, he remained obstinate, his fire still burning despite the torment. No sign of weakness, no flicker of surrender. But then, when he shifted on the cot he sat on, his face pale, I caught the briefest tremor in his hands as he gripped the edge, knuckles white. He clenched his jaw so tightly I thought it might crack. Doubt pressed in on me for a heartbeat. Would the pressure break him? Would he falter? I shook my head, pushing the thought away. Time and again he proved stronger than that, I convinced myself. But then the abrupt announcement cut through the air, and the ground beneath me seemed to shift, revealing a dangerous undercurrent.

Draven.

Dread crept through my thoughts: had the mind-sweep already begun? The thought of Thomas eroding until nothing of him remained made my skin crawl.

I knew Lyonal wasn't in the control room as he prepared for Saria's extraction, and I couldn't be sure where he might be to seek help. But one thing I knew for certain: I wouldn't just stand by and let this happen. Thomas needed someone to reach him, someone he might still recognize and trust. And that someone wasn't me.

Levity.

I would find her. She might be his only hope—perhaps the only one who could halt the misconduct before it set in. My chest tightened at the thought of involving her, putting her at risk, but no other option remained. Levity needed to know. She needed to get to Thomas.

I slid open the door and hurried through the dark corridors to the Sanctioned living quarters. My heart raced, chaotic thoughts swirling in my head. I urged my body to move quicker, my legs faster.

Arriving at her room, I placed my palm on the door with a force that echoed down the hall. The guards outside her room looked at me, but I paid them no attention. Each second felt like an eternity until finally, the door slid open.

Levity stood before me, lips pressed. "Betta? What's going on?"

I stepped inside and let the door close behind me.

"Thomas," I blurted, voice trembling despite my best efforts to remain calm. "Something's happened. His Sanctioning—it ended too soon. Dorian Ballister won, and I'm afraid… I'm afraid Thomas might be in the process of the mind-sweep."

Levity's expression hardened, concern morphing into a fierce courage. "How could this happen? Did he concede?"

"I'm not certain yet, but I suspect Draven manipulated the outcome. He must have," I said, words spilling in a rush. "You need to get to Thomas, now. If there's any chance of stopping what they're doing to him, it's you. You can reach him."

Fear flashed across her face. "I'll go," she said, voice resolute despite the tension of the moment. "I'll find him."

I nodded. "Hurry, Levity. There isn't much time."

Reaching Draven's quarters next, I didn't bother knocking. The door slid open under my urgent shove, revealing Draven exactly where I expected him to be. His expression was a mask of calm that only fueled my rising fury.

"Draven!" I demanded, voice raw with emotion. "What have you done?"

His dark eyes met mine, and for a split second, I saw something unexpected—surprise, maybe even guilt. But the moment passed, replaced by a guarded, inscrutable show.

The tension in the room felt like a coiled spring, ready to snap. Shadows clung to the corners of the room, giving the space a bleak, claustrophobic feel, as if the walls were conspiring to keep us locked in this moment. Unspoken words and unresolved anger lingered between us, as an almost tangible barrier of separation.

Draven stood up from the desk, straightening his body to his full six-feet-four-inches of towering height. The coldness in his appearance returned with a palpable force. "Betta," he replied as if trying to contain something beneath that smooth exterior. "You need to calm down."

"Calm down?" The words burned in my throat, disbelief sharpening every syllable. The heat of my anger surged. I stepped closer. "You think I'm going to calm down. I know you meddled in the results!"

He scoffed before he scowled. "What exactly do you think I've done?"

"You sabotaged The Sanctioning," I spat, the bitterness of betrayal twisting in my chest. "You rigged it for your brother. I know it, Draven. Thomas was fine a moment earlier. You've turned this whole sick game into your personal battlefield."

He didn't flinch, but his jaw tightened, betraying his composure. The small space that remained between our bodies crackled with tension, our wills clashing. "And what would you have done, Betta? Watched as my brother failed? Watched him almost die? You promised you'd help him—"

"I promised to help him *survive*, not win through deceit!" The words lashed out, fueled by the deep well of fury and disappointment I could no longer suppress.

"He was dying, Betta!"

Could that be true? No, he was manipulating me. Manipulating the information.

"What kind of man are you, Draven? To use your own brother in whatever convoluted scheme you're working on."

He crossed his arms, the scent of leather and mint, once comforting, now felt like an intrusion. It reminded me of the closeness we once shared—a closeness now shattered beyond repair.

"What kind of woman are you?" he countered, voice laced with menace. "You promised to be on my side. But where were you when Dorian needed you most? Where have you been these past weeks? Helping everybody but Dorian!" His gaze darkened, the words sharp. "Death... it's always been a possibility, hasn't it? You should know that better than anyone, considering what happened to Edward. You think Dorian was immune to that fate with what he was being put through? Lyonal never changed his simulation. It was always the desert."

His accusation stung, but I refused to let him see the pain it caused. I squared my shoulders, meeting his glare with a defiance that matched the storm raging inside me. "Don't you dare turn this on me. I was there, watching, doing what I could to assist him in being more comfortable. But you—" My voice faltered, the enormity of his betrayal choking the words in my throat. "You made this into something it was never supposed to be."

Something I couldn't quite place flashed across Draven's face, but it disappeared as quickly as it came. The shadows now carved deep lines into his expression, making him look almost like a stranger.

"You don't understand," he said, his voice rough, the cold veneer cracking. "This isn't just about The Sanctioning. It's about ensuring that the right people are in power when all of this is over."

A tense silence followed. A mutual anger. A shared betrayal. It lingered between us. His breathing matched mine, harsh and uneven, as if the very act of drawing breath had become a struggle.

Draven's next step removed what space remained. He looked down into my eyes as his hard body hovered over me. "And what about you, Betta? You think you're so righteous, so above all this, but you're playing the same game. You've been lying, manipulating, pretending to be something you're not. You think you're any better than me?"

His words cut deep, stripping away the last vestiges of my control. I stepped back. "I never pretended to be perfect," I retorted, my voice tight with barely contained rage. "I never wanted this. I never wanted to become the thing I hate most." I stared up at him, tears pricking at the corners of my eyes. I refused to let them fall. "You're no better than your father," I finally said, my voice seeping venom. "Maybe you're even worse, because you pretended to be different. You made me believe you could be different."

The words hit their mark. I saw the flash of pain before the mask slipped back into place. And in that moment, I knew. I knew that whatever trust we built, whatever feelings we shared, were now tainted, irreparably damaged by the lies, the manipulation, the choices made on both sides.

I watched Draven, never breaking eye contact, waiting for a response. A denial.

Something to justify the hurt and betrayal, but Draven remained silent.

And that spoke louder than any defense he could've given.

I took another tentative step back. The room felt colder, the air sharper, as if the very atmosphere shifted in response to our war-torn words.

"Tell me the truth," I demanded. "What's really going on here, Draven? What orders did your father give you?"

His brow dipped—confusion, fear—but he regained composure. "You're talking nonsense, Betta. My father isn't involved in this. He has nothing to do with The Sanctioning beyond helping my brother into his elected seat."

I narrowed my eyes, refusing to be swayed by more lies. "You think I'm stupid." I scoffed. "You expect me to believe that? After everything I've seen, everything I know? You've been pulling *my* strings, Draven. And for what? To secure power for your brother? Or is there something bigger at play here? Something you're not telling me?"

His jaw clenched, the tension in his large frame becoming even more rigid. "This isn't about my father," he insisted, his voice tinged with frustration. "You're letting your imagination run wild. Dorian was about to die. I'm doing what I have to, Betta. To protect my brother, to ensure he survives my father! That's my only purpose!"

I shook my head, unwilling to accept his explanation. "No, it's more than that. I can feel it. You're hiding something from me, something beyond The Sanctioning, beyond your brother. What is it, Draven?"

Draven's calm demeanor faded. He ran a hand over the slickness of his head, and he paced like a tiger in front of me. "This isn't some grand conspiracy, Betta. It's survival… that's all it's ever been. For all of us."

"Survival?" The word felt hollow. Empty. I hated that fucking word. "Or obedience? You *are* a soldier."

"Stop it, Betta," he warned. Yet, an edge of desperation lingered, a hint of vulnerability that urged me to press on.

"No, Draven. I won't stop. Not until I know the truth. You talk about survival, but I see the bigger picture. I see the way you've been manipulated, the way you're trying to manipulate me. And I won't be a part of it anymore."

A deep, aching hurt cut through the tension and I no longer could tell if it was mine or his. "You think I'm just like him?" he said, his voice rough with emotion. "You think I'm like my father."

It wasn't a question.

I met his astonishment, unflinching. "You're acting a lot like him, Draven. Like what I expect from a man of Brawn. And that terrifies me."

For a moment, the room seemed to hold its breath.

Draven's shoulders sagged, the fight draining out of him. "You don't know him like I do," he said quietly, the anger replaced by something far more fragile. "You don't know what he's capable of."

"Maybe I don't," I replied, my voice softer but no less determined. I crossed my arms on my chest. "But I know what I see in front of me. And I see a man who's willing to sacrifice everything to follow orders. To win at any cost. I see a man who's losing himself in the process. The self he so badly needed me to see."

His head dropped, eyes unable to meet mine.

"I never wanted this," Draven muttered. "I never wanted any of this."

"Then why, Draven?" I pressed, my voice barely above a whisper. "Why are you doing it? What's so important that you're willing to destroy everything we could have built?"

His eyes met mine, and I saw the man I once believed in—the man I could have found more with. But then it was gone, leaving only the cold, hard reality of who we'd become.

"It's too late to stop," he said, his voice devoid of hope. "I'm in too deep. Dorian and I both are."

His admission. The point of no return. He couldn't come back from this.

I turned to leave, my heart heaving with all we lost. But before I could step away, I looked back at him one last time. "You're not like him," I said, the words penetrating the silence. "But if you keep this up… you will be."

With that, I turned and walked away, leaving him to languish in the darkness—a shadow of the man he once was, lost to his own demons.

The door slid shut behind me, severing the final, fragile connection that tied me to Draven. The tension wrapped around me as I stood in the lit corridor of the Sanctioned living quarters. Draven's guards looked at me, devoid of expression. I couldn't help the single finger gesture I gave them as I headed away from his room.

My heart pounded in my chest, a dull, relentless throb that echoed the tumultuous swirl of thoughts and emotions churning inside me. As I neared my room, I leaned back against the cold wall, the chill seeping through my thin white shift dress and into my skin. I closed my eyes, willing myself to block out the moments I shared with Draven. But they flooded my mind, each one laced with betrayal.

How could I have been so blind?

How could I allow myself to believe, even for a moment, that something genuine existed between us?

You stupid, stupid girl.

The man I thought I knew, revealed himself to be nothing more than a marionette, dancing to the sinister tune of a father he claimed to despise. The thought twisted the knife of foolishness, each turn drawing blood, each rotation reminding me of the fragility of my situation.

My breath came in shallow, uneven gasps as I grappled with reality.

The trust I allowed myself to feel for him now felt like a pitiful joke.

Every instinct screamed for retreat, urging me to gather the remnants of my shattered resolve and shield myself, to protect my mother from further harm. The idea of rebellion, which once seemed like a distant hope, now felt like an insurmountable challenge.

But so much more than my feelings were at stake. Others were depending on me—people with no idea of the treachery lurking beneath the surface. If I let this pain consume me, it would mean the end for more than just me. It would mean the end for those I cared about. The end for the cause I committed myself to.

I pushed myself away from the wall, forcing my feet to move even as my heart ached. The corridor stretched before me, uninviting. I made my choice. Draven's actions, however cold-blooded, only solidified my stance. He might have played a part in shattering my trust, but, by the Cird's breath, he wouldn't break my will.

The cold air bit at me as I moved away from Draven's quarters, pulling me back into the safety of my guarded self—a woman taught to trust no one, to see the hidden threats in every extended hand. My mother's lessons had built walls I swore no one would breach. I should have known better. Draven didn't deserve my trust, and now, after his betrayal, I felt those walls rebuilding, stronger than ever.

That icy feeling solidified around me, forming an invisible armor. If Draven was truly complicit in his father's plans, if he knowingly deceived me, then I would find a way to outmaneuver that asshole. I quickened my pace, footsteps echoing off the walls.

The path ahead bristled with unpredictable dangers, but that's the fight I'd chosen. I'd see it through, whether I had allies I could trust or not. I wasn't backing down—this was my battle to win.

At the corridor's end, I shot one last glance back. Draven's door closed, sealing away secrets I'd leave behind. There was no turning back—and

I could live with that. Whether by his side or in opposition, I'd keep fighting, unbroken, no matter how many pieces they tried to shatter me into.

The Revelation of Ancestors:

I stumbled upon an old record that suggested not all descendants of the ancient people were lost to The Depths of Sandric. There are those among us, living quietly, who carry the blood of the Cird, their powers intertwined with the very fabric of our culture.

This revelation ignites a spark within me. Could it be that someone close to me has roots in this storied lineage? The implications are staggering. The potential for collaboration with a living embodiment of Cird heritage could alter our approach to the resistance I've been considering. The abilities tied to the Cird's legacy—those of terra illumination—might not be as dormant as I once believed.

The realization that someone could harbor such secrets, cloaked beneath layers of ordinary existence, fills me with both excitement and apprehension. This changes everything. The unearthing of Cird ancestry brings with it the possibility of awakening the past and reestablishing a connection to a powerful legacy long buried beneath the surface.

What does this mean for our mission? What hidden strengths could lie dormant, waiting to be unleashed? I must explore this new angle, for the stakes have never been higher.

From darkness, we rise. For light, we fight.

—H. Wilhoph

Chapter Thirty-One

LEVITY

My lungs burned. My breath came in ragged bursts. But I couldn't stop.

I wouldn't stop.

Thomas needed me and the clock ticked closer to that inevitable outcome. I could almost feel it, the inexorable countdown to the moment they would erase him.

His kindness. His warmth.

The passageways that held our nightmares twisted and turned, each corner revealing another stretch of the same dark abyss. My footsteps pounded against the floor, the only sound in the suffocating silence. My dress gathered around my legs in a feeble attempt to slow me down.

The ink-black hallway turned in a familiar direction, guiding me toward Thomas's room, adjacent to where mine previously existed. As I neared his door, my pulse reverberated in my ears. I couldn't believe I found it again so quickly with the lack of light, but I let my heart lead me.

Directly across from his room, I spared no glance at the door that once trapped me. That door loomed like a grim reminder, as if the walls themselves held onto the terror they witnessed. My stomach churned, but my mind could only focus on what I might find beyond this door I now stood in front of.

This wouldn't be another desperate attempt at escape—this was life or... not death... an existence that would no longer resemble life.

Wiping my hands against the smooth fabric of my dress, I tried to calm myself, but the trembling in my fingers refused to cease. My hand hovered over the metal door, cool against the sweat-slicked skin, and I hesitated. The memory of my own ordeal clawed at the edges of my mind, but I pushed it aside. I wasn't the one in danger, not now. Thomas was behind this door, and inaction would mean losing him.

Drawing a shaky breath, I pushed open the door with my newly obtained access. The hiss of the pressure gasped into the silence, filling the space. This room felt like a tomb. The dim light barely reached the corners, and thick darkness pulsed with an almost tangible presence.

In my mind, I was back in Marmarie's room with Thomas, the day we stumbled upon it during our brief escape.

The void.

This room looked completely different from the last time. Gone were the haunting images of crumbling walls and empty shelves that spoke of a life ravaged by poverty. The harrowing vision of scarcity and despair that tormented Thomas had dissipated, leaving behind an unsettling emptiness. A silence that terrified more so than the nightmare itself.

On shaky legs, I moved, the coldness of the room wrapping around my core. My footsteps echoed, the sound muted and foreign, as if the room itself rejected any sign of life. The air felt substantially different—a sense of abandonment. The faint flickering of a swinging light overhead struggled to stay alive, casting weak, trembling shadows that danced across the walls.

In the center of this void, Thomas sat in a metal chair, his figure barely distinguishable from the surrounding darkness. His once broad shoulders were slumped forward under something far greater than physical exhaustion. He looked so small and diminished.

Drained. The essence of who he used to be had been siphoned. I was too late. A perceptible hitch in my breath broke the silence.

No straps bound his arms, yet he made no move. He gave no sign of noticing my presence. His hands were limp in his lap, fingers curled as if he'd been holding onto something but let it slip away. His head drooped, chin nearly touching his chest. His eyes looked empty—vacant. Thomas's spark had vanished, replaced by a dull stare.

I took a hesitant step closer. I searched his face for any sign of recognition, any flicker of the man I knew. But his expression remained flat, devoid of emotion. My throat tightened, a lump of despair began to choke me. This wasn't Thomas sitting here; it felt like a ghost.

The silence pressed against my ears until it roared, drowning out my thoughts.

I wanted to reach out, to shake him, to do anything that might bring him back to me, but I was frozen, trapped by what I saw.

I stared into the abyss where Thomas's soul should be. I heard his sweet, smoky voice. The kindness that would never return…

I couldn't afford to break.

Not now.

Not when he needed me most.

A desperate idea stirred in my mind—something that might reach a part of him still holding on. If The Sanctioning shattered his will, maybe I could find a way to piece him back together.

He needed to remember home. The world outside these walls. Something beyond the darkness that claimed him.

I moved to his side, the cold floor chilling my knees as I knelt beside him. My white dress pooled around me, the fabric whispering against the ground. His breath came shallow and faint. The scant warmth in his brown eyes pierced through me, cutting deeper than I thought possible. My heart ached.

I gently rested my head on his lap, hoping that the touch, the closeness, might stir some memory, some trigger of life.

My fingers brushed against the rough fabric of his jeans as I closed my eyes, searching within for the one thing that always brought my siblings comfort, that always brought me back.

A hymn.

The one my mother sang to me. The one I'd sung to the children when fear knocked at our hearts.

The melody pulsed like a heartbeat, steady and warm. I let it rise in my chest, and the words began to flow, soft and tender, carrying the affection of home, of the sea that nurtured us, of the shorelines we roamed as children.

> *"Hush now, child, the sea is near,*
> *Waves will whisper, calm your fear.*
> *Tides will carry you safe to shore,*
> *In the ocean's arms, you'll roam no more."*

My voice wavered at first, the words shaky and uncertain, but as I continued, the lullaby embraced us like a comforting blanket. Soft. Nonthreatening.

Each note carried a piece of Sertoda's spirit, of the life we knew before everything turned so dark.

> *"Feel the warmth of the sunlit sea,*
> *Let the waves set your spirit free.*
> *Softly now, let your worries fade,*
> *In the ocean's embrace, you've always*
> *stayed."*

I sang as if the sea itself could hear me, as if the waves might rise up and wash away the torment that held him prisoner.

> *"Beneath the moon's gentle, silver light,*
> *The shore awaits through the quiet*
> *night.*
> *Drift away on the ocean's song,*
> *Where your heart and the sea belong."*

I poured my heart into each new verse, into the melody.

I hoped against hope that Thomas would remember.

I sang until the words blurred with tears. Until my voice cracked under the weight of emotion. Until only the quiet echo of the song remained, floating in the air like the final trace of a summer breeze.

As the last note of the song faded from my lips, the room fell silent.

I waited, body tense, straining to catch any sign of movement from Thomas through our connection. My forehead rested against his lap. My spirit teetered on the edge of a precipice, ready to fall into the same void that claimed him.

Nothing.

Doubt crept in, whispering unkind words in the back of my mind. My fingers dug into the material of his pants, clutching it like a lifeline. Was I too late? Had he already gone too far, lost to the darkness that now surrounded us? The thoughts clawed at me, threatening to pull me under, but I forced myself to stay still...

...to keep hoping...

...to keep waiting...

And then, I felt it—a faint, almost imperceptible touch, brushing against the strands of my hair.

The sensation felt so delicate, so fragile, that at first, I thought I'd imagined it. But then it came again, a gentle stroke along the length of one of my long, brown curls.

My breath caught in my throat, and I didn't dare move. Dared not even breathe, for fear that this small, precious moment might slip away. His hand, warm and trembling, glided through my hair. Each stroke was slow with intention as if he sought to remember how to move, how to feel.

Relief washed over me in a powerful wave, almost knocking me off balance on the floor where I leaned into him. Tears sprang to my eyes, hot and unchecked. They spilled onto my cheeks as I remained still. I let him take his time and to find his way back to me.

I stayed there, letting his touch soothe the ache that lodged itself deep in my heart. I clung to our connection with every ounce of my strength, drawing him to the surface, pulling us into the light.

Amidst the quiet, I caught it—a faint whisper.

Then it came again. Barely a breath, but unmistakable.

"Happiness."

My heart ached. The word that carried a memory. A shared moment between us from that day on the train when he'd told me what my name meant.

It was him.

Thomas.

My pulse quickened, and I dared to lift my head, blinking back the remaining tears as I looked up at him.

His eyes, now searching mine, filled with confusion. He was there. The man I knew was fighting his way back.

His lips trembled as he spoke again, the words barely audible and choked. "Is it... over?"

My throat tightened. The tears I'd held back now spilled freely down my cheeks once more. I managed to nod, my hand gently reaching up to cup his face, lingering on the bristle of his dark stubble.

"Yes," I whispered, my voice trembling with the force of my relief. With my love for him. "It's over, Thomas. It's over."

His eyes closed as if the words were a balm, a release from the torment that held him captive for so many weeks.

"I think I used too much Widow's Source. I lost consciousness."

Slowly, gently, I crawled into his lap. I wrapped my arms around him, pulling him close as if by holding him as tightly as I dared, I could shield him from the horrors that still lingered in his mind.

His body trembled beneath my embrace as I buried my face in the crook of his neck. The scent of him, salt like the sea air, filled my senses. His firm arms encased me, tentative at first, then stronger, as if he, too, needed the comfort, the reassurance that we were both still here. Both still alive.

Being this close to him drew up a desperate, raw need for more. Thomas's grip tightened, his hands gripping my back with a fierceness that belied the vulnerability of his condition. Tremors ran through his body, a silent echo of the torment. My heart ached with the need to take away his pain and help bring him back to himself. Completely.

His breath came in ragged gasps against my neck. His lips brushed my skin with a touch so light it made me shiver. Then, he pulled back just enough to look at me. His look pleaded for solace, for connection, for something real.

I cupped his face with my hands. My eyes darted between his. He in turn searched mine with an intensity that made my heart pound and the blood in my body sear.

"Levity," he said.

"I'm here," I whispered.

Without another word, his lips collided with mine, desperate and insistent. The kiss carried the urgency of someone clawing their way back from the brink of oblivion. His mouth moved over mine with a fervor that spoke of all the pain and longing he'd endured. This kiss served as a cathartic release for everything he'd held back. It embodied desperation, relief, and the feelings he couldn't articulate.

I gave it all to him. My fingers tangled in the longer strands of his hair, pulling him closer. I pressed against his body. The heat of his mouth, the feel of his tongue, the roughness of his stubble against my skin, all of it ignited a fire within me that burned away the last remnants of our anguish.

His hands roamed my back, exploring every inch of me as if memorizing the feeling of being whole again. Each caress begged for reassurance that we could still find our way through this shattered world.

When we finally broke apart, the world felt different. Our breaths mingled together. Our foreheads resting against one another. The darkness in the room seemed to recede, replaced by a fragile glimmer of hope. I looked into his eyes, clearer, more focused.

We stayed like that for what felt like an eternity, clinging to each other in the dim light of the nightmare room. The world outside forgotten. Irrelevant. The only thing that mattered remained: he was here with me, I was with him, and that, somehow, we had found our way back to one another to finish this together.

"It's over," I repeated, my breath against his skin. It was a promise, a prayer. And as I held him, I felt the tension drain from his body, his breathing evening out as he absorbed the truth of those words.

Wrapped in his arms, I let myself believe that we could find a way through, that the nightmare might finally be behind us. But the room's intimate silence shattered abruptly as the door gasped open.

Thomas stiffened, tightening his hold on me, his body.

Lyonal entered first, his presence a dark silhouette against the dim light.

Behind him, Betta followed, her eyes darting nervously between us.

I held Thomas's hand as we stood together, then stepped in front of him, shielding him with my body.

Lyonal's vision swept over the scene, taking in the tangled embrace we shared with a mixture of disapproval and calculated intent. He approached us with a firm, commanding presence.

"Thomas," Lyonal said, his tone clipped, "it's time. We need to move."

Thomas looked from Lyonal to me, skepticism clouding his judgment. His hand lingered on mine, yet Lyonal's command held an undiscernible weight.

Betta stepped closer, her eyes raised to meet mine. She leaned in, her voice barely a whisper. "Levity, Lyonal is taking Thomas to the tunnels. They're planning an escape, a chance to get out before it's too late. This isn't the last time you'll see him, I promise. But he has to go now if we're going to make it work."

Her words were bittersweet. I nodded, swallowing the lump in my throat as I fought to keep my composure. The thought of losing Thomas again, even temporarily, felt almost unbearable, but I knew this may be his only chance of escape.

Lyonal gestured for Thomas to follow, his eyes flicking to Betta as if seeking her approval. Thomas hesitated, then slowly stepped in front of me, his focus lingering on my face. I could see the concern in his eyes, the struggle to reconcile the comfort of our shared moment with the harsh reality of our situation. His hand lingered on mine until our fingers finally broke apart.

As Thomas moved toward Lyonal, Betta stepped in front of me, her expression resolute. "Levity, stay back," she ordered far louder, her voice firm and hiding compassion. She dropped to a whisper. "We need to make this look convincing. I'll handle the rest."

Before I could protest, Betta turned to Lyonal, his iron grip seizing

Thomas's arm. Lyonal's expression hardened as he began to drag Thomas away, each movement deliberately forceful. The scene played out like a conflict—a forced separation crafted to satisfy any onlookers.

Thomas's eyes locked onto mine one last time. I reached out, my fingers brushing against his, as he struggled to move closer, but the distance between us grew as Lyonal pulled him further away.

The room constricted around me as Betta blocked my attempt to move with them toward the door. She placed a comforting hand on my shoulder, her touch a silent promise of solidarity.

"Just a little longer," she whispered. "We're close to making this work. You and Thomas will be together again, I swear."

As Lyonal and Thomas exited the room, the door closed behind them. A cold emptiness settled over me. The illusion of normalcy, the meticulously orchestrated coup, now unfolded before us. Betta's hand remained on my shoulder, a grounding presence as I fought to maintain my composure.

"Levity," she said, her voice piercing through the quiet, "Lyonal is helping plan an escape that is bigger than just Thomas. Thomas will head back to Sertoda to secure your family, to make sure they're safe from harm. This is our chance to get them out of danger."

Her words hit me like a rescue buoy thrown into turbulent waters. The idea of Thomas returning to Sertoda, to protect my family, brought a wave of relief. But I also felt fear. Relief because they would be safe—at least for now. Fear stemming from the fact that the path to securing their safety bristled with potential danger.

I swallowed hard, trying to process the enormity of her words. "And what about us? What happens next?"

Betta's expression softened, though the urgency in her eyes remained. "We'll be following close behind. Lyonal and I are creating a diversion, staging a conflict to distract any watchers. Once Thomas is back in

Sertoda and your family is secured, we'll regroup and find a way to get everyone out safely."

I nodded, my fingers twitching at my side as anxiety throbbed through my veins.

"Thank you, Betta," I whispered, my voice cracking with the emotion I barely held in. "For everything. I'll be waiting. I'll do whatever it takes to make sure we all get out of this."

Betta's hand lingered on my shoulder, a brief, reassuring squeeze before she stepped back. Her demeanor shifted once more to match the façade we now were expected to enact. Her golden eyes met mine one last time.

"Stay strong," she said softly. "We'll find a way through this."

With that, she removed herself from the room, her steps purposeful and deliberate.

As I looked toward the door—the barrier to the world beyond—a steely determination settled over me. This wasn't the end, but a turning point. Leaving this nightmare meant closing a chapter of torment no one else should endure.

I took a final, steadying breath, resolved to make sure these walls would never again imprison another soul.

No Entry Name:

She is Cird.

I didn't think it possible for her to keep anything from me.

The revelation feels like a tide pulling me under. Everything shifts; my understanding of her, of our potential, and of the very foundations of our struggle.

She said there are tens of thousands of them left, maybe even a hundred, not counting the ones that live above ground.

Nothing stays the same after this.

—Hophsted

Chapter Thirty-Two

BETTA

In the wake of the Noble Warrior Sanctioning ending, mere moments slipped away as we hurried back to the control room. Together, Lyonal and I secured Thomas in the tunnels using the blind spots Draven showed me. Now, we quickly needed to enact the next part of the plan.

The diffused light hung low, casting a muted glow over banks of silent, dormant screens. Only two displays remained active, their faint illumination stretching across the vast array of control panels, keyboards, and switches. Lyonal's face bathed in soft radiance, his expression teetered between contemplation and strain as he focused on the scenes, watching his daughter.

The monitors showed Garon and Saria, their horrors unspooling within the frames like a live transmission from some far-off battlefield.

Lyonal's fingers moved over the controls with the precision of the system's maker. The screens before us presented two contrasting nightmares: Garon, lost in a frozen tundra, and Saria, standing alone at a funeral.

I sat in the second chair of the control room, the same spot where Garon once positioned himself to gather the evidence. My heart raced as I absorbed the pain etched on Saria's face, recognizing the moment as a critical turning point—not just for her, but for all of us.

On one screen, Garon's simulation was an endless white canvas stretched beneath a dark sky. Biting winds whipped across the tundra, clawing at him with icy ferocity. His breath hung in thick clouds as he struggled against the snow, each step an agonizing fight through the cold. The desolation of the scene—the unforgiving frost and relentless wind—made his isolation and desperation painfully real. The frigid landscape seemed intent on consuming him whole.

Saria's simulation manifested as an agonizing tableau of grief and loss. She stood in a shadowy chapel, the scene filled with wilting flowers and muffled sobs. Mourners blurred into indistinct figures, their faces hidden behind veils of sorrow, leaving her adrift in a sea of despair. The coffin, draped in somber fabric, loomed at the front of the room, open for her to look upon what I assumed to be her husband's lifeless body.

Strain was etched in Lyonal's eyes as he bounced his attention between the screens, his brow furrowed in concentration. The intensity of his focus shone through, a veneer barely concealing the immense pressure of the task at hand.

When his gaze finally met mine, his piercing blue eyes, framed by his sleek glasses, spoke volumes in a silent exchange. He removed his glasses, running a hand down his face, drawing down his chin. The time for intervention fast approached, and every detail needed to be flawless.

"Ready?" I asked, my voice no more than a strained whisper amidst the relentless hum of the technology.

Lyonal dropped his head in a nod and locked his concentration onto the array of controls before him, his fingers poised over the keys. Ready. "As soon as I signal, I'll simulate Saria's defeat. But you need to move quickly and get her out before anyone who could potentially be watching realizes." His tone was stern—*that of a father's.* "This is crucial, Betta. I need her out of here and into the tunnels where Thomas is waiting. I'll ensure the simulation makes it look like she's being processed. If they think she's still undergoing the mind-sweep, it will buy us the time we need. I'll have maps, flashlights, supplies, everything, ready to make their way out of this Cird-damned hell when we meet back up."

The control room's lights glinted off Lyonal's sweat-slicked brow. I stood from my chair next to him and moved to the door, leveling my stare with his as I said, "We've come too far for this to fail. I won't let you down."

As I approached Saria's room, my heart pounded so hard in my chest, I reached a hand out to the wall for balance. My focus remained fixed, bracing myself for the announcement that would crackle over the speakers, signaling the end of the Perpetual Sense Sanctioning. The end of The Sanctioning in its entirety. Time slipped through my fingers, and I would need to act quickly to extract Saria before the mind-sweep claimed her.

As my eyes zeroed in on the end of the hall, trying to focus on the continuously dim passage, Draven materialized. His tall, imposing figure, clad in black, came to life like a shadow.

I felt like an animal caught in a trap, and I no longer knew where to look. As he approached, his midnight eyes pierced with an intensity that sent chills down my spine.

For a heartbeat, the world fell silent.

Panic gripped me.

I didn't have time for his shit.

"What are you doing here, Betta?" His voice emerged as a low growl. Draven's predatory gaze shifted into realization. "You're helping Lyonal, aren't you? That's why you're here. What are you planning?"

I stiffened, my breath catching in the back of my throat. The pressure of timing this moment perfectly felt almost unbearable. "Lyonal can be trusted. You? Not a chance. Not Brawn," I shot back, my voice rough with frustration. Each word ripped from my mouth, hard and defiant. I wouldn't give him an inch.

The announcement system crackled overhead, the familiar mechanical voice declaring the end of the Perpetual Sense Sanctioning. The urgency now pressed down on me like a vice, the gears beginning to tighten.

My heart raced even faster as I tried to push past him, desperation fueling my steps, but his size made it impossible for me to get by. "I don't have time for this!" I exclaimed, my voice trembling with anger, but now also fear. "Saria needs me!"

Draven's face contorted, but his voice dripped with mockery. "You really believe you can waltz out of here without facing any consequences? Lyonal is just manipulating you like everyone else."

I placed two hands on his chest and pushed with all my might, my anger bursting forth like a storm. "Everyone like you!" I spat, my voice slicing through the charged air. The raw fury coursing through me matched the intensity of his stony bearing. "How could you look me in the eye, kiss me, come on to me, make me believe that I could actually trust you?"

I pushed him again, but he'd already moved out of my way. My breaths came in ragged bursts, each one fueled by the betrayal that defiled my insides. "You made me feel safe, like I found something real amidst all the lies and deceit. You let me break the walls around my heart, walls I used to keep myself protected. And now I see it all for what it really was—a pathetic illusion. You shattered my trust as if it were nothing more than a toy to be played with and then discarded."

My voice broke, the pain spilling over into every word. "How could you be so callous? How could you rip it all away and leave me exposed and vulnerable? I trusted you, Draven. I let you into the deepest corners

345

of my heart, and you turned it all into a sick game!"

I pushed against his chest again and again with a force born of betrayal. He stood and took it all. Tears of frustration burned at the corners of my eyes, and I shoved him one last time, the intensity of my emotions spilling over. "I don't understand how you could do this. How could you be so heartless? I gave you my trust, and you threw it all away."

His dark eyes softened, revealing a guilt buried beneath his hardened exterior. But nothing would soothe the ache in my chest. "Betta, you don't know the whole story—"

I didn't want to hear it, so I turned my back to him.

As I did, his hand shot out, seizing my arm in a grip that felt both bruising and desperate. His fingers dug into my flesh, a visceral expression of his refusal to let me go. The sharp pressure ignited a flash of anger that flared hotter than the pain in my arm.

"Let go of me!" I shouted, my voice echoing off the cold walls. I twisted against his iron grip, every ounce of resistance fueled by the fire raging within me.

Draven's eyes locked onto mine. "You're making a grave mistake, Betta," he snapped, his tone sharp enough to cut. "You think Lyonal's your answer? He's part of the same system you're trying to destroy. You're running straight into the web, blind and unarmed."

My free hand moved. A flash of movement honed by years of lessons I never thought I'd need to use. I grabbed the pistol holstered at his thigh. With practiced efficiency, I flicked off the safety and had it pointed at him in the span of a breath.

Draven froze, releasing my arm, and slowly raised his hands in the air. His lips parted, but no sound came as he stared down at the barrel aimed at his chest. Whether he underestimated me or thought our intimacy meant I wouldn't dare, I didn't care.

"Your mistake," I said, my voice calm despite the adrenaline surging through my veins. The pistol felt steady in my grip, the coldness of the steel reminded me of every lesson my mother drilled into me. She taught me how to handle a weapon, not just for defense but for survival. A medic's daughter, prepared to protect herself in a world that gave no guarantees.

Draven spoke softly, as if to placate me. "I didn't expect this from you."

My jaw tightened, but I didn't falter. "Funny... this is exactly what I expected from you, and yet I still told myself not to."

I cleared the chamber and ejected the magazine, the metallic clatter of bullets hitting the floor cutting through the tension. Without a word, I tossed the now-useless pistol back to him.

He caught it, his reflexes quick despite the surprise still etched across his face. I turned on my heel, refusing to linger any longer.

"Betta—"

I didn't stop. The sound of his voice wouldn't slow me. My focus stayed razor-sharp as I stormed down the corridor, leaving him and his warnings behind.

His lies and manipulations were no longer my concern.

My only thought was getting to Saria.

The tunnels stretched out before us like the shadowy veins of a vast, subterranean beast. Every step inward promised salvation, or perhaps just more dread. The intermittent sconces in this area illuminated the uneven stone walls and not much more. The cold served as the only constant presence. It seeped into my bones and reminded me of the magnitude of our task.

As Saria and I rounded a corner, the sight of Lyonal and Thomas standing in the gloom with flashlights stopped me in my tracks. They were waiting with canvas bags of supplies slung over their shoulders—a testament to the journey that lay ahead.

Lyonal's usually unflappable demeanor melted away before my eyes as he reached out to clasp Saria's trembling hand. I watched, my ribs tightening, as his stoic exterior gave way to an almost unbearable surge of emotion. His usual keen eyes turned to puddles. He traced the contours of Saria's face. His attention lingering on the bruises and her sunken eyes.

Lyonal's laughter—sharp, almost hysterical—cut through the tense silence, a jagged release of pent-up agony and dread. The chuckle trembled on the edge of tears, a bittersweet attempt to mask the deep relief he felt.

"Dad," Saria whispered, her voice a fragile thread that seemed to weave through the chaos around us.

When Lyonal spoke, his voice was raw and rough with emotion. "You're here," he said, sounding almost in disbelief. "You're really here."

Saria, pale and bearing the scars of her ordeal, looked up at him with eyes that witnessed too much, yet now, glimmered with fragile light. Exhaustion weighed heavily in her face, but a flicker of resilience sparkled.

Lyonal fought to contain his emotion.

As Lyonal gently brushed away one of Saria's tears, the world around them shrank to just the two of them. The chaos of the system fell away in the face of their tender reunion. Lyonal's fierce voice cut through the air. "We're going to get through this," he promised. "I won't let anything happen to you."

A pang of longing tightened in my chest. I saw in their embrace a glimpse of what I yearned for—a reunion with my mother.

"Thomas," I called out. I reached out, gripping his arm with a firm resolve. "You need to get out of Mass. This isn't just a matter of escape; it's crucial. You have to make your way discreetly back to Sertoda. They will be looking for you."

His attentive eyes met mine, unwavering.

I continued, each word measured and intense. "When you get there, find Levity's siblings. They're vulnerable, and they need someone they can trust."

I hesitated, searching for the right words. "I know you've been through hell, and I don't want to ask too much of you, but… my mother is in Sertoda as well. If you can, I need you to secure her. She'll be in danger, too, and I can't bear to think of her being left behind. She's in the city." I quickly relayed her address to him, and he seemingly was familiar with the area.

Thomas's face, etched with exhaustion, nodded solemnly. "I'll get them out, Betta. All of them. I'll make sure they're safe."

He promised protection. A pledge that transcended the immediate danger and reached into the conjectural future we were striving to secure. The trust I placed in him felt difficult and immense. His success was now tied to the safety of everyone I held dear.

"Thank you," I said, trying to bring stability to my voice. "Once you've secured them, we'll have a plan for what comes next. Do whatever it takes to keep them out of danger." I motioned to Lyonal and, from one of the bags, he pulled the gun that Garon previously strong armed from the guard in the control room. I placed it in Thomas's hand.

Lyonal turned to Saria, placing his hands on each one of her shoulders. "Saria, we need to move. It's not safe here. Go with Thomas."

Saria's azureth blue eyes, wide with a fear she could not shake, darted between Lyonal and the dim tunnel before us. "But what about you? You'll come with me, won't you?"

Lyonal's hand, firm yet comforting, remained on her shoulders. "I'll be with you every step of the way." He looked at me before turning back to his daughter. "We have to make sure everything's secure."

I watched the exchange, my heart clenching with collective desperation. Lyonal's promise of safety to his daughter cut through the darkness of our predicament, a fragile beacon in an unpredictable ocean.

"We'll meet after the induction ceremony," Lyonal continued. "I have a warehouse in Sertoda. Brawn doesn't know about it. It's secure—a hidden refuge where we can plan our next move."

Saria's eyes scanned me and Thomas with caution. "Are you certain it's safe?"

Lyonal's nod was resolute. "Yes. You remember where it is? It's off the grid, well-hidden. It'll be our sanctuary until we can regroup and strategize. We will meet you all there as soon as we can make it."

I glanced at Saria, whose brows dipped with worry. Her gaze intensified on her father as she memorized the lines of his face. I then looked to Lyonal and finally Thomas, their features illuminated by the harsh light of the flashlights Thomas and Saria would use to guide them out.

Lyonal quickly showed them the map inside their bags that would help them find their way just above ground, right outside of Mass, in Sertoda territory. From there they would need to cautiously make their way to The Divide, the city, and then finally to Lyonal's facility.

Saria and Thomas turned to head into the dark tunnels. I watched them with intense feelings of relief and anxiety. Their silhouettes faded into the darkness, carrying our hopes and the promise of a better future with them. The next time we saw them, we would be on the other end of revealing the deceit of Sandric rule.

The significance of our choices, the lives we vowed to protect, and the ever-present threat of Brawn filled the air with tension. Once a symbol of unity, the tunnels now served as a desperate escape route from the city—a chance to rebuild and reorganize that unity elsewhere. Their scarred walls, marked by time and past struggles, bore witness to the new world order.

A Path to the Cird:

Tomorrow, we embark on a journey into the depths of the Sea of Impassis, seeking the Cird and the strength of their legacy. I now understand the path to reach them through my wife. The way she spoke of the hidden routes awakened something deep within me, a sense of urgency and purpose.

Today, I kissed each of my children goodbye, aware that I may be gone longer than originally planned.

Levity, with her fierce spirit, is destined for greatness. I find solace in the thought that she will carry on our family's legacy should anything happen, but the thought of leaving her fills me with a bittersweet ache. Tivian and Triad, both blossoming into remarkable young individuals, remind me of my own youthful courage. Their laughter will echo in my heart as I navigate the unknown.

Little Blue, with her mother's eyes—those piercing blue, wise eyes I now recognize as the essence of the Cird—holds a special place in my heart. There's a spark in her gaze, a reminder of the connection we share to a past both vibrant and painful. And our newest baby, Evie, her innocence a stark contrast to the challenges that lie ahead, serves as a reminder of all that we fight for.

Each kiss felt like a tether binding me to home, a promise to return and protect the world we hold dear. They are the light that guides me. I must believe that our journey will lead us not only to the Cird but also to the hope of a brighter future for them all. Tomorrow, we dive into The Depths, the unknown, but tonight, I hold them close in my heart, fortifying my resolve for what lies ahead.

From darkness, we rise. For light, we fight.

—H. Wilhoph

Chapter
Thirty-Three

LEVITY

The arena buzzed with an electric fervor; a cathedral of celebration bathed in the harsh brilliance of countless floodlights. It was a marvel of modern technology, stretched out in a sprawling expanse of polished stone and shimmering screens.

Holographic projections of the Sandric emblem floated above the crowd, their ethereal glow casting a surreal light over the sea of spectators. Interactive displays and augmented reality panels showcased the faces of the representatives, their names and titles flashing in vibrant hues that danced across the walls.

Before we entered, Betta shared crucial details of our plan with me, along with last-minute advice on my demeanor and the precise moment in the ceremony when she would step forward. After the newly Sanctioned finished speaking, she would return to the stage and expose Brawn's secrets and the evidence, for everyone to see.

I stood among the gathered representatives on the expansive stage, my heart pounding in my chest, in my temples, in my fingertips. The ceremonial platform, an imposing structure of gleaming steel and glass was draped with banners and emblems that proclaimed the unity of Sandric. The insignias shimmered under the harsh lights, their colors bold and merciless.

The elite and the powerful filled the front seats, their faces a blend of excitement and guarded apprehension. Did they know the true cost of the unity they celebrated?

Only the citizens of Mass were in attendance, their cheers loud and charged by the government's influence. Likely, ten thousand or so present on this day. But I knew this moment would reach far beyond these walls, broadcast to every corner of Sandric.

The crowd, dressed in their finest, immersed themselves in their excitement and blissful ignorance. To them, this was a grand display of unity and triumph. But for me, it represented something far darker—the end of The Sanctioning that attempted to twist me beyond recognition, wringing every ounce of hope from my soul.

While they celebrated, I stood ready to help reveal the truth, a truth that would shatter their illusions and change Sandric forever.

To my left, the other Sanctioned stood, new and old, with calculated poise for the cameras, their expressions composed like silent sentinels. Behind us stood the remaining representatives from our term—the small council. Each fixed their gaze on a singular point in the crowd, exuding nothing but obedience. Their once-vibrant minds mere whispers of what they once were.

Marmarie stood stiffly among the voided. Her vacant regard and eerily serene features absent of recognition. No spark of familiarity, no trace of the bond we once shared as people of Sertoda. Her essence wiped clean, replaced with a cold, mechanical compliance. The sight chilled me, a haunting reminder of what could have become my own fate.

Two spaces were kept empty for the missing representatives, adding to the tension in the air. It had been two days since Thomas and Saria escaped. The silence around their missing forms unnerved me. The atmosphere on stage brimmed with dread, a gnawing undercurrent that slithered beneath the surface of the spectacle, never fully breaking through. And yet, here we were, standing on the precipice of a future none of us could fully comprehend, the cheers of the crowd a meaningless echo in the vastness of the arena.

Betta stepped forward to the center of the stage, and the crowd fell into a hushed reverence as if the very air around her demanded their attention. She embodied authority and elegance, draped in a flowing gown that shimmered like liquid silver. It caught the light with every movement, sending gleaming refractions across the arena. Its texture was a perfect blend of traditional Sandric design and the cutting-edge technology that defined our world. Symbols of Sandric's history and the unity we were meant to uphold wove into the intricate patterns.

She embodied the very spirit of this false nation.

Her silky black hair, styled into an intricate braid, crowned her head like a halo adorned with tiny, glistening crystals. She wore a pendant—a simple yet powerful emblem of the five territories, fused together to form a single, unbreakable whole. It symbolized the dream, not the reality.

I touched the humble wave pendant I wore around my own neck.

Her voice resonated across the arena when she spoke, amplified by technology. The impact of her words captivated the crowd. Warmth infused her tone, carrying a sincerity that reached and touched each person. She made them feel seen, valued, and part of something greater. Beneath that warmth lay her undeniable strength—a core of steel that promised she would pass on her status of Sanctioned while championing the new leaders into this era with unwavering boldness.

Watching her, my heart swelled with admiration. Her grace inspired me, and I channeled the familiar pang of anxiety, letting it fuel me rather than hold me back. This ceremony signified the future of everyone we loved, and it carved Sandric's path forward.

Soon, I would stand beside her as a source of inspiration—ready to lead and strong enough to face whatever lay ahead.

Dorian Ballister, the newly appointed Noble Warrior, stood to my left, his presence marked by a stoic calm that seemed almost at odds with the vibrant energy of the ceremony. Clad in an impeccably tailored uniform of deepest black, his appearance reeked of Brawn's military precision. The fabric of his uniform seemed to devour the light, its rich texture adding to the imposing figure he cut. Silver insignias gleamed on his shoulders, symbolizing his rank and the authority he now held... but something more grabbed my attention.

As I looked over him, expecting the hardened demeanor typical of Brawn's warriors, I noticed a softness in his features that contrasted with the severe lines of his uniform. His posture exuded rigidity and discipline. Yet, his eyes told a different story. Deep and stormy brown, they reflected the light with a subtle sheen, revealing a hint of unease and a flicker of something almost vulnerable. Beneath the composed exterior, a part of him seemed misaligned with the stoic image that Brawn demanded.

Our eyes met, and I offered him a small nod, a gesture of reassurance that felt strangely necessary. He returned the nod, his lips twitching as if he were on the verge of a smile, but it never fully formed. The brief exchange left me curious.

Garon Fiore stood to my right, anointed Perpetual Sense, bearing the weight of an entire territory's hopes and aspirations. As the first representative from Dobia to reach Sanctioned, he transcended ordinary status. He embodied Dobia's potential and its struggles and aspirations. His presence on the stage reflected the resilience and strength of his people, witnessing one of their own rising to heights never before attained.

Garon's long silver hair, shaved on the sides, cascaded down his back, bestowing upon him an aura that radiated both fierceness and dignity. The woven braids reflected the meticulousness of a man who fought his way to this position, not just with muscle, but with mind and spirit.

He wore a light gray suit. The color echoed the muted hues of a snow-laden sky. It was tailored to his muscular frame, the fabric accentuating his broad shoulders and powerful build. Beneath the suit, a white shirt lay partially unbuttoned, revealing the upper edge of a tattoo that sprawled across his chest. It looked ancient in design. It pulsed with a meaning I was not aware of. Perhaps a mark of his heritage or the battles he endured in the name of Dobia. He wore the formal attire with a casual confidence that spoke volumes about his inner strength and self-assurance.

Garon's ruggedly handsome features were accentuated by dark stubble across his jaw. As he surveyed the vast arena, he appeared to be assessing, as though plotting a move in a game only he could fully see. The crowd viewed the induction ceremony as a celebration, a public spectacle, but for Garon, it appeared to represent something far deeper.

I glanced past my fellow leaders to the vast crowd filling the arena, finally landing on the imposing figures near the podium where Betta spoke. The Brawn military. Their presence seemed like an obvious overreach of power in Sandric, a silent assertion of authority that I could no longer ignore. Each soldier was dressed in dark, menacing formal uniforms, that opposed with the vibrant, celebratory banners decorating the ceremony.

Among the sea of hardened soldiers, one older man stood out with his unsettling aura. He towered over those around him. His broad shoulders and imposing stature made him impossible to ignore. His black uniform adorned with intricate patterns and symbols spoke of a long and distinguished service.

His face bore the marks of countless battles, deep lines etched into his skin by years of hardship and command. His jaw set in a firm line. His lips pressed into a thin, unforgiving slash, as if smiling represented a long-forgotten art. But his dark brown eyes truly unsettled me. They swept over the arena, taking in every detail, every possible threat, and every potential opportunity. I watched as they landed on Betta.

General Ballister.

Those eyes, sharp as a predator's, seemed to bore into her.

The flesh on my exposed arms began to rise.

It felt as though he saw through her, through us all, dissecting thoughts and intentions with a single glance. No warmth or empathy existed in that look—only the ruthlessness of a man who spent his life mastering the art of war.

He commanded not just the soldiers in front of me, but the very fate of Sandric.

The living embodiment of the ruthless territory he served.

As I watched him take his seat, a part of me understood why Brawn became such a dominant force in Sandric. It involved not just their military might but the sheer, unwavering will of people like General Ballister—individuals who would stop at nothing to achieve their goals, no matter the cost. Seeing him sit there, unyielding and ever-watchful, served as a sobering reminder of the challenges ahead—not just for me, but for anyone who dared to oppose the power he represented.

The crowd's murmur swelled, their collective breath held in expectation as the time for the final address from the newly Sanctioned approached.

Betta stepped back into the line, positioning herself between Lyonal and Draven. She motioned with her hand for Dorian to step forward.

Dorian Ballister, the newly appointed Noble Warrior, walked a few steps to the front of the stage. The murmurs of the crowd faded into a tense silence as he prepared to speak.

"People of Sandric," Dorian began, his voice deep and steady, carrying the pressure of his title and the lineage he represented. "Today marks the beginning of a new chapter for our world. We have faced trials that have tested the very core of our strength and unity. We stand here, not as victors, but as survivors—survivors of a challenge that has forged us into the leaders you see before you. Our duty now is to carry forward the lessons we've learned, to protect and serve our people, and to ensure that Sandric remains strong and united, no matter the obstacles we may face."

As he spoke, a quiver of recognition resonated in his features. His eyes locked onto his father's within the crowd. There was an unmistakable change in Dorian. The stoic mask he wore slipped, revealing a flash of fear. He quickly raised the back of his hand to his forehead and wiped at the perspiration forming before continuing, "We are committed to serving Sandric with honor and integrity, and we will not falter in our duty. Together, we will face whatever lies ahead and emerge stronger for it."

With that, Dorian stepped back, his address complete.

My heart pounded deep within my chest, creating an acidic churn within my stomach, as I realized my turn approached. I could feel the eyes of the entire arena on me, and for a fleeting second... I hesitated.

Could I find the words to inspire hope without betraying the truth of The Sanctioning?

As I scanned the faces in the crowd—the ordinary citizens of Mass with wide, expectant looks—I felt a surge of resolve. These were the people we fought for. The innocents. They deserved a leader who could rise above fear and speak for them.

Drawing a deep breath, I stepped forward.

The arena fell into a hush as my secure voice poured into the air before me. "Our lives are not defined by the trials we have faced," I began, my voice gaining strength with each word. "They are defined by how we rise from the depths of our struggles, how we emerge from the shadows of our fears and doubts. It is our actions that define us. Each one of us"—I scanned the crowd, meeting the faces of those like mine—"have been met with moments that seemed insurmountable, moments where darkness threatened to swallow us whole and despair seemed to be the only companion left."

I stole another deep breath, pacing myself. "But it is in those moments of darkness that we discover our true strength. It is when we are tested to our very limits that we find the flicker of light within ourselves, the spark that refuses to be extinguished. We are not just survivors; we are warriors of hope. We are living proof that even the deepest wounds can heal, that the most profound sadness can be transformed into the greatest resilience."

I looked out into the eyes watching me, seeing the glimmers of hope and the hesitant belief. "It is this spirit, this unbreakable will, that will propel us forward into a brighter future. Each of you carries within you the power to overcome the obstacles that lie in your path. You have the strength to rise above the difficulties, to reclaim your light even when it feels like it's fading."

I pushed a thick dark curl from my face, feeling our objective solidify within me. I could see the impact of my words spreading before me, and it gave me the strength to continue. "We are the architects of our future, and together, we will build a world where hope triumphs over despair." Dipping deep into my soul, I pulled the words of my father to the surface. I raised a fist above my head. "From darkness, we rise. For light, we fight!"

The crowd erupted in cheers, but I barely registered their jubilance. General Ballister's menacing focus locked onto me, penetrating my soul. My final words hung between us, charged as a perceived threat that sent electricity racing through my body.

With that, I stepped back from the podium, the applause swelling around me. I felt a sense of relief and pride.

Garon stepped forward next, lightly brushing my shoulder with his as I returned to my spot. A collective breath held in expectation of what he would impart. As the Perpetual Sense, Garon embodied logic and philosophy, a role revered for its depth and insight.

The arena, previously abuzz with celebratory energy, now felt like a taut wire of suspense. Every eye was on Garon—including General Ballister's—the crowd's murmurs again fading into a hushed reverence. The audience waited for Garon's words to fall, anticipating a rhetoric from the first Dobian leader that would undoubtedly redefine their world.

"I am Garon Fiore," he announced, his tone resonant and clear.

Standing on that stage, time seemed to freeze as we endured his pregnant pause. The arena, brimming with anticipation.

Garon's next words carried the weight of an entire epoch.

"I am Cird!"

The world tilted on its axis. The impact of his declaration was seismic, rippling through the crowd like a thunderclap.

It was not just a revelation…

…it was a declaration of war.

Epilogue

GARON

The uproar of the crowd swelled like a fast-pacing storm. I stood on the expansive stage in the arena, observing the grandeur that belied the turmoil roiling beneath these seats. The ceremony's splendor—gleaming banners, cascading lights, intricate holographic displays—contrasted sharply with the darkness from which I emerged. This arena, intended as a spectacle of unity and progress, was about to bear witness to a truth that would shatter its gilded veneer.

Last night, I guided the Cird military through the hidden tunnels beneath Mass—those dark veins meant to suffocate us. Instead of a prison, those underground passages became our gateway to freedom. We endured the shadows and relentless oppression for a century, our strength quietly building. Now, the very tunnels designed to confine us would serve as our path to the surface—a passage to reclaim our rightful place.

"No longer will we be forced to dwell in darkness!" I shouted, my voice booming across the sound system, piercing through the rising clamor. "The time for silence is over!"

I turned to face the bodies behind me.

I noted the shocked face of Lyonal first.

Levity, mouth agape with startle, would soon get the answers she needed.

A furious growl broke from Draven's throat, and I questioned if he would rush me. I was prepared if he did. I welcomed it even.

But then Betta stole my focus.

Her golden eyes filled with moisture, and a single tear ran down her cheek.

Fear.

Fear I'd never recognized in her otherwise steadfast, confident demeanor. She couldn't truly believe the lies they fed her about the Cird, the lies she in turn fed to Sandric, *could she?*

I wanted to reach out, to touch her. The truth of it all sat between us like a stone—*my truth.* The part of me I'd kept from her, the part that made it harder for her to trust me. I could see it now, the confusion in her eyes. She didn't want to believe it, couldn't. To do so would mean everything she'd fought for, everything she'd stood by, crumbled into a lie. And I'd been part of that lie.

I could've told her who I was from the start. Hell, I kept half of what I already knew—and what she needed to know—from her as I sifted through the control room files. I should've stepped in, should've saved her from the hurt Draven would cause when I realized, back at that damn luncheon, that he coveted her. But I stayed silent. I didn't protect her then, when I should've.

Did I make it worse? Did I betray her trust before I even earned it?

I hated that fear in her eyes. Hated that it came from me. I never wanted to hurt her like this. Not her. Not the woman I believed could be more to me than I ever imagined possible. More than just a mission. More than a cause. More than an ally.

I would fix it. I would make things right.

As I surveyed the arena, I felt the crowd's anticipation crackling in the air, mirroring my own tension. What would come next? It took us a century to rise from the brink, to hone our powers, and prepare for this pivotal moment. Our patience, silence, and strategic planning fueled our readiness. We would emerge not just to be seen but to challenge and dismantle the false peace projected by those who suppressed us for so long.

Our subterranean world, shrouded in black, bore a unique supernatural power most only speculated: terra-illumination. With this ability, we could manipulate the land and create light. With a mere touch, I could shift the world, expanding and reshaping it into new forms—tunnels, caverns, or fertile patches. This power was crucial for our survival, transforming barren spaces into habitable sanctuaries. They wouldn't fear us for long. Not once they knew the truth of our culture and how we would help the surface thrive once more.

Despite our terra-illumination abilities, resources underground were scarce. Our environment could no longer sustain our growing population, and vital materials were becoming increasingly out of reach, which led many of us above ground and into the mountains of Dobia. Our desire to revolutionize and take back our rights to the surface stemmed from a deep-seated need for resources, as well as justice.

Before any words of incentive could pass, chaos erupted.

The stadium, once echoing with celebration, now drowned by the sound of panic. People stepping over one another to get out. The Brawn military that lined the rows of seating sprang into immediate action. Forcing people to remain in their seats. Pulling weapons to their ready, they pointed them directly at me.

Boom!

The colossal doors at the far end of the arena exploded open with a resounding bang, shattering the illusion of peace we hoped to retain. A regiment of our soldiers stormed into the stadium, their stark white and gray uniforms gleaming under the harsh electric lights. They moved with discipline that spoke of our rigorous training.

The Cird soldiers formed an imposing phalanx, our own weapons glinting menacingly as our soldiers pointed a barrage of firearms directly at the podium. Directly at past and future leadership. The sight of our guns, poised and ready, transformed the arena from a symbol of ceremonial unity into a stage for impending conflict.

Tension crackled in the atmosphere, the festive air dissolving into one of palpable dread. The presence of the Cird on this day tore the fabricated unity wide open. We planned for the shattering. This would be the big reveal of the unvarnished truth of Sandric's dark history.

The moment for reckoning dawned.

Something ancient and powerful surged within me. Tonight, choices would be made. The Cird's long exile would transform into strength. The real battle had flared into existence, and with this crucial moment upon us, I saw our truth poised to ignite a raging firestorm that would tear through the darkness—filling the world with our light.

Acknowledgements

Without Light has been an incredible journey, and I wouldn't be here without the support of the amazing people who stuck with me through every twist, turn, and snack break. To all of you, this book is as much yours as it is mine.

First up, and the biggest acknowledgment goes to my best friend and fellow nerd, Jena Kassay. Without you, Sandric wouldn't exist, and I probably wouldn't have taken on the challenge of building a world to center this book around. We bonded over dragons, Game of Thrones, and Fortnite, and through all our epic (questionable?) "safe space" conversations, you inspired me to reach for something more than a simple story. Your endless enthusiasm, our brainstorming sessions, and your beta reading shaped this book. You even got yourself written into it (by sheer necessity after all the support you gave me). Thank you for being my most promising beta reader and the friend who keeps me grounded, laughing, and inspired.

Of course, a huge thank-you goes to my mother. Mom, you've supported me through every crazy life decision, and this one was no different. You've been there cheering me on through all the ups and downs, twists and turns that I call my life. You've liked all my posts, reels, and stories and for that I'm indebted to you. Whether it was home renovation, bodybuilding, furniture salvage, event marketing, and now writing, you didn't miss one post! That leads me to say, I'm concerned about how much time you spend on social media. Thank you for always being my biggest fan and showing me that no dream is too big (or too weird). I'm grateful beyond words for your faith in me.

To my editor, Laura Pu-Syska: I knew you were the one when you were the only editor who replied with emojis in our first email exchange. I took a chance, and it turned out better than I could have hoped. You were more than just an editor—you were a steady guide through the sometimes terrifying publishing process. Your depth of knowledge in the industry made me feel confident putting Without Light in your hands, and you went above and beyond. Whether you were enlightening me on trending topics or helping me navigate sensitive themes, your guidance was indispensable. I truly can't recommend you enough.

To my two little guys, Ezra and Axel. You may be too young to understand why Mommy's computer became her best friend, but your snack requests and constant bathroom breaks were little reminders to take a step back and breathe. You kept me smiling, even if it felt like I was on snack duty every other sentence. Someday you'll read this book (at least the parts I'll let you read), and I hope you'll understand that it was all for you.

To my family and friends, thank you for being my support system, even when I rambled about characters and plot twists that probably made no sense out of context. Some of you were brave enough to read my early work (for which you truly deserve a medal of honor). You were there to cheer me on and pick me up when I got discouraged, and I'm endlessly grateful to each of you.

I can't leave without acknowledging the friends I've made on Bookstagram and the friends I've made all around the world because of this silly little social app.

To Jessica and Jaime specifically—beyond your encouragement and support, your second and third set of eyes in the last hour was invaluable. I can't wait to share the wild world of indie writing with you guys!

And finally to my writing community friends I've met through IG, both near and far—every message, every shared post, every word of motivation has helped bring this book to life.

This book was a labor of love, and it wouldn't have been possible without every one of you.

About the Author

Megan A. Rockwell is a storyteller with a passion for creating immersive worlds and deeply relatable characters. Her narratives often explore themes of resilience, trust, and personal growth amidst challenging circumstances.

Now that formalities are out of the way, I am a mother of two rowdy little boys, living in North Carolina. I have an extensive background in Marketing, a degree in Communication Studies, and the creative soul of a houseplant—I'll shrivel up and die if you don't water me with new projects and challenges daily. I renovate extremely old homes, salvage vintage furniture, and oh yeah, I write fictional novels with extensive world building!

· · · · ● · ● · · ·

Betta, Levity, and the entire world of Sandric have so much more in store for you, with history to unravel, alliances to test, and battles yet to be fought. This is just the beginning of The Sanctioned Series, and there's plenty left to resolve as our characters face new challenges and darker secrets.

To stay updated on the next book in the series and all things Without Light, make sure to visit www.meganarockwell.com. Exciting news and more adventures await!

Let's Connect on IG: @Megan.A.Rockwell